Multi-award-winning author L[...] novels featuring strong heroines, the heroes who love them and the bad guys who fear them. She called Denver home until she married a Texan without reading the fine print. Now she lives halfway between Houston and Galveston and embraces the humidity. When Leslie's not writing, you might find her camping at a lake, fishing pole in one hand and a book in the other. Visit her at lesliemarshman.com, on X @lesliemarshman, on Facebook and on Instagram @leslie_marshman

Justine Davis lives in Puget Sound in Washington State, watching big ships and the occasional submarine go by and sharing the neighbourhood with assorted wildlife, including a pair of bald eagles, deer, a bear or two, and a tailless raccoon. In the few hours when she's not planning, plotting or writing her next book, her favourite things are photography, knitting her way through a huge yarn stash and driving her restored 1967 Corvette roadster—top down, of course. Connect with Justine on her website, justinedavis.com, on X @Justine_D_Davis or on Facebook.

Discover more at millsandboon.co.uk

RESOLUTE SECURITY

LESLIE MARSHMAN

OPERATION RESCUE

JUSTINE DAVIS

MILLS & BOON

First Published in Great Britain 2025
by Mills & Boon, an imprint of HarperCollins*Publishers* Ltd
1 London Bridge Street, London, SE1 9GF

www.harpercollins.co.uk

HarperCollins*Publishers*
Macken House, 39/40 Mayor Street Upper,
Dublin 1, D01 C9W8, Ireland

Resolute Security © 2025 Leslie Marshman
Operation Rescue © 2025 Janice Davis Smith

ISBN: 978-0-263-39737-6

1125

RESOLUTE SECURITY

LESLIE MARSHMAN

This one's for Joan, because I love a good villain.

Chapter One

Boone County, Texas
The Montgomery Ranch

"Walk," Erin Montgomery commanded in the soft, firm voice she used with all her animals. She took a step forward and the jet-black horse fell in behind her, kicking up dust as they rounded the corral for another lap. Trained to perform specialized movements at the direction of his rider, Redemption had been limping since his last dressage competition. After the vet diagnosed ligament inflammation, the valuable Dutch Warmblood horse had come to the Montgomery Ranch for physical therapy.

"Halt."

Redemption stopped, shaking his head and snorting. Erin leaned forward until her forehead rested against the gelding's neck, stroking him with a gloved hand. "Yes, I feel it too, boy." It was an uneasiness that came from more than just the stiff wind that suddenly kicked up, cutting like a blade of ice. Dry leaves and dirt took to the air as the sky darkened to a slate gray.

Erin turned up the collar on her thick barn jacket, then reached around her neck for her bandanna, pulling it up over her nose and mouth. "Might be one of those winters when we get some snow, boy." But it wasn't the weather making her as skittish as the gelding.

Choices she'd made ten years ago were reaching out from the past like poison tendrils of acid rain. Burning into her soul, her confidence, even her ability to discern good from evil, right from wrong. She'd made so many poor decisions that she no longer trusted herself, and that insecurity had led to her current purgatory—stuck on her parents' dressage training ranch. It wasn't that she didn't love horses, but dressage was not where her heart lay.

You don't deserve your heart's content.

And she didn't. Not after everything she'd done, and no amount of penance would ever wipe that slate clean.

Redemption lifted his head with a jerk, nostrils flaring. Erin tightened her grip on the training rope as the prized animal pulled back from her.

"Settle down, boy," she cooed. But when he refused to be calmed, she yanked her bandanna down in case it was spooking him. "Easy, boy, e—" Another icy gust blew dirt into her mouth and whipped away her words.

She and Redemption danced in an awkward circle until Erin finally saw the reason for the horse's distress. A man, leaning his forearms against the top rail on the far side of the corral, was staring them down.

Erin squinted against the swirling dust, trying to figure out who he was. He wore a heavy jacket, with the hood from a sweatshirt underneath pulled over his head. Between that and his dark beard, mustache and sunglasses, not much of his face was visible.

Redemption pawed the ground, and Erin refocused on the horse. She calmed him down enough to tie his lead rope to the nearest fence post before striding toward the stranger, one hand curled around the pepper spray in her jacket pocket. Erin wasn't normally so jittery, but ever since—

From the corner of her eye, she saw her family's longtime ranch hand, Hank Caldwell, standing in the open doorway of the barn. He was nearing seventy but was still strong enough to take down a stubborn calf that didn't want to be branded. And Hank always wore his gun.

"I don't know who you are, but you're trespassing. And I'm sure you know that, considering all the signs posted along the fence lines." Inside her other jacket pocket, her fingers rested on her phone. "And that you need a security code to open the gate."

The man didn't move. Didn't smile. Didn't speak. His silent stare spooked her far more than if he'd made an aggressive move.

"Fine. Have it your way." Erin pulled her phone out. "I'm calling the police."

"Ah, come on, *Eriss*. Is that any way to treat an old friend?"

She froze at the sound of his voice. A voice she hadn't heard in years. The deep Texas twang he'd acquired and then kept to convince others he was born here.

He'd convinced a lot of people.

Including her.

But what really sent a shiver down her spine was hearing the nickname Alex Townsend had given her after the first time they kissed. An endearment that combined Erin and heiress, a shared intimacy that had once made her smile but now turned her stomach.

Calling on years of hiding her true emotions to keep the shock and fear from her face, Erin forced a hard edge to her tone. "I heard you finally made parole."

"Yeah. Finally." His mouth twisted into a smirk. "For

some strange reason, time off for good behavior eluded me."
He pushed his hood back, revealing scars on his forehead
and closely shaved scalp.

Erin studied his face, at once familiar to her and yet
changed in a way that defied definition. Older, obviously.
Harder, maybe. His once straight nose now bent to the right,
the center of it a mass of scar tissue. A jagged line crossed
up one cheek and continued through his brow, just missing his eye. Souvenirs from his time in prison, apparently.

She made a show of looking toward Hank. "I suggest
you leave now."

Alex flashed her the smile that used to make her insides
flutter, that charmed her into believing every word he said.
That even convinced her to take part in a crime. "Come on,
Erin. I'm just here to talk. I've missed you. Thought you
would have visited me once in a while, or at least accepted
a collect call or two."

Funny how that smile did nothing to her now. "Leave or
I'm calling the police. Your choice."

"Whoa, baby. Relax. If you don't want to get back together, fine." He gave her an exaggerated shrug. "Just give
me my half of the haul plus interest, and I'll be on my way."

Still trying to get past the *get back together* comment,
it took Erin several seconds for the rest of what he said to
sink in. "Interest? Half of the haul? What on earth are you
talking about?"

Alex glanced over at Hank, then leaned closer to Erin.
"You're the only one who could have taken everything we
stole. I just want my fair share, plus a bit more for my pain
and suffering. Ten years behind bars and this—" he pointed
to his damaged face "—are worth the extra."

Erin frowned. "You're crazy." She regretted the phrase
the moment the words left her mouth, remembering how

it affected him. He'd donned an almost flawless persona during his con years. Being everyone's friend, convincing the special few he'd chosen at the charity where they'd met that his ideas were actually theirs. But even a joke about Alex or his ideas being crazy brought out the darkness in him. A darkness Erin eventually learned was his true self.

His hands shot over the top rail and grabbed her jacket collar on either side, yanking her hard against the fence. "I've waited a long time for this, Erin. And your innocent act ain't working. Everything we stole that night didn't just up and disappear into thin air. The cops never found it, not even after you turned traitor and told them where it was."

Alex jerked her harder, and Erin dropped her phone and braced her hands against the fence to keep from having her face smashed into his. She tried to pull away, but his strength was too much. He leaned even closer, his face almost touching hers, his eyes burning with malice. Having the fence as a barrier between them should have afforded Erin a modicum of safety, but it didn't.

His breath hot and foul on her face, Alex continued. "Three of us went to prison and Jensen ran. You're the only one who could've taken it."

Erin's mouth went as dry as the West Texas plains, and her heartbeat kicked into double time. "Jensen must have taken it, then. Because I don't have it."

"I already tracked him down. He died a month after he left here, shot while holding up a convenience store in San Antonio and buried in a pauper's grave. Trust me, he didn't take the jewelry."

"All you have to do is read the police reports." Erin spoke with the soft but firm voice she used with her horses. All the while, she pulled against his grip. "I was still sitting in the police station when the cops went to retrieve the bag. I couldn't have moved it."

Alex scoffed. "Not my problem, sweetheart."

Hank, by now standing behind Alex, leveled his gun at him with a steady hand. "Get your hands off her, or I'll drop you where you stand."

"Take it easy. We're just having a little reunion." Alex released her, his hands up in mock surrender.

"I suggest you reunion yourself off this property." Hank moved a step closer.

"On my way." Alex turned his glare back on Erin. "If you don't already have it, you best get to treasure hunting, and fast. I got to you once. I can get to you again, and no old man is going to stop me. You've got until the end of the month. Once I get my share—and don't forget the interest—you'll never hear from me again."

"That's just two weeks away."

"Yep. You better get busy."

"You're wasting your time, Alex. Trust me, I have nothing to give you and no idea where the jewelry could be. Now get out of here before I have Hank shoot you."

"Trust you? Traitors don't inspire trust, sweetheart. I suggest you rethink your answer. Because one thing I've learned is, you don't get people to do things for you by threatening them. You get people to do things by threatening the people they love." Alex looked at Hank. "Better sleep with one eye open, old man."

"I sleep with my gun in my hand, cocked and ready, you punk. Now git!"

Alex looked back at Erin, his smile lazy and cruel. "Give my regards to Ma and Pa Montgomery." And with that, he turned and sauntered away.

Hank came up to her. "You okay, Erin?"

"A bit shaken, but fine."

"I'll let all the ranch hands know to watch out for him. We won't let that son of a— We won't let him back on the property."

"Thanks, Hank."

"Nothing to thank me for."

Hank left her there, staring after Alex's retreating form long after he'd disappeared, the cold seeping into her bones having nothing to do with the weather.

MATT FRANKLIN PUSHED through the front door of Resolute Security, humming an old '60s tune still popular with surfers. What he wouldn't give to paddle out into the surf and catch a good wave. When he'd joined Nate in Texas, he lamented leaving the West Coast behind. Nate had mentioned how close Resolute was to Matagorda Bay, but the warm, murky waters of the Gulf were a far cry from the blue chill of the Pacific Ocean, especially when it came to surfing.

Still, working with Nate was worth the sacrifice. Becoming a partner in Resolute Security was worth even more.

"Hey, boss man." Matt dropped into the chair facing the reception desk. "You've got a job for me?"

The storefront office had three rooms: Nate's office, a space to meet with clients and the small reception area. Its location next door to a private investigator's office was perfect, especially since the PI was Nate's brother-in-law Trevor Bishop, and referrals between the two businesses helped both companies grow.

"Yes, and it's a well-paying one." Nate opened a file folder and glanced at the paperwork inside. "Jim and Holly Montgomery live on an eight-hundred-acre ranch up in Winston. They're part of what you'd call Boone County's elite. Jim's an international venture capitalist. Holly, aside from being a prominent socialite, runs a dressage training and rehab business."

"Boone County has an elite? And socialites?" Matt chuckled. "I must have missed that in the orientation meeting."

Nate looked up, smiling. "I'll grant you that Boone County doesn't compare to the glamour of Hollywood, but the Montgomerys are heavy hitters in the political arena and are always on the A-list for charity galas, stuff like that." Nate leaned back in his chair. "Holly called first thing this morning, requesting a bodyguard."

"So, what's the job?"

"Mr. and Mrs. are overseas on one of Jim's business trips, and their daughter Erin's home alone. She needs round-the-clock protection."

Matt groaned at the thought of babysitting some rich kid. "Don't they have staff to take care of their children?"

The smile—no, smirk—taking over Nate's face made Matt cringe. He'd seen that look before, always followed by a punch line. "Erin is twenty-eight."

Matt raised a brow. "Okay, you got me. But you still haven't explained why she needs protection."

Nate's grin vanished. "She had a threatening visit from Alex Townsend, thirty-four, an ex-boyfriend who thinks he has a pretty big ax to grind. Her parents are convinced he poses a real danger and have hired us to keep her safe." He slid the file across the desk. "Long story short, Erin got into trouble when she was a teen. Part of a group that robbed the guests at her parents' charity gala."

"Wait. If her family's so wealthy, why…" Matt shook his head as his words trailed off.

"She was in love." Nate shrugged. "Anyway, they caught her, but she cooperated with the police by turning in her boyfriend and the other three men involved. Also told the police where the gang hid the stash, although it was never recovered. There's still a reward for anyone who turns it in. Because of her confession, her age and her parents' influence with the previous county judge, she was released on probation."

Matt flipped pages in the file. "What about the other three? Are they bothering her, too?"

"Brad Parker and Kevin Moore are still in prison. Billy Jensen died during another robbery ten years ago. But now Townsend, the leader of the gang, is out and harassing the daughter. Says he wants his half of the loot, which Erin claims not to have."

"You believe her?"

"It doesn't matter whether I do or not. What matters is—"

"Keeping the client safe." Matt rested one ankle on the opposite knee. "Is ten years the usual term for robbery in Texas?"

"*Armed* robbery and aggravated assault."

"And yet the girl walked away with no jail time?" Matt blew out a breath. "Unbelievable."

"She wasn't armed, she was young and she cooperated with the police." Nate gave Matt a pointed look. "So yes, she got a second chance."

"Bottom line, she wasn't held accountable for her actions."

"Bottom line, she's in danger and we've taken the job of protecting her." Nate leaned forward, resting his forearms on the desk blotter. "This is a high-paying job from people who could refer other wealthy clients to us. And we need the money."

"You know how I feel about second chances."

A moment of silence hung in the air between them. "I

get it, Matt. If your mom hadn't given your dad a second chance, she'd still be alive. But you and I have protected plenty of people we wouldn't want to be friends with. And this job is nothing like what happened with your parents." Nate drummed his fingers on his desk. "It could bring in a good chunk of what you need to buy your half of the company. That's why I want *you* to take it."

Matt's goal was to become a fifty-fifty partner with Nate, just as they'd been in California. When they'd sold Reed and Franklin Security in Los Angeles and Nate returned to Texas, Matt made the mistake of staying in the Golden State for what he thought was a combo job/romance gig, emphasis on the romance. Boy, had he called that one wrong. Although he'd invested what he had left when he arrived in Resolute, he still needed to chip in more to become an equal partner. A lot more.

He shrugged. "A job's a job." Matt stood, holding up the folder. "This my copy?"

"It is." Nate paused, then added, "I'm sure I don't need to remind you of this, but…"

"I know, I know—"

In unison, they both said, "Don't fall in love with the client."

"I promise you, boss man, there's not a snowball's chance in Texas of that happening."

After his fiasco in California with Meryl Duncan, agent to the stars, Matt was on the wagon where women were concerned. Not that he had much to worry about with this case. He knew from firsthand experience that giving someone a second chance was for chumps, and he was no chump.

Chapter Two

After swinging by his shabby but affordable apartment to throw some clothes in his duffel bag, Matt headed north-west toward Winston, Texas. Although Resolute was the county seat, Winston, according to Nate, was bigger and had its own police force.

Thirty minutes later, a low whistle escaped his lips as he drove along the fence line of the Montgomery Ranch. When he reached the locked entrance gate, he stopped and stared. This place might be called a ranch, but instead of a large rustic house made of logs and beams, Matt gaped at what looked like a contemporary mansion plopped down in the middle of Texas.

Pressing the buzzer for the gate several times brought no response, so Matt tapped in the code Nate had gotten from Mrs. Montgomery. A barn and another building sat a good way off to the left and behind the house. A note in the file from Nate directed him to go past the big house and find his client at the barn or the bunkhouse near it. He followed the interior paved road to the house, where it made a circle drive around a life-size bronze statue of a horse, its mane in weird little knots.

A gravel road split off to the right and curved around the back of the house. Matt followed it to the barn, parked next to a shiny red pickup and turned the key in his ignition to Off.

As the cooling engine pinged, he sucked in a breath and exhaled slowly. Time to put on his poker face. A good bodyguard never reflected their true feelings about a client, especially if those feelings were negative.

He stepped from his truck. A chilly day for sure, but his heater worked like a champ, keeping him toasty. He left his jacket and duffel bag in the vehicle for now while he got the lay of the land.

As Matt walked toward the buildings, he checked out the property, assessing avenues of potential threats and means for protection. So much open space was both a good and bad thing. Easy to spot incoming threats while at the same time hard to cover all potential places of ingress.

He'd have his work cut out for him.

He reached the closed-up barn, surprised to see another security code lock on the doors. With no one in the nearby corral, he headed to the log cabin. It was farther from the barn than it had looked from a distance, sitting on higher ground.

Another door bearing a security code lock. After knocking and getting no response, he peered through the windows, seeing no signs of life. His client could be off running errands. Or she could be lying inside, dead at the hands of her ex-boyfriend.

Matt tried the front gate code on the door and it opened. He took in the log walls, rustic wood ceiling with beams and a small kitchen off to one side. Three doors led to rooms partitioned off along the back wall of the building, and he peered into each one. A bedroom with a freestanding wardrobe, dresser and a bed. A small bathroom. And behind door number three, what looked to be a combination junk/

storage room, jammed with boxes and bins, a full garment rack and more pairs of Western boots than a shoe store.

But no Erin Montgomery.

He jogged back to the barn and punched in the same code there. When he swung the door open, the view inside the barn grabbed his attention.

A woman, presumably Erin Montgomery, stood in the middle of the barn with her back toward Matt, brushing a horse as gold as a ray of sun. She wore a heavy jacket, jeans and cowboy boots, and her long dark hair hung in braids, swinging with each sweep of the brush across the horse's flank.

"Hello," Matt said, still at the barn's entrance.

Nothing.

He tried again, louder. "Hello!"

Still no response.

Matt walked up behind her and tapped her shoulder. The woman jumped, and the brush flew out of her hand, straight up in the air and down. Right on top of his head. Swearing under his breath, he reached up and rubbed the spot where a lump was already forming.

The woman spun toward him. Matt had only a second to confirm her face matched the picture in the file before Erin's hand disappeared into her jacket pocket and reappeared, holding a small cylinder in her fist.

"No, no—" was all he got out before she shoved her hand toward his face and pepper-sprayed him. "Son of a—" Ducking his head, Matt yelled, "Stop! I'm Matt Franklin, your bodyguard!" His face burned, his mouth burned, his eyes burned most of all. Tears streamed down his face and he coughed as he stumbled blindly back toward the door and outside.

"I don't have a bodyguard!" Erin yelled back at him as

if she thought blinding him also rendered him deaf. "I'm calling the police!"

"Go ahead. I'll have them arrest you for assault." Man, his eyes were on fire. He could not get them to stay open.

"And I'll have them arrest you for trespassing."

"Fine, but could you get me some water while we wait?" Matt wheezed before dissolving into another coughing fit.

"Why should I?"

He used his shirttail to wipe his watering eyes, but it did nothing to ease the pain. "Look, lady, I'm here by invitation. How 'bout you cut me some slack?"

After a moment, Erin yelled, "Stand still!"

A wall of water hit him full on in the face, drenching his whole upper body. "Are you kidding me?" He tried to squint, but his eyes remained closed. He yanked apart the snaps on his shirt and dropped the wet garment on the ground in case another dousing was coming.

The cold air latched on to his wet skin and drew out goose bumps by the score.

"Here." Erin grabbed his hand and yanked him forward a few steps. "If you don't like the way I do it, you can do it yourself. The water's right in front of you."

Matt groped until his hands made out the edge of a metal pail of water. He wrapped one arm around its middle and hoisted it to his chest. Cupping his free hand, he splashed water on his face over and over.

"Listen, buster, you've got one minute to explain yourself before I call the police."

Matt's eyes still burned, but he was no longer having coughing spasms. His temper, however, hung by a thread that was getting thinner by the moment. "No, you listen, Princess. Your parents hired a bodyguard from Resolute

Security. I'm that bodyguard." Matt kept splashing water on his face as he spoke. "And why are you yelling?"

"Oh. I forgot I had my earbuds in."

She must've removed them, because Matt could hear the song playing even from where he stood. He stopped splashing water on his face and turned his head to where he guessed she might be. "And the music wasn't a clue?"

"Hey. You're the intruder here. No one hired a bodyguard for me, and when I prove it, I'm having you arrested."

"Bring it on."

ERIN FISHED HER phone out of her pocket. The only thing that could make things worse right now would be confronting her mother, so she called her father.

"Erin? Is everything all right?" Her dad's concerned voice boomed in her ear.

"I'm fine, Dad. Listen, I'm putting you on speaker." *Let this jerk hear Dad's denial himself.* "There's a guy here who says he's my bodyguard. I say he's a liar. You didn't hire a bodyguard for me, did you?"

The beat of silence that followed chipped away at her certainty.

"Ah, that's your mother's doing."

Of course.

"She heard you were having trouble with that guy from before and wanted to make sure you're safe."

Guy from before. The closest anyone in the family ever got to mentioning Alex's name. Or the robbery.

"I'm sure she meant to call you about it."

"Well, she didn't, and I nearly killed the man when he showed up here." Erin turned away from Matt and spoke through gritted teeth. "Dad, you need to talk to Mom. Tell her I don't want this bodyguard. Any bodyguard. Hank is here. He'll watch out for me."

"Sweetie, you know how your mother gets when she sets her mind to something. It's easier to just accept it."

"Yeah, Dad, I know." Erin sighed. "I just wish you would…" *stand up to her.* She couldn't bring herself to finish the sentence aloud. She may not respect her father for always giving in to her mother, but she'd never tell him that to his face.

"Sorry, Erin, you caught me just as I was walking into a meeting." And just like that—just like always—her father was back to his upbeat, path-of-least-resistant self. "I've got to go. Love you."

Erin closed her eyes and took a deep breath. "Love you, too, Dad." Her anger toward Matt for scaring her faded, but the anger at being handled by her overbearing mother still simmered under the surface. Resigning herself to her fate, as well as an apology she needed to make, she turned back to her injured bodyguard.

"I guess I owe you an apology." She cringed at the sight of his red and swollen eyes. "My mother didn't bother to fill me in on her little plan." Then, trying to regain a modicum of dignity, she added, "But you shouldn't have snuck up on me. If you'd buzzed from the gate, we could have resolved this without the pepper spray."

"I might be more inclined to accept that apology when I can open my eyes without pain." Matt wheezed and coughed some more. "And I did buzz. No one answered. Maybe because, *earbuds*?"

She ignored the dig. "So, how *did* you get in?"

"Your parents gave us the security code for the gate."

Alex's visit had scared her plenty, but the last thing she wanted was some stranger underfoot. Hank would have everyone on alert, and she was half tempted to arm herself full-time.

"Look, I don't need a bodyguard. Our ranch hands are aware of the situation, and they're armed. So, if you need me to call your boss to cancel this, I will."

"First, that's not how this works. Only the person who hires us can cancel the job. Second, is pepper-spraying people something you do on the regular?" Matt put a thumb below his right eye and a forefinger on the upper lid and tried to pry it open. "Because it's not usually a thing someone does who's not afraid for their life."

The remark stoked her anger, but mostly because he was right. She'd started carrying the pepper spray after the robbery. After she'd seen Alex's dark side the first time. Erin grabbed the empty bucket from him and refilled it. "Here." She shoved the pail against his chest. "I'm going to finish brushing my horse."

"Don't wander off when you're done."

"Or what?" she threw back over her shoulder. Blind as he was, he'd be hard-pressed to stop her. And she needed to be away from him, away from every controlling person in her life. Space. That's what she needed. And the comfort she got from the horses she cared for.

Fear gnawed at her, but even more overwhelming was the exhaustion and frustration of having no control over her own life.

HALF AN HOUR LATER, her horse was back in its stall, and Erin had calmed herself enough to check on Matt. It would be a whole lot easier to stay irritated with his presence if he'd left his shirt on. Although not bulked up like a bodybuilder, his six-pack rippled with each splash of water to his face and, well, she was used to judging fine horseflesh.

Not much difference in judging a fine male form; nothing more than an analytical, objective perusal.

"Are your eyes feeling better?" She picked up the pail at his feet and refilled it again.

His red-rimmed eyes squinted at the water she scooped up. "You've been giving me water from a horse trough to rinse my face?"

Erin almost laughed out loud. "That's a rain barrel, not a horse trough. It's clean water." Erin shook her head. "You aren't from around here, are you?"

Matt picked up his shirt and shook it out. "California. But even if I *was* from Texas, I wouldn't be living on a ranch with—" he waved his hands in the air "—horses and troughs and…and stuff like that."

"A city boy, then. And here I thought you must be a genuine cowboy, what with that pearl snap shirt and all." Erin smiled as her gaze drifted from Matt's broad chest down to his chiseled abs and narrow waist. Analytical and objective. Nothing more. "I bet you'd make a good one."

"Trust me, I'm about as far from cowboy as you can get. And the shirt was a gift." He pulled the damp garment on but left it hanging open. "Now, how 'bout you show me where we're sleeping?"

Where *we're* sleeping?

Forget that. If it was the last thing she did, she was getting rid of Matt Franklin and his shirtless abs. He'd see. Her mother would see. Alex Townsend would see. It was all a part of her grand plan to take control of her life.

MATT PICKED UP his duffel bag and jacket that he'd retrieved from his vehicle while Erin finished grooming her horse.

"Where we're sleeping?" Erin repeated in a tone reminiscent of his third-grade parochial teacher. The one who'd smacked his knuckles with a ruler more than once. "*I* sleep in the bunkhouse. I have no idea where *you'll* be sleeping." She glanced at his old, beat-up truck parked next to hers. "Don't you stay in your truck for stakeouts?"

"This isn't a stakeout. I'm providing round-the-clock protection. Which means I go where you go, and I live where you live."

"That's not going to work for me." She tipped her head toward the small log cabin bunkhouse. "There's barely enough room in there for me. And I value my privacy."

"I like my privacy, too, but this isn't forever. We'll figure it out." Getting new clients familiar with protection protocols was always a process. Matt found it best to just rip off the Band-Aid. He started across the shallow incline toward his soon-to-be temporary home. "Best place to start is with sleeping arrangements."

Quick footsteps pounded behind him. "Wait a minute. You can't barge into someone's home uninvited."

Matt turned to face her while walking backward. "I already have. Technically your parents own the bunkhouse, and your mother invited me here." He tried not to laugh as she raced ahead to reach the front door first.

"What do you mean, you already have?" She spoke through clenched teeth while blocking his entrance.

"Relax." He stepped onto the porch. "I couldn't find you, and I needed to make sure you weren't hurt. Or, you know, dead."

Erin's eyes narrowed. "My parents are away, so there's no reason you can't stay in the main house. You'll have the place to yourself, and you can see the bunkhouse from there."

Her response confirmed that he'd accomplished step one: getting the client to accept that a bodyguard was a part of their life. Now Erin needed to accept that he, the body-guard, set the rules.

"When a bodyguard guards a body, both the bodyguard and the body need to be near each other at all times." Matt reached past her, turned the handle and pushed the door open. "After you."

From the set of her jaw, she had no intention of moving. Time for a little truth strategy.

"Look, I'm not here to ruin your life," he said. "I'm here to do a job. And you… Well, I read the file on Alex Townsend. He was a nasty piece of work before he went to prison, and trust me, he didn't improve any while serving time. He spent more time in solitary confinement because of fighting than he did in gen pop." When she raised a questioning brow, he clarified, "General population."

She gave a nod as if she'd known that.

"The owner of Resolute Security is the brother of Boone County Sheriff Cassie Reed. She's aware that Townsend is back in town and that he threatened you. Winston Police Chief Simpson knows as well. It seems he filed your restraining order request with the judge, but they haven't been able to serve it yet because Townsend keeps disappearing."

"Of course he does," Erin muttered.

"Unfortunately, even if he had been served, there's no proof Alex trespassed or violated it."

"Hank was here. He can testify."

"It's still 'he said, she said.' And by the time he's found and hauled to court, it could be too late for you." He softened his tone even more. "Your parents think he poses enough of a threat that they hired me. And you carry pepper spray, so you must be worried. How about, just for now, we figure out a way to make this work?"

She hesitated, then said with an imperious lift of her chin,

"For your information, I always carry pepper spray." She arched a brow, reminding him she wasn't afraid to use it. Then she spun around and clomped across the hardwood floor, holding out her arms. "This is it. Home sweet home."

Step two, check.

Having already been inside the cabin, Matt crossed the threshold and began a mental list of security needs. Locking pins for one, two…four, five, six windows. Motion detectors, too. The front door had a keypad dead bolt lock, but he wanted to add a manual dead bolt only operable from the inside. Lighting needed to be added around the perimeter, and the shrubs under the windows needed to be clipped back.

"Like I said, I didn't expect anyone to stay here. But if you're determined to, that's the only spare room." She twisted her mouth to the side as she pointed to the junk room. "Sorry."

Oh, she wasn't sorry at all, but Matt refused to give her the satisfaction. "No problem. I can sleep on the couch." He crossed the room and sat, sinking into the oversize piece of furniture. "Ah, this will be just fine."

"You can't sleep there. That's where I relax in the evenings. You'd be in my way."

"I won't stretch out with my pillow until after you go to bed."

"Nope." Erin shook her head. "You on the couch just won't work for me."

Matt arched a brow at her when she offered no solution to his lack of sleeping accommodations.

"Well, make yourself at home. I have an appointment in town this afternoon and need to shower off the barn dust and horse dander." Erin didn't exactly slam the bathroom door but closed it with…emphasis. Then locked it.

Matt chuckled. She was a spitfire.

As soon as the water came on, he headed into the junk room. He stood with his hands on his hips for a moment, surveying the mess, then got to work.

He was back on the couch by the time Erin appeared in clean clothes. She'd been cute in the barn with braids, but cute gave way to pretty with her long, dark hair hanging loose and framing her face. Not that he was interested in second-chance socialites.

"As long as we're heading to town, I need to pick up an air bed."

"An air bed?" She made a point of surveying the couch, coffee table and TV that took up most of the small living area.

"Not for out here." Matt stood and walked toward the extra room. "But there's plenty of space in here."

"You must be out of your—" She stopped at the doorway.

He'd moved the boxes and storage bins until they lined two walls, stacked three high. The garment rack, holding an assortment of long-sleeved shirts, Henleys, tank tops and T-shirts, with folded jeans on the bottom shelf, sat against the wall with the door. And he'd arranged her many pairs of boots in two rows along the fourth wall.

"See? Plenty of room for an air bed." Matt held his breath. People seldom appreciated uninvited guests moving things around.

Erin chuckled, her reaction surprising him. "Wow. I hope you don't charge extra for housework." When she smiled, all her hard edges softened.

"First time's free. Part of our introductory offer." He winked, then followed her into the room. "I'm curious. What's with all the boxes? Is that where you store your ball gowns and diamond tiaras?"

She'd been facing away from him, but at his question,

Erin turned back, her smile gone. She walked past him and out the front door.

Matt hadn't seen anyone's demeanor change that fast since his ex-girlfriend changed her locks. Something had set Erin off, putting him back to square one with her. Just when things had been going so well.

He joined her outside, sitting beside her on the porch swing. "I'm sorry if I said anything to offend you."

"No reason to apologize. It just reminded me of something unpleasant from a long time ago." Erin stared off across the property. "You better get a move on if you want to get that bed before the stores close."

With the sun high above them, Matt looked at his watch. "It's not even noon."

"It's a small town. You might have trouble finding one."

"Then get your shoes on and let's go." Matt stood, but Erin stayed put.

"That's okay. I've got some things to do around here while you're gone." She finally looked at him, her face showing no anger, no emotion at all.

"You said you have an appointment in town."

"I can reschedule it. You run along, and I'll see you when you get back."

Oops. Apparently step two needed a refresher course. "That's not the way this—" he pointed back and forth between the two of them "—relationship works. The bodyguarding has begun. I won't be going anywhere without you, and you won't be going anywhere without me."

"In other words, if I don't go, you don't have anywhere to sleep." She folded her arms across her chest. "That's a shame, but not my problem, Mr. *Bodyguard*."

Matt hid a smile. So, she wanted to play hardball, eh? Fine by him. He may not be a cowboy, but this wasn't his first rodeo. "It will be your problem, because I plan to sleep in a bed tonight, and right now the only available one in this bunkhouse is yours." Matt mirrored her folded arms and stubborn glare. "So unless you want to sleep on the couch, I suggest *you* get a move on."

Chapter Three

Erin stewed as she stared through the windshield during the quiet ride into town. For someone determined to take charge of her life, she seemed to have less control by the second. Her mother's infernal interference, her dad's apathy. A bodyguard in her life, in her home, in her business. And he came with a passel of *don't-do-this* rules. Alex back, threatening her and those she loved, demanding jewels she didn't have.

She felt like a passive participant in her own existence. And she hated that feeling.

Though unfair, Matt proved a convenient target for her frustration. True, he was part of the problem. True, she still planned on getting rid of him, the sooner the better. And yet, it was unfair to take it all out on him. Even so, she was giving him the silent treatment. And all because of his crack about gowns and tiaras. How mature was that? No way he could know how close he'd come to Alex's past comments about her family's wealth. It had been how Alex preyed upon her, capitalizing on her feelings of privileged guilt.

Erin broke the silence when they passed a speed-limit sign. "Don't go over the limit by even one mile. The Winston cops are famous for their monthly ticket quotas."

Matt eased his foot off the gas, coasting as they approached the first buildings. "Any idea where we should try first?"

"The hardware store should have the air bed." She didn't mention it was also where she'd planned to go today, but by herself. "Take a right at the stop sign. It's down about a block."

"Okay. After that, I need to swing by the grocery store, pick up a few things."

"I've got a fully stocked kitchen."

"Yeah, I checked it out while you were in the shower." Matt pulled into a parking space in front of Hudson's Hardware. "But there are some things I like that you don't have."

By the time Matt killed the engine, Erin had unfastened her shoulder harness and had her hand on the door handle.

"Not so fast." He pushed the door-lock button. "We went over this. Wait until I get around to your side, then unlock the door."

"Seriously?"

"I'm dead serious. If someone wants to hurt you, they could get at you as soon as you step out of the truck."

"Trust me, Alex isn't going to hurt me unless I—" Erin snapped her mouth shut and turned her face away.

"Unless you what?"

Unless I don't find the jewelry.

"Unless I'm isolated," she improvised. "You really think he's stupid enough to come after me in a town full of people?"

"I have no idea how stupid he is, just as I'm pretty sure you're not telling me everything I need to know about this whole situation."

Was she that obvious?

He climbed out, rounded the front of the truck and unlocked her door with his key fob.

"This seems like overkill." Erin climbed out into what amounted to a wide, loose embrace from Matt.

"Just pretend I'm being a gentleman."

She looked up into his eyes. "*Are* you a gentleman?"

Matt's only answer was his sly smile, combined with the twinkle in those impenetrable blue eyes.

They entered the store, and Erin was glad to be out of the cold. But Matt was stuck to her side like they'd been superglued together. She needed an alternate plan to buy her supplies without him being aware.

While Matt shopped for an air bed that suited his apparent Princess-and-the-Pea syndrome, she pulled a scrap of paper and a pen from her purse. At the checkout, Erin insisted on paying for the mattress, and passed her note to Betty, the cashier, with her credit card.

The note had her shopping list and a request to deliver the items to the main house. Mission accomplished.

Twenty minutes later, they'd worked their way through almost every aisle of the grocery store except produce and health foods.

"You do know that most of this stuff will kill you, right?" Erin rummaged through the cart filled with what she considered stress-eating foods: packages of cookies and crackers, bags of chips and candy, protein bars of questionable nutritional value.

Matt tossed a bag of kettle corn into the cart. "Sometimes you have to weigh the balance between physical and mental health. And based on today, which is barely half over, I'm more concerned with my sanity than my glucose or cholesterol levels."

"Are you implying that I—"

"I'm *implying* nothing." One corner of his mouth kicked up in a half smile, bringing out a small dimple.

Obviously, she was the reason for his stress eating. "You can always quit, you know."

"Nice try."

"Hi, Miss Erin."

They both turned toward the youthful voice behind them.

"Tommy! How are you?" Erin approached the nine-year-old boy and crouched to give him a hug.

"Who's that?" Tommy pointed at Matt, then whispered, "Is he your boyfriend?"

Laughing, Erin stood. "No, no, no. This is my friend Matt. Matt, this is Tommy Barrows. I give him riding lessons."

"Nice to meet you, Tommy." Matt stepped closer to the boy. "You like horses, huh?"

Tommy tilted his head back and looked up at Matt. "Yep. Miss Erin says I'll get to ride outside of the corral pretty soon."

"Dude!" Matt held his hand out for a high five. "*I* can't even ride outside the corral."

Tommy smacked his hand, a smile overtaking his face. "Wanna see what I found?"

"Sure." Matt crouched next to him while Tommy dug in his jeans pocket.

Just then, Tommy's mother rounded the corner, pushing a cart. "Tommy! I've been looking everywhere for you."

"Hi, Jill." Erin joined her friend near the end of the aisle. "He's okay. Just showing my…friend his latest find."

Jill gave her a questioning look that said she wanted to know more about Erin's friend but kept the conversation on Tommy. "I swear, that boy and his gewgaws. He found a big, old marble, what we called shooters in my day." Jill chuck-led. "He thinks the twists in the center look like an eye."

Erin's gaze drifted down the aisle to the boy and the man. Tommy, his arms and hands moving as he spoke, and Matt nodding, smiling and widening his eyes as if in awe. No way a grown man could be that astonished by an old marble. But Matt acted as though it was the most amazing thing he'd ever seen.

Jill stepped closer and nudged Erin. "So, who's your friend?" she whispered. "Don't think I've seen him around before."

Erin wasn't about to share the ex-boyfriend/bodyguard story with anyone. "Not what you're thinking. He's just a friend, visiting for a week or so."

"Well, that's a shame, 'cause he's definitely got a new fan. He sure is good with kids."

"Yes, he is," Erin murmured. "Isn't he?"

"Don't be surprised if Tommy brings his whole triple S collection to his next lesson."

Erin cocked her head to the side. "Triple S?"

"Shiny, sparkly or strange." Jill laughed. "That pretty much describes everything that catches his eye."

"You've got that right," Erin agreed, smiling. But her attention was still drawn to the attractive bodyguard who could make a little boy happy so quickly.

There was more to Matt Franklin than she'd assumed, and that troubled her for reasons she couldn't define.

"WHERE DO I TURN?" Matt had reluctantly agreed to stop at a long-term care facility on the way back to the Mont-gomerys' ranch so Erin could visit a friend. Reluctant, be-cause this was yet another stop, after the liquor store, she hadn't informed him of when they set out. He'd been clear on travel protocols for leaving the ranch, but she wasn't complying. That didn't bode well for his ability to keep her safe. He needed to set her straight.

As she sorted her grocery purchases, transferring items from one bag to another, Erin said, "Turn left just past the giant live oak."

Matt glanced at her. "I might need a little more detail. There are a lot of oak trees out here."

Without looking up, Erin sighed. "Don't worry. You'll know it when you see it." She scraped at a price label on a jar of gourmet jam with her thumbnail.

"So, who are we going to visit?"

Erin lifted her head. "Liam O'Roarke. He's an old friend of my father."

"You're visiting him because your dad's out of town and can't?"

"No." A shadow passed over her face. "I visit him every week."

Huh. Not something he'd expect a spoiled socialite to do.

The biggest oak tree he'd ever seen loomed ahead on the left, and he slowed to take the turn. A sign announced the Hidden Oaks Care Facility. An apt name.

"This is the driveway. Keep straight, and it's just beyond the rise in the road."

Matt pulled into a parking space near the front door. "Not many visitors here, based on the empty parking lot."

"It's busier on weekends and holidays. A lot of people swing by after work." Erin opened the passenger door. "Some residents have spouses who still live in their own homes but can't drive, so they have to wait until someone can bring them. Luckily, Mrs. O'Roarke is younger than her husband and still going strong, so she comes by often."

Matt raised a brow at her, his eyes moving from her to

the door and back. Shaking her head, Erin pulled the door closed and waited for him to come around and let her out.

"You know this is ridiculous, right? There's no one here."

"It's good practice, so it becomes a habit." Matt walked next to her toward the entrance.

"Good luck with that, Mr. Bodyguard. It takes six weeks to form a new habit." Erin scoffed. "And this—" she pointed back and forth between them "—is not going to be going on for six weeks."

"We can only hope." Matt followed her inside and waited while she signed them in, then they walked through a maze of hallways to a private room with an open door.

Erin crossed the room in a few long strides and set her bag down on the bed.

"How are you today, Liam?" She bent over, gently put her arms around his shoulders and gave him a long hug.

The smile on the old man's face was lopsided but big. "Ah, grand, I am. And you, my girl?" Despite a shaky voice, his words carried across the room to Matt.

Erin straightened. "Pretty darn close to grand."

The old man's gaze drifted past Erin to Matt. "And who might this strapping young lad be? Don't tell me you finally took my advice and found yourself a gentleman friend."

Erin's face reddened, but to her credit, she recovered quickly. "You better quit your teasing, or I might stop sneaking contraband to you." They both laughed over the shared secret. "This is Matt Franklin. He's just a friend who I'm spending the day with."

"Well, the more the merrier, I always say." The old man smiled at Matt. "Pleased to meet you."

Matt stepped closer and offered his hand. "The pleasure's mine, sir."

The old man grimaced as he shook Matt's hand with his

left one. "Oh, none of that *sir* stuff, now. I'm Liam." He sat in a wheelchair positioned close to his bed. Erin dropped onto the bed and motioned for Matt to take the recliner.

"Take care not to fall asleep in that thing, Matt." The old man chuckled. "When I sit there to watch TV, I can't even make it through a half-hour program."

"How's your shoulder feeling?" Erin set her hand on Liam's closest shoulder. "The other day you could barely move it."

"Much better. Between the ice, heat and massages, the old biddies have loosened it up."

Erin glanced at Matt. "He calls the nurses and aides here 'old biddies.'" She rolled her eyes. "Last week he got into a wheelchair race with one of his neighbors and overdid it."

"I was sure I could beat him, even with only one good arm. But I should have made him tie one hand behind his back. *Then* it would've been a fair race."

"And you'd likely be just as sore."

For the next hour, Matt watched as Erin asked Liam questions about his days, about what he'd been up to since her last visit, about his wife. She held the old man's left hand, and Matt noticed that Liam's right hand hadn't moved from his lap since they'd arrived.

She smoothed back a wisp of white hair falling over Liam's forehead, touched his arm with loving familiarity and leaned into him as they shared a laugh about something. Matt's opinion of her went up by a couple of notches, and he admitted, if only to himself, that there was more to the second-chance rich girl than he'd originally thought.

"I got you more of that fig jam you like. And look, your favorite cookies." As Erin pulled items out of the bag and showed off each one before setting them on his tray table, the old man's off-kilter grin grew bigger and bigger.

"You're going to get me in trouble if the old biddies find this stuff in my drawer." Liam laughed.

"What won't they let you have in here?" Matt asked.

"Pretty much everything." Liam winked at him and patted Erin's knee. "But I've got my own secret supply line." Erin pulled the last item from the bag and held it up for both men to see.

"Ah, bless you, my girl. 'Tis my favorite brand of Irish whiskey." Liam glanced at Matt. "I like a wee nip before sleep takes me."

"And a wee nip in his morning coffee and a wee nip—"

"Hush now, Erin. Don't tell all my secrets."

A knock on the door brought a flurry of activity as Erin grabbed the items, put them back in the bag and slipped it into a drawer of the nightstand.

"Come in," Liam called out.

One of the aforementioned old biddies breezed into the room with a blood pressure cuff and a small paper cup of pills. "Time for your medicine, Mr. O'Roarke."

The old man grumbled while Erin offered a smile to the aide.

"We'll get out of your way." She rose, and Matt followed her cue and stood. "I'll be back soon, Liam. Be nice to these wonderful people who take good care of you."

He waved at her to go away while he grumbled some more.

The aide laughed. "He just talks big to impress you, but when you or his wife aren't around, he's a sweetheart."

"Erin, wait," Liam said. "I nearly forgot to mention that your friend stopped by. Kept thinking I should know him from somewhere, but he said he only just arrived in town. Said his name was Allen. Nice enough fellow, and I was glad for the company. Told him he could stop by anytime. Wanted to thank you for sending him my way."

"Allen? I don't recall… What did he look like?"

"About as tall as Matt there, beard and mustache. Poor guy looked like he lost a fight, had a scar across his face."

Matt grabbed Erin by the elbow when she teetered. Her face had gone sheet white and her eyes rounded like saucers.

"What's the matter, my girl?" Liam asked.

Erin took a deep breath. "Nothing. Just a bit hungry, is all. What did this man say to you, Liam?"

"Oh, nothing much. We just chatted about this and that. Nothing of real consequence."

"Okay. Thanks for telling me. You'll let me know if he comes back again, won't you?"

"Sure, if that's what you want."

"I do. You know how much I enjoy keeping tabs on you," she said, her voice shaky, a false smile plastered on her face.

Liam appeared not to notice. "Ack! You're worse than my wife."

"I'm telling her you said that."

"Nah, you'd never betray me like that."

Erin's smile was genuine this time. "You're right, I wouldn't. See you next time."

"Sit still," the aide scolded, "or I'll never get this cuff on you."

"Hate having my blood pressure taken. That cuff of yours pinches." Liam's complaints continued.

Matt held Erin's arm as he led her out of the room and down the hall. "You okay on your own?" he asked when they reached the front door.

She nodded.

"Wait here." Matt went to the desk and spoke to the receptionist, telling her that Alex Townsend should not be allowed into the facility again under any name. He promised to email them a picture of the man within the hour.

"Thank you," Erin said to Matt as they left the building. Then without speaking further, she went to the passenger side of his truck and waited obediently for him to unlock it. She got in, buckled up, then manually locked the passenger door.

After he jogged around to the driver's side and climbed in, Matt cranked the engine and headed out of the parking lot. "Anyplace else you need to go?"

"No. Just take me home." She leaned back against the headrest and closed her eyes.

It seemed he wouldn't need to revisit security protocols with her after all. Alex had taken care of that for him by scaring the living daylights out of her, and now Matt burned with a sudden need to punch something.

Something like Alex Townsend's face.

Chapter Four

Alex Townsend rode the borrowed Harley back to his friend's place, where he was crashing for now. His visit to the old guy in the rest home, so soon after confronting Erin, was just to let her know how accessible her friends were. He didn't want to *really* threaten anybody. At least, not yet. Just a reminder that time flies.

He wouldn't be mooching off his friends from the bar for long, though. As soon as Erin did what needed doing, he'd be leaving Texas in his rearview mirror, just like the song.

And she needed to do it fast, because Cowboy didn't bluff.

Alex hadn't thought twice about sharing details of his crimes in prison. Even exaggerated them to build his reputation. But his last cellmate, Cowboy, had latched on to the story of the stolen jewelry from Winston, and he wanted it.

Explaining the loot was missing didn't matter to Cowboy. When he wanted something, he got it.

And all of a sudden, Cowboy had the name and address of Alex's ma, who was raising his son.

The kid's baby mama had handed a then-twenty-year-old Alex an unnamed bundle of dirty diapers on her way out the door, and Alex handed it to his ma. But during all that handing off, he'd named the kid Justin because it sounded like a smart person's name, and they were his favorite brand of boots.

Alex hadn't seen Justin since, but he'd sent money home whenever he could. The kid must be close to fourteen by now. But he wouldn't get much older if Alex didn't get the stolen goods to Cowboy's man outside the prison. The man willing to wipe out two generations of Townsends at Cowboy's command.

And Alex wasn't about to let his son, or his ma for that matter, die because Cowboy didn't get what he wanted.

Chapter Five

Well before dawn the next morning, Erin crept out of her room, her feet covered in socks. After a quick and quiet detour to the bathroom, she tiptoed past Matt's open door. This was her chance to sneak away and search for the stolen goods without him knowing. A trace of guilt spread through her about the guest room's condition yesterday when he arrived. But with no advance notice of an incoming bodyguard, she'd had no reason to organize the room. And yet, the guilt didn't evaporate, because she wouldn't have organized it even if she'd known he planned to stay with her.

Passive-aggressive much?

Frustrated, Erin grabbed her jacket and boots, eased open the front door and slipped through, closing it behind her without a sound. The predawn chill sank into her bones before she could get her jacket buttoned up. By the time she stepped off the porch and into her boots, her entire body yearned for the warmth of hot coffee, but there was no time today.

Yes, she was frustrated, because deep down guilt was needling her for more than just the condition of Matt's room.

Right out of the gate, she was breaking Bodyguard Rule

Number One: don't go anywhere without him. But despite the additional guilt brought on by sneaking away, she knew it wouldn't stop her. Her mind set on finding the missing jewels, she couldn't let her mother's hired babysitter interfere with that.

In the barn, Erin worked as fast as she could to saddle Shadow, one of her own horses. With the door closed, she worked beneath the overhead lights to attach her pickax and folding shovel to the saddlebag. The same tools she'd stealth-ordered from the hardware store the previous day. She said a silent thank-you to Hank for leaving the delivery in the barn, unopened.

Flashlight in her pocket, she turned off the overhead lights and led Shadow out through the barn's rear door. The inky darkness made it too dangerous to ride, so she and the horse would walk until her eyes adjusted. When the sky lightened a bit, she'd mount up and they'd pick up the pace. Although going off by herself broke Matt's number one rule, she made a mental one-sided compromise with him that seemed fair: she wouldn't leave the property.

Last night before sleep finally took her, Erin had wracked her brain, thinking of places where one of Alex's accomplices might have hidden the stolen goods. She'd finally settled on an area along the eastern property line of the Montgomery Ranch that sat far from all the post-robbery activity at the house, but close enough to the county road behind the property for quick access.

Shifting the loot back onto the property would have been a clever move, not that any of Alex's cohorts possessed much intelligence. But the police search had focused on public land. Whoever took the haul may have figured sneaking back onto the ranch was a risk worth taking.

Darkness slowed her progress, but Erin was determined

to stick to the dirt road that cut across the property from front to back. When the dawn's light peeked above the horizon, she'd veer to the east. Drawing images of that part of the ranch to mind, she mentally pinpointed possible dig sites.

"Where the hell do you think you're going?"

Erin screeched. Her heart came to a full stop, then roared back to life with the thunderous booming of a kettledrum. She whipped around to find Matt ten feet behind her, shining a flashlight at her face.

Damn it!

She slapped her hand over her pounding heart. "You really need to learn how to approach people without scaring the daylights out of them. And would you get that light out of my eyes?"

"I asked you a question." Matt lowered the flashlight, but only a little.

Asserting his dominance, was he? Erin shone her flashlight in his direction to let him know two could play this game. The scowl on his handsome face brought her a small sense of satisfaction.

Matt shaded his eyes to block the light. "You can't sneak off like this. I thought you understood that."

"I'm not sneaking. I'm going for an early morning ride. I like watching the sunrise from on top of a horse. Besides, it's not like I left the property."

"Remind me where it was that Alex first approached you?" Matt asked. "Oh, yeah. *On* your property."

He certainly had her there.

"Come on." Matt motioned with his light. "We're going back."

Erin's huff of frustration formed a white cloud in the chilled air. She needed to stop letting him get under her skin. At the same time, she managed to remind herself what was at stake. Her parents. Liam. Hank. Tommy. They might all be in danger if she didn't find the missing haul, and now she'd blown her best chance to hunt for the loot. Even worse, Matt would now be more vigilant than ever.

Her brain spun with ideas of what to do. Stewing in anger or arguing with him wouldn't help. Erin drew in a deep breath. Since she wasn't going to give up hunting for the loot, and she doubted she'd get another chance to do it alone, she had no choice but to bring him along.

She tugged Shadow's reins. "I'm not going back. I'm going for a ride, just like I said. Come if you want, but it's a long walk."

She half expected him to stop her, but he stepped up to the other side of Shadow's head and walked with her. "What's your horse's name?"

"This is Shadow." Erin ran her hand over the mare's withers. "The palomino in the barn is Blaze."

After a few more steps, Matt asked his original question again. "What's so doggone important that you're willing to risk your life for?"

In the misty darkness of the quiet morning, separated only by a horse, the sense of intimacy surprised Erin. Intimate, and yet anonymous, like having the privacy screen of a confessional booth between them. She may as well come clean with him. "There's another reason I wanted to ride this morning."

"You don't say."

She ignored the twinge of sarcasm in his voice. "I'm trying to find the stolen jewelry."

Only the clop-clop of Shadow's hooves broke the silence. Then, "Let the authorities handle that."

"You don't understand."

"Then explain it to me."

Erin pressed her lips together. She wasn't used to explaining herself to anyone. But like it or not, figuring out a way to make this work with Matt was imperative. "When Alex was here, he threatened to hurt the people I care about. That's why he paid a visit to Liam."

"How is Liam involved in this? How did Alex know who you visited?"

"Liam attended the party that night. He's the man Alex sent to the hospital after pistol-whipping him."

"That's why his name sounded familiar. I must've seen it when I skimmed the police report." Matt reached for the reins, and Erin let them drop, curious to see what he intended. He brought Shadow to a gentle halt, along with Erin. "Has Liam lived at Hidden Oaks since that night?"

Matt's incredulity almost distracted her from his subtle attempt to end her hunt. Almost. She allowed him to turn her back toward the barn. Well, he'd need a horse if he came with her. No harm in letting him think, for the moment anyway, that he was winning their war of wills.

"Alex hit him so hard, it caused a stroke. Left Liam partially paralyzed, and he needs more care than his wife can handle at home. They're wealthy, so at first they tried keeping him home with private nurses. But he still had a lot of anger. The nurses kept quitting. His wife believed Hidden Oaks would be a good solution until he calmed down. But by the time he had, they'd both developed their own routines and decided not to rock the boat."

"So that's why you visit him? Out of guilt?"

The disdain in Matt's voice made her angry about his presumption. But how could she be and stay honest with herself? "It started out that way, sure. And every time I went, he raged at me." Erin kicked a rock in her path. "I deserved it. Eventually, though, his anger faded. It's taken years to develop the relationship we have now."

"Okay, Liam. Got it. One box checked." Matt continued leading them toward the barn. "But let's circle back to that night. I'm curious about something. After the heist, an anonymous call notified the authorities. EMT and the police arrived within minutes of that initial 911 call. But the report states that someone cut the landline, and your gang took everyone's cell phones."

Erin's posture stiffened, and in the pale gray light of the cold dawn she held his gaze without blinking. "They weren't *my* gang."

"Semantics. And not the point. What I find odd is no one had access to a phone, yet someone reported the crime almost immediately after it happened."

Erin gave a noncommittal shrug.

The deep creases across his forehead softened. "You called the police, didn't you?"

Interesting that Matt deduced what everyone else had missed. "No one was supposed to get hurt. I didn't even know anyone had a gun." Her throat tightened at the memory of Liam lying crumpled on the floor, blood pooling around him from the gash on his head, his face as pale as a sun-bleached skull. Afterward, what had kept her awake at night was knowing that if she'd possessed even half a brain back then, she could have prevented it. Matt was right. She did have guilt. A mountain of it.

"Alex had given us all burner phones, and Liam needed help. I called as soon as the others left the woods."

Her gaze clouded over as horrible memories of that night continued to rush forward. The people she'd known her whole life, their faces filled with terror. The shouts, the screams, overturned tables, broken china and crystal. And then there'd been Alex.

"I'd never seen Alex like that before," she said. "He swore to me that no one would get hurt. But once inside the house, he became a monster. He pistol-whipped Liam just to show everyone he meant business, that they'd better do what he said or else. I was afraid Liam would die. What else could I do but call 911?"

Matt's tone softened. "Did you tell the police you made the call?"

"No."

"It might have helped your case if they'd known that."

Erin's eyes refocused. The way he said it, the look on his face… She could almost think it was empathy.

"That's not why I did it."

"How'd you get involved with Alex in the first place?"

"As a teenager, my mom wanted me to play the socialite's daughter and assist her with charity galas. But I had a rebellious streak and instead volunteered at one of the charities she supported." Erin smiled to herself, remembering her mother's reaction.

Matt snorted.

"What?"

"You and I have different concepts of a teenage rebel."

"I'll have you know, rebels come in all shapes and sizes." She straightened her back, clenching her teeth. Why did this man make her want to argue every little point? "But I thought you wanted to know how I met Alex."

"Sorry. Go ahead."

"As I started to explain, Alex showed up a few months later, also as a volunteer. He was charismatic, and when he showed an interest in someone, they fell under his spell." Erin rubbed her hand over Shadow's neck. "My mother ran off any boys I wanted to date, setting me up instead with the sons of those in her social circle."

"What? You didn't like the rich boys?"

"You can't help it, can you?"

Matt flinched. "What are you talking about?"

"Is it part of your job description to constantly needle me, or do you just enjoy it? Maybe both?"

Putting his hand to his heart, he said, "I'm sorry. Really. Continue, please."

Sucker that she was, Erin chose to believe in his sincerity. "Mainly, I didn't want to turn into my mother." She shuddered at the thought. "Anyway, back to Alex. While a volunteer, he also made friends with a few guys who worked there. I found out later they were on probation and working there as part of a community service program."

"Were you the only girl in the group?"

Erin ducked her head to hide the blush warming her cheeks. "Yes. Alex cultivated a relationship with me separately at first, then started taking me to the bar where he met with the others. He argued, and very convincingly, that less waste on an expensive charity gala would mean more money for the people who needed it. What can I say? I was in love. Or at least thought I was. Plus, I'd witnessed firsthand what my mother shelled out for one of her parties, so I completely bought his argument. He made it sound romantic, like a Robin Hood caper, and I was too young and naive to see it for what it was." She scoffed. "Obviously, the other three knew no money from the stolen goods would make it any farther than their own pockets, but I didn't."

She fell quiet then, unsure of herself. Other than her initial statement to the police, she'd never talked about the burglary with anyone but her lawyer. Never spoken about it aloud in such a detached, fact-based way. Strange that

Matt could ask a couple of questions and parts of her sordid past came pouring out.

"What exactly was Alex's plan?" Matt asked.

"You read the police report."

"I'm sure it's difficult to talk about, but I'd like to hear it from you."

She massaged the back of her neck. "Fine. My parents had a charity gala planned. Alex had magnetic signs made for the charity's van we, uh…borrowed, that made it look like one of the catering vans."

"And that's how you got in?"

Erin paused. "Well, that, and me knowing the gate code. My job was to drive the van. We met at a spot in the woods that Alex had chosen, where the guys hid their bikes. I'd told my parents I wouldn't be home for the party, and we all wore ski masks. I waited by the door while Alex and two of the others collected everyone's jewelry, money and phones and the fourth guy emptied all the women's purses into a bag. There was no one to stop us as we drove back to the woods. They transferred the phones and wallets to one bag that Alex kept with him. We hid the bag of jewelry in a hole already dug, then they all took off in different directions on their motorcycles. I removed the magnetic signs and hid them in some bushes, then I was supposed to drive the van back to the charity."

"But the police stopped you at one of the roadblocks."

She nodded.

"And that happened soon after you left the woods?"

"Not too long after."

"Why didn't any of the others get stopped by roadblocks?"

Erin sighed. "I headed into town, to the charity, and the

cops had *just* set up the roadblock. The others took back roads away from town."

Matt appeared to be making mental notes, and then his tone changed. "Since you were the last to leave, you could have moved the jewelry before you drove away."

"Yeah, right." Erin laughed. "I'm the one who told the police about the hiding place."

"Misdirection. You tell them where the original spot was only after you hide the stuff somewhere else." He shrugged. "You have to admit, it's a possibility."

Erin felt his eyes on her, watching for her reaction. "So you think I'm lying about the loot, and I'm going through all this, this charade, for…what? Fun?"

"Think about it." Matt held up a hand and began ticking off items on his fingers. "You didn't want a bodyguard. You just tried to sneak away. You didn't tell me you were going to go look for the stolen goods. Hell, you didn't even tell me you *planned* on looking for them. Not a lot in there to make you believable."

Though he spoke the truth, his words stung. "Believe me or not. Doesn't matter to me. But then tell me this. Why would I be sneaking off to find the loot if I already have it?"

"Possibly to throw everyone off. Or maybe you just want to move it again. To a safer spot this time. And that's why you didn't want me with you."

"Think what you want. But heads up, Mr. Bodyguard. I *am* going to be looking for the loot, so either get out of my way or put on your spurs and grab a shovel."

They resumed their walk to the barn in silence.

After a few minutes, Matt said, "Okay, say for the sake of argument I believe you and you don't have the stuff. And let's even say that after ten years, you're somehow able to miraculously find this pot of gold. What then? Hand half of it to Alex and keep the rest? Give it all to him so the others won't come after you when they get out?"

And there it was. Judgment once again imbued with his disdainful tone. Erin finally had him figured out. Matt seemed incapable of forgiveness, as his blatant disapproval of her past made clear. "I have no control over what you think, but just to set the record straight, I intend to turn it in to the police. If they have it, there's no reason for Alex to harass me any longer." Erin added in a biting tone, "But I really appreciate your high opinion of me."

"What I think doesn't matter."

"You got that straight."

Matt drew in a sharp breath, then let it out. "Look. We got off to a rocky start. What do you say to me helping you search for the jewelry if you'll agree to wait for full light? Maybe until after I've had some coffee and breakfast."

Erin nodded. Although grateful he'd agreed to help, her ire still simmered. True, her past was against her. And she'd snuck away and omitted telling him about her plan to find the loot. But one thing she'd never been was a liar. And for some reason, it was important to prove that to him before this whole thing was over.

BY THE TIME they finished a quick breakfast and Matt filled two thermoses with hot coffee, the sun was hard at work burning off the ground fog. In his professional opinion, finding the loot was about as likely as a blizzard in Los Angeles, but if nothing else, it would keep Erin close while giving him a chance to map out a good-sized portion of the property.

"Come on." Erin's eagerness to get going annoyed him.

He zipped his jacket, grabbed the thermoses and followed her outside. As he watched her sashay toward the barn, he replayed one portion of their earlier conversation. She'd surprised him with her plan to turn in the stolen jewelry instead of giving it to Alex. Matt frowned. He'd been burned before, so he'd believe that if and when it happened.

As far as her overall character was concerned, the jury was still out on that, but he conceded that perhaps he had judged her without knowing all the facts.

Erin hadn't unsaddled her horse before they ate, and as Matt followed her into the barn now, he realized this meant trouble for him. With Shadow's reins looped over a post, she walked to the third stall down and opened the gate. Patting the neck of the gold horse who must be Blaze, Erin gave her a quick brushing and led her from the stall. She grabbed another set of reins and fit the bit into the horse's mouth, then threw a blanket across the broad back before reaching for a saddle.

Matt rushed to intercept her. In a casual tone, he said, "Why don't we just walk? I'll carry the tools."

Cinching the saddle straps, Erin smirked. "This is an eight-hundred-acre ranch, and we're going to a section on the far southeast side."

Matt was a whiz with numbers, but he didn't know the calculation of acres to miles off the top of his head. "Still—"

By now, Erin was reaching for Shadow's reins. "We'll be out searching all day. I'd prefer riding, though you can walk if you want. Of course, you won't be able to keep up. But trust me, that won't bother me one bit."

"I guess you can't help it either."

Her head cocked in confusion. "Help what?"

"Needling me. Just part of your charming personality, I guess." Matt enjoyed the sour look that crossed her face when her words were thrown back at her.

She surprised him again with her measured response.

"Touché." She dug into her jacket pocket and brought out some chunks of carrots, which she offered Shadow. Those large square teeth chomped on the treat as Erin grabbed Blaze's reins and offered the gold horse some carrots as well. Then she led both animals outside.

Despite the crisp morning, Matt began to sweat. "Why don't we drive? We can take my truck."

"Very kind of you to offer, but the terrain where we're going isn't conducive to vehicles like your truck, even if they're four-wheel drive. And both of the ranch's off-road utility vehicles are in the maintenance shed, you know, being maintained." She gave him a dry smile as she loaded the saddlebags on both horses with tools, emergency supplies and the thermoses.

Apparently, his attempts at disguising his discomfort weren't succeeding, and Erin was enjoying herself way too much at his expense.

"Besides which—" she went on, swinging up onto Shadow in one smooth motion "—the maintenance shed is in the opposite direction from where we're headed, way over on the northeast side of the ranch, near the stable and main bunkhouse."

"Wait. There's another bunkhouse and stable?" This was something he would need to inspect for possible safety concerns.

Her laugh hung in the chilled air. "Where do you think all the rest of our horses are? And where our ranch hands stay, except for Hank, of course? And the grazing pastures are that way, too."

"I thought this was it." He waved his hand to indicate the barn behind them.

"An eight-hundred-acre horse ranch with only two horses?"

"Three horses. What about the black?"

"Redemption is a client's horse. I'm helping him recover from an injury." Erin motioned Matt toward the gold horse. "Mount up."

Damn it. The moment of truth. Matt refused to swipe at the perspiration dripping down the sides of his face. "Look, I've never ridden a horse before."

Not entirely true. He *had* ridden a horse. Once. For about two minutes. But he'd been a kid, and the ornery beast had reared up. Matt had screamed bloody murder and tried to leap off, but his fright spooked the animal and it careened down the trail. Matt's foot got stuck sideways in the stirrup. Before the instructor could get to him, he fell off and landed in a fresh, stinking pile of horse manure. The other kids had still been laughing at him as the bus took them back to school.

All in all, not the worst thing that could've happened, but trauma at that age left scars. To this day, horses petrified him.

Erin's eyes widened. "Never?"

Matt shook his head.

Erin blew out a breath as she walked Shadow over to the gold horse. "Blaze is calm, gentle and absolutely won't buck you off. All you need to do is hang on." She leaned down, grabbed Blaze's reins and handed them to Matt. Then, looking down at him like the Queen of Boone County, she said, "Take hold of the reins in your left hand, up near her neck."

Matt did as she instructed.

"Good. Now put your left foot in the stirrup." Erin gave him an encouraging smile.

Lifting his left leg, Matt tried slipping his toe into the stirrup. But Blaze sidestepped, and his boot slid off the metal.

"Come on, Mr. Bodyguard. We don't have all day."

"Hold your horses." He wasn't amused when Erin laughed at the unintended pun. The only thing that kept him from snapping at her was his concern about provoking her. She might decide to take off and leave him in the dust. Literally.

"Hold the stirrup with your right hand if you need to."

He didn't need to. He didn't even need her instructions. All those years ago, he'd gotten *on* the horse just fine. Getting *off* had been the problem. And he'd let that humiliating and painful experience fester into a phobia.

Matt went for the stirrup again, and this time his boot slid in. Before Erin could tell him what to do next, he swung his right leg over and settled into the saddle. His anxiety settled in too, gripping his guts in a fist of apprehension, because at some point he'd need to get off the horse.

"That was great. You look like you were born to ride." Erin gave him a playful wink. He liked her this way. Not the part about him being the target of her teasing, but the way her joking softened the lines of her face and added a sparkle to her eyes. With the soft light of the rising sun illuminating wisps of her hair like a halo, she looked downright angelic. Beautiful, actually. And that made her dangerous.

"Yeah, right."

She stopped poking fun at him as they took off down the dirt road at a slow walk. "Try holding just the reins."

Matt glanced down at his hands, gripping the saddle horn as well as the reins. "I'm good."

Erin's mouth kicked up at the corners with a smile she couldn't hide. "Seriously, let go of the horn. Between the reins and your thighs, you'll have more control. And it's safer."

Safer. That, more than the smile, made him tighten his

hold on the reins and lift his hands from the saddle. When Blaze tossed her head and snorted, Matt tensed, reins still in a death grip. He wiped sweat off his forehead with his jacket sleeve, then grabbed the horn again. *To hell with what she said.*

Erin blocked his path, stopped and brought her phone out of her pocket. "Let go of the horn, or I'll take pictures of my big, strong bodyguard who can't ride a horse."

Just what he needed. A social media hit to his professional reputation. "Put the phone away."

"I will, but only if you let go of the horn. For real, it's the only way you'll learn how to ride." Erin's mouth set in a firm line. "Or do you want to be afraid of horses the rest of your life?"

Blaze shook her head, snorting at Matt's tight hold.

Matt mimicked the sound but did as Erin demanded.

With a satisfied nod, Erin put away her phone and clicked her tongue. Both horses started moving again.

Matt had planned to get a look at the safeguarding measures implemented at the rest of the ranch's operations, but Erin made it clear they were headed in a different direction. Maybe he'd have time later in the day. If not, he might need to have Blake, the security system installer Nate used on a contract basis, come back out and do the inspection. The ranch had a lot of real estate to cover.

For now, Erin might be able to provide some info. "Why are the big stable and bunkhouse so far away from your parents' house? It doesn't make sense to have a mini setup where you live and all the rest at the back of the property."

"This ranch has three purposes, at least for my mom." Erin's huff of exasperation reeked of sarcasm.

Man, she really doesn't seem to like her mother.

She lifted a hand, her index finger jutting straight up.

"Number one, convey wealth and status. Number two, breed, raise and board horses, and number three, train dressage horses for competition." She rolled her eyes. "Mother used to compete. I think she hangs on to the world of dressage to retain her illusion of youth." Erin scoffed. "Or should I say her *delusion* of youth?"

Oh, yes. The mommy issues came in loud and clear. He'd need to tiptoe around that minefield. "I've heard of dressage, but I don't really know what it is."

"It's a style of riding where the rider uses invisible communication to make the horse go through a series of distinct movements. When done correctly, the harmony between the horse and rider is a beautiful thing to watch. Anyway, the ranch exists because my mom wanted it," she said. "My dad lives to make money and to make my mom happy. Not sure of the order of those two things, but when they planned the layout of the ranch, the only thing my dad requested was that the horse business wasn't in his daily line of sight. He doesn't hate the animals. He just doesn't want them front and center. Personally, I think he dislikes the smell, which is crazy. Nothing beats the scent of horses and hay."

"Then why is your barn, corral and bunkhouse near the front?"

"My place sits behind and to the side of the main house. You can't see it from the front of the house, and the house is angled so the back of it doesn't face it either. Approaching the property and main house, I'm far enough away that the buildings aren't noticeable unless you're looking for them." Erin led the way along a narrow path between towering live oaks. "It was originally built so my mom could train a few dressage horses without having to cross the whole ranch. Eventually, she quit training and assigned me the job."

"So why, with that enormous house, do you live in the bunkhouse?"

"To get away from my mom."

That answer didn't surprise Matt.

"She micromanages every aspect of my life and has since…well, you know. Made sense at the time, since I don't have the best track record when it comes to making good decisions. After the robbery, I didn't trust myself at all. And for a while, after the case was adjudicated, it was easier to let her have her way." She shivered, but Matt doubted it was from the morning chill. "Until one day I just couldn't breathe. So I moved to the bunkhouse."

The horses splashed across a shallow stream.

Matt surveyed the terrain. Fields of winter-dead wild grass stretched away to the west. To the east, the trees grew sparser and the ground vegetation gave way to dirt and rocks. "What makes you think the loot might be buried on your property, and why out here?"

"There've been rumors over the years that Alex or one of the other men doubled back and moved the loot right after the robbery. I know it wasn't me, and I think we can cross Alex off the list since he thinks I have it. That leaves Billy Jensen, who's dead, Brad Parker and Kevin Moore. I can only assume Alex has already talked to Brad and Kevin, especially since they had their prison sentences extended. So, my best guess is that one of them lied, or Jensen moved it but was killed before Alex could question him. It really doesn't matter who moved it, only that it was moved. And whoever did it couldn't get back to retrieve it."

"Except you."

Erin turned her head and narrowed her eyes on Matt. "Except I didn't. And I'm not going to say that again. Got it?"

"Got it." Although she could be lying, somehow Matt didn't think so.

She loosened the reins and Shadow continued at a somewhat faster pace. A pace that Matt didn't care for. Not one bit. His backside was bouncing up and down, hitting the stiff leather of the saddle each time with a hard smack, like swats he'd taken in some of the foster homes he'd lived in while growing up. How the heck did Erin make trotting look so easy and natural?

She moved out in front, telegraphing her displeasure with Matt's speed in a clear message. "So, the way I see it, if no one retrieved it, then it could still be where it was left."

"*Could* be. But someone unrelated to the crime might have found it. Hell, someone who never even heard about the crime could have happened upon it."

"I guess that's possible," Erin conceded. "But not likely if it's on our property. Besides, none of the jewelry ever turned up in a pawnshop. And if one of Alex's guys moved it, then this would have been the perfect hiding place since the cops focused their search in the area where the jewelry had originally been hidden. They didn't search the ranch, because who in their right mind would chance coming back to the scene of the crime? But whoever took it could have planned on waiting until the commotion died down, then slipping back onto the property to recover it later."

"I still say it's a long shot, but my money's on Jensen."

"Jensen was killed within a month of the robbery, ironically while robbing a convenience store. How's that for karma? If he knew where the loot was, why would he do something so stupid? "

"A lot of *ifs* in your thinking, which is why I think this hunt of yours is a colossal waste of time. Not to mention leaving you exposed to any number of potential threats."

Erin glared at him from over her shoulder. "I don't remember asking for your opinion, and it's not like you have anything more important to do right now. Or do you? Maybe you want to quit. There's always that option."

Matt's silence answered her.

"That's what I thought," she muttered.

After a long, excruciating ride, they approached a wooded area interspersed with large boulders, rock piles and scrub brush. Erin dismounted in one smooth move and wrapped her horse's reins around a tree limb. Matt stayed in the saddle, his clammy hands tightly wrapped around the horn again.

"You're going to have to get down if you plan on helping me search." Erin's lips curled into a wry smile. Apparently, her temper had cooled, and she was back to mocking him. "Or have you become enamored of horses and never want to leave the saddle?"

"Getting down seems the more difficult choice."

With the sun above the horizon, Erin squinted up at him. "It's not. You just do everything you did to get on the horse, but in the opposite order."

"Gee, why didn't I think of that?"

"Oh, come on, you big baby. Kids can do this."

Some kids can. Matt exhaled in resignation, then swung his right foot over the horse's back and toward the ground. But his childhood nightmare returned to haunt him. The toe of his left boot slid forward. With Matt caught in the stirrup. Blaze, curse the beast, refused to stand still. She moved sideways, apparently trying to get away from her rider. Matt held on to the horn for dear life, his left foot firmly stuck while his body hung down the horse's flank, his right foot hopping awkwardly on the ground. He and

Blaze did a circular five-legged dance to the tune of Erin's laughter.

"A little help here?"

Still chuckling, Erin grabbed Blaze's reins and, with one word, commanded the mare to stand still. "Get back on her, then when you dismount, don't tip your left foot forward."

Matt followed her instructions and ended up standing on two legs instead of sitting in the dirt. Or worse, in another pile of steaming manure.

"You're doing pretty well with the riding itself, at least at a walk. We can increase your speed gradually. But you need to work on your unhorsing." She gave him an encouraging smile. "Don't worry. If I can teach Tommy Barrows how to ride, I can teach you."

Matt walked Blaze to the tree and wrapped the reins around a branch, repeating her last words in a sarcastic tone too soft to hear. At least this time he'd only bruised his ego.

And while Erin reminded him of his bruised ego with good-natured teasing throughout the day as they poked into rock formations and dug around trees, it didn't bother him nearly as much as he thought it would.

Go figure.

Chapter Six

When they reached the barn, Erin dismounted and took Blaze's reins from Matt. "I'll just hold on to these until you have both feet on the ground." She tried her best to keep a straight face, but the smile playing at the corners of her mouth won.

"Very funny." Matt swung one leg over the horse and managed to get his other foot out of the stirrup without an encore performance of his and Blaze's five-legged boogie.

"You're making progress." Erin handed the reins of both horses to him, then opened the barn doors. "I'll make a cowboy out of you yet."

She replaced Shadow's bridle with a halter and lead rope and knotted it to a tie ring, pleased to see Matt studying and then copying her every move with Blaze. She handed him a brush and showed him how to use it by keeping her hand over his for the first few strokes, ignoring the tingles and sparks in her fingers.

"As you brush, examine every part of her. Look for rubs or chafing from the saddle. Feel her legs for cuts or bumps." Erin returned to Shadow and began brushing. "Between how cold it is outside and how slow we were walking, they won't need much of a cooldown period."

"So what do we do after brushing and checking them over?"

"Give them some hay in their stalls. It was a long day, even moving slowly, so I don't want to feed them grain right away." She glanced at Matt, who seemed to almost enjoy working with Blaze. At least his fear of horses was lessening.

Once the horses were squared away, Erin walked with Matt to the bunkhouse. "Think we need to move the search off the ranch tomorrow?"

But Matt didn't answer, his attention focused on the building's roofline. "Excellent. Nate had the cameras installed." He turned and looked back at the barn, a smile spreading across his face. "And he had enough in stock to send extras."

Erin pulled her gaze from the unfamiliar protrusions adorning the cabin and followed Matt's line of sight. "Why are there cameras on my barn?" Her fingers curled into fists as her mood took a dive.

"I just told you, Nate must have sent extras." Matt climbed the porch steps.

The frustration of once again not being in control, the anger of losing even more privacy, burned through Erin like a river of lava. "I didn't give you permission to install cameras all over the place. You never even asked."

"You must've been too busy trying to think of a way to get rid of me yesterday to pay attention when I took an inventory of the security measures that needed to be beefed up." Matt chuckled.

Erin joined him on the porch, despair drilling a hole in her gut as she noticed even more cameras attached to the porch roof, at least one facing the front door. "Look, I appreciate you wanting to make sure I'm safe. But this is overkill. I don't want cameras on me every time I step out of my house."

"Once this job is over, I'll gladly remove everything we've installed if you no longer want it." One corner of his mouth lifted into a sly grin. "But for now, it all stays. Come on, let's see what Blake did on the inside."

"Who's Blake?" Erin asked.

"The guy Nate uses to install alarm systems."

"I swear, if there's so much as one camera *inside* my home—"

Matt punched in the code and opened the front door. "Relax. No cameras inside." He moved through the rooms, checking the windows, new dead bolts on the doors and everything else he'd had installed without her consent.

While Erin paid attention to everything Matt was looking at, she also checked the ceiling corners and beams for cameras. When she glanced again at Matt, he stood there, grinning.

"What'd I tell you? No cameras inside." Matt held his arms wide.

Erin planted her fists on her hips. "Hmm. I wouldn't put it past you to hide one of those pinhole cameras or baby monitor ones. I should probably check to make sure there aren't any cute stuffed animals sitting around."

Matt barked out a laugh. "You watch a lot of true-crime shows?"

"I know those things exist." Erin examined everything that faced the front door, figuring that was the view Matt would most likely be interested in. "Are the cameras outside to watch for someone trying to break in or to watch for me trying to sneak out?"

Matt, confirming the new thumb locks prevented the

windows from opening, glanced at her. "It's always a good thing when you can kill two birds with one stone."

"Hmph." Erin toed off her boots and dropped onto the couch. She didn't like losing even more privacy, but she understood the need for the cameras—she just wouldn't let Matt know she understood.

"I really can't see checking much more of your property for the loot," Matt answered her earlier question as he sat near her. "Tell me about where you all took the stolen stuff when you left your parents' party."

"Alex had already picked out a spot in the woods. Not too far from here so the stuff could be stashed quickly. Into the trees, a ways in from the road so no one in passing cars would see us, but there's a turnoff where I drove the van in to hide it."

"And you don't know what any of the guys did after you all left the woods?"

Erin shook her head. "They arrested Alex and Brad in the wee hours of the next morning, and brought in Kevin not long after that. Somehow, Billy evaded all the blockades and disappeared."

Matt tapped a finger against his chin. "What if the cop who was supposed to retrieve it only *said* the hole was empty?" Matt leaned forward, his forearms on his knees. "What if *he* took it?"

"He didn't."

"How can you be so sure?"

"The Winston PD got one body camera way back when they first became popular in the US. They wanted to make sure it was worth spending the money before they bought more of them." Erin closed her eyes in shame, recalling the time spent being interrogated. "Chief Simpson told the cop to wear it so they could test its efficiency in the dark."

"There goes that theory." Matt drummed his fingers on his knee. "But even if we only have your gang to work with, we're still narrowing it down. If Brad or Kevin re-hid the stuff, where would they have put it?"

"Would you please stop referring to them as *my gang*?" Erin glared at him before she picked up her phone and opened a map app. Matt slid closer to her and leaned in to view the screen over her shoulder.

"Here's where the stuff was hidden first." She tapped her screen, dropping a pin at the spot in the woods. "The police arrested them here and here." She dropped two more pins at locations on the far side of town.

Matt stayed quiet, focusing on the map. "If we concentrate on the areas between the woods and where the cops picked them up, that will narrow down our hunting ground."

Erin nodded. "At least to start."

"We can do a little more research in the morning about the geography of our target areas, and then I'd like to start out at the original burial spot." Matt tapped her phone screen to indicate the pin.

"Sounds good to me." Erin's stomach growled. "I'm starving."

"That pizza I bought is in the freezer."

"That'll work." Erin stood and stretched, then headed for the kitchen. "I'll turn on the oven, then you can put the pizza in while I take a shower."

After checking the temperature and bake time on the pizza box, she opened the oven door before turning it on. She'd developed this habit after hiding some dirty dishes in the oven and forgetting about them. She never wanted to smell the reek of toxic fumes from melted plastic again. And cleaning up shattered glasses had not been fun.

Erin bent over for a quick peek inside. The oven light

shone like a spotlight on something in the middle of the top rack. Something her mind refused to compute.

"Matt!" Not quite a scream, but loud and shrill.

In seconds, Matt stood by her side. "What?"

Erin pointed at the oven. "There's an eyeball in there."

Crouching, Matt looked inside, then grabbed a paper towel and brought out the item without leaving his fingerprints.

Tommy's latest find, the large marble he'd shown Matt yesterday, sat glued to the center of a white plate. The message, finger-painted in blood, circled the marble.

Tick Tick Tick

BEFORE MATT COULD say a word, Erin rushed to her phone. While it rang, he said, "Put it on speaker."

Tommy's mother picked up.

"Jill? It's Erin."

"Are you all right? You sound funny." Jill kept her voice low.

"I, um, can I speak with Tommy?" Erin eyed Matt, her face a picture of panic.

"He's already in bed. What's going on?"

Matt glanced at his watch, unaware of the late hour.

"This must sound strange, but I was wondering if he still has that marble he showed Matt in the store."

Jill let out a small laugh. "Well, yes it *does* sound strange, calling this late about a marble." The clink of ice cubes in a glass came through the phone. "And even stranger, that marble seems to have disappeared."

"How did it disappear?" Erin asked, sounding calmer.

"Well, Tommy was playing marbles on the front porch when I called him in to put on a warmer jacket. He couldn't have been in the house more than a minute or two, but when he went back out, he claimed that marble was gone. His whole marble collection was out there, but only that one disappeared." Ice clinked against glass again. "It probably just rolled into the bushes."

Matt met Erin's eyes as she raised her hands in a question: *Should she tell Jill what they found?*

Instead of speaking through Erin, Matt said, "Jill, this is Matt. Can we stop by to show you something? It'll only take a minute."

"I guess so. Y'all are starting to worry me."

"No need to worry," Erin said. "We'll see you soon." As soon as she ended the call, she glared at him. "Are you out of your mind? You want to show her what happened to his marble?"

"Of course not." Matt shook his head, surprised she would think that. "We need to show her a picture of Townsend so she can make sure he doesn't get anywhere near Tommy." He pulled a picture from the police file and put on his jacket.

Erin grabbed her coat, and Matt escorted her to his truck with one hand on her shoulder and the other on his gun.

"TOWNSEND IS TRYING to prove he can get to anyone you care about," Matt said as they left the Barrowses' house half an hour after they'd arrived.

"He's done more than try." The anger and bitterness in Erin's voice filled the truck. "He's gotten to Liam and gotten close to Tommy. You should be protecting everyone I know instead of me."

"You think Jill's going to be okay?"

"I hope so." Erin wrapped her arms around herself, as if more than the night air chilled her. "We definitely gave her a scare. At least she agreed to start using her alarm system again."

Matt snapped his fingers. "That reminds me." He tapped a button on the steering wheel. "Call Blake."

A deep voice came through the truck's audio system. "Hey, Matt. What's up?"

"I need you back at the Montgomery Ranch pronto. We need the digital locks for the bunkhouse and barn changed. Front gate, too."

"I didn't change any of those when I was there." Blake sounded wary. "Was I supposed to?"

"No, I didn't think it would be necessary." Matt blew out a frustrated breath. "When you were installing the equipment today, did you see anyone?"

"Just some guy named Hank. Said he was Ms. Montgomery's ranch hand. He offered to help, but you know we can't risk someone getting hurt." Based on the sounds of a car door closing and the engine starting, Blake was already on the move.

"Blake, this is Erin. What did this guy look like?"

"Hmm, probably in his thirties, slim, dark hair, beard and mustache. Looked like he broke his nose at least once." Road noise could be heard in the background now. "I'm on my way. Should be there in about twenty."

As soon as they heard the description, Erin grabbed Matt's arm, her eyes wild. "We have to get to Hank's. Alex might have hurt him."

Stepping harder on the gas pedal, Matt spoke to the phone. "We might not be there when you arrive. Go ahead and change them, then send me the new codes." Erin directed him to continue past the Montgomery Ranch gate. "Do you carry, Blake?"

"Of course. And I never go out for a night job without Brutus."

"That's what you named your gun? Brutus?" Another

mile, and Matt took a sharp right onto a minor road Erin pointed out to him.

A loud bark came through the phone.

"No, man. That's what I named my Rottweiler. He's a big baby, but if anyone even looks at me cross-eyed, he'll protect me or die trying."

"Watch your six. That guy at the house today was the jerk I'm protecting Erin from. We're on our way to check on the real Hank." Matt slowed and took another right turn. "I'll talk to you soon."

Hank's property was a small fraction of the size of the Montgomerys'. The dirt drive led to a small two-story house that looked less out of place in the countryside than the Montgomerys' modern mansion. White clapboard needed paint, a sun-faded red barn leaned a little.

He'd barely stopped in front of the house when Erin opened her door and jumped out.

"Erin!"

"Move faster or yell at me later. I'm not waiting for you to open my damn door." Even so, before she'd made it five steps toward the house, Matt was beside her, gun in hand as Erin bounded up the front steps and pounded on the front door.

Erin pounded again.

"Hold your horses. I'm on my way." Hank's distinctive, gravelly voice sounded from inside.

The door swung open and Erin almost fell into his arms. "Are you all right, Hank?" Her eyes scanned his body.

"Why wouldn't I be? Except for freezing my family jewels. Get in here before we're heating all of Winston on my dime." He opened the door wider and ushered them inside. "What in tarnation is going on?"

"Can we sit down? This may take a few minutes." When

Hank nodded, Matt moved into the small living room on their right. He waited until Hank and Erin had taken seats on the small couch, then sat in the remaining chair. "Erin had a scare tonight and was worried that you might have been hurt."

Hank's head snapped back in surprise as he looked at Erin. "Why on earth would you think I got hurt?"

"Remember I told you about Matt's plan to install a security system at the ranch today?"

"Of course I do. That's why you told me to take the afternoon off." Hank glanced at Matt and stage-whispered, "She wanted to make sure I stayed out of the way while your man was working."

"That's not the reason." Erin frowned. "But Alex pretended to be you, and he walked right into my bunkhouse."

"We worried he might have made sure you wouldn't show up while he was impersonating you," Matt added.

Pulling his lips into a tight line, Hank muttered a string of curse words.

"I would never forgive myself if Alex hurt you while trying to get at me." Erin dragged her jacket sleeve across her eyes.

"Don't be foolish." Hank shook his head. "I've told you before, you're not responsible for what someone else does. And believe you me, if that boy comes prowlin' around you again, I'll be loaded for bear."

Matt rested his forearms on his thighs and leaned forward. "I'm assuming you've had previous contact with Alex Townsend?" He raised a brow and Hank nodded.

"Hank was there the other day when Alex approached me. He ran him off for me." Erin grasped the older man's hand and held it between both of hers.

"Kiddo, you know I'm never going to allow anyone to

hurt you. I knew that boy was trouble waiting to happen when you first started seeing him all those years ago." Hank reached over and wiped a tear off her cheek. "But you were at that age when you were going to do what you wanted, not about to take advice from your parents or some dusty old cowboy." He shrugged. "When he went to prison, I figured he'd be back someday, and I've been ready for ten years. So don't be crying on my account."

"Would you like to stay at the Montgomerys' ranch until this problem is solved?" Matt smiled at Hank. "I think we can fit another air bed into Erin's bunkhouse."

"Or you could stay at the main bunkhouse, with the other hands," Erin suggested.

Hank shook his head. "I appreciate the offer, but I'm fine here. I'll just be more on my toes, now that I know that no-good bum is skulking around."

"Then let me at least install a security system here at your place." As the old-timer shook his head again, Matt continued. "Just a couple of cameras and an alarm. At least until we've taken care of this Alex business."

Hank stood. "I've done fine by myself for this long. Figure I can last until that little thug is gone for good. However the good Lord might choose to make that happen."

Matt and Erin stood when Hank shuffled toward the front door.

Matt shook his hand. "If you change your mind, let me know."

"You kids stop worrying about me. And, Matt, you focus on keeping my kiddo here safe, all right?"

"Will do." Matt paused as he and Erin walked down the porch steps. "The gate, barn and bunkhouse lock codes are being rekeyed tonight. I'll text you the new one as soon as I know it."

Hank gave him a thumbs-up before closing his front door.

On the way home, an oncoming car's headlights washed through the truck cab and Matt glanced at Erin. With her brows knit into a frown and her skin pale in the unnatural light, she resembled a frightened child. He had seen her mad, seen her laugh, seen her determined. But tonight was the first time he'd seen her scared.

His eyes back on the road, he asked, "Do you think you can talk him into the security system?"

"I doubt it. We could install some cameras and ask for forgiveness instead of permission. But I don't think he'd use an alarm. They take a while to get used to, and in the meantime he'd either be setting off false alarms or just not setting it."

"I get it." Matt's job was to protect Erin, not her ranch hand. But if anything happened to Hank, it would destroy Erin.

And somewhere deep in his gut, a suspicion stirred that *that* would destroy Matt.

Chapter Seven

The following afternoon, his empty stomach rumbling with embarrassing sounds, Matt held the door to Bo's Bar-B-Q Bonanza for Erin. The place was one big room with picnic tables and benches lined up in rows across the concrete floor. Erin led him to the back of a small line of people waiting to order at the counter.

"This might be the best smell I've inhaled since landing in Texas." Matt studied the menu on the wall, settling on a brisket sandwich with fries. He kept pace with Erin as they moved through the line, then handed the cashier his credit card. "I've got both of these trays."

Erin side-eyed him. "You don't have to buy me lunch."

"I know that."

"Then why—"

"Because I want to, okay?" Matt picked up his tray and headed to the drink station, where he filled a glass with iced tea.

"Thanks." Erin reached past him to grab a glass, playfully nudging his hip with hers. "I'm just used to paying my own way." Her voice didn't carry the same playful tone as her actions.

"I'm not sure using your parents' money is exactly paying your own way." It was a harsh thing to say, but Erin lived in a bubble of advantages and seemed not to appreciate it.

Gathering silverware from containers on the drink station, Erin paused at his words and faced him. "I do have a trust set up by my mom's parents, but I won't have access to it until I'm older, and I have no idea what the contingencies will be. I receive a small monthly allowance from a trust my dad's parents set up for me. And when I say small, I mean it. The only other money I have to spend on myself now is what I make through riding lessons and dressage training. Maybe you shouldn't be so quick to judge when you don't know the facts." Erin strode across the room and sat at the end of one of the tables.

Ashamed of judging and embarrassing her, Matt hurried after Erin and took the seat across from her. "I'm sorry. You're right, I shouldn't have said that."

"I'm actually glad you did." With jerky movements, she unwrapped her silverware from the paper napkin rolled around it. "Otherwise, I might not have known what you thought about me." With the napkin covering her lap, she picked up her fork and stabbed at the food on her plate. "Or been able to straighten out your misconceptions."

Matt reached across and stilled her hand, holding it until she met his gaze. "I'm sorry for assuming something that's not true about you. It wasn't fair."

"I accept your apology." She pulled her hand from his. "But as for *fair*, look around. I'm still the black sheep of Winston after ten years." Erin scoffed.

Matt surveyed the room, noticing whispers aimed at Erin from other customers. "People around here really carry a grudge, huh?"

"Some of them have good reason to." She met Matt's gaze. "But I didn't expect so much animosity from you."

He fought against looking away from the hurt in her eyes. He'd caused that pain, and the least he could do was accept her silent reproach. "I really am sorry, Erin. I guess sometimes I'm quick to judge, and I have a tendency to say what I'm thinking."

"Forget about it. Let's just enjoy lunch." Her resigned smile didn't reach her eyes, a clear indication she'd not soon forget anything about his hurtful misconception.

When Erin finally focused on eating her food instead of stabbing it, Matt took a bite of his sandwich and changed the topic. "This is amazing. I definitely need to come back here and try the ribs."

With a forkful of pulled pork halfway to her mouth, Erin paused. "I hope you mean that."

"Why do you say that?" Matt tried for levity. "You hoping for another meal on me?"

But instead of smiling at his lame attempt at humor, Erin's expression darkened again. "Brandon and Lisa Bauer own this place. It's named after their son, Bo. He loved barbecue, and he loved the old cowboy TV show *Bonanza*."

Was. Loved. Past tense. A lump of sandwich seemed stuck in Matt's chest as he anticipated what she was about to say. He chugged some tea before Erin continued.

"Bo was their only child. He died from cancer when he was eight."

"So this restaurant is a sort of tribute to their son?" Matt asked.

Erin nodded. "They were already planning on opening a barbecue joint. Bo was super excited about it. But then they put it on hold when he was diagnosed. Later, they went forward with the plans, renaming it for Bo. Part of every dollar they earn goes to cancer research. And they hold benefits twice a year."

Impressed by the depth of Erin's caring about others, Matt made a mental note to not make any more ignorant assumptions about her. And especially not to voice them aloud.

Erin cleared her throat, this time giving him a genuine smile. "Anyway, back to our search."

They'd spent the morning visiting the places Matt had asked Erin to show him—the stolen goods' original hiding spot, and where the police had stopped her.

"How far from the roadblock was the charity you were supposed to return the van to?"

"Only a block away." She shook her head. "If I'd circled around the long way, in the direction Alex and Brad took, I probably would have missed the cops completely."

"Maybe so. But then who would you be today?" Matt arched a brow.

Erin's lips twisted to the side. "Not sure I want to consider the possibilities." Her expression fading, she shrugged. "Looking at it that way, I guess I'm lucky I got arrested."

"That's one of the toughest things about life. Learning lessons the hard way." Finishing his sandwich, Matt wiped the barbecue sauce from his fingers on a paper towel. "So, where to next?"

"The bar. We were supposed to all meet at Mom's."

"Your mom has a bar?" Matt couldn't picture the Southern society queen who'd hired him as a bar owner.

Erin laughed. "Mom's is a biker bar out on the southwest side of town. The guys all had bikes and hung out there, so they figured Sonny and the regulars would alibi us."

"Who's Sonny?"

"Mom's son."

"Of course he is."

"Mom owned the bar until she died. Sonny was always the bartender, and he became the owner after her death." Erin's words spilled out now. "That's where we need to go. See if any of the guys showed up that night."

"Hang on a minute." Matt massaged his temples, trying to slow down and think this through.

"Don't you see?" Her excitement grew. "If any of them did get there, they might have slipped up and said something."

"I don't feel comfortable walking into a biker bar without knowing the layout or anything else. Especially with you."

"What's the difference between Mom's and this place? You didn't have a problem walking in here without knowing anything about it."

"One potential difference could be a bunch of big bikers who don't like us asking questions on their turf."

"I used to go there all the time with Alex. I know Sonny. We'll be fine." Erin drained the last of her tea and stood. "Let's get going."

Matt sighed. It might not be the worst idea to check out Mom's. At least Erin wasn't just sitting around, scared of everything. She was being proactive, taking the bull by the horns, so to speak. But if it *was* the worst idea, it'd be too late to do anything about it by the time the door closed behind them.

SINCE MATT HAD offered to help her look for the loot, and especially since he'd agreed to go to the bar with her, Erin stayed in the truck until he went through his process of letting her out at Mom's.

As Matt took in the old, dilapidated building, Erin tried to see it as if it were her first time here. A faded wooden sign above the door that read *Mom's*. Neon beer signs in the two tinted windows, making it harder to see in than out. A long row of bikes in front of the bar, most of them backed in to make for an easier, quicker getaway.

Matt held the front door open for her, but stayed tight to her side as they entered. Erin's eyes took a long moment to adjust to the dim room, and when they did, every person in there was staring at them.

Erin faltered for a moment, then approached the bar with a big grin. "Hi, Sonny. It's been a while."

Sonny, a glass in one hand and a dish towel in the other, smiled at her, just as he always had in the old days. But back then, that smile had been almost pitying. Like she was in over her head, hanging out with Alex and his friends, and it was only a matter of time before she figured that out, too.

The burly man glanced at his watch. "About ten years, give or take. How you doin'?"

Shuffling of feet throughout the room, a few low comments between men at the tables, and Erin's memories of being a teenage rabble-rousing rebel evaporated, leaving behind images of a naive do-gooder who had fooled herself into thinking she could hang with the tough crowd.

"I'm good." She took a step back. "This is my friend Matt."

Both men nodded at each other, which apparently took the place of a handshake in situations like this.

Erin settled onto a barstool. "Can we get a couple of drafts?" While Sonny filled two mugs, Erin motioned for Matt to sit next to her instead of scanning the room like… well, like a bodyguard. "You hear Alex is back in town?" she asked the bartender.

Sonny glanced at her over the mugs as he set them in front of Erin and Matt. "A few of the guys mentioned seeing him. He hasn't been in here, though. Pretty sure having a beer with some of my clientele would violate his parole." He chuckled.

Erin took a long draw on her beer. "I know we were in here a lot, so you might not recall just one specific time, but do you remember if Alex, Brad, Kevin or Billy came in here the night of the *Charity Hold-up*?" Yes, their crime caper had an official name around town. "We were supposed to meet here afterward. I obviously didn't make it, but I was wondering if any of the guys did."

A man in biker leathers yelled from one of the tables. "You mean, did they stop in here for a quick beer while you were ratting them out to the cops?"

Brad Parker, Kevin Moore and Billy Jensen had been working at the charity for community service as part of their probation terms. But they'd been bikers long before that, and this bar had been their favorite haunt. Of course everyone in here hated her for snitching on their friends.

Her idea to come to Mom's for information seemed less and less like a good one.

Since the robbery, Erin had dealt with her guilt about stealing valuable items from her parents' guests, friends and neighbors. She'd sought redemption for being part of a caper that caused a man to have a stroke. Now she faced the flip side of the coin. She hadn't turned in Alex and the others to save herself from prison, although that's what most people thought. She did it because what they'd done was wrong. The moment Alex had pistol-whipped Liam O'Roarke, causing him to collapse, Erin knew she couldn't live with herself if she didn't report him. It was the same moment she'd realized what she thought was love was as nonexistent as Alex's *good* intentions.

But now she was seeing herself the way these men saw her—as a backstabber. A snitch.

She understood why they wouldn't want to help her. The code they lived by wasn't one of right and wrong, at least not in the sense of most people. It was based on loyalty to each other, regardless of what any of them had done.

Erin spun her barstool around and faced the room. "I'm sorry that you consider me to be the bad guy. But Alex put an innocent man in the hospital that night. And the police found out that he was my boyfriend before I even told them anything."

One of the men at the pool table walked toward her, slapping his cue against the palm of his hand. "Still doesn't make it right. Either you're loyal or you're a rat."

A chorus of *yeah, that's right, tell her* rose from various tables.

Matt stood and moved in front of Erin, and she finally understood how dangerous his job could be.

But before anyone made a move, Sonny wadded up his towel and threw it on the bar. "Y'all shut up and sit down. You're getting all worked up about something that happened years ago." He moved into the room, giving those still on their feet a hard look. "You think beating up on a woman is going to make bigger men of you?" His sneer as he went back behind the bar answered the question for them.

Matt sat again, rested his forearms on the bar top and angled himself toward Sonny. "Look, we didn't mean to cause any trouble. The thing is, Alex has been harassing Erin about the loot that disappeared back then. We thought if you could remember which of the guys made it to the rendezvous here that night, we might be able to help Alex find it and get him off Erin's back."

Sonny glanced at Erin, then back at Matt. But not before

she caught a glimpse of the Sonny from the past. The one who had felt sorry for her.

Erin leaned in. "Which of them made it back here that night, Sonny?"

"Townsend, Parker and Moore. All of them except you and Jensen." He kept his voice low.

"Did they say anything? Or did you overhear them talking?" Matt asked.

Sonny's eyes slid to the bikers before he grabbed his towel off the counter. "All they knew was the cops showed up way faster than they'd expected. They hung out here for about an hour, knowing most of the guys here would give them an alibi. And when you—" Sonny looked at Erin again "—didn't show after an hour, they figured you'd been picked up. The other two kept whining about how you were going to turn them in, but Townsend told them he had you wrapped around his little finger and you'd never do that."

Erin swallowed back regrets that always skimmed the surface of her emotions. Not regret for turning in Alex Townsend but regret for thinking he'd actually cared for her.

"The only reason I'm telling you this is because I never liked that guy," Sonny continued. "He was the new one in their group, but the other three acted like he could walk on water. Reminded me of those cult leaders you hear about on the news."

Matt nodded. "I'm aware of how easily some people fall under another's malicious spell."

Erin wondered for a moment if he meant her, or someone from his past. "Did they talk about the stolen stuff at all?"

Sonny shook his head. "They were trying to act natural. Didn't even get hinky about you until right before they left."

Matt leaned back when Sonny started wiping the bar

in front of him. "Did you know about the robbery before-hand?"

"Me?" Sonny paused, his bar rag mid-swipe. "Nah. I don't think anybody did until the police set up the road-blocks and word started getting out. I figured out the part about them setting up their alibi here after overhearing what little I did."

"Thanks, man." Matt stood and shook Sonny's hand. "We appreciate your help."

"One last word of advice." Sonny leaned closer and kept his voice low. "When word got out about the loot disap-pearing, every lowlife in this county searched for it. That stuff ain't hidden around here, and it's a waste of time looking for it."

"Thanks again." Matt grabbed Erin's elbow before she could respond and steered her toward the door. And he didn't let go until she was seated in the truck with the door locked.

Mulling over what they'd learned, Erin waited for Matt to start driving before putting her thoughts into words. "So, where should we look this afternoon? The woods where they were first buried, maybe?" She watched the bikes grow smaller in the passenger-side mirror. "If you think about it, the fastest way to get rid of the loot would have been to move it somewhere close to the original hole."

Matt was silent for a mile marker, probably wondering why she was still so insistent on the loot being around here, even after Sonny mentioned the treasure-hunt riot that en-sued after the arrests.

"It's clouding up." He craned his neck forward and looked up through the windshield. "And it'll be even darker in the woods. If you want to try for that area, I'd rather start early tomorrow morning."

Erin accepted his idea with a nod, thankful he didn't outright say that she was crazy to keep trying. She checked her watch. "In that case, I'd like to check in with Liam again. If that's okay with you."

"I thought you said you don't visit him this often."

"I usually don't. But I figure we'll be busy for the next several days, so this will be a good time to stop by."

"Next stop, Hidden Oaks."

Erin smiled as she watched the scenery pass by. It had been a good day so far, and nothing would spoil the rest of it.

Chapter Eight

Alex Townsend laughed as the truck he'd been following turned onto the road leading to the old folks' home. Erin had a surprise waiting for her there. Nothing gruesome. Just a little reminder that time wasn't on her side.

Twisting the throttle on his bar brother's bike, Alex continued straight on the main road, traveling like a bat out of hell. He preferred riding fast, especially after tailing Erin and her bodyguard boyfriend. That guy drove like Alex's grandmother used to—crawling along below the speed limit and slowing at every intersection. At least his grandmother had an excuse: she could barely reach the pedals and see through the windshield at the same time.

He couldn't understand why Erin didn't just hand over the loot and be done with it. She had to have it. Only thing that made any sense. Why she was dragging this out, pretending to search for it, was beyond him. But if she insisted, he'd keep having fun with her. At least, until Cowboy's deadline caught up with them.

The kid's marble in the oven had been perfect. And easy, too. Then all that running around to the kid's house and the old-timer's ranch. They'd been so upset, no one had noticed Alex. Hiding in the dark, but always one step ahead.

Unable to follow them into Mom's today, he'd called a friend inside the bar while he waited outside. He got the gist of why they were there. But it bothered him that Sonny had huddled with them at the bar. He might need to pay a visit to his favorite bartender and learn what the big secret was about.

But now, as he slowed to the town speed limit to avoid getting pulled over, full-visor helmet hiding his identity, he focused on his next plan to light a fire under dear *Eriss*. And it was a real humdinger, all right.

Chapter Nine

Matt noticed the receptionist's brows pulled into a worried frown when they approached the front desk. "I'm not sure how well your visit will go today. Liam is a bit frazzled."

Erin signed in and handed Matt the pen. "Why? What's happened?"

"He had another visitor a while ago, and after he left Liam seemed very upset. He's calmed down a little since then, but not much." The receptionist answered the ringing phone and placed the caller on hold. "We've notified Mrs. O'Roarke, and she's on her way. The police are already here."

"The police? What did this visitor do?" Erin pulled the sign-in sheet out from under Matt's hand before he could finish his signature. Skimming down the list, she tapped her finger on the name of Liam's last guest. *Alan*, followed by a squiggly line. "It has to be Alex. That's the same name he used last time he came here."

Replying to Erin's last question, the receptionist said, "Apparently, he threatened Liam. That's why we called the police."

"Who was on duty at this desk when the visitor checked in?" Matt turned the register sheet around and held it in front of her nose.

"Well, that would be... Let me just check the sign-in time—"

"Come on. We can deal with whoever screwed up later." Erin speed-walked through the maze of hallways to Liam's room.

The door stood open, and the small room seemed to overflow with people even before they stepped inside. Two policemen, an aide, a woman in a suit with a calm demeanor that practically screamed, *We are not responsible and you can't sue us*, and Liam, dressed in a somewhat fashionable sweat suit, sitting in his wheelchair, his hands in his lap, trembling.

"Liam!" Erin rushed across the room and crouched next to the elderly man. "Are you all right?"

As she laid her hand on his arm, he slowly lifted one of his to cover hers.

"What happened?" Erin spoke softly. "Who came to see you today?"

Liam's eyes closed. "When he was here the other day, he said his name was Alan and that you'd told him to come visit me." His voice fluttered like a newly hatched butterfly. "But today he told me he's Alex Townsend, the one who..." He opened his eyes, lifting his hand again to gesture to the room. "The one who put me in this place. I thought I recognized him the other day. Just couldn't think of the name."

Although he'd expected Liam's answer, Matt's pulse accelerated at the name of the man he was protecting Erin from. He stepped closer to the older gentleman, needing more information. "What exactly did he say to you today?"

One of the cops interrupted. "Just hold on here. Who are you two?"

Steve Folsom, the other officer and someone Erin knew well, answered. "She's a good friend of the victim."

"And I'm her bodyguard, protecting *her* from your suspect."

Pulling his eyes from Erin, Liam pinched his brow together as if trying to remember Alex's words. "He said if you don't give him all the stuff you stole, he was going to put me out of my misery."

"Liam..." Erin seemed at a loss for words.

"Threatening an old man in a wheelchair? That didn't upset me so much." He smiled wanly at Erin before turning back to Matt. "But when he said he'd pay a visit to my wife..." His voice broke, and he looked away, unable to hide the fear in his eyes.

Erin wrapped her arms around his shoulders. "It's okay. He's not going to hurt you *or* your wife. We'll make sure of that." She looked at Matt over Liam's head, her eyes holding as much desperation as Liam's did fear. "Right?"

No. Not desperation. Matt tried to sort the many thoughts running through his head. Hope. Erin was looking to him to help keep her hope alive. Hope that he'd be able to keep not only her but also Liam safe. Hope that he'd help ensure an end to Alex Townsend's evil machinations and threats.

But could he? He'd never felt the pressure of his job as much as he did in that moment. Oddly, most of the pressure stemmed from his heart.

Shaking off his doubts, he organized his thoughts.

His number one priority was Erin. But he'd call Nate about the O'Roarkes. His partner—no, boss—would agree they couldn't leave the older couple to the mercy of Townsend.

"Yes, of course." He managed a smile at both Erin and Liam. "We'll speak with Mrs. O'Roarke when she arrives and discuss security measures."

Erin's eyes softened, and the smile she returned his way

did more to ease his doubts than all of Nate's pep talks combined.

After a few moments, Liam had calmed down enough to want a cup of coffee.

"You got it." Erin straightened out of her hug, brow raised at Matt. "You want one?"

Matt nodded. "I'll go with you so you don't have to balance three cups. I'm sure the police would like to finish taking Liam's statement."

It wasn't until they were several doors down the hall from Liam's room that Erin spoke. "I can't believe Alex threatened a sick old man. As if Liam has anything to do with me finding the jewelry."

"I'm sure it's meant as added motivation for you." Matt tried to keep his tone level but felt as enraged as Erin sounded. Only truly vile people went after children and the elderly. "Probably thinks his threats to hurt the O'Roarkes will make you try even harder, and faster, to find the stuff. Remember the message with Tommy's marble."

Erin, mouth pressed in a flat, firm line, turned a corner and stepped into a small kitchenette.

"How many other people do you think he's running around trying to intimidate?" Matt asked.

Erin filled three paper cups with coffee from a large carafe. "Not that many, to be honest. My parents will be in Europe for at least another week, and I don't really have any close friends anymore. Liam and Hank are about the only people I spend any time with at all, other than those I give riding lessons to. And there haven't been any lessons since before Alex got out of prison, so I can't think of a way he could find out who they are. The only reason he found Tommy was because he followed us to the store."

Matt picked up two of the cups, leaving one for her to

carry. "That's good." Good for potential people Alex could threaten, but sad that Erin had only an old man in a care facility and her ranch hand as friends.

A few minutes after they returned to Liam's room, Maeve O'Roarke arrived, quick to sit by her husband's side and take his hand in hers. "The front desk said a visitor upset you and I should come right away." She looked around at Erin and Matt. "Who was it? What's going on?"

The police and staff had left, so Erin took a deep breath, then repeated the whole story. "I'm so very sorry. I feel responsible for him coming back into your lives."

The older woman left her husband's side long enough to give Erin a hug. "Don't be ridiculous. You've more than made up for your small part in that…past incident." She glanced at Matt.

"This is Matt. He's not just a friend." Erin looked at Liam, her cheeks flushed from her previous fib. "He's my bodyguard. My parents insisted on hiring him when they heard Alex was back in town."

"I think we need protection for you too, my love," Liam said to his wife. "He's threatened both of us, and I don't want to take any chances that he'll show up at our house and hurt you."

"I'd be happy to call my boss, see if he has someone available," Matt offered.

Maeve gave him a firm nod. "Can you check with him right now? I'd like to get this taken care of so Liam can stop worrying."

"If you'll excuse me a moment, I'll make a call to get the ball rolling." Matt fished his phone out of his pocket. "And afterward, I'll need to have another word with the facility's administration. I'm not too happy that after I informed the receptionist of the possible danger Alex represented and to be on the lookout for a man of his description, he was able to walk into a resident's room unchecked."

"Really?" Maeve's countenance darkened like a storm rolling in. "Well, we'll just see about that. With as much as this place is charging, along with the status of most of its residents, they should be able to keep every one of them safe from ill-intended visitors. I'll be right back, dear." She laid a kiss on her husband's forehead and steamed out of the room, Matt following to make his call.

After speaking with Nate to arrange a bodyguard for Maeve, and an hour-long meeting with the owner of the facility, the head administrator, the chief financial officer and the front desk receptionists, the agreement reached provided 24/7 protection outside Liam's door by Resolute Security, with the facility and the O'Roarkes splitting the fee.

And as much as the increased revenue for his future co-owned business was appreciated, it was the warm glow in Erin's eyes when she looked at him when they left for the ranch that revived his spirit.

ON THE WAY HOME, Matt glanced at Erin. Her satisfaction with the security arrangements for the O'Roarkes no longer had her glowing. "You okay?"

"I'm furious." She leaned back against the headrest. "Ten years later, and the first thing to make me this mad since Alex hit Liam has to do with Liam again."

Matt understood her frustration. "We'll make sure Liam and Maeve are safe. Don't worry."

"The thing is, I've always hated physical violence." Erin's hands, resting on her thighs, curled into fists. "But right now, I want to punch Alex Townsend all the way back to prison."

"I'm sure you do, especially since he's messing with people you care about."

"We need to find him." Erin drummed her fisted hands on her thighs. "Today. Right now."

"Aside from the fact that my job is to keep Alex away from you, we have no clue where he is. And even if we did, beating him up would only put you in jail, not him." Matt kept his voice even so as not to aggravate her even more.

Erin fumed the rest of the way back, jumping out of the truck the moment Matt parked it next to the barn. She strode toward the building.

Still trying not to add to her ire, Matt refrained from reprimanding her on not waiting until he opened her door. "Where are you going?"

Erin yanked open the barn door but stopped long enough to answer him. "I need to go for a ride. Blow off some steam. Clear my head."

Dread that had nothing to do with Alex Townsend punched Matt in the gut. "You know I have to go with you, right?"

"I'm aware. But if you can't keep up, I'm not stopping to wait for you."

Matt followed her inside, and as Erin saddled Shadow, he did the same with Blaze. Thankfully, by the time they were done, she seemed a bit less combustible.

"I'm impressed." Erin handed a pair of gloves to him before pulling on her own. "You remembered how to do it."

"I might've snuck a look or two at what you were doing, just to make sure." Proud of getting the hang of some of this horse stuff, Matt pulled on the leather gloves with polar fleece lining. At least his hands wouldn't freeze as the late afternoon temperature dropped.

They led the horses out of the barn, and Matt made sure

the door lock clicked before they swung into their saddles. He kept up with Erin's trot along the ranch road, but when they reached a grassy meadow off to their right, she kicked her heels once, and Shadow took off at a gallop.

Matt watched her go, knowing he wasn't ready to match her speed and keep up with her. But he also knew she wasn't trying to lose him, so he kept his anger in check and trotted after her. As his backside banged against the saddle, Matt winced and shifted as best he could.

Although he could still see Erin, her unbraided hair flying behind her, the distance between them grew. As if sensing they needed to catch up, Blaze segued into a lope that helped Matt sit rather than bounce.

Normally unwilling to tolerate pushback against his rules from his clients, Matt had surprised himself with cutting Erin some slack for this ride. It had been a roller coaster of a day, and as she herself had told him, Alex wouldn't hurt her as long as he thought she'd find the jewelry for him. Maybe her willfulness with him served as a counterbalance for her deference to almost everyone else in her life.

Blaze snorted.

Breaking out of his reverie, Matt gazed across the meadow. Tall grass, wildflowers, trees here and there. But no Erin. A jolt of panic kicked him in the chest. He let out on the reins, but white-knuckled the section he held, and let his horse do what she'd wanted to do all along. Gallop.

He had to trust that the horse knew its way across the property, because Matt's steering skills were limited to low-speed jaunts. But as they covered more ground, his fear of riding faded and he began to enjoy the ride. Almost the same exhilarating experience as riding a wave.

Matt leaned forward, his eyes watering from the cold air. A blurry shape materialized up ahead and transformed into

Erin as he gained ground. She must have heard him, because she looked over her shoulder and reined in Shadow to a stop.

Blaze's primary goal must have been to catch up, because she slowed on her own and stopped next to Erin.

"Well, look at you." Erin arched a brow as Matt's horse circled around and nuzzled hers. "You galloped."

"I did." Matt gasped for breath. "But it's a good thing she stopped, 'cause I have no idea where the brakes are on this thing."

A faint smile curved her lips.

"I get it now. How it pulls the tension and stress from your body and frees your mind."

Erin nodded. "It's the only thing that does it for me."

"It's the same with surfing. Slide into the pocket of a barrel wave or catch a point break, and it's just me and the wave."

Erin climbed down from Shadow, walked her to a tree and draped the reins around a branch. "You'll have to explain all those surfing terms to me one of these days."

"Happy to." Matt got off his horse and tied her next to Erin's. "Did the—" he turned to find her pacing in circles, her hands curling into fists and then opening, again and again "—ride help?"

"Yes, but that's the thing. When the ride's over, everything you're running from catches up with you again and fills your head and your heart and your soul." Erin massaged the back of her neck. "My entire body is like one big knot, and I just can't relax."

"I know that feeling, and I've got the perfect way to help you blow off some steam."

ERIN FROZE MID-PACE at her bodyguard's words. "What could I possibly do out here that would calm my anger?"

Matt raised his gloved hands in a defensive position. "You've been wanting to punch someone, so come on. Hit me."

Erin took a beat to stare at Matt in confusion. "What on earth are you talking about?"

"Trust me." Matt demonstrated what he meant by punching his right fist into his left palm. "This will make you feel better. There's nothing like pummeling a boxing bag to release all that negative energy. We don't have a bag, so use me."

Erin tilted her head to one side and considered Matt as an opponent. She'd never hit anyone in her life. "I don't know..."

"Just try it." Matt widened his stance.

With nothing to lose, Erin approached him. Her gloves were a far cry from what boxers wore, but at least they offered her knuckles some protection. She balled her hands into fists, raised them and—

"Put your thumbs on the outside of your fists. Otherwise, you'll break them."

After a quick adjustment of her fingers, Erin pulled back her right arm and drove her fist into Matt's palm with all the force of a gnat landing on an overripe banana.

"Seriously?" Matt scoffed. "I know you're packing a harder punch than that. *Hit* me."

"Fine. I'll *hit* you." This time she slammed her fist into his hand, satisfied when she felt him bracing for impact. "Happy?"

"Ecstatic." Matt reset his stance. "Now this time, say what you're upset about when you punch me."

With her lips twisted to one side, Erin imagined the cause of most of her torment. "Alex Townsend." *Punch.*

"Be specific," Matt demanded. "Why him?"

Saying his name aloud lit a fire in her veins, and she answered Matt with loud conviction. "For screwing up my life." *Punch.* "Twice!" *Punch. Punch.* "For Liam." *Punch.* "And threatening everyone I care about." *Punch.*

"What else are you mad about?"

Erin's answer came as swiftly as her punches. "My mother."

"Why?"

"For holding me hostage." *Punch.* "Controlling me." *Punch. Punch.* She alternated blows with her right and left hands. The crisp air chilled her cheeks, and she realized they were wet.

Not possible. She never cried.

"For hiring a bodyguard without even discussing it with me." The punches came fast and furious now. "And I have no privacy. You invaded my house. Put up cameras. Don't let me out of your sight."

Though she'd aimed the last words at him, Matt's tone never became defensive. "Who else?"

As her tears flowed, Matt blurred into an indistinct shape. "Me."

At that, Matt's expression faltered.

As did her punches.

"I'm mad that I let Alex ruin my life. That I played a part in Liam's injuries. That I don't have the backbone to go against my mother or to start my own therapy ranch." Erin's fists fell to her sides, her ragged breaths disintegrating into sobs.

Matt wrapped his arms around her, his punching-bag hands holding her close.

Physically exhausted, mentally drained, Erin rested her cheek against his chest.

"Feel better?"

Although he kept his arms around her, Matt loosened his hug as Erin lifted her head and looked up into his eyes.

The silent moment held as Erin slid her arms around Matt's neck and kissed him. Probably breaking another one of his rules, but she didn't intend to break it alone. She kept her lips pressed against his until he kissed her back with a passion that chased away her demons.

At least, for now.

Chapter Ten

Matt sat on the front porch steps with his hands wrapped around a steaming cup of coffee, watching Erin work with the dressage horse in the corral. His momentary panic from waking up and finding her gone for the third day in a row had eased when he checked the security cameras and saw her in the barn with Hank.

His first instinct, anger at her not following his rules, had faded as he backed up the footage and reviewed it. She'd taken the same precautions before leaving the house that she had yesterday. And to be honest, he appreciated the extra shut-eye. Sleep had been a long time coming as he tried to make sense of what happened last night. Although Erin had initiated it, he never should have kissed her back, regardless of how much he'd enjoyed it. But he'd been ambushed by the sudden desire that overtook him when her sweet tongue slipped between his lips and the length of her body pressed against his.

I made a mistake. It won't happen again.

A tone from his phone alerted Matt to the front gate opening. He jumped to his feet, unzipped his jacket for easier access to his gun and rounded the bunkhouse. A truck made its way around the main house and continued toward them.

About to race to the corral and get Erin inside, a text chirped on Matt's phone. A quick glance showed Nate's name.

Don't get your panties in a bunch. It's just me.

"What is it?" Erin called to him.

Matt headed toward the barn's parking area. "Nothing to worry about. My boss is paying us a visit."

Leaning against the barn, Matt waited for Nate to climb out of his truck. "A heads-up would have been nice *before* you came through the gate."

"What would be the fun in that?" Nate grinned. "Figured a mini readiness test couldn't hurt."

"Your sense of humor could use some work." He led Nate toward the bunkhouse. "Seriously, what are you doing out here?"

"I want to go over the logistics of our new clients." Nate waited for a response before knitting his brows. "The O'Roarkes?"

"Oh, yeah. Man, that seems like it was weeks ago instead of just yesterday."

Nate pulled the collar of his jacket up. "I don't suppose you have any coffee."

"Coffee's the first thing that happens around here. Come on, I'll introduce you to Erin on the way."

They shifted their direction and walked down to the corral, where Erin waited inside the gate.

"Erin Montgomery, Nate Reed."

Nate reached across the fence to shake her hand. "Nice to meet you, Erin. I trust Matt's been taking good care of you?"

"I guess if I have to have a bodyguard, he's not too bad." She glanced at Matt. "He's come in handy a time or two."

"Good to hear."

In an innocent voice, Erin asked, "Are you here to do a quality-control check?"

Nate snorted. "I've worked with Matt long enough to know he's the best there is. Well, second best, after me." He gave his friend a sly wink. "I just came by to review the additional security we're putting in place for the O'Roarkes."

"Thank you. I appreciate you taking care of them." Her expression darkened. "If Alex hurt Liam or his wife, I couldn't live with myself."

"We aim to make sure that doesn't happen," Nate said.

"It was a pleasure meeting you." Erin turned and walked Redemption toward the center of the corral.

Inside the bunkhouse, Matt poured Nate a fresh cup and refilled his own.

"What was with the weird mane on that horse?" Nate asked.

Happy to know something about horses that his friend didn't, Matt said, "It's how they fix them for dressage horses. Don't you know anything about elite horse competitions?"

"I see she's rubbing off on you. Let's hope the opposite's not true."

"Ha! She should be so lucky."

Nate's eyes scanned the bunkhouse. "So, this log cabin is where she lives?" Nate took a sip and swore. "Damn it, this is hot."

"Give it a minute and it won't be. I never thought Texas got this cold." Matt led his friend back out to the front porch. "And yes, this bunkhouse is where she lives. And me, too, for the duration."

"It's small."

"Tell me about it." Matt grimaced.

"How many bedrooms?"

Matt gave his friend a wry smile. "Two, of course. Which reminds me, I've got a receipt for an air bed to turn in." He added, "I'm in the junk room."

"How fitting." Nate laughed. "Just so you stay there. You don't need any more complications like you had in LA with Meryl Duncan, mixing business with pleasure."

"Hey, everything seemed great until she started getting serious." Matt shrugged. "It was never meant to last, anyway."

"Have things been going better between you and Erin since the first day?"

"Definitely. It's still a bit of a battle from time to time, but she's not as hostile as she was on day one." Matt's gaze drifted to Erin, directing the black horse in movements.

"Exactly how much better *are* things going?" Nate asked, pulling Matt's attention to his boss's raised brow. "It's hard to believe you could go from not wanting to even take this job to that wistful stare when you look at her in a matter of days."

"Wistful?" Matt scoffed. "Did Bishop give you one of his word-of-the-day calendars?"

Nate sipped his coffee, apparently waiting for a serious answer.

But Matt changed the subject. "Speaking of Bishop, has he had any luck tracking down Alex?"

"Not a trace." Nate had given the job of finding their nemesis to his brother-in-law and convenient office-next-door private investigator. "The guy hasn't met with his parole officer since he got out, and there's a warrant out for him on that. Not sure how his escapades at Hidden Oaks will factor into the whole situation." He paused. "I'm still waiting to hear why you look at Erin like a lovesick puppy."

"Give it a rest, Nate." Matt shrugged. "She's just not… who I thought she'd be. I admire her for trying to make up for her mistakes."

"Matt—"

"Chill, *boss*. I know you're just worried about the company's reputation if Mrs. Montgomery disapproves of us, but she won't. What happened with Meryl was a one-time thing. A job opportunity as her personal bodyguard that turned *personal* after I moved into her house." Matt side-eyed Nate. "But you have to admit, considering how things worked out for you and Sara, this feels like the pot is calling the kettle black."

Falling in love with Sara, the woman he'd been protecting in Resolute, was the reason Nate hadn't returned to their business in California.

"That's different. We'd known each other years earlier."

"Uh-huh."

"She was my sister's best friend. Practically part of the family."

"Uh-huh."

Nate blew out a breath.

"Don't worry. Nothing will ever happen between Erin and me." *And nothing* serious *will ever happen with anyone.* Matt's parents had shown him the worst-case scenario of a marriage—one that ended in tragedy. And most of the foster families he'd lived with hadn't been much better. They had all taught him well. He stuck to casual relationships and ended them as soon as they took a turn toward long term.

Although the passion of their kisses still lingered within him, Matt's determination to avoid getting too close to anyone stayed resolute. And especially with Erin. Because it would be unprofessional. It would jeopardize a renewed partnership with Nate. It would mean he believed she deserved her second chance. And giving someone a second chance could kill you.

"Glad to hear it," Nate said. "Now let's go over the plan for keeping the O'Roarkes alive."

Matt shook off old memories best forgotten. "Finally. I thought you'd never get to it."

"I'm assigning Charlie to Mrs. O'Roarke. She'll be with her 24/7, like you are with Erin."

"What about Liam?" Matt asked.

"Hidden Oaks has a contract with a security agency. They agreed to post one of their men outside Liam's door until this is resolved. Hidden Oaks decided to pick up the full bill since we're not providing the man, and because they don't want the O'Roarkes to sue them."

"That's good news."

"Liam and his wife wanted one of our men instead, but I don't have anyone else available." Nate stretched his legs out to a lower step. "I assured them the other company has an excellent reputation. They don't provide bodyguards, just big men with bigger muscles who guard doors. And they do it well."

"That will make Erin happy." Matt focused on his coffee mug to avoid looking at her. He didn't need another round of Nate's unsolicited and unnecessary advice.

"So, you've obviously kept our client safe. Any updates for me?"

After Matt gave his boss a rundown of the week's activities so far, Nate let out a low whistle. "You've been busy."

"Yep. And as soon as Erin's done working with the horse, we'll head out to look for the stolen goods again. We've got more precise information on where the police searched during the original investigation. We're going to move beyond that perimeter."

"Is it wise to take Erin out on these searches? It seems like a risk."

"Alex Townsend won't bother her because he wants what we might potentially find. And unless the police find and arrest him for parole violations, this will never end. If we locate and turn in the loot, he has no leverage over her."

Nate tipped his head back and looked toward the sky with his well-known thinking look. "He might want to take revenge if she foils his plans."

"Look, the day after I arrived, Erin tried to sneak out to search. Agreeing to help her was the only way I could get her to stop doing that." Matt chuckled. "Short of handcuffing her to something sturdy in the house. But if I have any reservations, I'll end the searches. If things get that dangerous, I know she'll sit tight inside."

"What makes you so sure?"

"Because she agreed to my rules." *Sort of.* "And rule number one is to stay near me and do what I say."

"Let's hope it doesn't come to that level of danger." Nate stood. "Keep in touch with Charlie, okay? If either of you run into trouble, y'all can back each other up faster than anyone else can get here from Resolute."

"Will do, but I doubt it'll be necessary." Matt walked Nate back toward his truck. "Erin and I will be just fine."

"WE KNOW THE police already searched here." Impatience filled Matt's voice.

Erin looked up at him. "Why are you so grumpy?"

After Nate left, he and Erin had gone over their printed maps one more time before beginning their search where the jewelry had originally been buried. With their heads together, shoulders touching, fingers brushing, when Erin had gazed into his eyes with the same passionate fire as the previous evening, it took all of his willpower to not take her in his arms and kiss her again. He couldn't, because he'd already decided their first kiss was a mistake.

And he'd assured Nate nothing was going on. Which was why he was grumpy.

"I'm not grumpy."

"I just want to look around here first before we move farther out." Erin crouched next to an oak tree and sifted the detritus at its base through her fingers. "Five more minutes. That's all I ask." Erin crab-walked to another tree and dragged handfuls of dirt and decomposed leaves away from its trunk.

"We're wasting time." Matt compared the police report map on his phone with the area. "The perimeter of the original search is another fifteen feet out from here."

Erin looked up at him. "You shouldn't be so eager to give up. You do know there's a reward for finding the jewelry, don't you? And if *we* find it, *you* get the reward."

He remembered Nate mentioning a reward. But that wasn't why he was there. "You're the one who's searching. I'm just along to keep you alive."

"You say that now. But wait until they hand you that big old check." She looked up at him and winked before digging her hands deep into the mulch again. "Ouch!"

"What happened?" Despite his frustration with her a moment ago, Matt raced to her side.

"Not sure." She brushed dirt off her hand and inspected it. "Something bit me, or maybe I cut my finger."

Matt took her hand in his and examined it. "Looks like a puncture. Could it have been a poisonous snake?"

Erin scoffed. "Unless the snake only had one fang, I'm pretty sure I'm safe on that account."

"We still need to see what it was." Digging through the handful of leaves she'd dropped, Matt added, "I'll have to get you to the emergency room if it was a bug carrying a virus. Ticks carry Lyme disease, right?"

As she poured water on her hand from her bottle, Erin scoffed. "You really are a city boy, aren't you? Ticks don't bite and go on their merry way. They latch on and don't let go."

"Still… Wait a minute." He twisted his fingers in the crumbled leaves and lifted them, holding a mud-encrusted earring toward her.

A ray of sun sparkled through part of the earring, and Erin took it from him. "This stone is an emerald."

"How can you tell it's real?"

"I've seen enough of them, I *own* enough of them, to recognize one." Erin turned it every which way. "I guess it could be a fake, but you can tell the setting is genuine gold because it's not tarnished." Her face lit up. "See? The loot is still here. Somewhere."

Matt dreaded ruining her hopes—trusting her gut and being right must rate almost as high as finding the piece of stolen jewelry. But for all they knew, this could be dime-store costume jewelry. "Let's not get too excited until we check the earring against the list of stolen items in the police report."

"Don't be such a Donnie Downer." Erin ran back to the truck and grabbed her folding spade. Returning to the tree where they'd found the earring, she dropped to her knees and dug.

Matt frowned as he watched her. "It just dawned on me, shovels are useless. Whoever took the jewelry wouldn't have had time to bury it again here before the cops arrived."

Erin paused, both hands on the spade. "I'm an idiot." Standing, she brushed dirt off her jeans. "I should have thought of that."

"Then I'm an idiot, too. Don't be so hard on yourself."

With slumped shoulders, Erin trudged back to the truck and put her folding shovel in the bed.

Matt berated himself. To him, searching for the loot was a lost cause. But for Erin, it was a way to own her previous actions and try to make up for them. He couldn't stand seeing her so defeated. And he *had* promised to help her.

"All he could have done was hide it somewhere no one would look," Matt said. "He must have planned on coming back later and getting it, but either he got arrested or left town."

"So we need to figure out the routes they each took after they left the woods and check along them." She straightened, her voice filling with enthusiasm. "Come on. There's enough daylight to start looking for hiding places before we call it quits for the day."

After mapping out routes for each accomplice from the earring's location to Mom's bar, Matt drove along the most likely one that Kevin took. It cut across the state road on a diagonal, connecting directly with another side road. "Where do these smaller roads lead to?"

"Other wooded areas, houses here and there for people who like their privacy, a ravine, an abandoned mine and a lot of old abandoned houses. Ramshackle messes, mostly. But some people own seasonal cabins, either for hunting or just a break from the city."

"People who like their privacy," Matt repeated. "Like reclusive millionaires?"

Erin sputtered a laugh. "More like reclusive meth cookers. Sheriff Reed and her department bust them from time to time, but new ones always spring up." She turned toward him. "We don't want to go searching anywhere near them."

"What if Kevin gave a meth-cooking friend the loot to hold for him?"

"Then it's gone for good. Either in an explosion and fire or pawned for more cooking supplies." Erin grimaced. "Either way, whoever he gave it to would be dead by now. Most cookers don't last ten years."

Matt continued driving the route, for now ignoring the even smaller roads branching off. "I'm curious about something you mentioned yesterday."

"What did I say?"

"Something about wanting to start your own therapy ranch." He glanced at her lips, curving into a smile. "You mean like what you're doing with Redemption? Working with injured horses?"

Erin shifted in her seat, turning toward Matt as much as the shoulder harness would allow. "No. An equine therapy ranch works with people who are dealing with physical injuries or emotional trauma. Mental illness sometimes, too."

"I don't understand—who does the therapy? The horses?"

She laughed. "In a way. I'm not a licensed therapist, so I'd hire at least one, maybe more." Erin grew more animated the longer she talked. "They would work with the clients in conjunction with the horses. Someone may just want to pet or brush a horse. Someone else might want to ride. I knew a guy in college, a paraplegic, who learned to ride after his accident. It helped him regain a sense of control in his life."

Matt's opinion of his client rose once again. Despite his assurances to Nate, as well as his pledge to himself to not get involved, something about Erin drew him in. His interest in her was going beyond a professional need to keep her safe. "What got you interested in that?"

"I've worked with horses my whole life. But after the burglary, I had a lot of anxiety and I realized that being around them, even just grooming Shadow and Blaze, calmed me." Her voice took on a pensive tone. "I already knew about equine therapy, and that was when I first considered getting involved with it. I figured if the horses had that much of an effect on me, they could help others who had even bigger issues. It can help people learn to communicate, cultivate trust, and so much more. I wanted everyone who needed it to experience it. So I learned everything I could about it."

Turning onto a road Erin indicated, Matt said, "Sounds like a big undertaking."

"It is, but it'll be worth it. I'm hoping Mom will let me tap into the trust her parents set up for me. Technically, I can't touch it until I turn thirty. But this may qualify for an exception. Regardless of the trust, the ranch will be a nonprofit. I'll have to depend on donations, grants and fundraising events for revenue."

"Maybe your parents can host one for you."

Erin snorted. "I won't hold my breath, but you never know."

He glanced over and caught her watching him. "What?"

"Just wondering what the dream is for you. Got any particular life ambitions?"

It wasn't that Matt wanted to keep his goal a secret from Erin. He rarely spoke to anyone about stuff like that. Nate, once in a while. Between a father who would ridicule and beat him, a mother who had her own life to worry about and several foster brothers and sisters who used information to gain favor, he'd learned to keep his cards close to the vest. But Erin had shared her plans with him.

"Nate and I were partners in our security company in California. My goal now is to buy into Resolute Security as a fifty-fifty owner. He had started the company before I moved to Texas, but from the moment I arrived, resurrecting our partnership has been the plan."

"So you're already doing what makes you happy?" Erin asked.

Matt nodded. "I enjoy it, and I'm good at it."

"It must be nice to have found your passion at a young age." Her tone seemed almost envious as she looked through the side window and pointed to what looked like a dirt parking lot.

He pulled into the lot and stopped the truck. "What is this?"

"People who hike this area leave their vehicles here. The ravine's a little way beyond it." Erin reached for her door handle, then rolled her eyes when he shot her a look. "I'm getting out, so if you insist on doing your bodyguard thing, you best hurry."

Blocking her door seemed pointless out there unless Alex was playing sniper, but Matt figured reinforcing the rules couldn't hurt. There could come a time when his rules defined the line between life and death for Erin.

She led the way through trees, shrubbery and rocks until they came to the edge of the ravine. "See the piles of boulders along the ravine floor? There are crevices between the rocks that create perfect hiding places."

"Worth checking out, I guess. But how do we get down to the bottom?"

"There's a trail that leads down. Like I said, people hike through here. Usually when the weather is better, but not having an audience while we search is probably a good thing."

"Drop a pin here on the map." Matt glanced at his watch. "Let's head home, and we'll come back tomorrow."

Between the icy breeze and her huge grin, Erin's face glowed. Although the ravine seemed like another long shot, Matt crossed his fingers that they'd find the loot here. It would bolster her confidence in this decision, and maybe others she'd make in the future.

Tomorrow would tell.

Chapter Eleven

Saturday morning, Matt parked in the area near the ravine where they had stopped the day before but left his truck idling for heat. Leaning forward, he looked up through his windshield at the dark, threatening clouds gathering above them. It snowed in the California mountains, but this damp, frigid weather in southern Texas blew his mind.

"Looks like rain." Erin tugged on gloves.

With his weather app open on his phone, Matt disagreed. "Says it might sprinkle a little, that's all. Heavier rain possible later in the week."

"Well, let's get to gettin', then." Erin waited until Matt turned off the truck, then picked up her backpack and climbed out without waiting for him to open her door.

"Hey, you know—"

"Yes." Layered in clothes, Erin hunched down inside her barn coat. "I know we're the only two people dumb enough to be out here in this weather."

Matt followed her since she knew the way to the trail that led down. The ravine, not too wide but deep, stretched out in front of them until it curved out of sight.

"This is what I'm talking about." Erin approached a grouping of boulders. "These crevices where the rocks meet make perfect hiding places. If Kevin shoved the bag in far enough, no one hiking past would even see it."

"*If* Kevin took the stuff." Matt scanned the floor of the gully, discouraged by the number of rock piles. "And *if* he hid it here." He moved to a nearby pile and reached into a crevice.

"Check for snakes first."

Matt yanked his arm out. "You couldn't mention that sooner?"

"I keep forgetting you're not much of an outdoorsy nature guy," Erin said.

"I thrive outdoors. But Texas is a far cry from California."

"Well, you live in Texas now. Maybe read a book about your new home." Erin glanced at him with a straight face. "At least learn about all the ways you can die here, so you can avoid them."

Matt's huff of exasperation formed a cloud in front of his face. "Are you going to tell me how to check for snakes?"

"Find one of these lying around. Make sure it's strong enough that it won't break." Erin raised her arm and waved a long, sturdy stick in the air. "If you see a snakeskin without a snake, there's a good chance he's in there somewhere."

As he looked for a stick amid the piles of wood debris on the floor of the ravine, Erin added, "They like to hide in the wood, too."

Regretting his decision to help her search this area for the loot, Matt picked up a stick with care, tested it to confirm its sturdiness and began poking into crevices.

While they worked their way down the ravine, the sky darkened even more, and Erin pulled her knit beanie down over her ears. "Looks like some rain is moving in."

"The weather forecast this morning said a chance of

showers farther north, but we shouldn't have any problems around here." Matt fished his phone from his pocket and opened the weather app. "And this still says just a chance of sprinkles."

Erin raised a brow. "If you believe the weather forecasters in Texas, I've got some swampland to sell you."

They continued the search for the stolen jewelry until lightning streaked the sky and thunder bellowed a few seconds later. Matt bent his head back to look up, blinking against fat drops of rain that splatted against his face.

Erin—one; forecasters—zero.

"We should go home and wait for the storm to clear, then come back." Erin turned around, toward the way they'd come.

"We've already come this far. I'd rather finish this area today and be done with it." Matt wiped his face. "Let's give it a few more minutes. Worst-case scenario, we get wet."

Erin shook her head. "Worst-case scenario, we drown."

"What are you talking about?" Matt asked. "It's just a little rain."

"You ever hear of a gully washer? It's a storm in a ravine that can cause a flood. And we've had so much rain lately, the ground is already saturated."

Matt shrugged. California sometimes had flash floods in the desert, and along the coast mudslides took houses over the edge of cliffs. But this ravine seemed safe. "Let's just make it down to that curve. Then we'll take a break and go back to the truck."

"Matt, you know a gully is a ravine formed by water flow, right? Like the one we're standing in?" Erin shouted over the rain that had become a downpour. "We need to get out of here."

With the conditions worsening by the moment, Matt

didn't argue. He'd been searching close to one wall of the ravine and turned to head back to the trail. But he waited for Erin, several paces behind now and working her way toward him from the center of the gully.

"Do you need help?" Matt yelled to her. He took one step in her direction before water surged over the edge of the ravine in every natural depression. Cascading down and filling the gully floor, it raced toward them. Matt's heart stopped and he could barely breathe as he lunged toward Erin with his hand outstretched.

Erin glanced at the flash flood, back at Matt, her eyes wide with terror. She reached for his hand. Their fingers touched.

The narrow ravine forced the flash flood into a wall of water bearing down on them.

Matt wrapped one arm around a boulder and grabbed Erin's hand with the other. But his strength couldn't match that of Mother Nature.

"Erin!" Matt's bellow evaporated within the roar of the flood as Erin disappeared into its depths.

ERIN'S EYES OPENED. She lay flat on the ground, Matt leaning over her. "You're alive." Her voice, raw and relieved, faltered. "Or am I dead?"

His smile tentative, Matt said, "We're both alive."

"But how—"

"I was behind you the whole way. It took a few minutes to work my way to your tree, but with my weight on it, too, it snapped. The water swept us here to the mouth, and I managed to get us up on the bank." He glanced at the violent sky. "Right now, we need to find shelter." Taking hold of her arms, Matt pulled her into a sitting position.

Her howl of pain froze him on the spot.

"My…shoulder." She gasped, tears stinging her eyes as she got to her feet unassisted. "I think it's dislocated."

"Let me take a look." With gentle fingers, Matt probed her left shoulder and disagreed with her diagnosis. "Definitely subluxated, but not fully dislocated. I can pop it back in."

"Oh, no you can't." Erin wasn't about to chance permanent damage to her arm by trusting her bodyguard's diagnosis and battlefield remedy.

The steady look in his eyes calmed her even as he took hold of her arm. "Our security training included first aid. I've done this before." He pulled it straight, then eased the ball back into the joint before she realized what he was doing.

After another gasp of pain, Erin smiled with relief. "I take it back. You *can* fix it." She lifted her arm in amazement. Sore, but mobile.

"Be careful with it. Once it gets subluxated, it's easier for it to pop out again." Matt scanned the area. "I'm sure the parking area is a mudflat by now. You have any ideas for shelter around here?"

Erin looked around, trying to get her bearings. "I've seen a few hunting cabins not too far east of here when I've been out riding."

Matt took hold of her uninjured hand and they battled against wind gusts and sheets of rain, this time searching for protection from the elements.

ERIN STUMBLED TOWARD the vacant cabin, Matt's arm around her waist to support her. "Check under everything on the front porch. There's a good chance they hid a key somewhere." Her body shivered against the cold.

Matt found the promised key inside a faded garden

gnome. "Got it." He shepherded Erin inside, then shut and locked the door behind them.

"I can't believe we survived that." Erin's voice trembled as she realized how close to death she'd come.

Wrapping his arms around her, Matt pulled her into his embrace. His steady heartbeat drummed against her, calming her frenzied pulse. "You're safe now." His reassuring words soothed her even more.

The shock of nearly drowning still knotted her stomach, but in his arms she found momentary peace.

"I'll keep you safe, Erin," he whispered into her ear.

She heard the sincerity in his words. And the way he held her made her feel she was the only thing that mattered to him.

But the cold still lingered under their soaked clothes in the frigid cabin. Matt pulled her even closer, careful of her sore arm. "We need to get you warm."

She'd never felt more vulnerable—or more safe—than at this moment. As the storm raged outside, Erin recognized the subtle shift between them as Matt moved her near the fireplace.

"Sit here. I'll find some blankets and, hopefully, some dry clothes for you." He glanced around the small, rustic cabin. "But first, I'll get a fire started with these." He moved to a pile of dry logs in a corner, next to a bundle of kindling and a container of matches.

Erin sank down by the hearth, desperate for the warmth she hoped would come. At least the cabin was dry, offering refuge from the unrelenting rain that drummed against the roof.

Kneeling by the stone fireplace, Matt arranged the wood. With the strike of a match, flames flared in the kindling and reached up to the tented logs above it. As the fire grew, its bright glow chased away some shadows, creating an unexpected coziness.

Matt glanced at Erin, still shivering, and disappeared into another room. When he returned, he carried a pile of blankets and quilts. "You need to get out of those wet clothes," he said, his voice gentle but firm.

She hesitated, her eyes dropping. "Just give me a blanket and some privacy," she murmured, her voice barely audible over the now-crackling fire. After Matt helped her shrug off her coat, Erin's fingers fumbled at the buttons of her shirt. But they were too numb with cold to cooperate.

Kneeling in front of her, Matt reached out and stilled her hands. "Let me help." He kept his eyes on hers as he worked the buttons free. The shirt slid off her shoulders and she drew in a sharp breath as the cold air hit her skin. Matt grabbed a thick quilt from the pile and wrapped it around her. "This will help."

Erin pulled it tighter, grateful for its warmth, before she stood and toed off her soggy boots. Matt helped unfasten her jeans, then she turned away from him and peeled everything else off within the privacy of her quilt cocoon.

Back in her seat by the fire, where Matt had already spread several blankets to make a pallet, she watched him take off his own soaked jacket and shirt. The fire's glow highlighted lingering drops of rain on his chest and cast shadows that defined his muscles' sharp lines and angles.

When he caught her looking and gave her a faint smile, heat blazed in her cheeks, and she looked away. Wrapped in another of the blankets, he sat next to her, his body close but not touching. "Lean against me. Shared warmth will help."

Erin's instinct was to refuse, to continue to grasp for her elusive independence, but she was too cold to argue. She shifted closer and rested against him. He rubbed his hand up and down her uninjured arm, attempting to chase away the lingering chill.

As the fire grew warmer, Erin relaxed for the first time since the water had dragged her under. Her head leaned against Matt's shoulder, and she closed her eyes.

"Thank you," she whispered.

Matt's arm tightened around her. "Always."

As the comfortable silence between them grew, Erin lifted her head. Her eyes met his, and for a moment neither of them moved. He stared at her openly, his gaze moving over her face as if to commit every detail to memory. Her pulse quickened again, this time not from fear but from the undeniable pull between them.

"You know, you're not just someone I protect." Matt spoke in a low voice, rough with emotion. Almost as if the words cost him something to say. His hand moved from her arm to her face, his thumb brushing against her cheek. "You're much, much more."

His eyes searched hers as his words set her world spinning.

Moving with care, Matt closed the distance between them, brushing her lips with his. A question more than a demand.

Erin's breath caught, and everything slowed down. Pressing her mouth harder against his, her fingers tangling in his damp hair, she gave him an answer he couldn't misinterpret. The kiss deepened, shifting from hopeful to desperate.

The blanket slipped from Erin's shoulders, and Matt drew her closer, his hands sliding down her back as she responded by tracing the planes of his chest with her fingers.

"Are you sure?" he murmured against her lips.

She pulled back and met his gaze. "Yes." And while her heart agreed, the voice in her head threw up roadblock after roadblock. *Is this the right decision?* But the desire within her banished the voice. "I want this."

Moving together, they shed the barriers between them just as they'd shed their wet clothes. Each passionate kiss, each tender touch, reinforced the trust they shared.

Matt's hands slid down to her waist, his firm touch guiding her to lie back, his body following hers in a seamless, natural motion. His lips trailed kisses from her mouth to her breasts and down, farther and farther. Erin arched into the warmth of his tongue, losing herself to his touches. Time and place disappeared as her release careened toward her and hurled her into an alternate dimension she hadn't known existed.

When Matt reached for his pants and pulled a condom from his pocket, Erin shook her head and switched positions with him. "My turn." She nipped at his earlobe, then let her lips wander, leaving a path of kisses along his jaw and across his chest, all while the crinkle of foil sounded nearby.

Her movements, unguarded and free of hesitation, were cut short of her goal when, seconds after Matt finished rolling the condom on, he wrapped his arms around her and turned until she lay beneath him once more.

With an achingly beautiful expression that she wanted to remember always, he whispered, "I can't wait."

Her shoulder pain a fading memory in the moment, Erin wrapped her hands around his shoulders, her legs around his back. "Yes."

Before she could take another breath, he thrust inside, and a silent scream pulled from her mouth.

Hands clutched at skin, then twisted in blankets as she soared higher than she'd thought possible with each subsequent movement.

And when they stilled, lying entwined and their breathing heavy, Erin rested her head on Matt's chest, noticing how the rhythm of his heartbeat matched her own.

Matt lifted his head just enough to look into her eyes. "You're beautiful."

Her breath caught. She'd been called beautiful before, but never with such awe, as though the word itself was inadequate.

"I don't—" she began.

But he silenced her with another kiss, one filled with an intensity that left no room for doubt.

She felt beautiful. And more importantly, for the first time in what seemed like forever, she felt whole.

She hadn't expected the emotions to hit her with such force. At first, it had only been the pull between them, especially after just escaping a watery death. But now it transcended that. She couldn't deny their connection.

But a moment later, that discouraging voice she'd banished earlier rallied.

I thought I could trust this decision, but now... I don't know.

Her mind went back to the struggles she'd had trusting herself, trusting him. Trusting anyone. She had felt safe in his arms. But now she wondered if these new feelings were real, or had she just fallen into old patterns, making decisions based on the need for someone to rely on?

Is it him I want? Or...just comfort?

She couldn't ignore what had just happened. But could she trust her own instincts? Wanting Matt frightened her, but she had to believe he was worth it.

This vulnerability exposed her in a way she hadn't expected. But it also made her realize something. It wasn't just about trusting him. It was about trusting herself. Her ability to navigate this whirlwind of emotions, to believe she could make the right decision for once, even if it wasn't the easiest one.

And maybe, just maybe, trusting him was the right decision.

MATT LAY IN the flickering firelight, Erin's warmth pressed against him. His heart still pounded in his chest, and though the physical release had been intense, the emotions seemed almost unbearable. He'd had no intention of developing personal feelings for her. But now that he'd crossed a line that he couldn't uncross, the possible consequences tormented him.

It hadn't been just the possibility of losing a client on his watch that had tightened his chest with fear in the gully. It had been losing Erin. The rising waters had swept her away, shaking him to his core, and he'd discovered his feelings toward her were complicated. Different from those he should have for a client. Stronger than he experienced when attracted to a woman. His gut told him if he fell for Erin, it wouldn't be his usual casual fling, but instead a serious relationship.

And serious wasn't something he'd been looking for.

Matt's mind went to his training, to the number one rule he lived by—let nothing interfere with the job. But with Erin, things weren't that simple. She wasn't just his client anymore. She was the woman who had changed everything he thought he knew about self-control. About boundaries.

"I never thought I could trust anyone like I trust you," she whispered.

Matt's breath caught in his throat. Her words were like a thread pulling him further into her, into something he wasn't sure he was ready for. He had always kept women at arm's length—had always been the one to step back, to guard his heart, his feelings. But here, with her in his arms, he felt something shift within him. Something soft, something he hadn't realized he'd been craving.

His gaze drifted to Erin's face, a slight smile curving her lips. He brushed a strand of hair from her forehead, his fingers lingering a moment on her skin. The impulse to pull her closer was overwhelming.

I'll never be able to go back to being just her bodyguard after tonight.

Chapter Twelve

Alex Townsend crept from tree to tree on the Montgomerys' property, nearing the closed-up barn while avoiding
the security cameras that bodyguard's lackey had installed.
He snickered as he pictured Erin's face when she'd found
the surprise he'd left in her oven.

But his amusement soon faded. The little boy's marble
had been meant to light a fire under her search for the missing jewelry. And yet, Saturday morning had arrived and
still no results.

Well, today she'd understand the consequences of her
*in*actions.

Less than an hour earlier, Alex had watched Erin drive
off with her hired protector, which meant only Hank, the
over-the-hill cowboy who fancied himself a gunslinger,
would be around.

The big black horse stood inside the corral, right where
he'd seen it when he paid Erin a visit on Monday. And
the corral was one area the security cameras didn't cover.
Keeping an eye on the barn, he ran to the corral gate and
let himself inside.

He'd never ridden but had always admired horses. Proud,
powerful, majestic. And this one, as black as the devil himself, held him in awe.

It was a shame what he had to do to teach Erin a lesson. A damn shame.

Speaking in a soft, calm voice, he approached the horse with slow steps. When he got close enough, he grabbed hold of the halter so they stood side by side.

Then Alex reached with his other hand to the hunting knife on his belt.

He sensed the horse's nervous energy pulsating through the air and tightened his grip on the halter. The animal's dark eyes rolled and its hooves shuffled in the dusty corral, as if it understood Alex's intent.

As he raised the blade toward the horse's neck, something caught his eye. The barn door stood wide-open, and Hank headed toward the corral with two more horses.

"Stop right there!" Alex yelled.

"Alex!" Hank's shout cracked through the tension. The older man unsnapped the lead ropes and smacked the horses on their hindquarters, sending them in the opposite direction before he continued toward the corral gate with his revolver pointed straight at Alex. "Drop the knife and let the horse go. Now."

Alex sneered, tightening his hold. The horse jerked its head, testing his grip. "One step closer, old man, and I'll do it."

Hank froze for a heartbeat, his eyes narrowing. Alex saw the hesitation and knew he had the upper hand. Hank opened the corral gate wide and stepped inside, the revolver in his hand.

They circled each other, Alex holding tight to the horse's halter to keep it between them. The animal's panic grew, and its hooves churned the dirt.

"You're not walking out of here if you hurt that horse." Hank's voice was steady.

"Big talk from an old-timer who's too scared to pull the trigger." Alex barked a laugh, but he knew darn well if the horse went down, he'd be the fool who brought a knife to a gunfight. "What's it gonna be, Hank?"

Hank answered by firing a shot into the air. The loud crack shattered the standoff. The horse reared, its front hooves lashing at the air as it pulled free from Alex's grip. He stumbled back, and when the horse's hooves came down, it backed into Hank, knocking him to the ground. The revolver slid across the dirt and landed beyond his reach.

"Damn it!" Alex snarled, lunging to grab the halter again, but the horse fled through the open gate.

Hank scrambled to his knees, but Alex was on him in an instant. With a wild roar, he slammed into Hank, driving him back down. The older man grunted, his hands coming up to block Alex's fists. They rolled in the dirt, a chaotic blur of swinging limbs and raw desperation.

Hank landed a solid uppercut to Alex's jaw, snapping his head sideways. His skull blossomed with pain, making him even angrier. He jabbed a fist into Hank's ribs, knocking the wind out of him. Hank gasped, and Alex seized the advantage.

"Should've left it alone, Hank." Alex drove his fist into Hank's face, over and over again until the older man lay almost motionless beneath him, his breath wet and uneven.

Panting, Alex stumbled to his feet, spotted the knife and picked it up. Turning back to Hank, he hesitated for a moment. The old man was barely conscious, his bloodied face turned up to the cloudy sky.

This hadn't been his intention, but he did pride himself on taking advantage of an opportunity.

"At least the horse got to live," Alex muttered. Then, gripping the knife, he stepped forward to finish the job.

Chapter Thirteen

Erin woke to silence. The wind no longer howled, rain no longer beat upon the cabin's metal roof. Matt spooned her in a cocoon of warmth, his breath on her shoulder a rhythmic pattern of exhalations. She snuggled in closer, and his arms tightened around her in a reassuring embrace.

She'd made the right decision last night.

"Morning." Matt nuzzled her neck, sending a shiver of pleasure through her.

She twisted around in his arms and gazed into his smiling eyes. "Sounds like the storm's over."

"Uh-huh." He kissed her.

"We should probably get going."

"Uh-huh." Another kiss.

As much as Erin would love to spend the day cuddling with Matt in front of a cozy fire, Alex's catastrophe countdown clock ruined the moment. "We've got to search the other areas we marked on the map."

"We will. Right after we—"

Erin turned her cheek with a soft laugh. The other day in the barn, Hank had told her it was past time for her to trust her instincts. And after ten long years, she was finally coming to believe that herself. But part of internalizing that belief was not allowing herself to be controlled by her baser needs. "Search now, play later." She mustered some country-girl fortitude, slipped from his grasp and rose from their makeshift bed.

With an exaggerated sigh, Matt rolled to his feet just in time to catch the clothes Erin tossed to him. "At least they're dry."

"You're dead wrong about that. They're still damp on the inside, but they'll do to get us home." She hopped on one foot, trying to pull on her stiff jeans without straining her sore shoulder. "Man oh man, do I ever need a hot shower. And clean clothes. And food. And lots of coffee."

"And not necessarily in that order." Matt caught Erin as she lost her balance and dragged her back down on the blankets with him.

"Stop that. We can't," she scolded, laughing as he kissed her neck.

"You sure can be stubborn when you want to be." Matt released her and they stood.

She helped him fold the blankets and quilts and set them on a chair. With her jacket and gloves on, Erin stepped into the sunshine and looked up at the cloudless sky. "What a difference a day makes."

Matt locked the cabin door and put the key back in its hiding spot. "Let's hope that's true when we get to the truck." He pulled his phone from his pocket and checked their location. "*If* we can get to the truck."

Erin tapped his phone map to enlarge it. "We can circle around this way to get back to the parking lot."

Trusting her knowledge of the area, Matt followed her in a roundabout detour to the far side of the ravine.

When they reached a washed-out part of the trail, Matt

stated the obvious. "It doesn't look like this route goes through."

Biting her tongue against a sarcastic retort, Erin checked the phone map again. The remnants of a fast-flowing channel of rainwater rushed past them. "We'll need to backtrack and hike farther to the west. Try to find a narrower spot to cross this, then double back on the other side."

They traversed the difficult landscape, climbing past mudslides and negotiating rivulets and streams that didn't exist before the storm.

By the time they arrived at the truck, they were covered in mud. Erin's stomach growled for food and her head throbbed from lack of caffeine. "I think I'm hangry."

Matt kicked at the thick, wet sludge encasing the truck's tires. "Then this won't help."

Erin knew soil in this part of Texas consisted primarily of clay, which wreaked havoc when caked around vehicle tires. Ideally, they'd let it dry and then knock it off, but they didn't have time for that. The other way to clean them was to pressure-wash the thick goop off. Another non-option for them out in the middle of nowhere

"Where's your tire iron?" Erin took off her jacket while Matt rummaged in the back seat and came out with a hammer and the iron. Erin chose the hammer and went to work scraping away the mud.

While she worked, her mind drifted back to the night before. To Matt's soft kisses and gentle touches. To the taste of his mouth, his body. To the intensity ramping up until she flew high and then crashed to the ground, pleasure filling every inch of her body, every corner of her soul.

Erin glanced at Matt, who had worked his way around the truck to her side. With each downward stroke of his tire iron against the mud, her thoughts went to a place they shouldn't be. Not when they needed to get back to the ranch, change clothes and start searching again. So she fought the smile trying to hijack her mouth, averted her eyes and focused on her own tire.

An hour later, the tires were clean enough to rotate within the wheel wells. Matt put the truck into four-wheel drive to navigate the storm-ravaged terrain, and they headed home.

ERIN STEPPED OUT of the truck, the hairs on the back of her neck standing on end. The ranch was silent, but not in a tranquil way. This stillness pressed on her chest and made it hard to breathe.

"Something's wrong."

But what? She glanced at the bunkhouse, then panned back up the road they'd just driven in on. Nothing to arouse suspicion, and yet her heart jackhammered in her chest. Why? What had her subconscious realized that her waking self was missing?

She heard snorting and turned toward the barn. The door stood open and hooked to the wall. Perfectly normal, and yet from the sounds inside, the horses seemed as uneasy as she was. They pawed at the ground, stomped their hooves.

Without thinking, Erin wandered in that direction, moving with caution.

"What is it?" Matt asked, walking by her side.

"I'm not sure. Maybe nothing." But she didn't think it was nothing, and Matt didn't seem to think so either.

Still a ways out from the open barn door, Erin made out Blaze, Shadow and Redemption standing loose just inside, dried sweat showing on their coats. They whinnied, their ears flicking back and forth.

No, no, no, she screamed inside her head. She sprinted toward the barn, Matt's bodyguard rules forgotten.

"Wait!" he shouted, matching her pace. "What's wrong?"

"Hank wouldn't leave them loose like this. And the only way they'd have sweat residue in this weather is if they've been running."

Matt grabbed hold of her arm and yanked her to a stop, keeping her from rushing headlong inside. "Damn it, Erin. Stop! Let me clear the area first." He pulled his gun from its holster with one hand. With the other, he shoved her behind him. "Maybe Hank's in the back."

They approached Shadow, the nearest horse, who raised her head, shaking it and flaring her nostrils. "No," Erin whispered, a tight knot of tension gripping her chest. "Hank would have groomed them."

Matt pointed out damp areas on the floor. "Looks like the door was open during yesterday's storm. Maybe Hank's sick or hurt himself."

Erin pulled her phone from her pocket and tapped Hank's number. After each ring on her phone, a fainter ring followed from somewhere outside. She pulled open the barn's front door, and she could hear the ring a little better. Her gaze settled on what looked like a pile of rags inside the corral.

"Matt…" Her voice was tight and loaded with fear. She knew firsthand the danger Alex represented, but she'd denied to herself that he would carry through with the worst of his threats.

Please let me be mistaken. Please, please let Hank be all right.

Matt joined her at the door and scanned the scene. "Wait here. Let me check it out."

But Erin ignored him. Her head on a swivel just as Matt's was, she followed him, the frosty morning air stinging her cheeks as together they edged through the open corral gate toward the bundle.

A bundle that was no mere bundle. Her breath caught in her throat. A camel-colored jacket, worn jeans, old boots. A crumpled body in the bloodstained mud. A familiar face, bruised and battered. Eyes milky and lifeless. Erin's knees buckled, and she fell to the ground beside him.

"Hank," she whispered, her voice breaking. Tears blurred her vision as she reached out, her trembling hand stopping just short of his cheek. "Oh, Hank." Her words came out in a low moan as she took in his face, turned to the sky as if he'd been looking to the heavens for help. Help that hadn't come.

"Don't, Erin. Don't touch him." Matt lifted her to her feet. His voice firm but gentle, his hand steady on her shoulder. "It's a crime scene." He pulled his phone from his pocket, his other hand guiding her away from Hank.

"This is Matt Franklin. We need law enforcement at the Montgomery Ranch immediately. Possible homicide," he said into the phone, his tone professional. Then he turned his attention back to Erin.

"He's gone, Matt. Hank's gone."

Matt wrapped his arms around her, pulling her against his chest. She buried her face in his shoulder, her tears soaking his shirt. "I know," he said, his voice low and soothing. "I'm sorry." He held her as she shook with grief. "I'm so sorry."

Like a collage of pictures projected onto a screen, memories of Hank flashed through Erin's mind.

The first time she sat on a horse, she'd been three. With her mother insisting she was too young, Hank had managed to find a moment when they weren't being watched.

He'd lifted her up and held on to her tightly while she experienced what would become her passion. Horses.

Their last conversation, just a few days earlier in the barn. Hank had urged her to trust her instincts. He'd always had more faith in her than she had in herself. And he had also been right about Matt. About the attraction between her and her bodyguard.

When Hank had observed things happening on the ranch, he hadn't just seen them at surface level. His perception had run deeper, allowing him to counsel Erin with down-to-earth cowboy wisdom. Hank had been her anchor. And now, without him, she was adrift.

The weight of her loss crushed Erin as she tried to process the impossible reality. Hank, her friend, the steady presence in her life since childhood, was gone. One more casualty of her past. She could barely breathe around the pain.

With his arm still around her, Matt said, "We should go wait on the porch for the police."

Erin let him guide her away, each step farther from Hank more difficult than the last.

"You know as well as I do, Alex did this," she said, not surprised by the rage bubbling deep inside her. But the amount of anger she harbored toward Matt *did* catch her off guard. If they'd left the ravine when she wanted to, Alex's confrontation might have been with a bodyguard trained for such situations instead of an innocent old man. She kept her feelings to herself, however. Matt was still her protector, and her only ally in finding the jewelry and ending Alex's reign of terror.

After settling her on the porch swing, Matt crouched in front of her, his eyes filled with concern. "And we'll make sure he winds up back in prison." Matt took her hand. "Just remember, I'm here with you. You don't have to handle any of this alone."

Erin clung to those words, but it was like grasping a small raft engulfed by the raging floodwaters of her grief. Hank had been more than a ranch hand. More than a friend and confidant. He had been family.

And now, because of her, he had died a violent, painful death. How could she ever forgive herself for that?

MATT WALKED OVER to the corral as flashing lights illuminated the ranch. The grounds had become a grim hive of activity, with police officers from Winston taking photographs of the scene and marking evidence with yellow placards.

What was it Erin had said just hours earlier—what a difference a day makes?

Ain't that the truth. From a storm to clear skies to murder in less than twenty-four hours. He went over those hours in his mind, guilt clawing its way through him. They had no idea yet what time Hank had been killed. And Matt had no control over the previous day's weather. But he should have heeded Erin's warning about a potential gully washer instead of insisting they'd be fine. It had been his fault she almost drowned during the storm. His fault they hadn't made it back to the ranch last night, possibly in time to save Hank.

And what if he and Erin had been making love at the same time a knife was draining the life force from the man? Matt's self-reproach deepened with the realization he was enjoying last night while Hank may have been lying out here, gasping his last few breaths.

His job was to protect *Erin*. But by not protecting all of those she loved, he'd exposed her to the results of Alex Townsend's savagery. Something she'd have to live with for the rest of her life. Matt had secured protection for the O'Roarkes. He should have pushed harder to keep Hank safe somehow.

But from here on, Erin and Matt would be joined at the hip. If Alex intended to hurt Erin, Matt would see him coming a mile away.

He looked toward the bunkhouse, where Erin sat on the porch steps, knees pulled to her chest, arms wrapped around her legs. Her eyes, puffy from crying, focused on the spot where Hank's lifeless body still lay. Matt's chest tightened at the sight of her, although he'd learned she was tougher than she looked. It would be difficult, but she'd survive this. He hoped their relationship would survive it, too.

"Mr. Franklin?" A young Winston officer approached him, appearing a bit overwhelmed. From what Matt had heard, murders weren't exactly commonplace out here. "Detective Martinez would like to ask you a few questions. If you'll come with me?"

Matt nodded, and after one last glance at Erin, followed the baby-faced officer to where Detective Martinez stood, holding a pen and a small notepad. The woman, who looked to be in her late thirties, was tall and imposing. Experience radiated from eyes darting here and there, taking in everything, trying to make sense of the senseless. She gave Matt a sharp nod as he approached.

"Mr. Franklin, I understand you're Ms. Montgomery's bodyguard. You work for Nate Reed over at Resolute Security?" Martinez asked, her voice calm but firm.

"Yes, ma'am."

"Can you walk me through what happened here?"

Scrubbing a hand across his face, Matt gave Martinez a concise replay of the morning's events.

Martinez scribbled in her notepad. "So, neither of you saw or heard anything unusual before coming outside?"

"No. We didn't come from the house. We got caught in yesterday's storm, hunkered down for the night and didn't make it back until this morning. When we arrived, Erin, um, my client, felt that something seemed..." He paused, searching for the right word. "Off."

Martinez gave him a nonjudgmental, but curious, look. "Where did you say you spent the night?"

He hadn't said, but best not to quibble with this all-business detective. "In a vacant hunter's cabin. We found the key hidden on the porch and let ourselves in. We left the place in the same condition we found it." Better to possibly get in trouble for illegal entry than become a murder suspect.

"I'll need you and Ms. Montgomery to come to the station later to make complete statements, including details about your entire day yesterday." She looked up from her pad. "I understand you both believe Alex Townsend should be considered a suspect in the death of Hank Caldwell."

"Yes, we do."

Martinez gave a noncommittal nod. "So, you were with Ms. Montgomery all night since you were hired to protect her from Alex Townsend's harassment. Correct?"

Matt's jaw tightened. He resented the implication in the detective's *all night* word choice, but he knew this line of questioning was necessary. Warranted. "Twenty-four/seven protection. Yes, ma'am."

She scribbled more notes, then gave him a hard look. "So, what can you tell me about Alex that I won't find in the police reports?"

"You've probably heard about the robbery back—"

She cut him off. "I know all about that."

Appreciating her brevity, Matt said, "Right. Well, since getting out of prison, Townsend has been making threats all week. Your department took a report on him for intimidating Liam O'Roarke and his wife. Here, I can provide you with a case number." He took out his phone, made a few swipes, then showed her a screen. "Resolute Security has provided protection for the O'Roarkes, but I'll be talking to my boss about tightening it."

Martinez jotted down the number. "Anything else?"

"Yes. He made another threat using one of my client's riding students." Matt filled in the detective on the incident with Tommy's marble and Alex pretending to be Hank for access to the bunkhouse. "I think you should send someone over to the Barrows household, provide protection for Tommy and his mother, Jill."

"Why didn't you file a report about that?" Martinez narrowed her eyes at him.

"I did. The officer I spoke with said he'd take my statement, but he needed proof it was Townsend. Said I was just speculating on the identity of the perp."

Martinez blew out a sharp breath. "We'll look into it. Do you have security footage on the property?"

"Yes. I'll show you." Matt slogged through the mud in the corral as he led the detective to the gate. He pointed up. "We installed cameras on two of these light posts, one facing the barn, the other aimed at the bunkhouse. And we have several on top of the barn and the bunkhouse. We also added a couple to catch the back of the two buildings." He indicated the trees marking the end of the road from the front gate.

Police officers crisscrossed the area, consulting with each other. Twice, Matt and Martinez were stopped so officers could clarify something with the detective. Glancing at Hank's body, Matt noticed a policewoman photographing and measuring footprints in the mud. *Erin and I will have to show them our shoes in order to exclude us from any suspicious prints.*

A justice of the peace stood by the corral gate, drumming his fingers on the top rail while waiting for the police to finish their footprint evidence collection before declaring Hank dead. Matt had learned that Boone County didn't have a coroner. The Harris County crime lab in Houston would perform the autopsy and handle the forensic investigation.

As Matt and Martinez finally approached the bunkhouse, he met Erin's eyes. She seemed lost amid all the chaos, and her gaze held the remnants of the morning's horror. But a glint of hope also shone in them. That, along with the determined set of her mouth, told him she still had a lot of fight left in her. And he intended to fight right alongside her.

After climbing the porch steps, Matt rested his hand on Erin's shoulder for a moment. As he gave a gentle squeeze, she covered his hand with hers. His resolve to keep her safe from that maniac Townsend tripled in strength.

Matt and Martinez sat on the bunkhouse couch while he pulled up the footage on his computer. Erin, despite her fragile state, insisted on joining them.

"You don't have to watch this." Matt worried what witnessing any portion of the violent death of her friend would do to her state of mind. Once seen, something that soul-stealing could never be unseen.

"I *need* to," she insisted, her voice raw with emotion.

Camera one, located on one of the tall light posts near the corral, showed Hank leading two horses out of the barn, then slapping their rumps to send them running. Then he drew his gun and ran toward the corral. There was nothing more until Redemption tore through the frame in the same direction the other horses had gone.

Although disappointed the footage provided no clues to the murder itself, Matt was glad Erin hadn't seen anything too traumatic.

Erin's breath hitched as the video looped again to Hank running. "That's the last time I…" Her voice broke as she stared at the screen.

To hell with Martinez and whatever she might think the relationship was between Matt and his client. He wrapped an arm around Erin's shoulders, his heart hurting for her. This was wrong on so many levels. He was breaking his word to Nate. He was setting himself up for another monumental fall. But in this moment, he didn't care.

Martinez leaned back, an unreadable expression on her face. "Do you have footage from any other angles?"

Hoping Townsend had been caught on camera on his way to the murder scene, Matt ran the recordings from every camera he'd had installed. But no luck. It seemed the killer knew how to avoid them all. "We focused on the buildings and areas between them rather than the corral."

Martinez stood. "Convenient for our perp that the storm washed away physical evidence," she muttered, more to herself than anyone else. "I'll need a copy of all this footage, as well as from the front gate camera, for us to review more thoroughly. But I'll be frank, Ms. Montgomery. Without more evidence or witnesses, we have nothing to charge Alex Townsend with."

Erin's large brown eyes glistened through her tears. She looked up at Martinez, pleading with the detective to believe her. "I'm telling you, it was Alex."

Martinez nodded. "So I've noted. I run my investigations

by the book, Ms. Montgomery, but I can assure you we will be looking into him as a person of interest."

Erin's shoulders sagged beneath Matt's arm.

They returned to the porch, where Matt stayed close to Erin, comforting her, while the police continued their work. They both knew who had done this. Now it was a matter of proving it.

Chapter Fourteen

Thursday dawned with a cloudless sky, too bright and clear for a funeral. To Erin, it seemed the weather should be as bleak and gloomy as she felt. The past three days had crept by in a blur for her.

As requested, she and Matt had visited the Winston police station to give their statements. Planning Hank's funeral had taken much longer than she'd expected. As had exercising Blaze and Shadow and working with Redemption without Hank's assistance. Matt had helped with her two horses while she fought back tears each time she'd taken out the dressage horse.

Taking into account the time difference, Erin had called her parents to let them know about Hank. Although upset, they couldn't come home for the funeral because of her dad's business obligations. But their worry for her had been evident. Her mother had insisted on talking to Matt, and apparently made it clear that if anything happened to their daughter, Matt would regret ever setting foot in Texas.

Erin and Matt had also managed a few more searches but found nothing, and a layer of dread rested just beneath her grief. Time was running out, and the question of whom Alex's next victim might be tormented her.

Erin entered the Cowboy Church of Boone County, Matt tight at her side, and made her way to the front row of folding chairs in the rustic barn that served as a place of worship. All of the hands who worked at the Montgomery Ranch were there, filling the first few rows. The rest of the room held everyone who'd known Hank and wanted to pay their respects. Not a suit in sight, just jeans, pearl button shirts and cowboy boots. Hank would be honored.

"Did you see Detective Martinez when we came in?" Matt whispered.

"Yes. She told me they'd keep a plainclothes officer with Jill and Tommy during the funeral and have more at the graveside service, too." Erin twisted a tissue between her fingers. "I just hope Alex shows up and they catch him without anyone else getting hurt."

"I'm more concerned that he'll take advantage of no one being at the ranch. Nate texted me earlier. He, Luke and Gabe have set up there and will keep watch until we all return," Matt said.

"Who are Luke and Gabe?" Erin asked, confused.

"Two of my fellow bodyguards at Resolute Security. There are four of us now, but Nate wants to hire more down the road." Matt leaned sideways and asked in a low voice, "How are Maeve and Liam doing at Hidden Oaks?"

"They're safe, but… Let's just say it's been an adjustment for them."

The O'Roarkes had moved into a double room at the facility, with both the hired guard Nate had arranged for and Resolute Security's Charlie with them round the clock. Erin appreciated the immediate increase in security after Hank's death, but after so many years of living apart, Liam complained to her that he felt stifled by Maeve's close attention. No more Irish whiskey for him.

A small grin tugged at Erin's mouth as she thought about the ruckus Liam had caused when his disapproving wife discovered his secret stashes. She'd removed all his contraband from the premises, despite Liam's loud and heated protests of their medicinal properties.

Somber music from a small country band pulled Erin away from her memory, and she braced herself for the funeral.

First, the hymns. "The Old Rugged Cross," "How Great Thou Art" and "Amazing Grace." Familiar songs that brought tears of sadness for the finality of death. But also brought comfort, at least for Erin. Bible readings proclaimed the promised hope of the afterlife, and friends stood and recounted stories that spoke of Hank's impeccable character and his abiding loyalty. The preacher then signaled Erin. She tensed, and Matt squeezed her hand before she rose and walked to the podium.

She took a deep breath and unfolded a paper with her notes. But then she realized her love for Hank didn't require her to read from notes after all. The words flowed directly from her heart. "Hank was like a grandfather to me in every way but blood," she began, her voice only quavering a little. "He may have been a paid ranch hand, but it wasn't in his job description to teach me to ride, to shoot. All the physical skills needed to run a successful ranch. Nor was it in his job description to bandage my scraped knees, wrap my sprained wrists and ankles and once, when I was twelve, promise me that I wasn't going to die when a horse stepped on my foot." Erin gave a small shrug. "What can I say? As a child, I had a tendency to be accident prone."

Chuckles and knowing nods came from Hank's friends and neighbors. Erin smiled out at them, tears forming in her eyes. The back of her throat was so tight it ached, and she took the moment to compose herself. Anyone who knew Hank had, at one point or another, been on the receiving end of his gruff but loving ministrations and generous nature.

She gripped the sides of the podium, steadied herself and continued. "But what he taught me that I value so much more than how to care for animals, how to operate farm machinery or the physical labor needed to build muscles on my skinny frame—" she mimicked Hank's voice on that last one, which earned another round of small chuckles "—were life's intangibles. Attributes like loyalty, persistence and fortitude. But most of all, love. John 15:13 says there is no greater love than to lay down one's life for one's friends. And that's just what Hank did. He saved three horses, protected the ranch and…and he gave his life to protect me."

Erin wasn't sure what people knew about the circumstances of Hank's death. They knew he had been murdered. By now everyone knew that. But what else did they know? That Alex was the prime suspect? And even if they did, did they remember him as one of the people arrested with Erin on that night ten years ago?

In Erin's mind, what they knew or didn't know wasn't important. What mattered was that Hank fought off Alex to protect her, and she would be forever grateful to him.

And for the rest of her life, she would miss his steadfast presence. But thanks to his wise guidance, she was not blaming herself for his death. Not anymore. Though no proof existed that Alex was the culprit, in her heart of hearts, she believed he was. And if it was the last thing she did, she would see to it that Alex paid the price.

She looked skyward. "Thank you," she said to Hank in a choked whisper. "For everything. I'm going to miss you so, so much."

Tears streamed down her cheeks, and she could barely

speak. "I love you," was all she managed. After that, she was incapable of saying more and returned to her seat.

Thankfully, her tears during the brief service ended with an uplifting message from the preacher. Pallbearers removed the coffin, and the crowd filed out of the building. Erin spotted Jill, Tommy and their policewoman escort, another harsh reminder of why they were all here today.

"I want to say a few words to Jill," Erin said.

Matt nodded, and they approached the trio.

Jill gave Erin a hug. "I'm so sorry. Tommy always looked forward to seeing Hank during his riding lessons."

Tommy tipped his head back to look up at Matt. "I lost my big marble, but want to see what I found the other day?"

"I sure do." Matt waited while Tommy dug in his pocket. "Sorry about your marble."

"It's okay. This is way better." The young boy held his hand up, something sparkling between his thumb and forefinger.

Erin, listening to Jill's condolences while at the same time keeping tabs on Tommy's conversation with Matt, turned her attention to the ring. "Can I see that?"

With only a small hesitation, he handed it to her, and Erin's stomach clenched.

"Why, this is beautiful," she said, not wanting the boy to become reluctant to share. "Like a pirate's treasure. Where on earth did you find this?" Erin rotated the diamond cocktail ring, sunlight flashing from its faceted surfaces.

Tommy glanced up at his mom before looking at his feet.

"Tommy?" Jill frowned at her son, waiting until he raised his eyes to hers. "It's okay. I promise you're not in any trouble. Tell her the truth, Tommy."

The boy hesitated, then hemmed and hawed.

Jill looked at Erin, her brow furrowed, then Matt squatted down to Tommy's level as if he sensed something wasn't going right. "Hey, man, I think this ring might be very, very important. Maybe even a clue to a hidden treasure." Matt gave him a conspiratorial smile. "Can you tell me where you got it?"

"I found it outside that old abandoned mine," Tommy said in an eager voice. "You know, the one with a tree on each side?"

"You mean the one with a live tree on one side and a dead one on the other?" Erin asked.

"Yeah, yeah. That's the one. It was the day before the storm."

Erin crouched down next to Matt. "Are you sure about that?"

"Uh-huh, Miss Erin. I remember 'cause my mom doesn't let me play outside after it rains on account of I always get so muddy."

"I see." Erin smiled at the thought of Tommy covered in mud.

"Yeah, so like I was over there, and I was digging up rocks like Indiana Jones 'cause I'm gonna be an archaeologist just like him, and I was near the entrance and saw this shiny thing."

"An archaeologist? That's cool," Matt said. "You're sure it was outside the mine? Not inside?"

Tommy nodded. "I'm not allowed to go inside the mine 'cause it's all boarded up. Mom said it might collapse on me and then she'd never find me."

"She's absolutely right about that. I'm glad you listened to her. I bet even Indiana Jones wouldn't go inside that mine." Erin held up the ring. "Would it be okay if I borrow this for a little while?"

"Um… Yeah, I guess so." Tommy's reply was soft. "But

you'll give it back to me, right? 'Cause I found it, and you know, finders keepers."

"I'll be honest, if it's what I think it is, I might have to give it to the police," Erin said. "But if that happens, you'll be a hero, and heroes get rewards."

"They do? So, maybe I could get another riding lesson?" His gaze slid to his mother before whispering, "Mom says we can't afford any more for a while."

Jill's cheeks flushed, but before she could refute Tommy's claim, Erin spoke up.

"Tommy, if I can't give this back to you, I'll give you free riding lessons for as long as you want to take them."

The boy's face lit up with delight. "You want me to see if I can find more stuff out there?"

"No. It would be safer for you to stay away from the mine for now." Erin held his shoulders and looked him straight in the eye. "Promise?"

Tommy scrunched up his face and looked away.

Erin pressed him. "You want free riding lessons, don't you?"

"I sure do."

"Good. Then promise me. You won't go back to the mine."

"Okay, I promise." His serious expression segued into an enormous smile. "Anything for more lessons."

Erin stood, and Matt followed suit, his knees popping in protest.

As Jill gave her friend another hug, she whispered, "This is so embarrassing, but I do appreciate the offer."

"Don't be silly," Erin said. "I've missed Tommy as much as he's missed riding."

"Thank you." The two women separated. "Again, I'm so very sorry about Hank." Jill took Tommy's hand and led him toward the parking lot, the vigilant police officer walking alongside.

"Is that a part of what I think it is?" Matt asked.

"I sure hope so." Erin pocketed the ring, its weight feeling heavier than its few ounces of metal and gemstone. "We need to hurry and get to the cemetery for the graveside service."

Erin noticed Matt's jaw tighten subtly. Lately, she'd found him easier to read.

"Something wrong?"

"I'm just not a big fan of funerals. Especially the part by the grave." Matt gave her a tight smile. "Don't worry. It's not a big deal."

She slipped her hand into his. "So, tell me. Who did you lose?"

For a moment, it seemed he didn't intend to answer. "My mom," he finally said, the two muted words conveying a loss that still hurt him.

"I'm sorry." Erin realized she knew very little about the man she'd been sleeping with the past few nights.

"It was a long time ago." He got her into his truck and then joined the line of vehicles proceeding to the cemetery.

"What about your father? Is he still alive?"

"Unfortunately, yes." The bitterness of his words shocked Erin.

"I take it you're not close?"

An ugly laugh broke loose from Matt's throat. "You could say that. We haven't seen or spoken to each other in twenty years."

"I'm sorry to hear that."

"Don't be. He's in prison." He glanced at her before turning his attention back to the vehicle in front of them. "For killing my mom."

Whatever Erin might have imagined as the reason for the rift between Matt and his father, never in a million years would she have guessed that. To lose your mother at the hands of your father. She couldn't begin to understand what that had done to the boy he'd been.

"Oh, Matt. I'm so sorry." Her words seemed so grossly inadequate, but what could one say when told something like that? What she did know was that her heart, already shattered from losing Hank, broke a little more.

"Like I said, it was a long time ago."

"How old were you?" Her voice came out in a whisper.

"Nine. The police arrested him for beating her up, but she took him back anyway. That's when he killed her." Matt's voice took on an even darker tone. "When she gave him a second chance."

MATT'S ANXIETY METER flashed red after the long, emotional day, and he was on high alert. Alex had crossed a line with Hank's murder. And now that he had, chances were high that if the killer didn't get what he wanted, he would kill again.

Not Erin, necessarily. Alex still needed her to find the jewels, but almost anyone else who attended the funeral services was at risk. And that's what worried him, because Erin also knew that. Matt's worst fear was that she would put herself in harm's way to protect those she cared about. Just like Hank had done.

On the way home, Matt called Nate for a ranch update.

"Everything's quiet here. Some of the guys who work here are returning to the big bunkhouse, so I've pulled Luke. The ranch hands all know who to watch for." Nate spoke to someone near him, then came back on the phone. "No activity near the big house or the barn and bunkhouse where you and Erin are staying. Winston police are posting one officer across the road from your bunkhouse for the night, so we're headed back to Resolute."

"Thanks, boss. Maybe we can finally unwind a little." Matt favored Erin with a weak smile. Despite her tears and anguish since Hank's murder, today she'd remained brave, determined to make the day only about the deceased. Oh, she had shed tears, and plenty of them. But she'd been able to give a fine eulogy for her friend. It seemed to be catching up with her, but his heart lightened when she gave him a faint smile in return.

"Here's hoping you do. Stay vigilant."

"Always. I'll keep you posted on any developments." Matt ended the call just as they approached the main gate.

Erin sighed. "All I want to do tonight is curl up on the couch in my warmest pajamas, have a beer and not cry."

Matt glanced at her again, her face the picture of exhaustion as she ran her fingers through her hair. "You grab the pajamas, I'll grab the beers."

"That sounds perfect." She paused. "Thank you, Matt."

"For what?"

"For being there with me today."

"It's my job."

"That's not what I mean." Erin gave him a pointed look.

"I know." He gave her hand a gentle squeeze. "And you're welcome."

It was testament to her exhaustion that Erin didn't even try to get out of the truck before Matt opened her door. Or maybe Hank's death had impressed upon her the need to adhere to safety protocols. Whatever the reason, he appreciated her cooperation. Made his job that much easier and lowered his anxiety by a notch.

With an arm around her, he ushered her into the bunkhouse and made her wait by the locked door while he cleared every room.

"No unwanted visitors," he said.

After toeing off her boots, she trudged to her bedroom like a zombie. By the time Matt sat on the couch with two open bottles of beer, Erin had already collapsed on it. He pulled her against him, wrapping his arm around her.

"I sure am going to miss him." Erin tapped her bottle against Matt's. "To Hank."

"To Hank," Matt echoed.

They sipped in silence, letting the toast fill the space between them.

After a beat, Matt broke the quiet. "Will you bring someone from the main stables over here to work with your horses?"

Erin shook her head. "I can't ask anyone else to risk their lives. For now, I can take care of them myself." She turned her head and smiled at Matt. "Especially if you keep helping me."

"I'll remind you that shoveling horse manure is absolutely *not* in my job description."

"City boy."

"Country hick."

"A country hick who will have you shoveling manure in no time."

"Says you."

"Says me." Erin kissed him on the cheek.

Their enjoyable banter lapsed into silence, and Matt's thoughts returned to their current situation. "You told me how much Hank and Alex disliked each other. Could Hank's death have been a personal vendetta and not part of Alex's quest for the missing loot?"

Erin blew out a hard breath. "Maybe, but I don't think

so, and I'm not endangering another hand on the ranch by recruiting one of them."

They again settled into a comfortable silence, Matt replaying the day's events in his head. Erin leaned against his shoulder, her eyes half-closed. Matt liked her nearness. Liked it too much for his own good.

Throughout the day, they had held hands in public several times, and Matt doubted that anyone who saw them confused Matt's job as Erin's bodyguard with the fact that he'd developed genuine feelings for her. Nate was going to come unglued.

Matt knew that by allowing his relationship with Erin to grow, he could be putting his partnership in Resolute Security in jeopardy. And yet, he felt powerless to stop. No, not powerless, he corrected. Unwilling. "So, you really think the ring Tommy had is part of the stolen jewelry?"

"I can't believe I forgot about it." Erin jumped up, retrieved the ring and dropped back down on the couch. "Here." She handed him the piece. "Since he found it near the mine, and the mine is near the ravine we searched, I'll bet you anything that's where the loot's hidden. I say we search the mine first thing tomorrow morning."

Matt's longed-for tranquility slammed into a brick wall. "Erin, listen to me. That mine is boarded up for a reason. It's too dangerous, and we're not going inside."

And there was his mistake. Telling her instead of asking this complicated, adorable, stubborn, caring woman not to do this.

She stiffened, moved off his shoulder and gave him a look of such intensity that he knew what she planned to say before she opened her mouth. Just as he knew he absolutely did not want to hear it.

"I'm going. If there's even a sliver of a chance the loot's

there, it'll be worth the risk." Determination laced Erin's voice, and Matt knew he was sunk. "Alex has already hurt too many innocent people, and I refuse to let Hank's sacrifice be for nothing."

"Erin, try to be reasonable—" *Another mistake.*

"What?" She got to her feet, each fist stubbornly planted on her hips.

"Calm down. All I meant—" *And yet another mistake.*

"Calm down? Hank is dead, we finally have our first real clue, and you want me to ignore it?"

"Yes, I do. We can report it to the police and wait for them to send in a professional search and rescue team."

"Alex isn't waiting, and neither am I."

There was a finality in her declaration. Still, Matt had to try to make her see reason. "The police will catch Alex, and he'll be back in prison in no time."

She narrowed her eyes. "The evidence against him is circumstantial. You said so yourself. What happens if the police question him and have to let him go? He'll be angrier and even more vengeful. So what would we gain except potentially putting more people in harm's way?"

Reasoning with Erin wasn't working. Time to put his foot down. Matt rose from the couch and crossed the room to the small kitchen. "We're not searching the mine. My job is to protect *you*. And whether that's from Alex Townsend or your own misguided ideas, I intend to do just that." Opening the fridge, he asked, "You want another beer?"

"No, thank you. I need a clear head to finish this conversation."

He shrugged. "Suit yourself." He hoped taking his time would dampen her hostility, so he popped the cap off, then returned to the couch at a leisurely pace.

Erin glared at him. "And exactly what did you mean by 'protecting me from my own misguided ideas'?"

Matt closed his eyes. *Jeez.* How was he supposed to continue this conversation without upsetting her even more? "Erin, I swear. I understand your concern, but you need to understand mine. This guy isn't just hurting people now. He's killing them." Matt patted the couch cushion, wanting her to sit back down next to him. To hear what he was saying, to heed his warnings. She didn't.

"That's my point. We have to do whatever we can to make sure he doesn't kill anyone else."

"The authorities are looking for Alex as a person of interest in Hank's death. In the meantime, we have eyes on everyone who you've deemed a potential target. If Alex shows up, we'll nab him."

"Great. So, that's your plan? We wait?"

"Yes, and while we wait, I believe we should limit our movements to the bunkhouse, barn and corral."

"So, you're turning me into a prisoner on the ranch, even more so than my mother did."

"That's not fair."

"No more unfair than what you're suggesting."

He wasn't suggesting anything but decided not to press the point. "Erin—"

"So, what happens if Alex doesn't show up? What then? Why not search the mine as a backup plan?"

Damn it, he didn't want to scare her, but at this point he didn't think he had a choice. Not if he was going to keep her in one piece. "With Alex escalating his threats and time running out, I'm concerned he'll come after you."

"If you come to the mine with me, there's no reason why you can't protect me there the same as you can protect me here."

"Think, Erin. There are cameras here. Alarms. Help within minutes. Out there, we're isolated. And once we set foot in that mine, we're at the mercy of crumbling shafts and falling debris." Matt crossed his arms over his chest. "I believe the rational thing to do is just stay here and let the police catch Alex."

But it seemed only one word penetrated Erin's brain.

"So now I'm misguided *and* irrational? Have I got that right?"

"No, that's not what I… I guess I wasn't clear about what I meant."

Erin stalked to her bedroom. "Well, let's see if *this* is clear enough for *you*." She went in and slammed the door behind her, the lock clicking loudly into place.

I guess it's back to the junk room for me.

EVEN WITH BONE-CRUSHING EXHAUSTION, Erin couldn't fall asleep. She stared at the ceiling, indignant, hurt and angry. Matt had been willing to search the long shots, like the ranch and the gully. But now, with their best clue so far for the most likely hiding spot of the jewelry, he shut the whole thing down. He expected her to listen, to be rational, to understand the safety concerns. But he didn't listen to her. Just like he hadn't listened to her about the storm in the ravine, and she'd been 100 percent right about it. He didn't respect her decisions. He didn't understand her intensified desire to find the jewelry.

Jill and Tommy had police protection. Liam and Maeve had top-of-the-line security. Hank was dead. The only person close to Erin that Alex could go after now was Matt himself. The man Erin was, without a doubt, falling for. Alex would only have to take one look at her face when Matt was around, and he'd know she was in love.

And Erin was about to blow that.

Matt had already caught her trying to sneak away once. When he caught her again, and she had no doubt he would eventually, she'd lose the trust of Mr. I-Don't-Believe-In-Second-Chances. No way would he forgive her. And after tonight, he'd be watching her like a hawk. She'd wracked her brain trying to figure another way out of this mess, but after hours in the dark, only two options remained. Either she broke his trust and he lived or she kept his trust only to lose him to Alex's madness.

Not really a choice at all.

Chapter Fifteen

After a few hours of sleep, Erin performed a replay of her first covert escape. Confirming that Matt had gone back to his air bed, she disarmed the security system, saddled Shadow by headlamp and took off for the mine. She would have preferred driving, but the truck engine would awaken Matt.

The full moon lit the way as she guided Shadow alongside roads, watching for vehicles or any sort of lights. Once at the mine, she draped the horse's reins around a tree branch and approached the entrance. Bright yellow danger tape crisscrossed plywood boards bolted into the rock that barred access.

One attempt at pulling off the plywood with her gloved hands, and Erin returned to Shadow to retrieve her folding spade and a crowbar. With the crowbar's help, she pried a piece of board away until it cracked in two. Exposed to the elements for years, the wood continued to crack and splinter, and soon she had an opening large enough to walk through.

Not sure what she'd need inside, Erin tossed the spade, crowbar and an empty saddlebag through the opening, patted her zippered pocket for the flashlight and turned on her headlamp. She squeezed past the broken pieces of plywood and entered the mine, the air turning cool and damp. Her light's beam danced across enormous spiderwebs and rough walls streaked with memories of mineral deposits.

The shaft's wooden support beams creaked above her, and each step she took stirred dust that hung suspended in the air. She pulled her bandanna up to cover her mouth and nose as she ventured deeper inside.

Erin followed the main shaft until it split into smaller tunnels. Ducking beneath a low beam, she chose the passage farthest to the left. The walls closed in around her, and when her headlamp flickered, she tapped it until the light steadied.

She came to a cave-in that blocked part of the tunnel. Her pulse sped up as she squeezed past the collapse, every sound exaggerated: loose debris as it slid to the ground, the creaking wood supporting the shaft, even her own breathing. Each step was a gamble, but one she intended to win.

The tunnel continued to narrow, and Erin walked hunched over for as long as she could before dropping to her knees and crawling, pushing her bag and tools ahead of her. After a few minutes, she stopped to catch her breath, glad she didn't suffer from claustrophobia, but the enormity of this escapade suddenly hit her. The mine had been boarded up because it was dangerous. She'd already passed one cave-in. No one knew where she was.

Well, Matt would figure it out fast enough, but he'd be so mad at her, he might just leave her here.

For a moment, Erin considered giving up and returning to the entrance, but she couldn't even if she wanted to. Only a contortionist could turn around in the small space. She pulled her bandanna back up over her mouth and crawled forward, sharp rocks bruising her knees.

Her breath hitched when the tunnel appeared to end ahead of her. The headlamp flickered again, and she struggled to get her flashlight out of her pocket. The brighter beam revealed not a solid wall or another cave-in, but an opening ahead. Relief washed over her, and she pushed through the hole and emerged in an enormous cavern, its floor littered with rocks and loose debris.

Shining her flashlight around, she noticed a pile of rocks on the far side of the room. It seemed unnatural. Out of place. Man-made. She ran to it and pulled away rocks, tossing them to the side. Her excitement grew as she uncovered a black plastic bag hidden under the rubble.

Erin pulled off her gloves and grabbed hold of the bag, only for it to disintegrate in her fingers. But within the shreds of plastic, jewelry glittered in her flashlight's beam.

She retrieved her saddlebag from where she'd dropped it and loaded the jewelry into it until the weight of the bag equaled the weight of her regrets. As she worked, a distant rumble vibrated, and dust rained down on her.

In a panic, she scrambled toward the tunnel. Erin retraced her route in reverse, again pushing the tools and bag ahead of her. She had almost reached the area of the cave-in she'd passed on her way in when more rumbles and vibrations surrounded her. She ran to the space she'd squeezed through earlier. The ground shook. Dirt fell in her eyes. Mid-step through the tight passage, it collapsed.

Everything went dark except the excruciating pain in her shoulder. That blazed with the brightness of a million suns. Dust filled her mouth, her nose, her lungs. Coughing, choking, her eyes watering, Erin suddenly knew what it was like to be buried alive. And standing up, at that.

If her situation weren't so terrifying, the irony might

make her laugh. After finally finding the jewelry, she was now buried with it.

But she refused to surrender to the circumstances. She had raised her good arm to chest level in a pushing position when the cave-in happened. An empty space right below it allowed a tiny amount of movement. She pawed at the debris with that hand. Dust thickened the small amount of available air. Each inhale made her cough out more oxygen than she took in. Sweat ran down her face, turning the dirt on it into mud. A small hole appeared, and she put her lips to it, trying to pull in a breath of air.

But it wasn't enough. She couldn't breathe.

Even the fresh pain in her dislocated shoulder faded away as her entire world turned black.

"ERIN!" MATT'S SHOUT echoed through the mine.

When there was no answer, part of his anger turned to worry. Erin had snuck out on him again. Put herself in danger because of Alex as well as the hazardous mine. Put Matt's reputation as a security specialist at risk. He was still mostly furious with her, but concern had definitely joined the party.

Matt continued deeper into the mine. "Erin!" Either she didn't want to answer him or she couldn't. If it was the first, she'd be sorry. If the latter... He wouldn't allow himself to consider that. Not yet, anyway. Instead, he kept going, calling her name, until he came to multiple tunnels branching off in different directions. "Erin!"

Still no response.

Starting with the first smaller tunnel to his right, he went to the mouth of each one. Examined the floor for recent footprints, any clue that might point the way. Matt yelled her name at the top of his lungs into every one of them.

When he reached the last one, he noticed disturbances in the dirt at its entrance. After he took several steps into it, his flashlight revealed boot prints that could be Erin's.

He called her name again. This time, he felt vibrations through his feet. He heard a sound he couldn't identify. A cloud of dust rolled toward him from the belly of the mine. Moving as quickly as he could, Matt kept going until his light bounced against a solid wall of dirt and rocks.

Damn it.

He'd chosen the wrong path. But before turning around, he approached the wall to confirm its solidness. There was a small hole, about chin level. Trying not to think about snakes or any other Texas critters that might be inside that hole, Matt pushed his finger through it.

And felt something soft.

Something that felt like…lips?

"Erin?" As he pulled his finger out, Matt hooked it on the edge of the hole and pulled more dirt away. After a few more times of doing that, he shone his flashlight into the hole. Still couldn't see. He shoved two fingers in and pulled. Then four. Then his whole hand. He tried the flashlight again. This time, it revealed part of a face. A nose streaked with dust. A mouth that he would recognize anywhere, even covered with granules of dirt and sand.

But Erin wasn't responding.

How long had she been without air? Matt dug his hand through the hole and pulled. Instead of the hole getting bigger, dirt and debris from around it slid down, hiding her face again. Matt kept clawing at the cave-in, his arms moving like a windmill. One after the other. Never slowing. Never stopping.

As the mess piled up around his legs, Erin began to sag.

Matt wrapped an arm around her waist and pulled her to him. Limp as a wilted flower, she slumped against him, her head lolling to the side. She wasn't breathing.

Matt felt for a pulse. Weak, but it was there.

He backed away from the cave-in and laid her on a relatively clean part of the tunnel floor and began CPR. Each time anxiety threatened to seize control, Matt pushed it away.

I don't have time to panic.

Alternating between chest compressions and breaths, Matt fought to save her life. When not holding her nose and breathing into her mouth, he muttered to the count of the compressions.

"You-bet-ter-wake-up-you're-in-so-much-trou-ble-I'm-fur-i-ous-with-you-you-broke-rule-num-ber-one-don't-leave-me-now-I-love-you."

During the second round of compressions, Erin sputtered, coughed out dusty spit, then inhaled a breath. Matt sat back on his haunches, fighting back tears of relief.

Erin looked up at him, dragging a filthy hand across her dirty mouth. "I found the jewelry."

Matt stared at her in silence for a moment and then got to his feet. "What the hell were you thinking?" His angry tone wiped her excited smile right off her face. "I told you to stay away from here!"

"I had to find it." Erin coughed out more dust while she sat up, then stood, unsteady and flinching when she moved her shoulder. "Alex can't keep hurting everyone I care about." Her voice sounded like gravel in a tin cup.

"You injured your shoulder again, didn't you?"

"No." She walked over to the cave-in and dug through the debris with one hand.

Matt followed her. "Yes, you did." He took hold of the arm she'd hurt during the flood and popped it back into place as Erin's scream filled the mine.

"Let's get out of here." Matt grabbed for her hand, but she yanked it away and kept digging.

When a corner of her saddlebag appeared, she turned and grinned at him. "See? I found it." Coughing and gasping for breath, she stepped back. "Would you mind pulling it out?"

Matt knew this was huge. They'd been looking for this stuff for the better part of two weeks, and Erin had found it. They could turn it in, and the police could maybe use it to catch Alex. But he couldn't get past his anger at her. His short-lived relief that she was alive evaporated. Instead, he was infuriated because she'd given him a taste of what it would feel like if she died. And he didn't like the deep ache it had caused in his chest. The sense of loss.

After grabbing the saddlebag, Matt led the way back through the tunnels without another word.

As they approached the entrance, a figure silhouetted in the early morning light stood just outside the mine.

"I knew you could do it, *Eriss*. You just needed the right incentive." Alex backed away. "Throw out the bag, then come out one at a time."

Erin leaned against the mine wall, fished her phone from her pocket and dialed 911. "Damn it! There's no reception inside."

"Think you can manage to pay attention to me this time, and stay here?" Matt whispered to Erin as he dropped the bag next to her. Moving toward the entrance, he called, "Get out of the way, Alex. This ends now."

"Are you sure about that?" Alex grinned as he pulled a knife from his belt, the blade flashing in the pale light.

MATT STEPPED THROUGH the mouth of the mine, ready to stop this guy once and for all. The faint morning light filtered down on Alex, bouncing on the balls of his feet while tossing a knife from hand to hand like some street thug in a dark alley.

"That the same knife you used to kill Hank?" Matt moved farther into the clearing as he spoke, giving himself more room to maneuver.

"The old guy had more muscle than I figured. Had to sharpen it after I gutted him." Alex held the blade up between them, his eyes cold, his tone taunting.

"Drop the knife." Matt's hand drifted close to his holstered gun as he took a step forward. "You're done harassing Erin. Done threatening and killing her friends."

"You think *you're* going to stop me?" Alex's laugh infuriated Matt.

But before he could respond, Alex lunged. Matt stepped to the side and grabbed Alex's arm, twisting it backward, forcing him to let go of the knife. Alex drove his shoulder into Matt's chest and they fell to the ground, Matt struggling to suck in air beneath Alex's weight. He rolled to the side just as Alex's punch grazed his cheek.

They scrambled to their feet, circling each other like wrestlers inside a ring. Alex feinted to the left, then came back with a right cross. Matt blocked the first blow, then took a savage hit to his gut, doubling over in pain. He got even with an uppercut that snapped Alex's head back, then followed with a jab that sent blood spraying from the felon's nose.

But that didn't stop Townsend, who slammed into Matt, driving him into the wall of the mine. Fists flew, Matt's knuckles split against Alex's jaw, but a sharp jab to his ribs left him gasping.

While Alex rained punches into his side, Matt used his superior strength to push him back. They tumbled to the ground again, battling for control. Alex managed to grab Matt's gun from its holster, but Matt yanked it from his grip and sent it flying.

He pinned Alex, holding him down and landing blow after blow. Alex twisted beneath Matt, throwing him off-balance, then rolled away and dived for the knife on the ground. Matt cursed under his breath as Alex rose, flashing the blade as he advanced.

"Stop!" Erin's voice rang out, raw and rough. Both men froze. Matt's gaze slid to her, a few feet away and holding his gun. Her hands trembled, but her tone was steady. "Drop the knife, Alex. Right now!"

Alex hesitated, his eyes darting between Matt and Erin, his lips twisting with anger. Matt thought he might charge at her, but then Alex let out an unsettling laugh and threw the knife down.

Matt snatched the gun from Erin and leveled it at Alex. *His* hands didn't tremble. "Don't even think about moving."

Alex raised his hands, expressions flickering across his face. Anger. Failure. Maybe regret?

Behind them, Erin already held her phone. "I'm calling the police."

Matt kept the gun trained on Alex as he tried to catch his breath, his ribs throbbing with every inhale. Seconds stretched into minutes before the welcome sound of sirens wailed in the distance. Only then did Matt spare a quick glance at Erin.

"Good work," he said in a soft tone.

"Even though I didn't *stay*, as you ordered me to?" She stared at him, her face a blank canvas. As if she'd packed away her emotions and wouldn't need them again anytime soon.

"IT MUST BE a slow crime day in Winston." Erin's throat ached with each word as she counted police cruisers parked along the dirt road near the mine.

"Every day's a slow crime day in Winston." Officer Steve Folsom arched a brow. "Except the ones when *you're* involved."

Erin had gone to school with Steve and knew him well enough to take his teasing in stride. He'd been assigned to stay with her until Detective Martinez took her statement. She followed his eyes across the clearing to where Martinez stood next to Alex, reading him the Miranda warning from a card she held.

"She's not taking any chances with this guy," he said. "Usually Martinez just recites Miranda from memory."

"Bless her for dotting all the *i*'s and crossing all the *t*'s to make sure he stays locked up for the rest of his life." An image of Hank flashed in Erin's mind. "He deserves everything he gets."

"So, you really found the stuff y'all stole?" Steve asked, then dropped his gaze when Erin scowled at him. "Sorry. I'm just impressed."

Holding the saddlebag tight against her chest with her good arm, she nodded. "It's right here, and I'm not letting go until I hand it to Martinez directly." She leaned toward him. "You know, chain of custody and all that."

"Don't suppose I could just take a quick peek?"

"Not a chance." Erin tightened her grip on the bag as she watched Matt talk to another police officer near the back of an ambulance. "I hope they know he's not going to let them transport him to the hospital in that thing."

As if on the same wavelength, Matt looked across the clearing at her. Maybe he didn't smile at her because his battered face hurt too much. Maybe he didn't raise a hand to wave because his bruised ribs wouldn't allow it. Or maybe he was as mad at her as she was at him. Whatever the reason, he just stared at her for a moment, then turned his attention back to the officer.

"Here comes Martinez." Steve straightened, and Erin wondered if he hoped to move up the ranks to detective someday.

"Ms. Montgomery." The detective nodded. "Quite the week you're having."

"I could have done without it, but you know what they say. All's well—"

"Yes. I do know." Flipping open her notebook, Martinez sighed. "Let's just do a quick rundown of the day to make sure your story matches your friend's over there." She tipped her head toward Matt. "We'll save the long version for your statement at the station later, after you've been checked out at the hospital."

"Oh." Erin looked toward Shadow. "I rode my horse here this morning, and—"

"Officer Folsom here can get the horse back to your ranch. You sound like a bass singer who's gargling with rocks." Martinez raised one brow. "And every time you cough, I could swear I see a puff of dust come out."

The detective couldn't be much older than Erin, but Martinez's matter-of-fact manner intimidated her. Hopefully, she'd intimidate Alex even more.

"Why don't you tell me how all this happened." She raised a hand and gestured around her.

Beginning with Tommy's ring, Erin gave the detective a condensed version of the past twenty-four hours, minimizing the argument with Matt.

With her head still bent over her notepad, Martinez raised her eyes and met Erin's gaze. "And that's the *loot*, as you call it?" she asked, indicating the saddlebag.

"Yes. I wanted to give it to you myself. For chain of custody." Erin held it out. "I've got Tommy's ring and the earring I found in the woods in my pocket. I'm not positive they're part of it, but I figured you, or forensics, or whoever, could check them against the list." For the life of her, she couldn't seem to stop talking.

"Right." Martinez took the saddlebag, unfastened its strap to peer inside, then closed it back up before holding out her hand, palm up.

It took Erin a moment to realize she was waiting for the other two items. After placing them in her hand, she said, "If the ring isn't part of it, I promised Tommy he'd get it back."

Martinez gave her a deadpan look, did an about-face and started toward the bustle of police activity. She called back over her shoulder, "Oh yeah, don't leave town."

"I won't. Wait. What?" Erin looked to Steve, who fought a losing battle with a laugh. "Why did she tell me to stay in town?"

"Calm down. She's pulling your leg." Steve patted her shoulder. "Martinez is an acquired taste, but she's a brilliant investigator. You're lucky she wasn't a detective ten years ago, when, you know, you—"

"Yes, Steve. I know," Erin said, taking a page from the brilliant detective's playbook and cutting him off. She loosened Shadow's reins from the branch and handed them to him. "See you at the station."

She crossed the clearing to the ambulance and approached Matt with a smile. "How are you feeling?"

"I'll live. You?" Exhaustion replaced any warmth in his tone.

"I have to get checked out at the hospital, but I'm okay." Erin paused, the conversation starting out more awkward than she'd hoped. "By the way, thank you for saving my life in there." She tipped her head toward the mine.

"Just doing my job. No matter how hard you made it." He perched on the back of the ambulance, grimacing with the movement.

"I'm sorry, Matt. I had no way of knowing Alex would show up here. But now it's done. He's been arrested, and we recovered the stolen jewelry." She shrugged her good shoulder. "At least I was right about where it was."

"Well, so long as you were right, that's all that matters."

Erin's head snapped back as if he'd slapped her. "No, what matters is you never believe I'm right about anything until after the fact, when it's too late. You didn't listen to me about the ravine, and I almost died. If you'd listened to me about the mine and come with me, maybe neither one of us would have been hurt."

Matt shook his head. "If you'd listened to me and stayed home, *definitely* neither of us would've been hurt."

He just doesn't get it. "And Alex would still be on the loose, threatening people I care about. Maybe worse." Erin blew out a frustrated breath. "He'd already threatened or killed everyone else in my life he could get to. You were the only one left. I went after the jewelry because I didn't want him hurting you."

Matt closed his eyes for a moment before replying in a softer voice. "I appreciate that, but it was my job to keep you safe, not the other way around. All you had to do was follow my rules, but right up to the end, you refused to do that."

"Well, I hope you and your rules live happily ever after together." Erin leaned toward him and lowered her voice, but it held a bitter edge. "Because if I had followed that last rule of yours, your order to stay in the mine, you might not have a future to look forward to. But hey, no need to thank *me* for saving *your* life."

She walked off toward the second ambulance, blinking the sudden dampness from her eyes. Because Erin Montgomery didn't cry, damn it. Especially not over some control-freak bodyguard who refused to acknowledge her worth.

Chapter Sixteen

The day after Alex's arrest, Matt eased his truck up to the Montgomerys' front gate and buzzed the intercom. Yesterday had dragged on endlessly, and this was the first chance he'd had to swing by and pick up his belongings.

He pressed the buzzer again, but there was no response.

He'd refused the ambulance ride from the mine only by promising the paramedics that he'd drive himself straight to the hospital from the crime scene. And as much as he despised hospitals, it had been the right call. One cracked rib. A deep gash in his cheek that needed stitches. A bruised kidney that still ached with every step.

Hours later, when the emergency room doctor finally released him, Matt had made good on his word to swing by the police station and give them the full version of his statement. By the time he'd finished that, he barely had enough energy to drive to his apartment, climb the stairs and collapse face-first onto his bed.

True, Erin's place was closer than Resolute. But the way things had ended between them at the crime site, he'd been confident she wouldn't let him in to spend the night. Even on the air bed.

Giving up on the intercom, Matt punched in the gate's

security code, let himself onto the property and parked near the bunkhouse. He climbed out, grimacing as his ribs protested every movement.

He needed to grab his duffel bag and go. But a stubborn part he couldn't shake hoped to see Erin before he left. He should have kept his mouth shut at the mine. Anger and worry had consumed him when he found Erin gone yesterday morning. She'd betrayed his trust again, put herself in danger and still seemed only to care that her hunch about the loot was right.

He regretted not keeping his reactions under control. Some of what she'd said had been valid but hit too close to the truth, and he'd made things between them even worse by holding his ground. And now he honestly wasn't sure where his emotions lay. Thirty-six hours ago, Matt would have bet every surfboard he owned that he and Erin would make it long term. And though he still wanted to be with her, that old reliable voice in his head urged him to run without looking back.

He knocked on the bunkhouse door, wincing when his raw knuckles hit the wood.

Again, no response.

"I'm coming in," he called out.

Still no answer, so he unlocked the door and stepped inside.

Everything looked exactly the same.

Matt scoffed at himself.

Of course it does. It's only been one day.

But it felt longer. It felt permanent. As if he were trespassing where he no longer belonged. A heavy shadow settled over his heart.

He headed into the junk room. The air mattress sat in a corner, deflated, the pump next to it.

She had wasted no time erasing him from her life.

He packed his clothes into his duffel, and by the time he walked out of the room, nothing remained to show he'd ever been there.

Except now, it was all organized.

A dry chuckle escaped him, one tinged with irony. He remembered his first day here and how Erin had made it clear she wanted him gone. Well, now he was going.

He pulled the front door closed behind him, making sure the lock clicked. Glancing at the security cameras mounted on the house and barn, he made a mental note to have Nate check with Erin about keeping them. And to remind her to reset the code combinations for the whole ranch.

Almost at the front gate, he caught a glimpse of movement in his side mirror. A figure on horseback. His heart hammering, Matt braked and twisted around in his seat to peer through the truck's back window.

Erin sat astride Shadow, her back straight and tall. Her gaze met his across the distance, felt more than seen.

She didn't ride toward him. She didn't wave.

Instead, she guided Shadow around and rode away, her silhouette fading into the landscape.

Matt gripped the steering wheel, his raw knuckles turning white. He fought the urge to turn the truck back and go after her.

She'd made her choice.

REDEMPTION PRANCED ACROSS the corral, no hint of a limp in his step.

"Good boy." Erin slipped him a piece of carrot. "I think it's time for you to go home."

She glanced at her watch and noticed the day of the week. Monday. A violent shudder wracked her body.

Today was the deadline. Two weeks ago, almost to the hour, Alex Townsend began his reign of destruction. Erin's eyes drifted to the spot where Hank's body had lain, her mind only too willing to manufacture the pools of blood staining the earth around him. How much more devastation would Alex have wreaked by now if he hadn't been arrested?

Shrugging off these morose thoughts that had settled over her like a shroud, Erin led Redemption to the barn. Although glad the horse had recovered from his injury, she would miss him. His workouts helped fill the empty hours she faced now that Matt had left. After grooming the gelding and moving him into his stall, she brought out Blaze.

"It's your turn to lead today, you beauty." Erin brushed the mare, then saddled her for riding. After opening Shadow's stall, she clicked her tongue to bring her out. "And you get to run free this time."

When she exercised both horses by herself, Erin rode one and had the other follow alongside. She'd trained Blaze and Shadow well enough to not worry about either one running off on their own.

The late morning sky was clear, the air frigid enough to see the horses' plumes of breath each time they exhaled. They'd get a good run in when they reached the meadow. But they walked in the meantime, Erin in no hurry to end this part of her day. Her animals brought her comfort.

Erin's mother's call, perfectly timed to come through after all the Alex furor had ended, brought excellent news. Her dad had extended his business. Erin would have the whole ranch to herself without having to answer to dear old Mom. But for the first time in her life, she experienced loneliness, not simply solitude. Without Matt around, and without the nonstop activity of the past two weeks, she didn't know what to do with herself.

I was fine before him, and I'm fine now.

It angered her that she even cared he was gone. He hadn't trusted her to make a good decision. He'd been angry that she followed her gut and wound up being right. He hadn't even said goodbye when he left. With a heavy, aching heart, her choice to turn away had been her only recourse to avoid more pain.

When they reached the meadow, the horses took off at a gallop, their hooves thundering across the ground. Erin's discontent lifted away, and she intended to let it stay gone. She had trusted herself and been right to do so. The time had arrived to make more life-changing decisions on her own. She didn't need her mother's constant disapproval. She didn't need to lean on Matt, or any man, for support.

Although the path to the future was still unclear, the destination wasn't.

Erin's equine therapy ranch would happen.

Chapter Seventeen

After adjusting her attitude about herself, her plans and life in general, Erin enjoyed two more months of freedom before her parents returned. Their extended trip translated to a grand tour of Europe, Asia and parts of the Middle East. Combining business and pleasure had always been a sound financial tactic for her dad. And the very few phone calls home meant her mom had planned the itinerary and was too busy enjoying herself to worry about the ranch.

All good news for Erin. And the recent meeting she'd had with the family attorney had left her downright euphoric.

But now, she meandered around the main house, waiting for her parents to arrive home from the airport so she could greet them. As was expected of her. Her stomach roiled in anticipation of what she thought of as *THE CONVERSATION.* Inhaling deep breaths, she trailed her fingers along the mantel, not surprised to find it dusted and polished. The Montgomerys' housekeeper hadn't slacked off for a moment, even with her parents on the other side of the world.

An engine purred in the circular drive out front, and car doors opened and closed. Erin shook out her arms to release her nerves, pulled her mouth into a loving smile and opened the door.

"Erin, darling." Her mother entered the house, air-kissed her daughter and left her in a cloud of perfume. "Have you lost weight? You're so thin."

"Hi, Dad." Erin hugged her father as he came through the door.

"You look wonderful," he whispered in her ear.

"No, Mother, I haven't lost weight." She opened the door wider for the driver, who struggled to haul what looked like twice the luggage her parents had left with into the house.

"We had the most wonderful time. It was a shame you didn't join us." Her mother took off a fashionable coat Erin had never seen before and draped it over a chair. "Especially considering all that ugly business going on here."

"Why don't you tell me about your trip." Now that she was face-to-face with her mom, Erin needed some time to gather her nerve about her own news. "Where did you go? What did you see?"

"Oh, where didn't we go?" Her mother settled on the couch, shooting a glare at her father as he fled to his office. "After we left Paris, we went to Japan. You know I've always wanted to go there, and it was as amazing as…"

Sitting in a nearby chair, Erin only half listened while her mom recounted every city in every country they'd visited, every purchase in every store she'd made and every delectable morsel from every restaurant that passed her lips. What she did hear sounded like it had been an incredible trip.

Meanwhile, the other half of her brain rehearsed the already memorized speech planned for her mom. And as had become her habit during all the years of squabbling with her mother in her head, she'd also prepared her mother's side of *THE CONVERSATION*. For every argument her mother would make, Erin had a counter. For every reason why not, Erin had a reason why. For every threat, emotional plea and criticism, Erin had a spine of steel and she wasn't afraid to use it.

As soon as she gathered her damn nerve.

"...but your father decided it was time to come home, so here we are."

"Wow."

"Now tell me what you've been up to. But before you start, I heard about all that nasty business at that old mine, and I'm going to give that security company a piece of my mind." She crossed the room to the bar cart and poured herself a sherry. "Would you like one, dear?"

"No thanks. I'm fine."

Returning to the couch, her mom continued, "That bodyguard they sent out here, Mark, Mike, whatever his name is, had no right to put you in such danger. And poor Hank, getting killed like that."

"His name is Matt, and he never put me in danger, Mom. He kept me safe while he was here." Erin's thoughts drifted to the hunter's cabin during the storm. If only her mother knew about that and the flood. "I was the one who decided to go to the mine. Matt didn't want me to."

Her mother paused, sherry glass an inch away from her mouth. "*You* decided to go. Now, why doesn't that surprise me? Your father and I spent a great deal of money for your protection, and you just go chasing after that...that *criminal* on your own." She tossed back her sherry and set the glass on the end table next to her. "Good grief, Erin. You're almost thirty years old, and you still don't have the sense God gave a goose."

Wait...wait... Yes, there it is.

It seemed Erin's nerve just needed a slight nudge from her anger.

"I had enough sense to want to make things right." Erin

rose and paced around the room as she spoke. "I went to the mine, I recovered all the stolen jewelry from the robbery. Matt subdued and held Alex until the police arrived and took him into custody."

"You never should have—"

"For the first time in ten years, I trusted a man. And it was the right call." Erin stopped in front of her mom. "For the first time in ten years, I trusted myself, and it was the right call. I do have good instincts. And if I put myself in danger, it was a risk I was willing to take to make up for my past mistakes. It was my choice, and I don't care what you or Matt or anyone else thinks about it."

Her mother stood, refusing to meet Erin's gaze. "Well, I'm exhausted from traveling. I think I'll go freshen up."

"That's not all, Mom." She waited her mother out, until she looked Erin in the eye. "Hank left everything he owned to me. I won't bore you with the details, but because he set everything up in advance, the attorney is already probating the will."

"What exactly do you mean by 'set everything up'?"

"I mean his property will become an equine therapy ranch." Erin watched her mother drop onto the couch. "He knew my dream was to use horses to help people deal with mental or physical challenges."

"That's ridiculous." Her mother held out her glass to Erin. "Would you please bring me a refill, dear?"

Erin rolled her eyes but did as she was asked.

"That will never work, Erin. I'm sure you don't have the necessary education for something like that."

"You know darn well my bachelor's degree is in veterinarian technology. I have plenty of certifications to work with horses. But I'll hire an actual therapist, and who knows? Maybe I'll go back to school for my master's, maybe even my doctorate."

Her mother almost snorted sherry out of her nose. "How do you plan to pay for all that?"

This was where Erin's plan to be self-sufficient ran into a hitch.

"Since you control Grandma's trust—"

"Those payments don't start until you turn thirty."

"But she told me she'd specified certain circumstances under which money could be released early. I believe starting my own business qualifies as one of her exceptions."

"Early release of any money from that trust would be at my discretion. And I'm certainly not doing it for some silly pipe dream that will never get off the ground." She set her glass on the table and stood. "Besides, we need you here to work with our dressage clients."

Erin's gut churned with anxiety, but she straightened her spine and met her mother's gaze. "I am moving to Hank's property, and I will be turning it into a therapy ranch. It's time for me to take control of my own life."

"Then you'll be doing it on a shoestring budget, dear, because the trust is locked for another two years." Her mother's brows struggled toward a frown, but the latest round of Botox injections won out. "Although I don't approve of this, when you're finally ready to face reality, we'll welcome you home again. Just like we did the last time you exercised such poor judgment." She turned away and, without another word, went upstairs.

Although Erin had trudged to the main house, dreading with every step the talk with her mother, she seemed to almost float above the ground during the return trip to the bunkhouse. As if she'd removed the proverbial millstone from around her neck that she had carried for the past ten years.

A range of emotions as wide as Texas itself tumbled through her, and she tried to focus only on the positive ones. Relief, excitement and self-confidence topped the list. Disappointment in her mother's attitude toward Erin and her plans hurt, but not as much as she'd expected. She pushed that one away. When she did, two more rolled into its spot. Sadness. Regret. They merged to form an image in her mind.

Matt Franklin's face.

Chapter Eighteen

After finishing up two jobs near Austin, Matt met Nate at the Busy B Café in Resolute.

"I emailed you my report this morning." Matt took a bite of his burger and chewed slowly, savoring the flavor.

Nate nodded. "I got it. Sounds like these last two assignments were your easiest of the year so far."

"Considering the Montgomery job was the only other one, that's not saying much." He shifted in his seat, wincing at the residual pain in his ribs.

"It's been a few months. Shouldn't you be all healed up by now?" Nate drained his coffee cup and held it up in Marge's direction.

"You would think. At least the ER doctor's teeny, tiny stitches in my face maintained my rugged boyish charm." He laughed when Nate almost choked on a french fry.

Marge, the owner of the diner, worked her way to their table, her orthopedic shoes squeaking across the linoleum floor. "You boys need refills?" She held up the carafe of coffee she'd brought with her.

After filling both cups, she leaned in close to Matt's face, squinting. "I can barely tell where that big old cut was."

She straightened. "Must have been a plastic surgeon wannabe who stitched you up."

Matt smiled at Nate and spread his arms wide. "What'd I tell you?" He looked up at Marge. "Do I still have my rugged, boyish charm?"

"Sure you do." The older woman patted him on the shoulder. "And just enough of it to woo that Erin Montgomery and take her off the market before some other charming boy snags her."

Matt glanced at Nate, who stayed quiet while he dipped a fry in ketchup.

"I'm not so sure Ms. Montgomery wants to be taken off the market." Matt shifted again, now uncomfortable *and* feeling awkward.

"And I'm not so sure discussing women being on or off the market is socially acceptable these days." Nate shrugged.

Marge glared at Nate. "It's my diner, and I'll talk any way I want to." She then turned to Matt. "I heard tell you two had something going on while you were protecting her. If you ask me, you should figure out why you don't anymore, fix it and get it going again."

"Thanks for the advice." Eager to change the subject, Matt added, "And these are the best burgers west of the Pecos."

Marge and Nate looked at each other, then burst out laughing.

"I appreciate that, honey. But when you look like one of them surfers from California, trying to talk like a Texan just don't work." She leaned in again and stage-whispered, "And we're east of the Pecos. Not west."

She squeaked off toward the kitchen, laughing and muttering, "West of the Pecos. Don't that beat all?"

Nate held his napkin to his mouth to hide his chuckles.

"Whatever." Matt shrugged it off and took another bite of his burger. "At least I tried."

"Check a map next time." Nate leaned back against his bench seat. "You know, Marge might not be wrong."

"This from the man whose company motto is don't fall in love with the client?"

"You can't put that toothpaste back in the tube." Nate arched a brow.

Concentrating on his condiments, Matt said, "How'd you figure it out?"

"Give me some credit." Nate snorted. "And you haven't been yourself since the job ended. What happened between you two?"

"Well, we got caught in the storm—"

"Not that part. What happened that you're not even talking to each other?"

Matt thought about it before answering. "I was more concerned with my rules than listening to Erin's opinions. I guess I should have done a better job of balancing the two." He popped another fry in his mouth. "But what's done is done, and she made it clear I've lost my chance with her."

"I know this is the opposite of what I usually say, but you shouldn't give up on her so quickly. I almost made that mistake myself with Sara, and I'm really glad I came to my senses in time." Nate nodded, as if agreeing with himself that he'd done the right thing. "Maybe it's not too late for you and Erin."

Matt shrugged but didn't reply. He wished Nate was right, but at this point, that was another decision Erin would have to make.

"I do have some good news." Nate grinned. "Winston PD

is processing the reward, and you should have the money any day."

"That's nice," Matt mumbled, still thinking about Erin.

"Nice? It's enough to buy back in as a partner."

Matt perked up at that. "Seriously? But shouldn't it go to Erin? Technically, she's the one who recovered the jewelry."

"She's not eligible for it because she was involved in the original crime." Still smiling, Nate added, "Plus, she made it clear, even if she were eligible, she wouldn't take a dime."

Matt tried to ignore his guilt about the way he'd ended things with Erin. "So, you and me—we're partners again?" He lifted his water glass and waited for Nate to clink his against it.

"To partners."

"This is the best news I've had since I moved to Texas." Matt couldn't wipe the grin off his face. He would finally share ownership of *their* company with his best friend again.

"Scooch over." Charlie, the bodyguard who had stayed with Maeve O'Roarke, dropped into the booth next to Nate while Gabe forced his muscled self in on Matt's side. "What's this confab about?"

"Matt's buying into the company as an equal partner," Nate said.

"Oh, man. We're gonna have two bosses now?" Charlie rolled her eyes.

"It was bad enough with just the one." Gabe stared at Nate with a straight face.

Matt could never tell when the big man was joking. "Yeah? Well, get used to it." He elbowed Gabe in the side.

"Just kidding, Matt. I'm glad you did it so quickly," Charlie said, then kicked her Southern drawl up a notch. "Y'all goin' to the barn raisin'?" Her eyes twinkled.

"What barn raising?" Matt asked.

"The horse therapy ranch." Charlie widened her eyes in surprise at Matt. "Figured you'd know all about it, since she was your girlfri... Ouch, why'd you kick me?" She glared at Nate.

"I was going to tell Matt about it." Nate fortified himself with more coffee. "Erin inherited Hank's property, and she's turning it into a therapy ranch. But the place needs a lot of work, and rumor has it Erin's mom won't release any of her trust money early. So some businesses in Winston are donating supplies, and we're all going to build her a new barn and whatever else we can."

"She still won't be able to open anytime soon," Charlie said. "She'll need to buy horses and hire a therapist and a bunch of other stuff. But at least the property will be ready."

"We're all going, and my sister and brothers and their spouses will be there." Nate avoided Matt's eyes.

"When is it?" Matt asked.

"Beginning of the month." Gabe glanced at Charlie. "Are we eating here or what?"

"Hold your horses. Marge is heading this way." Charlie flashed her dazzling smile at Marge.

Gabe grumbled about needing sustenance.

And Matt realized he had no one to blame but himself for being out of the loop when it came to Erin and her new ranch.

But maybe it wasn't too late to help.

Chapter Nineteen

The first Saturday of June dawned cooler than everyone had expected—welcome news for the passel of friends and strangers who'd volunteered for the grueling work of a barn raising for Tranquil Trails Equine Therapy Ranch. Matt parked his truck and walked across grass damp with early morning dew, the last of the ground mist swirling as he passed. Long into his sleepless night, he'd debated the wisdom of coming here today. But like that moth to a flame, he craved nearness to Erin.

Maybe I am a chump after all.

Sure, he was gratified to play a part in her dream. What she was trying to accomplish was admirable and would help a lot of people. But to be so close to her and not tease her, laugh with her, touch her would be torture. His version of the moth's death from the light that attracted it.

The sight of the Montgomery Ranch foreman directing volunteers surprised Matt. "Morning. Erin's mother okay with you being here?"

The man chortled. "Hell no, but they have no say about what I do during my day off. She okay with you being here?" he asked with a wink.

Matt grinned. "I expect she wouldn't be, but I don't work for her anymore."

"Figured as much, what with that creep out of the picture. But, you know, after you and Erin... Well, I flat out didn't expect to see you here either."

Matt gave him a small, one-shoulder shrug. "Worthy cause."

"A very worthy cause," the foreman said with another wink, and Matt knew he wasn't referring to the ranch.

Given the job of directing supply trucks just arriving, he waved his arms to direct one loaded with tools and a second, longer flatbed piled high with donated boards and posts to the spot where the builders waited.

Once they'd parked, he greeted each truck driver with a handshake, and introductions were made before the real work of unloading began. The aroma of freshly cut lumber reminded Matt of the times he'd spent in the woods with Erin. A warm, earthy scent that he found pleasing.

Not that he found much to be pleased about these days. *And whose fault is that?*

After the trucks were emptied, Matt spied his boss. He headed toward Nate and Nate's very *un*identical twin, Noah, and the three began laying wood studs on a framing table, measuring the wall studs according to blueprint specs, then sawing them to length.

"Slow down, Noah," Nate said. "Measure twice, cut once."

Noah inhaled. "I was distracted. The smell of those grills warming up is making my mouth water." He turned to Matt. "Our brother, Adam, is the best home chef in the county, and he excels at grilling."

"You and your stomach," Nate grumbled. "It's dawn,

you blockhead. Hours before lunch. How can you already be thinking about food?"

Matt laid a stud on the table, and Nate redirected his attention. "Wait, Matt. Not like that. Here, let me show you."

Clearly, the Reed brothers had more construction know-how than Matt, but he was always willing to learn.

Like horseback riding.

He swore under his breath. Why did every action, every thought, always circle back around to Erin?

"Stop harping on the man," Noah said. "Anyone can see we got us a city boy here."

Nate nodded. "A useless city boy."

Matt's brows shot up. "You clowns work that out ahead of time?"

They grinned, and Matt got an inkling of what they must have been like as kids. "You're on your own. I'm going to take my city-boy ways and help elsewhere."

He walked away to the sound of their laughter. The Reeds were like that. The twins, Cassie, Adam, even their spouses. If they didn't tease you, they didn't care about you. At least, that's what Matt kept telling himself.

As he made his way to the slab for the new barn, he noticed vehicles now lined both sides of the state road for a half mile or more, parked on the shoulders along the Montgomerys' property and Hank's—no, Erin's—property. Hank would have loved this.

Over near Hank's old, small barn, scores of people moved about like ants at a picnic, issuing directions, offering advice or just chatting. Children ran around, squealing and laughing. Women shooed them away while working under pitched canopies, organizing a water station, first aid station and a food station. Hammers pounded, saws buzzed.

A day of organized chaos with an atmosphere of raucous anticipation.

When the Reeds showed up for an event, apparently they brought the entire town of Resolute with them. To be fair, Winston's townsfolk were nearly as plentiful. Matt surveyed the spectacle. All of this, the planning, donations, supplies and people, were here for one reason—to help Erin realize her dream of opening a therapy horse ranch. The turnout was beyond amazing. Matt thought back to his own childhood and wondered how different his life might have been if there had been a place like this for him.

A pang of envy shot through him. He was tired of not belonging. To a community. To someone.

To Erin.

His chest burned with a stabbing ache, one that happened frequently these days. He did his best to ignore it, but fools deserved what they got.

Charlie appeared to be in charge of the barn construction, so Matt headed for her. Tall and well-muscled, she'd tied her blond hair in a ponytail that hung through the back of a gimme cap with Resolute Security's logo. She wore a sleeveless T-shirt under overalls and old work boots, yet she somehow managed to make all that look feminine.

"Put me to work," Matt said.

She tugged a bandanna from her back pocket and blotted the sweat on her forehead. "Luke had to bail. Got called out on a case. But you can help Gabe." She shoved the bandanna back into her pocket. "I was happy to see the foundation already set. Nice job, that."

Matt saw nothing but an ordinary concrete slab. Whether it was a nice job or not, he had no idea. "So, you know about this stuff?"

"I've spent a lot of my vacations building homes for a charity organization, so yeah, I know a bit."

"Well, look at you, you big softy."

"Tell anyone and I'll have to take you out."

Matt held up two fingers in promise. "To the grave," he said, grinning. As a woman in a male-dominated field, Charlie worked hard to prove she was one of the best. And she was.

"Grab a two-by-six," she said, pointing to the stack of lumber. "Take it over to Gabe. He'll tell you what to do."

"You got it, boss."

He started to turn away when Charlie grabbed his arm and stopped him. "Listen, I wasn't going to say anything, but the hell with it."

"Mind telling me what you're talking about?" But he figured he already knew.

"I heard what you did. Giving up your shot at becoming *my* boss."

Matt's jaw clenched.

"Look, I'm not going to tell anyone. I know you want the donation to be anonymous and all. But I want you to know that gifting Erin that reward money is pretty awesome."

"Not very anonymous if you know about it. How'd you find out? Nate?"

"Indirectly. I accidentally overheard him talking to his wife about it."

Matt grunted, turned to go and stumbled, nearly doing a face-plant before regaining his balance. He looked down. "Whoa there!" Tangled up in his legs was young Tommy.

"Sorry, Mr. Matt. Glad you didn't fall. Gotta go." The boy dashed off, several children chasing him down in a mean game of tag.

"This is a dangerous place," Gabe said, coming up to

them to grab more lumber. "Matt, quit lollygagging with this pretty lady and get to work."

Matt winked at Charlie, picked up a wooden stud and followed Gabe. "Lollygagging?"

"Don't judge. That PI we use turned me on to word-of-the-day calendars."

For several hours, Matt, alongside Gabe, members of the Winston police force and dozens of other volunteers, lifted and hammered together the barn's frame. Others worked on the trusses for the roof before lunatics with no fear of heights laid down the metal roofing sheets.

Throughout the day, Matt kept constant tabs on Erin as she flitted from place to place, speaking with everyone, it seemed. Everyone but him. He made sure to steer clear of her. It was one thing to lend a helping hand, it was another to let their personal stuff ruin her day.

"Lunch break, everyone!" Charlie shouted, and the hungry group of workers dropped their tools and stampeded toward the live oaks shading a grouping of picnic tables and benches.

Long tables were piled high with food. Potluck dishes of every type—casseroles, salads, rolls, sandwiches, plus all the fixings to go with Adam Reed's burgers and hot dogs. Marge, the owner of the Busy B Café, presided over the array like a sergeant major.

"Now, Bill, you go on and leave some of that pie for other folks."

"Yes, ma'am. It just looks so darn good."

"Well, of course it's good. I baked it. And watch that language. There are children about," she scolded. "Jace! Goodness me. Use the serving thongs and not your grimy fingers, if you please."

"Sorry, Ms. Marge. Real sorry."

"Why, Annabelle Gibson, you look rail thin. Take a second helping."

"Oh, no thank you. I'm full."

"Fiddlesticks. Here, you take this, and you eat it. You hear me?"

"Marge is a real force of nature, isn't she?" Erin, sweaty and disheveled and never more beautiful to him, moved along the other side of the table, casually scooping food onto her plate as if nothing had ever passed between them.

How had he let everything go so wrong?

Matt gritted his teeth. "She is that."

"I didn't expect to see you here." Her voice was soft, enticing, a siren's song making his nerves crackle.

Hoping he appeared indifferent, he shrugged. "Resolute Security is a donor. The boss wanted us here."

"Oh, I see. Makes sense."

Was that disappointment he heard? Or was his wishful thinking working overtime? He plopped a spoonful of something onto his plate. He didn't know what. Didn't really care. "It's a good cause. I would have come anyway."

"Well, thank you." Having reached the end of the table, her plate full, she said, "Take care, Matt."

And that was that. Whatever had been between them was over. He was certain now.

She turned and walked away, taking his heart with her.

No second chance for him. Irony was a vindictive shrew.

AFTER LUNCH, ERIN LED a group of volunteers to what would become the training paddocks. Never in her wildest dreams could she have imagined such an outpouring of support. A perfect reason to smile. And yet, her smile felt brittle and phony on the outside, while she felt miserable on the inside.

Matt didn't love her. He'd made that plain enough. She

wondered if he'd ever cared about her. It seemed impossible that she had misjudged the situation so completely. Again. But the evidence told her otherwise. What twisted irony that just when she'd decided to trust herself, Matt blindsided her with a sucker punch.

Can't blame Matt. I won't. I'm owning my life, screwups and all.

Growth only came when you learned from your mistakes, and her mistakes were telling her that love was not in the cards for her. At least not with Matt. Love for her would have to come from the gratification she'd find the first time some kid smiled down on her from the back of one of her therapy horses. It was enough. It would have to be.

"Hey, everyone, can I have your attention, please?" she shouted to the landscaping crews. "Team leaders, raise your hands. Great. Team A will be with Marcella over there. You're in charge of pulling weeds. Where's Cruz? There you are. His team, Team B, will be tying up the broken tree limbs. And my group, Team C, will be in charge of clearing brush. Everyone find a team. Don't all bunch up in one place. Spread out evenly between the groups. That's it."

Several minutes passed with people shuffling around before Erin could delineate three relatively evenly populated teams. "Okay, listen up. Whichever group finishes first—"

"Gets dinner on me at my place in Resolute," Adam Reed declared. He smiled at Erin as she mouthed, "Thank you." A much better prize than what she'd planned to hand out.

Charlie, on the brush crew, waved her gimme cap in the air. "Woo-hoo!" she hollered. "Best steaks in the county."

The crowd cheered in approval.

"Come on, team! Let's show these punks what we're made of," Charlie called out, clearly up for the challenge.

Erin laughed. Strange, really, that Charlie was becoming

a good friend in such a short time. One bodyguard coming into her life, one going out.

About two hours into the backbreaking contest, Tommy's mother came running up to Erin, her eyes wide, a piece of paper fluttering in her hand. "Erin! Erin!"

"Whoa, slow down, Jill. Is everything okay with Tommy?"

Unable to speak while she caught her breath, Jill nodded in the affirmative while bending at the waist to rest her hands on her knees. Finally, she stood and waved the paper in front of Erin's face. "You're never going to believe this. Look!"

Erin took the sheet. "My bank statement?"

Jill, who worked at the bank in Winston, nodded toward the paper. "Yes. And?"

Erin looked again. "And what?"

Jill folded her arms across her chest, almost as if hugging herself. "Seriously? You don't see it?"

Erin looked for a third time. "Um, no. I don't… What the—" Her head shot up. "Is this a mistake?"

Jill's smile stretched from ear to ear. "I thought so too, at first. So, I checked. Girl, it's not a mistake. That's one hundred percent legit."

The statement showed a deposit into her ranch operating account. A huge deposit, even by Montgomery standards. "Where did this come from?"

"I have no idea. It was tagged as an anonymous donation."

"Mom! Mom! Mom!" Tommy ran up to Jill and wrapped his arms around her legs. "You're here. Finally."

Over the top of Tommy's head, Jill told Erin, "I had to work, so my sister's been keeping an eye on him."

Jill extracted herself from her son's loving embrace. "Say hi to Miss Erin."

"I already did. What's that?" He pointed at the paper she held.

"Just some boring adult stuff," Erin said, still wondering if she was dreaming.

Jill scoffed. "Adult stuff, yes, but boring? Not by half."

Tommy looked from Erin to his mom. "How come?"

Jill squatted until she was face-to-face with him. She thumb-wiped dirt from his cheek. "Because Miss Erin has a secret admirer."

Tommy's nose scrunched up. "Does he want to kiss her? 'Cause that's gross."

"No, he doesn't want to kiss her. He wants her to have money for this horse ranch."

"She should say thank you."

Jill stood and finger-combed his tousled hair. "Yes, well, she would, except she doesn't know who gave her the money."

"I know. It was Mr. Matt."

Both Jill and Erin said, "What?" in unison, startling Tommy.

"It's okay," Jill assured him. "It just surprised us. How do you know that?"

"'Cause I heard him tell that lady over there." Tommy pointed to Charlie.

"What did he say, honey?" Jill asked.

"Um, I don't remember. Can I have a soda?"

"No, you may not. It's bad for your teeth. But I need you to think. What makes you think it was Mr. Matt who gave Erin the money?"

"Mo-om."

"Don't whine, Tommy." Jill looked at Erin and shrugged.

"I know for a fact Matt doesn't have that kind of money," Erin said.

"Oh, oh, oh," Tommy said, jumping up and down. "I remember! The lady," he said, again pointing to Charlie, "said he wasn't going to be her boss and he said so what it was his reward money."

Erin's mind spun. Matt wanted that partnership more than anything. She needed to return it to him somehow.

"Are we done now? Can I go play?"

"Sure, honey," Jill said, and Tommy darted off. "Well?" she asked Erin.

"Well, what?"

Jill gave her a knowing look. "Are you going to talk to him?"

"I am not." Matt had made his feelings, or lack thereof, well known. She'd blindly followed her heart once before, and that ended poorly. No way would she make the same mistake again. She was a stronger person now.

"I have a feeling the donation came from my father," Erin lied. Anything to keep from having to face Matt.

"I think you're being a fool."

"You're wrong about that. This is the least foolish thing I've done in a long while."

Anything more, her heart wouldn't survive.

WHY WAS HE LINGERING? There was no reason to stay, and yet he did. Matt could kick himself. If only he'd tried harder to mend the rift between them, maybe he wouldn't be here now, alone, leaning back against the new paddock fence, one boot braced behind him against the lowest rail.

To the west, the setting sun grazed the horizon, casting the newly completed barn in dark relief. A beautiful scene, solemn and lonely. Time to leave. Past time, if he was being honest.

Just a little bit longer, he told himself. Then he would go.

And yet, his thoughts were so full of Erin laughing at him, defying him, making love with him, that he couldn't bring himself to go.

He was a fool.

ERIN WALKED THROUGH the dim interior of the barn, the smell of new lumber teasing her nose. The volunteers had all left, the day was drawing down and she was enjoying a bit of quiet solitude. She surveyed the barn, marveling at how everything was so new and clean.

A nicker caught her attention, and she wandered over to Shadow's stall. She dropped his head over the Dutch door.

"That's right. Come here, girl." She rubbed the horse's soft nose. "What do you think about your new digs? Nice, isn't it?" Erin made sure there was plenty of hay for the mare to munch on and then wandered over to visit with Blaze.

"Hi there, Blaze. You didn't think I'd forgotten about you, did you? No, I would never do that."

At last, the day's activities began to take their toll. Exhausted, she shuffled over to the main door and prepared to close it up for the night. And gasped. Silhouetted against a sky ablaze with orange and crimson was Matt.

What was he still doing here? She hadn't seen or heard from him in months, and then today he showed up out of the blue to help out. And the donation, what was that all about? She was beyond grateful for it, but if she wasn't good enough for a second chance, why was he doing all this for her? Why didn't he just leave?

"You should talk to him."

Erin whipped around and slapped a hand over her thundering heart. "Jeez, Charlie. You scared the daylights out of me. What are you still doing here?"

"Love you, too."

"Sorry. I didn't mean that the way it sounded."

Charlie grinned. "Yeah, I know, but it's fun messing with you."

"Cute. But really, why are you still here?"

"Just checking the new security system. Once a security nerd, always a security nerd." She nodded in Matt's direction. "Whatcha gonna to do about that?"

"Wait for him to leave?"

"Chicken. Why not just go out there and talk to him?"

"I tried that earlier. It didn't work."

"Seriously? I've never met two more stubborn people." Charlie rubbed her forehead as if she had a momentous headache.

"He doesn't care about me. He's made that perfectly clear. I don't see what we have left to talk about."

"Don't you?"

The donation.

"Do you, um, I mean, what do you…do you know?"

"I'm really hoping you never seek a career in a clandestine service, because you have absolutely no skills ferreting out information."

Erin pointed out the barn. "Clearly, I'm not about to apply for a job at Spies R Us."

Charlie laughed. "Good thing."

"So, what *do* you know?"

"About what?" the bodyguard said with a smirk.

Getting frustrated, Erin said, "You know."

"Do I?"

"You're driving me crazy."

"And you're avoiding."

Erin was, but it was no fun being called out.

"Go on. Talk to him. What could it hurt?"

Charlie didn't understand. Being rejected again would tear Erin apart, shatter her heart. But hey, no big deal. So, like the fool she was, she walked outside.

In the shadows of early dusk, she approached Matt. She almost turned around, but he'd know she was chicken, just as Charlie had claimed. For that reason alone, she kept going.

She stopped a few feet from where he stood. "Thank you for all the work you did today. I still can't believe the barn and grounds are ready to go."

His voice, when it came, sounded almost like low, masculine music. "I'm glad I could lend a hand. I've got a lot to learn about construction, but I picked up a fair amount today."

Silence. Long and painful.

"Matt, I know you donated your reward money to the ranch."

"Does everyone in Boone County know?" Matt massaged his temples. "How did you find out?"

"Accidentally, but that doesn't matter. I can't let you do it." Erin planted her fists on her hips.

"Too late. It's already done."

"I can't accept it. I'll cut you a check for the full amount on Monday." She dropped her arms. "I appreciate the gesture, but you need that money for your partnership. That's been your dream, and you deserve it."

"It's not a big deal. It'll just take me a bit longer to become a partner."

"I don't understand you."

"Don't you? Can't you see how not being with you is ripping me apart?"

He'd raised his voice, but Erin was in no mood to be cowed. "No, I don't see! All I know is you can barely stand the sight of me."

"What the hell are you talking about?"

"Ever since the mine, you won't look at me except with a glare. You won't talk to me. And oh, yeah, you left without bothering to say goodbye. Was anything between us real, or was it all for the job?"

His voice lowered again, Matt said, "Everything I've done since the day I met you was to keep you safe."

"So it *was* all for your job."

Matt swiped his hand through his hair, leaving it standing on end. "When I thought I'd lost you in the cave-in, I died on the inside. I've never protected anyone like I did you, but it was more than that."

"Why? Help me understand."

"Can't you see? I love you, Erin Montgomery. Didn't want to. Tried not to. But I do. And nothing you say or do will ever change that."

"Even if I refuse to follow your rules?" She cocked one brow.

"Even then."

"Even if I think I'm right and you're wrong?" The other brow rose.

"I doubt that would happen, but even then." The corner of his mouth kicked up in a smile.

"Then why would I ever want to change that? I love you, too, Matt Franklin."

He curved one hand behind her neck and kissed her until she couldn't breathe.

Panting, Erin took Matt's hand in hers. "Come on. Let's ride the property."

ERIN AND MATT worked side by side in Hank's old barn, saddling her two horses she'd brought with her. She glanced across Shadow's back at him, a small smile tugging at the corners of her mouth.

"What?" he asked.

But her days of teasing Matt about his fear of horses or lack of knowledge were behind them. These days, he knew as well as Erin how to groom, saddle, mount and ride. He may not be quite as good as or as fast, but he knew how. He'd learned during the short time he lived with her, and he hadn't forgotten a thing.

"Nothing." But she widened her smile just because it would irritate him.

Once the horses were ready, they mounted and set off at a leisurely pace next to each other.

"All of the buildings and operating areas are near the barn. I want to show you the rest of it, the fields, the wild parts," Erin said. "It's a tiny fraction of the size of my parents' ranch, but it's plenty big enough for what I want to do, even if I get more horses down the road."

They rode in comfortable silence through pastures dotted with wildflowers and huge trees that provided shade. When the horses picked their way across a stream, Matt asked, "Is this the same one that runs across the Montgomery Ranch?"

"Yep." She gave him a mischievous grin. "Don't tell my mother. She might find a way to dam it up if she found out."

Matt laughed.

Crossing through more fields, he said, "Every acre of this place feels like you."

Erin glanced at him. "That's the plan. Make it mine. It already feels like it is."

The air was warm, carrying the faint scent of earth and grass, mingled with the subtle sweetness of blossoms.

Erin brought Shadow to a stop at the edge of a large field.

She dismounted and waited for Matt to do the same. When he landed on two feet with no hopping around, she smiled.

"Come on. This is my favorite spot. We'll tie up the horses here."

After knotting the horses' reins around a tree branch, Matt took Erin's hand in his and walked with her deeper into the pasture. They walked until they reached a small copse of trees surrounding a clearing. Erin stepped into the open space and sank down into the soft grass.

Without a word, Matt joined her. Stretching out beside her, he propped himself up on one elbow, his gaze never leaving Erin. She lay on her back, her arms folded beneath her head, gazing back at him with love-filled eyes. The scent of honeysuckle drifted on the air. One of the horses nickered, and Erin pulled her eyes away from Matt to look up at the millions of stars filling the sky.

"You ever seen anything like that?" she asked, her voice barely above a whisper.

"Not like this. It's beautiful," Matt agreed. "But it doesn't hold a candle to you."

Erin turned her head to look at him, at his eyes as they caught the faint glow of the moonlight. "It's why I love this place. No matter how hard things get, you look up at the sky, and it reminds you how small your problems are."

Matt reached out and brushed a strand of hair away from her face. "Your problems aren't small, Erin. But you're strong enough to handle them. You've proven that."

She rolled onto her side to face him. "I don't feel strong sometimes. Especially when I think about everything that's happened. Everything I've lost."

"You've also gained a lot," he said. "This ranch. The people who care about you. A future where you can make a real difference."

His gaze held hers, and neither of them spoke for a moment. The air between them seemed to crackle with tension.

Erin finally broke the silence. "You were here through most of it. And now you're here again."

"I should have been here through all of it." He took her hand and brought it to his lips, kissing it softly.

"No. Everything happened the way it was meant to." She caressed his bottom lip with her thumb. "I needed to make the decision. I needed to confront my mother. And I needed to start the journey of Tranquil Trails. By myself. For myself." Erin's heart told her all this was true. But it also told her that now she was ready to share her life with the right person. And Matt was definitely that person. "But I'm glad you're back now."

"I wasn't going anywhere," he said. "Maybe we both just needed to wait for the right time."

She sat up, leaning closer to him, their fingers intertwining. "I don't know what I would've done without you, Matt."

He cupped her cheek, his thumb brushing lightly against her skin. "You're never going to find out."

Their kiss was slow and tentative at first, then deepened as months of tension and longing melted away. Erin's hands gripped his shirt as if he might disappear, and she wasn't about to let that happen.

They sank back into the grass together, and soon the warmth of his body against hers, the softness of his touch, the way she couldn't breathe when he kissed her neck consumed her.

The moon and the stars bore silent witness as Erin and Matt gave in to the pull they'd been denying for months. It was a moment of connection, of healing, of peace.

Just like Tranquil Trails.

When it was over, they lay tangled together in the grass.

Erin rested her head on Matt's chest, her finger tracing a lazy pattern over his heart.

"I've never felt this safe," she said softly. "Even during the whole Alex thing—and you did make me feel safe then—somehow this feels different. Lasting."

"You deserve to feel safe." Matt kissed the top of her head. "And loved. Forever."

They stayed wrapped in each other's arms until even the breeze of a warm June night chilled them. They dressed and mounted the horses to ride back to the ranch house. As they rode side by side, Erin felt the bond between them deepen and strengthen even more, a quiet promise of a future they'd build together, one step at a time.

Epilogue

Boone County, Texas
Tranquil Trails Equine Therapy Ranch

The summer sun beat down on Tranquil Trails Equine Therapy Ranch as laughter and conversations filled the air. Erin had scheduled the grand opening for late afternoon, hoping to miss the worst of the July heat. But summer in Texas was what it was. She stood near the closest paddock with Angel, one of the therapy-trained horses she'd purchased a few weeks ago. The mare's ears flicked as a small child clambered onto her back with Erin's help.

"Hold tight to the reins, okay?" Erin adjusted the stirrups.

The little girl nodded, her face glowing with a wide grin as the horse whinnied. Holding the lead rope and staying alongside the saddle, Erin kept one arm looped around the child as they walked in circles. Within a few minutes, the girl was ready to get down and go play with her friends.

Erin tied Angel's lead to a hitching post and surveyed the crowd. She'd never expected this large of a gathering. Her heart warmed, knowing she owed it to her friends and neighbors.

People admired the newly built barn, now painted a

warm red, the color Hank's old barn had been before it faded under the relentless Texas sun. It stood as the centerpiece of her vision, a testament to the hard work and generosity of everyone who had come together to make it a reality.

"Looking good out here, Erin." Nate Reed's booming voice drew her attention. He approached with his usual easy grin, a plate of food balanced in one hand.

Beside him, his wife, Sara, nodded in greeting. "I hear you've also fallen victim to the charms of a bodyguard." Her smile and wink made Erin laugh.

"Ah, yes. They do grow on you, don't they?" Erin glanced around, wondering where Matt had wandered off to. She noticed the rest of the Reed family standing near the fence, chatting. Their children ran in the grass, playing tag and chasing bubbles blown by—Detective Martinez? *That is one interesting woman.*

The Montgomerys' ranch foreman joined them. "This place… It's special. Hank would be proud."

Erin's throat tightened at the mention of Hank, but she managed a nod. "I hope so."

In the distance, children's laughter rang out as Erin's other new horse, Daisy, carried a young boy around the paddock, assisted by the new ranch therapist.

Just then, Matt appeared from around the corner of the house, his tool belt slung low on his hips. His T-shirt hugged his biceps and abs, and sawdust covered his forearms from the house renovations they'd been working on together. He caught Erin's eye and gave her a small smile that sent heat spiraling through her.

He sauntered over and greeted the others before turning to Erin. "Everything seems to be running smoothly."

Their eyes met, and for a moment, the people, the noise,

the activity around them faded away. Matt reached out, brushing a stray strand of hair from her face. "You've done something amazing here, Erin," he murmured. "I'm so proud of you."

She gave a small laugh. "I had help."

His crystal-blue gaze steady, Matt said, "Still, this is your dream, and you made it real."

Before she could respond, another of the ranch hands from the Montgomerys' property approached. "Miss Erin, this place is incredible." He took his hat off and held it over his heart. "Hank... He'd be over the moon to see what you've done with his ranch."

Erin's chest tightened again, but this time with a mix of grief and gratitude. "Thank you," she said. "That means a lot."

The ranch hand nodded, setting his hat on his head again before walking off to join a group near the barn.

As the afternoon wore on, Erin watched the therapy horses work their quiet magic on the children, as well as a few teens and adults who ventured into the paddock. These people weren't even potential clients, yet the sense of peace and joy on their faces filled her with a deep sense of fulfillment. This was what she'd envisioned—a place of healing and connection.

After Matt had showered off the sawdust and changed clothes, he joined Erin. There if she needed him, but allowing her space to shine. She appreciated that as much as she did the frequent, loving glances he sent her way. But when all three of his bodyguard buddies kidnapped him for a beer, she wandered over to one of the long tables under a canopy, laden with food.

Erin greeted Brandon and Lisa Bauer, owners of her favorite barbecue place, with hugs. "I can't thank you enough for helping out like this." The Bauers had refused to accept a penny more than half price to cater her event.

"Are you kidding? Thank *you* for all the future business." Brandon spread his arms wide toward the crowd.

"Hopefully, we'll be doing more business together in the future." Erin leaned toward the couple. "You know darn well I won't be having any fancy-schmancy dining establishments cater my fundraisers."

"Damn straight," Lisa said. "And I'll bet those rich donors will be happy as hogs in mud when they're gnawing on rib bones and chugging beer."

Erin laughed at the visual, although she agreed. The guests at her parents' parties had always looked bored out of their minds.

Detective Martinez sauntered up to the barbecue spread and began loading a plate. "You've got quite the turnout," she said to Erin. "And quite the man, too."

Erin's eyes followed the detective's to where Matt helped a group of kids climbing on the paddock fence. "He's something else," she admitted, her lips curving into a smile.

Martinez chuckled. "Took you two long enough to figure it out."

Erin laughed softly, shaking her head. "It's been a journey, Detective. That's for sure."

As the sun began its descent, casting long shadows over the ranch, Erin gathered everyone near the barn. She stood on a small wooden platform, her hands clasped in front of her.

"Thank you all for being here today." Her voice was steady but full of emotion. "This ranch wouldn't be what it is without each and every one of you. Your support, your hard work, your belief in this dream, *my* dream, means everything to me."

She paused, her eyes scanning the crowd, hoping to see her parents but not expecting them. Despite most of the Montgomerys' ranch hands attending, her mother and father were clearly absent. But then she saw Maeve waving as she stood next to Liam in his wheelchair, a wide, crooked smile covering his face. A better surprise than even her parents.

"Hank believed in my dream and encouraged me to follow my heart. He believed in the power of horses to heal, to connect, just as I do. I hope Tranquil Trails can honor his memory and bring that same peace to everyone who comes here."

The crowd broke into applause, and tears pricked at the corners of Erin's eyes. As she stepped down from the platform, Matt was there, his hand outstretched. She took it, their fingers intertwining as he pulled her close.

"You did good," he said, his voice low.

"*We* did good." She leaned in and kissed him.

They stood together in the fading light, surrounded by friends and family, the promise of new beginnings woven into every corner of the ranch.

* * * * *

OPERATION RESCUE

JUSTINE DAVIS

It is with an aching heart and a bleeding soul that I take possession of this dedication space. You can guess why, if you've read these Cutter dedications before. Especially if you read the last one.

For those of you who have enjoyed coming along with Cutter on this string of adventures, you have a particular individual to thank. One who supported me, who made me laugh when I was down, kept me going when I wanted to quit. One who gave me a side-eye from the stair landing if I didn't get to work quickly enough to suit her. One who settled into my office as quiet, calm support staff, for hours every day, because she knew the rest of the day was hers, no matter how often she wanted to go outside or how much attention she wanted. One who reminded me constantly of the miracle that dogs are to us unworthy humans. One who gave me those same knowing, loving looks that Cutter gives to his people.

I adopted Elf from an unpleasant situation that involved a child tormentor who took everything she feared and used it against her. It was a couple of months before Elf trusted me, and nearly a year before she believed I wouldn't let any stranger hurt her. In the end, she became the absolutely perfect dog for my quiet, mostly solitary life as a writer. If I could have custom ordered the perfect dog for me, in looks, size, spirit, temperament and above all heart, it would have been her.

Now my beloved, beyond-sweet miracle dog is gone. I had to live up to the advice I was giving out in that last dedication a year ago, and give my girl peace and free her from pain and fear. And I am lost without her. Time will pass; I have been through this before. But anyone who's had dogs through their lifetime knows that there's always that one who leaves the deepest, most painful yet wonderful forever footprints on your heart.

Elf was mine.

So any time you read a Cutter's Code book and enjoy it, say a little mental thank-you to a certain real dog named Elf, who had Cutter's heart.

My Elfie
2009–2024

Chapter One

"I need some time off."

Quinn Foxworth blinked. Even his dog, Cutter, looked up at Rafe Crawford as if puzzled. Rafe, asking for time off? Would wonders never cease? Would the changes in the man ever stop?

The head of the Foxworth Foundation studied his usually reticent employee and trophy-winning sniper. The man who usually had to be flat out ordered to take a break, who seemed to be always working on something, be it a Foxworth case or keeping all the equipment they had—including their two aircraft, the helo and the Piper Mirage—working.

Of course, what had once been usual for Rafe seemed to have been blown to bits once he and Quinn's sister Charlie had torn down the wall Rafe had built between them. He'd had his reasons, Quinn knew, but the years of obvious tension between his sister and this man he respected, admired, even loved, had been wearing. Sparks—of all kinds—had flown whenever the two of them were in the same room together.

And still did, now that they'd worked things out and put their personal relationship back together. Rafe still managed to get everything done, but he was—on stern orders—taking time for him and Charlie to get settled, once she'd decided she'd be staying here at Foxworth Northwest instead of going back to headquarters in St. Louis.

It wasn't until his wife, Hayley, spoke that Quinn realized he'd been surprised into not even answering Rafe.

"Anything we can help with?" Hayley asked, very gently.

Belatedly Quinn realized she—as usual—had sensed something that he hadn't.

"I…don't know. Yet. But I need to be down south for a while."

Quinn snapped into prep mode, finally. "How far south? Do I need to call some friends in Mexico?"

Tuned in now, Quinn saw the flicker of surprise in Rafe's expression. Even after all this time, the man was still startled at genuine offers to help.

"You don't even know what it's about," Rafe said quietly.

"I don't need to. If you need Foxworth help, you've got it."

"Or if you need personal help, you've got it," Hayley added.

A soft but emphatic woof seemed to underline those last three words as Cutter gave his opinion on the matter.

Rafe took in a deep, visible breath, as if he needed to steady himself. "It's someone I owe," he said, his voice a little rough. Cutter heard it, got up and went to him, sitting down nearly on his feet. He leaned in hard, Quinn could tell by the way Rafe had to shift his feet to take the weight.

"Somebody called in a marker?" Quinn asked.

"Yeah," Rafe muttered, lowering his gaze to the dog before he added, "The biggest one of all."

Without knowing anything else, Quinn knew what that meant. And for him, it was the only thing he needed to know, except how to help.

Rafe bent slightly, ran a hand over the dog's dark head. Quinn knew quite well the steadying effect that had on a person, so he simply waited. And after a moment Rafe looked up and met his gaze.

"He's the helicopter pilot who saved my life."

Quinn's eyes widened. He knew that Rafe had saved Quinn's own Ranger team from near-certain death by picking off one by one the insurgents who had them pinned down—from a distance that still boggled Quinn's mind. Later Rafe had been injured while saving yet another team, a serious leg wound that he carried evidence of to this day with a twisted scar and a slight limp.

Quinn hadn't found this out until the next time they were at the Forward Operating Base, and he'd asked about the sniper who'd bailed them out. He'd learned that Rafe's situation had been so bad he'd had to be casevaced out—a casualty evacuation using the closest possible aircraft—under fire, and that the nearest option had been a SuperCobra attack helicopter whose pilot never hesitated to go get him, even flying solo in an aircraft that normally had a two-person crew.

"Whatever you need, you've got it," Quinn said.

He knew perfectly well that this was a "blood oath" kind of obligation, one Rafe would hold inviolate. As would he himself. He wondered briefly how Charlie was going to take this. Things were a bit new for them still. She knew now, from the experience that had brought them back together, exactly what Rafe did for Foxworth, and how well he did it. So now she might as well learn, as she'd had to with him, just how far they would go to pay this kind of debt.

Cutter woofed again, on his feet now, pressed against Rafe's leg—the wounded one, oddly—as if he were permanently attached.

"And there's your first volunteer," Hayley said with a wide smile.

Rafe looked down at the dog, a smile on his face. And

Quinn realized that was something they never would have seen before, either. A trace, maybe, but never the open smile he gave the dog now. And that had to be thanks to the mending of fences between him and Charlie as well. He and Hayley had taken to calling the rapprochement "The Great Reconciliation," in both amusement and relief.

"Thanks, buddy," Rafe said softly, stroking the dog's head again. "You just might come in handy." He looked up at his boss. "If you can spare him."

Quinn chuckled. "What makes you think I have any say in what that dog does? He decides, and he's decided he's with you."

Rafe's smile became a momentary grin. "I guess he has."

"Now," Quinn said briskly, "I assume time is of the essence?"

Rafe nodded. "There's…a kid involved."

Quinn drew up slightly, and felt Hayley tense beside him. But he merely said, "All right. Load up what you need while I call the airport and have them ready Wilbur."

Rafe blinked when he heard the nickname for Quinn's beloved Piper Mirage turboprop plane. "I…you don't have to fly me. I was going to drive. I'd appreciate bunking at Foxworth Southwest, though—" he glanced at Hayley "—if your brother's not using the accommodation at the moment."

"Last I heard they were on a case over in Arizona, but I'll call him right now to confirm."

"And do what I said," Quinn added mildly. "I haven't had a chance to take Wilbur for a long flight in a while. I'm feeling deprived. A nice thousand-plus-mile run will be fun. And then I might just hop on over to Arizona to see how the research is going there."

"Only you," Rafe muttered, but Quinn could see he was a little relieved.

"I assume you've already called and told Charlie?" Hayley asked. At the moment Quinn's sister was back in St. Louis, packing up the last of the things she wanted to bring here from her old base at Foxworth headquarters.

"I did," Rafe said, in the rueful manner of a man who had finally learned the price of not performing such niceties. He was studying his boot tips when he added hesitantly, "She said she understood why it was a no-choice thing." When he looked up he was smiling slightly. "She seems to think she owes him, too."

"She's coming right along," Hayley said cheerfully. "I'll make sure there's a car ready for you down there, too. I'd like to go, but…"

"You've got a wedding to help plan," Quinn said.

Rafe's head came up sharply enough that Quinn drew back slightly. But Hayley grinned. "Gavin and Katie's" she said, but then raised an eyebrow. "Unless you've got something to tell me?"

To Quinn's amazement, the ever-unflappable, self-confessed emotionally impeded Rafe turned the slightest bit pink. Barely enough to notice, but one of the many, many things Quinn had learned from his beloved wife was how to read faces better.

"Don't start," Rafe said, his voice almost a growl.

"I won't," Hayley promised as she pulled out her phone to no doubt call Walker. Then she looked back at Rafe with a wide, loving smile that melted Quinn no matter who it was aimed at. "Yet," she added pointedly.

"Let's get going," Quinn said, pulling out his own phone. "You've got a debt to pay."

"More than one," Rafe said softly, as the Foxworth Foundation once more rolled into action.

Chapter Two

Blaine Everett looked out the UC-35's window as they taxied off the runway and began to slow to a halt. It felt strange, being here in Southern California again. He'd grown up in South Orange County, so the territory was familiar, yet so much had changed since he'd last been here he felt as if it was someplace he'd never been. But he was sure it would all come flooding back the first time he got stuck in a freeway traffic jam.

Erin had grown up here, too, and after she'd left him she'd come straight back. Not to the old neighborhood, it was too expensive now, but close enough. Back to build the life she'd wanted, a life without the man she'd married, the marriage he'd thought would last forever. After all, he'd loved her since he'd been old enough to understand what the word meant. As little kids they'd done mischief and punishments together. They'd made big plans and carried out little ones. They had grown into the proverbial girl/boy-next-door romance, except it was across the street. As adults, they'd finally cemented it all.

The entire neighborhood had turned out for their wedding.

He'd signed the divorce papers alone.

He'd had no choice. Because he loved her. He would always love her. And so he wanted her to be happy. Which to her meant she couldn't be married to him anymore.

He leaned back in the comfortable seat, thinking he'd be sore and aching now if he'd gotten his usual ride on one of the big transports that would have him sitting on a hard bench with a sling around his shoulders for a seat belt. His body didn't tolerate such things so well anymore. But so far things had gone surprisingly smoothly. He'd wrangled leave, managed to get his duties covered. And then he'd been able to hitch a ride on the usually VIP jet that was on its way to pick up some big shot—he hadn't even wanted to know who—giving a speech in LA. It was stopping here at Camp Pendleton to refuel, which was the only reason he'd taken it, since he had no desire at all to set foot in what had at one time been a dream destination.

He'd been surprised when Rafe had texted that he'd pick him up here, at Pendleton. He'd expected to have to make his way to the address the former Marine had given him to meet up on his own. But he shouldn't have been surprised, he realized now. No Marine base anywhere was going to turn down a request from the most famous Marine sniper since Carlos Hathcock himself, except maybe for Chuck Mawhinney.

But the biggest surprise came when he spotted Rafe Crawford on the tarmac with a dog at his heels. A dog who, although with more fur, reminded him of the military K-9s who were often passengers on his own flights. Or at least, they had been, when he'd been really on active duty, doing something more than just training his replacements. But that was then, and right now it seemed the Corps had decided it was time to slowly ease him out, given his reup enlistment was down to its last six months.

At least they're not kicking you out the door like Erin did.

He shook his head at himself, then waved a final thank-you to the pilot as he passed the cockpit headed for the stairs that were already lowering.

He'd long ago accepted Erin's leaving, and didn't blame her for why. In an ironic sort of way, it just showed how much she had loved him. She'd even said as much, that she loved him too much to see him go through such pain again. It was an irony that bit deep, but still…

He looked at Rafe, remembering when, still on crutches from his own injury, the man had trekked all the way to see him after he'd finally ended up in a military hospital stateside after his crash. And he'd visited often after that. Blaine had still been hooked up to every medical machine imaginable, and from photos he'd seen it had been pretty bad, but the man kept coming.

At least he was doing well now. When Blaine had gone to see him in the field hospital after he'd pulled him off that battlefield, Rafe hadn't looked so great. He had barely managed to slow the bleeding from the gaping wound on Rafe's left leg long enough to get him out of there. He'd always been amazed they'd managed to save that leg. It had been a casevac, since he'd have bled out by the time a medevac unit could respond. Blaine had had to call up some long-unused first aid skills to get the bleeding slowed enough to load him up and go. Flying the big SuperCobra was interesting enough with the standard two-person crew, but alone it was…an adventure. He also could have used a hand getting Rafe aboard, but the wounded man somehow found the strength to help a little, and they'd gotten it done.

And he'd never forget what the man had said, lying there with his lifeblood literally pouring out of him.

"Thanks. I didn't want to die there."

Like it was only *where* that mattered.

He hadn't understood that at the time. But a year later he had, when his helicopter had been blasted out of the sky and he'd nearly disintegrated with it. Then he'd been the one saying to the evac crew, "Just get me, and yourselves, out of here."

He hadn't said he didn't want to die knowing they'd died, too, trying to save him, but he saw the understanding in their eyes. They knew.

They'd gotten out. And for him, once back at a hospital facility, the real hell had begun.

Rafe had spotted him now. He'd only had contact via phone or email since that day, so seeing the tall, rangy guy walking toward him with just the slightest of limps made him feel good, like he'd had a part in it. He knew too well the kind of work it had likely taken for the man to be this functional, since he himself had a couple of aftermarket parts now.

The combination handshake-shoulder slam got them through the initial greeting, but then the awkwardness of lack of contact set in. Blaine had been wrestling with what to tell the man on the entire flight, and hadn't really reached a conclusion.

"Nice ride," Rafe said, nodding at the Citation jet.

"Lucky timing," he said, but added with a wry smile, "Coulda' been worse."

"Yeah," Rafe agreed. "It could have been an Osprey."

Blaine chuckled at the old joke about the versatile but di-saster-prone aircraft. It was the first time he'd even smiled, let alone laughed, since he'd gotten that phone call from Erin.

"And this," Rafe said, gesturing at the dog whose steady gaze Blaine would have sworn he could feel, "is Cutter."

Blaine bent to offer a hand to the dog, who nosed it willingly. "He's yours?"

Rafe shook his head. "Belongs to my bosses, but they loaned him to me in case he could help." Blaine would swear the cool, gray eyes of the former sniper held more than a hint of amusement. "And believe me, he will, in ways you can't imagine until he shows you."

"I've seen some pretty smart war dogs," Blaine said.

"So have I. So mix that with incredible perception, cleverness, planning ability, and understanding of the crazy human brain, plus—well, that's enough for now. Just pet him, and that'll be your first clue."

Blaine's brow furrowed, but the dog nudged his hand again, so he complied and stroked the dark head. An unexpected and odd sense of calm flowed into him, as if the soft fur held some sort of magical drug that soothed his soul. His gaze shot up to Rafe's face. The man was grinning.

"Told ya," he said, in a jovial tone that surprised Blaine as much as the look in his eyes had. The Rafe he remembered had been as grim in demeanor as you would expect a sniper to be. But this man…this man had found peace. Maybe sometime before this was over he could ask him how.

"That's…really something. What is he, some kind of therapy dog?"

"Among several other things, including a tracker, an undercover agent and an attack dog when necessary."

"Jack-of-all-trades dog, is that what you're saying?"

"Trades you can't even imagine," Rafe said, and Blaine had the strangest feeling he was laughing to himself. "Come on, let's roll. You can fill me in on the way to Foxworth Southwest."

"To what?"

"I'll explain on the way. But first tell me what's going on with your boy."

Blaine sighed deeply as they started walking toward where he could see some vehicles parked. "I'm not sure. We usually text regularly, but that stopped last week. And... I haven't seen him in person in three months."

Rafe gave him a startled look. Blaine supposed he was remembering how obsessively proud he'd been of his son, always willing to talk about him, to anyone. "How'd that happen?"

"Long story. You want the whole sorry thing?"

"Up to you, but tell me what I may need to know to help. Are you saying you and... Erin, isn't it? Are you saying you're not—"

He hadn't realized he'd never mentioned that to Rafe. He sighed. "We aren't me and Erin anymore, no."

"Sorry. Sucks."

"In two words, yes." He sighed again, but stopped when he realized he was dodging. If Rafe was going to help, he needed to know the basics, at least. "When I crashed, it was...pretty bad." He shot Rafe a sideways glance. "Thanks for offering to help back then, by the way. But Erin—" he had to pause to swallow past the lump in his throat "—she took care of me. She never left my side when I was in the hospital. All the surgeries, all the setbacks, she was there. She made the doctors coordinate, fought with them if she had to..."

He couldn't stop the tightening of his throat, and for a moment he wondered if he'd be able to even breathe if he kept going. It was a moment before he could.

"I remember waking up sometimes and she was there sleeping on one of those lounger things they bring in, obviously exhausted, and usually...usually with her cheeks wet from crying."

Blaine couldn't remember the last time he'd poured all this out, and it still made him uncomfortable. But Rafe said nothing, just kept walking. He had that slight hitch in his gait, but it didn't slow him down any. And the dog, he noticed, was between them. He looked down to see the dark eyes—were those touches of gold he was seeing there?—flicking from him to Rafe and back again, as if he were assessing and wanted to be between them so he could help whoever needed it. Which was a crazy thought, no doubt brought on by Rafe's unexpectedly fanciful description of the animal.

He drew in a long breath and went on with the sorry tale. "When I got out of the hospital Erin was there every step of the way. She coaxed, pushed and shoved me through all the rehab and therapy it took to get me back on my feet. For a year she took care of both me and our boy, Ethan. As much as I hurt, as tired as I got, I don't think it was anything compared to what she went through."

They'd reached Rafe's car, a newer-looking, silver SUV Blaine had seen hundreds of on the road. But when they got in and Rafe started it up, the engine roared and then settled into a throaty growl that told him there was nothing basic about it.

Rafe caught his startled look and smiled crookedly. "I came down and did a little work on it after they bought it."

Blaine remembered something else then, from when he'd happened to be near the hospital Rafe was still in and had stopped by to see him. And had found him in a hallway outside his room, in a wheelchair, talking to another man in a wheelchair. Only this man's leg hadn't had the chance to heal: it had been ripped off by an IED. What had surprised him was that they were talking, not about their injuries or recovery, but about engines.

He fastened his seat belt. The dog, who had jumped easily into the back seat, plopped his head down on the console between them. And as they started to move, Rafe spoke again.

"Then what?" he said, prompting him to continue the sorry tale by saying the words in a knowing sort of way that somehow made it easier to vomit it out.

"When I was back on my feet, just when things looked like we could get back to normal, she told me she was leaving. That she couldn't go through anything like that ever again. Because…because…"

He stumbled on the word twice and gave up. Rafe finished it for him. "Because she loved you too much."

Surprised, because the man he remembered had not been one to talk about such things, he could only nod. And then he used his last thought as a way to divert from a subject it still gutted him to talk about. "You been studying human nature or something since you got out?"

A slow smile spread across the man's face. "In a way."

That clinched it. Whatever had happened to the top Marine sniper since he'd left the service, it had caused a sea change. And it was apparently for the better, because he'd never seen *that* kind of smile from the guy.

And he had to quash a stab of another feeling. The guy had dropped everything to help him, after all, so being even a tiny bit jealous of him being so obviously happy seemed wrong.

It was wrong, and it would end now. He needed to focus on the chaos of his own life, not envy someone else's.

Chapter Three

Erin Everett had to stop herself from rubbing at her aching, weary eyes again. She was where she'd sworn she would never be again, living every day in fear for someone she loved. It didn't matter that she'd found her niche—freelance graphic design for small local companies. It didn't matter that she now had her dream house. Old and somewhat small though it might be, it had space around it and she'd been able to garden to her heart's content until they were surrounded by color and scent and pathways that seemed out of a fairy tale.

It didn't matter that she didn't have to face the possibility that Blaine would be badly hurt again, or dread the arrival at her door of messengers delivering death. It didn't matter because now the one person still in her life who mattered most, her precious son, had finally acted upon the hatred he'd aimed at her ever since he'd realized she was the one who had broken up their family, who had taken him away from the father he loved and admired and so often said he wanted to be like.

And now that once innocent boy was a teenager in chaos, and at fourteen determined to make her pay for what she'd done.

How could you do it? After he got hurt like that, you just walk out?

I stayed until he was healed—

That's even worse! He thought everything was going to be okay, he told me it would be, that everything would go back to normal, we'd all be fine.

Ethan, I couldn't go through that again, and as long as he's in uniform, it—or worse—could happen.

You couldn't go through it? *He* was the one who was hurt! *But he got better, so you leave? And you make me go with you?*

I guess I'm a coward.

I hate you!

That had been their final argument, because the next day when, after he didn't get up on time for school, she went to wake him, he was gone.

I guess I'm a coward.

That final admission rang in her head now, as she sat in the garden that today brought her no pleasure or comfort, until she thought it would drive her mad. Because she couldn't deny the truth in it. She had been a coward; she hadn't been strong enough or tough enough to be a military wife. She'd coped with the moving from base to base, she'd coped with Blaine being away during important events in their son's life, she'd coped with their only communication often being via video calls or emails, she'd coped with the apprehension of being married to a helicopter pilot, she'd even coped with the fear—okay, terror—when he'd been in a combat zone.

But when it finally happened, when he'd finally come back so hurt, so broken, she'd gone almost numb. She'd done what had to be done—she'd supported him, she'd taken care of him, she'd pushed him through therapy and rehab until he was back on his feet again. The doctors had even told her she'd worked a miracle, getting him nearly back to his old self, apart from the occasional aches and stiffness.

And then she had told Blaine what was nothing less than the truth. She simply could not go through this again, seeing him like this. Or live in fear of him coming home in a flag-draped box. She could not do it, and she wasn't even going to try.

She thought the career he'd chosen had destroyed their marriage, although she knew others thought she had done it. But Blaine had never accused her of anything. He'd even said he understood, that last time they'd met before she went back to their housing, packed up and ran for home. Funny how her first and overwhelming instinct had been to return to where it had all begun, not the same tight-knit neighborhood but the same environs in the California county where she'd grown up.

She hadn't anticipated how hard that, too, would hit her, seeing the familiar places again, places she and Blaine had gone, from their favorite pizza parlor to their favorite hidden spot on the beach due west of their small apartment. The only way she could quash the fierce, fiery longing that erupted in her every time one of those memories hit was to summon up other memories, the ugly, bloody ones, of Blaine lying in that hospital bed, of him being readied for yet another surgery he dreaded, of him waking in the night in a cold sweat, a heart-wrenching shout ripping from his throat.

If not being able to risk seeing him like that again or, worse, having to sit at a funeral and be presented the carefully folded flag that had covered his casket, made her a coward then so be it.

And if nobody understood it wasn't because she didn't love him but because she loved him too much, then so be that, too.

Blaine Everett had been her center, her rock, her reason for being for so long it had taken her a year simply to get used to the idea that he would no longer be there. To try and fill that gaping empty spot with something, anything.

She found trying to rebuild around the hole his absence left so much harder than she'd ever imagined.

But easier than having to get used to the idea that he's dead.

She'd had some tangled idea that if she got used to being without him while he was alive, then it might be easier to deal with if that awful, final news ever came. Of course, now she wouldn't know, would she? Did the Marine Corps have a policy of notifying exes? Or…was there someone else to be notified?

He probably moved on long ago. If you want to prepare for something, prepare for him showing up with someone else's ring on his finger.

"Oh, stop it," she muttered aloud.

She knew that wasn't true, that he hadn't remarried, because he would have told Ethan and her son would not have been able to resist throwing that in her face. She could picture it perfectly. "Happy now, Mom? You got what you wanted. Dad will never be in my life again, not like a real dad."

And his anger had driven him so far from her. Far enough that he'd fallen in with a group of kids who seemed to idolize some sort of gang she'd heard about in the news. He'd narrowly escaped getting arrested with a couple of the rowdier ones, and she'd hoped that would rein him in a little, but it had only seemed to make him even more defiant. Made him hate her even more.

And now he'd vanished.

She walked down the short hallway to where the door

to his room stood open. How many times had she walked back here, thinking it was all a mistake and when she went there she'd find him burrowed into his blankets as usual, just oversleeping after a night probably full of furtive on-line activity or gaming. She'd told herself more than once she should shut down the internet overnight, but it would only infuriate him more. Besides, more than once she herself had spent some hours in the dark looking for solace or distraction via that means.

She'd done all the things you were supposed to do—called the police, who dutifully took a report, but the questions they asked about Ethan's life only made her feel worse. Because when it came down to it, she knew so little about his friends, enemies, his interests, any trouble he might be in or anything else relevant, and what she did know she'd learned from essentially spying on her son, since he barely spoke to her anymore.

After three days with no word, three days of hounding the police for any news, three days of her haunting every-place she knew that Ethan went, contacting every friend that she knew about, she had no more idea where he was than when she'd started.

So she'd called his father. Because she had no other choice. His father, who would stand strong where she crumbled, because he always had. Blaine had always had the courage she lacked.

She started to tremble, then her knees got weak. She slid down along the doorjamb to the floor, wrapping her arms around herself in an effort to stop shaking. It didn't work.

She sat there, useless, helpless, not even able to fight the tears that began again.

She truly was a coward.

Chapter Four

"Who are these people you work for?" Blaine asked as he tried to orient himself amid all the changes to what had once been his stomping grounds since he'd last been here.

"They're the best," Rafe said simply. Then, with a crooked smile he added, "Even if Quinn Foxworth is a former Ranger."

Blaine drew back slightly. "He is?"

"It's okay," Rafe said, the smile widening. "We've got Teague Johnson, too, and he's one of us."

"So the Marines outnumber the Army? Always a good sign."

"Exactly." Rafe said it with another grin. Blaine wasn't sure which was harder, adjusting to the changes they were driving through, or the changes in the guy driving.

"But what is it they—you—do, exactly?"

"We help the little guy in the right against the big guy in the wrong."

Blaine blinked. It sounded so simple, but he'd had enough experience with the big guys to know it had to be very far from simple or uncomplicated. "A lot of that last part going around these days," he said.

"We're rarely short of work," Rafe agreed as they pulled to a halt at a stoplight that had just turned red.

"How does that little guy you help pay for your ser-vices?"

Rafe looked at him. "They don't. We're very careful, and if we take a case, the only cost to the people we help is a promise to help us help someone else down the line, if they can."

Blaine stared this time. Rafe Crawford, toughest of the tough in the Marines, lethal sniper, was now a…do-gooder? For the first time since Erin's phone call, his brain locked onto something else.

"What is it, exactly, you do for them?"

"Whatever they ask." Rafe didn't even blink. "Including what I used to do in uniform, if necessary. Only now the goal isn't to kill, just to succeed."

Blaine recognized now what he was hearing in Rafe's voice. Satisfaction. The kind he used to get, knowing he was on the side of the angels. Not so much anymore, but once…

"If your…customers don't pay for it, who does?" he asked.

He wasn't prepared for the expression that he saw on Rafe's face then, a bemused but joyful look he would have never expected to see. The man he'd known had been a si-lent stoic, who, if he'd ever known how to be happy, had long forgotten the lesson.

But all Rafe said was, "Quinn's sister takes care of that. Among many other things."

"So this is a family business?"

"In more ways than one, yes."

Blaine thought he understood the implication there. That not only was this business owned and run by a family, ev-eryone who was part of it was also part of that family. He didn't know much about Rafe's blood family, but he knew all he needed to know about this new family just by looking at that expression. And at the changes in him. Now he seemed so darn solid it was almost hard to believe it was the same man he'd known.

"We're about twenty minutes out from Foxworth Southwest," Rafe said as the light changed and they moved on. "Want to use it to fill me in?"

"Foxworth Southwest?" The two words together tickled something in the back of his mind, but he focused on the first question that occurred. "How many are there?"

"Five, now. I'm stationed out of Northwest, but we've got one in all four corners, plus an HQ in St. Louis."

Blaine figured he was probably gaping now, but he couldn't help it. "And they all do the same thing?"

Rafe nodded. "Same mission. Quinn's wife is Hayley, and her brother, Walker, runs this office. He also happens to be married to Hayley's best friend."

Blaine gave a quick shake of his head. "This Foxworth…"

"Is as incredible as it sounds. Anyway, they're on a job over in Arizona at the moment, so we'll have the run of the place." He gestured at the dash of the SUV. "Including this or anything else we need."

"Where'd you fly into?"

"Closest. John Wayne Airport." Rafe's mouth quirked. "I liked the statue. Ironic, given I hear he hated the noise from the jets when they flew over his house on takeoff."

Blaine smiled. "I remember. It's a busy field, for being pretty small."

"Not so much on the private side." Another smile flashed. "My boss flew me down."

Blaine knew he was gaping now. "Flew? As in…you've got a plane, too?"

"We do. Named Wilbur. And perhaps more of interest to you, a sweet little helicopter, too."

And now laughter got through, because he couldn't stop it in his wonder at both what Rafe was telling him, and the fact that he was enjoying it so much. "Let me guess, Orville?"

"Nope. Try again."

It only took him a second. After all, Sikorsky had invented the things, and his name was still carried on many built today. "Igor?"

"Got it," Rafe said.

"And your boss…he flew you down himself? Just for this?"

"He understands," was all Rafe said about it. "Now, did you really want to know all that, or were you just dodging the question?"

Blaine sighed audibly. "Yes," he admitted.

"I'm not asking you to pour your guts out. Treat it like a mission and give me the need to know."

He sucked in a breath. Then, in the most neutral tone he could manage, he did as Rafe asked. "Ethan fourteen now, and he's been in a…teenage mood. Mad at her. Hiding things from her. Blaming her for…everything. Started hanging with some shady kids. A week ago he disappeared. Left their house during the night. Took a few things with him so it wasn't a case of snuck out and didn't come home. She hasn't seen or heard from him since. Me, either. He stopped texting, or any contact at all."

"She report it to the police?" Rafe's voice was as neutral, and even more businesslike than he'd been able to manage.

"Yes. They're looking, and she said they told her they were familiar with the group of kids she described."

"That's both good and bad."

He nodded. "That's how I felt. Last update I had was last night before I headed here—no news."

"All right. You have a recent photo of him?"

Blaine grimaced. "Most recent I have is from a couple of years ago when he started middle school." *And I had to beg for that.*

Rafe merely nodded. "We've got someone who can age that up a little, if necessary, but I assume his mother has something more recent?"

"Oh." He felt stupid now. He was so used to pushing Erin out of his thoughts he hadn't considered that. "I'm sure she probably does. She used to take pictures of him all the time."

"Good." Blaine caught his sideways glance as he said, "But you'll have to ask for it. Are you on speaking terms?"

"On this we will be," he said flatly. "Whether she wants it or not." Rafe seemed about to speak again, then he stopped. Blaine grimaced. "It's not as bad as that sounded. We're in touch, it's just always email or text. We never…talk. That's how I knew this was bad, when she actually called me. But she's never tried to come between me and Ethan, stop me from talking to him or seeing him if I can get here on leave. It just gets…difficult."

"She can't really stop you, can she? You are paying child support and then some, you said?"

That bit harder than he would have liked. He didn't want to think that was the only reason Erin was so reasonable about Ethan, but deep down he knew it well could be. Because he was sending her not just the court-ordered amount, but most of the rest of what he could spare. He supposed it was stupid, and more than one person who'd found that out told him he was nuts, but…he loved his son.

And then there was Erin…

Almost exactly on Rafe's stated twenty minutes, they turned into the drive of what looked like it had once been a typical residence in the tile-and-adobe style of many places close to the famous Mission San Juan Capistrano. Long and low, with arch-topped windows facing the street, the building looked solid and well kept. There was a sturdy gate across the driveway, which Rafe opened with a button above the rearview mirror. In the back, where the driveway curved toward the garage, there was a smaller building in the same style, apparently a guesthouse. As they got there, Blaine could see a tiled courtyard directly behind the main building. In the middle of the courtyard sat a classic-style, three-level fountain, which at the moment was apparently a birdbath for the local avian population. Beyond that was a grassy area shaded by a large tree, which he guessed would probably be a welcome cool spot in a hot California summer.

"Nice," Blaine said.

Rafe shrugged. "Opened this one about a year and a half ago. Quinn's thinking about getting out, though. Arizona, maybe. California's getting a little…cramped."

"Is that why…his wife's brother, you said? Is that why he's there?"

"Partly. He'll be checking things out after this case. So for now, it's all ours. Office is up front, and we can crash back here," Rafe said, nodding toward the second, smaller building.

"Not even a sign out front?" Blaine asked, wondering how anybody found this firm Rafe worked for.

"The Foxworth Foundation keeps as low a profile as possible. Which," he added with a wry grimace, "is getting harder all the time."

And suddenly that tickle in the back of his mind exploded. "Wait… Foxworth Foundation? Like in the people who took down Governor Ogilvie up north, and then that crooked former senator a couple of months ago, what was his name?"

"Maximilian Flood," Rafe said, and Blaine knew he hadn't mistaken the pure satisfaction in his voice.

"You're working for that Foxworth?"

"I am."

"Taking down crooked politicians?"

Rafe shrugged. "A couple. But that one was personal. He betrayed the country and us, and almost got our entire team killed. Including him," he added, with a nod toward the dog.

Blaine automatically reached back to pat the dog's head, and again felt that odd sensation that went beyond warmth into soothing.

"So, Foxworth is karma delivery?"

A grin flashed across Rafe's usually—at least, it had been—unreadable face. "You could say that. But on any level. One of Quinn's first cases was finding and return- ing a stolen locket that was a little girl's only memento of her dead mother."

Blaine drew back, staring.

"And then, about six months ago, we ended up helping the reformed thief who gave it back." That made him blink. "And he's now working for Foxworth, helping guys like him who have truly turned around and made their way back into society, with the Foxworth name behind them. Which means a lot in some circles. That one was Hayley's idea."

Blaine didn't think he could ever remember this man talking this much. But pride rang in every word. He wasn't just happy at this Foxworth place, he was proud. And given the medals that could hang on his dress uniform, that was saying a lot. More than a lot. He had a few himself, and he tried to think of something in the civilian world that would make him as proud, but right now saving his son was the only thing that really mattered at all.

"And," Rafe added, very quietly now, "you'll have all that team to back you up, if need be."

Blaine was beginning to think that calling Rafe Crawford hadn't just been the only thing he could think of, it was the smartest thing he could have done, for Ethan's sake.

Chapter Five

Erin felt like sinking down to the floor, dissolving into a puddle of tears, the moment she closed the door behind her. She fought it, because it was becoming a habit after every round of going to everyone she knew who knew Ethan, another round of questions until she'd irritated them all, with the same results she'd gotten every time. Nothing. Nobody had seen him since she had, nobody knew anything about where he might be. Teachers, parents of friends, even the clerks at the convenience store where she'd discovered someone had been sneaking them vaping supplies. Since it was against the law for anyone under twenty-one, she understood the hesitancy to discuss it, although she'd assured them she didn't care about getting them in trouble, only about getting Ethan home safely.

She felt so alone it seemed to twist her heart in her chest. *And whose fault is that?*

She didn't even try to quash the instinctive mental response anymore, not now. It was her fault, because she hadn't been strong enough, hadn't been resilient enough to deal with the reality of being married to a hero. She'd spent those seemingly endless days and nights at his side when he'd been in the hospital, and then months in rehab, and later on in out-patient therapy. She'd never faltered, but about halfway through, that little voice in the back of her mind had kept getting louder and louder.

Never again. Never again. Never, ever again.

She simply could not go through this again, could not bear watching this man she loved beyond measure suffer such agony, could not stand ever again finding him on his knees in tears when he thought she wouldn't see—this man who'd never come close to breaking in all the years she'd known and loved him.

She made herself go to her computer usually reserved for her graphics work, with which she helped support herself and her son. *Helped* being the operative word, because she knew that without Blaine paying his child support—and more—regularly, they would not be as comfortable as they were. It jabbed at her, but for Ethan's sake, she couldn't say no.

She pulled up the file she'd started last night when she'd finally accepted she wasn't going to get a miracle, that the police were not going to instantly find Ethan and bring him home. She knew that as scattered as she was right now, she needed to keep track of things, of people she'd spoken to and what they'd said, and of people she didn't know how to find or reach but had reason to think might know something.

She stared at the list of names, some with notes, some blank. If she kept this up, people were going to start running and slamming doors the moment they saw her coming. But she had to do something, she couldn't just sit around the house and hope he came home. She had to *do* something. She had to or she would go crazy with the ever-building worry. She had to or—

Her phone rang and she grabbed for it. It was an unknown number she probably would have blocked as spam a few days ago, but now…

"Hello?"

"I'm here."

Her breath caught at the deep, vibrant voice. The voice that had once sent ripples of sensation through her, head to toe with several stops in between. Blaine. If she'd been less rattled right now, she might have pretended not to recognize him. Play it cool.

She almost laughed at the idea that she could ever play it cool around Blaine Everett.

"Where?" was all she could manage.

"In San Juan Cap near the mission at the moment. I need that list."

She could hardly blame him for his short tone and blunt words. After all, she was the one who had walked out on him. But it still stung, and she didn't like that it did. After two years, she'd hoped to be further along in this journey she'd never wanted to be on in the first place.

You did it. You're the one who ran, not him. Never him. Never, ever.

"I have it all in a document I put together last night. Tell me where to send it. It's kind of long," she added in warning.

He gave her an email address that had no name connection to him that she could see, a .org address, and she couldn't help wondering if maybe it was a girlfriend's work address. Surely some lucky woman with more courage and endurance than she had had snapped Blaine up by now?

And if she was jealous at the very idea, that was her own stupid fault.

BLAINE STARED OUT the window at the fountain in the back courtyard while Rafe looked over the list showing on the screen. They were in the front building now, clearly the actual headquarters of Foxworth Southwest.

"I'll take the official ones, the cops and county sheriff," Rafe said, and Blaine turned his attention back to where it needed to be. "I can call and name-drop Foxworth on them and maybe get more than an anxious parent could." At Blaine's raised-brow expression, he shrugged. "We've got a rep, and with law enforcement it's generally a good one, because we don't care who gets the credit as long as the right thing gets done."

"Okay," Blaine said, becoming more amazed every time something Rafe said indicated the reach and influence of these people he now worked for. He supposed he should have guessed the crew that took out a governor and a sitting senator would have some pull.

But that feeling was quickly overtaken by apprehension when he realized he was going to be contacting people as Ethan's father, someone who as far as they knew was rarely in the picture.

At least there wasn't a stepfather to deal with. He'd made sure of that when she'd first called, because he wanted to know what he might be dealing with. Sort of like checking the weather one last time before you took off.

He get in a fight with your husband?

There is no husband.

Boyfriend?

That either, not that it's your business.

Oh, heck no, none of my business. Unless he's abusing my son and that's why he ran.

She'd almost hung up on him then, he could practically feel it over the phone connection. He supposed it was a measure of how worried she was that she didn't. Which in turn told him he had to take this seriously.

"—you can take the parents of his friends, get what you can," Rafe was saying, and he tuned back in, giving himself an inward shake at letting his focus wander.

"Okay. I'll try, but I'm no cop or trained interviewer."

"Do it in person." Rafe gave him a crooked, half smile. "You're less intimidating than I seem to be, to civilians."

"You do have that thousand-mile stare," Blaine said, only half kidding. There was indeed something about the guy that intimidated even combat veterans.

"And take Cutter with you," Rafe added.

Blaine gave him a startled look. "The dog?"

"He makes people react differently." Blaine was sure he must have looked doubtful, because Rafe went on. "Took me a while to accept the effect he has, but he calms people. Might help with the kids, too."

Blaine couldn't deny that. After all, he'd felt it himself. And he supposed having a dog as company would at least keep some kids, friends of Ethan's, from taking off the minute they found out who he was. Who knows what his son had told them about him. Maybe that he didn't even care enough to visit more than a few times a year. He figured that was what Erin had told him, to keep him from knowing he hadn't come more often because she made it so difficult.

He's your son, I'd never deny you visitation, but I need to make arrangements when you come, so I need plenty of advance notice.

Which had eliminated a few times when he'd had a couple of days drop unexpectedly out of his calendar and he could have visited, spur of the moment. He hadn't been sure at first what arrangements she had to make, but after the third time he'd realized the arrangements were for her to be elsewhere.

Ethan had always just said Mom had something to do, some extra class she was taking, some friend she was visiting, but Blaine knew perfectly well it wasn't what she was going to, it was what—or rather who—she was getting away from. Him.

And so he'd been forced to settle for texts and the occasional phone call to keep in touch with the boy he loved more than anything.

"Let me get hold of Walker and get some further local direction. Once we have that, I'll see what I can find from official sources, see if there's anyone they thought knew more but who was reluctant to talk to them. Then we'll go from there."

Blaine nodded, and while Rafe made his calls he wandered around the building. It was a single story, with several work areas with computers. He was drawn to one corner where there was a large, built-in fireplace, rounded and white, in the traditional adobe style. A curved sectional sat in front of it, along with a circular coffee table that echoed the theme. To one side of the fireplace was a large flat-screen on the wall.

There were a couple of individual offices around the outer edge of the spacious building, and one large room with an appropriately sized table, that looked as if it were reserved for meetings. The place was a combination of both businesslike and welcoming, unlike anyplace he was used to.

He'd never expected this. Or anything like it, when he'd called Rafe to ask for help. He'd just wanted some backup, in case he had to confront some nasty—and armed—gangsters to get Ethan out of whatever trouble he was in.

He thought about sitting down—he was more than a little tired—but with his luck lately he'd doze off. But then he realized how little chance there really was of that, with his mind racing full tilt. Still, he stayed on his feet, not pacing exactly, but going from window to window, room to room, trying to focus on this new place rather than the well-beaten path that had taken over his consciousness. The path that led to the inevitable conclusion.

This was his fault. At least, in part. He should have pushed harder, pushed to be a bigger part of his son's life. No matter that it was painful to see Erin dodge him when he was around, he should have done it anyway. But she'd made it so clear she didn't want to be anywhere near him, and he couldn't help wondering if that had something to do with Ethan's situation now. Maybe she'd told him his father didn't care about him, that was why he wasn't around. It didn't seem like something Erin would do, bad-mouth him to perhaps keep the boy loyal only to her, but then walking out on him after the worst was over didn't, either.

But she'd done it. After all they'd been through, after she'd been rock-solid through his entire recovery, after he was back on his feet and things were almost back to normal, that was when she'd walked away and never looked back.

Everyone around him had been stunned. She'd been an almost fiery presence in the hospital, in the rehab center and during the outpatient treatment, confronting anyone from therapists to doctors if she thought he was getting shortchanged. She'd fought for him, in a way that had surprised even him; he'd never seen this fierce side of her before. He, their son, and everyone else, saw it as evidence of just how much she loved him.

It turned out to be the last flameout of a dying star.

And now Ethan was on a path to a different kind of flameout. And Blaine's jaw tightened at the grim thought.

He needed to quit feeling sorry for himself, and focus on his son.

Chapter Six

"The general opinion from everyone I spoke to was that these kids are mostly gangster wannabes," Rafe said as they pulled out of the Foxworth driveway. It was getting late, and they were going to have to decide whether to press any of the people on his list tonight. "There is a gang active in the area, but they don't generally run that young unless it's family. And they don't usually spill over into that neighborhood."

Blaine grimaced as he made the turn onto the street. He was behind the wheel at Rafe's suggestion, since although it had changed, this was still where he'd grown up. Blaine suspected it was also as a distraction from his ever-tumbling thoughts, and the fact that they were on their way to see his ex-wife, who this time wouldn't be avoiding him.

Only because she couldn't, he told himself. She'd have to see him this time, because too much was at stake.

"Which means exactly what?" he asked. "That Ethan had to go and find them?"

"Pretty much," Rafe said. "Or else they're recruiting. Plus, I spoke to one of the detectives who's on Ethan's case, and she said the main operators in the area had some trouble last summer. Several of them landed in jail and are still there."

Blaine spent a moment being thankful he'd called this

man, even though at the time he'd had no idea about all the connections he—and the place he'd landed—had. But time to thank him again for that later.

"So they're shorthanded and need more bodies for whatever crap they have going on?"

Rafe nodded. "Quite the going trade in car parts, from what the locally assigned county detective said. There's the occasional house burglary when the opportunity arises and they know people aren't home, but they mostly focus on cars."

"But not the cars themselves, just car parts?"

"Easier to get away with. And the more expensive cars get, the more the parts are worth. And catalytic converters are the hottest part going. All those precious metals in them are worth a lot when melted down."

"But we don't know if that has anything to do with whoever Ethan's taken off with."

"No, we don't. It's just something to throw in the pot while we wait to see what bubbles up to the top."

One corner of Blaine's mouth twitched. "You sound like Rowdy, our old unit mechanic."

"Rowdy," Rafe said solemnly, "had a reputation that earned him the right to be quoted far and wide."

"He did indeed," Blaine agreed. He'd known Rafe would remember the man who had gotten his helicopter repaired in time to make the emergency flight that had saved Rafe's life.

Things had changed enough that Blaine followed the GPS instructions until he got onto more familiar turf. Which wasn't until he turned onto Camino Capistrano and headed south. Just past the mission itself he made the left onto Ortega Highway and headed inland, away from the more expensive real estate between Interstate 5 and the coast.

They'd driven in silence for several minutes before Rafe asked quietly, "How long has it been since you've seen her?"

"A long time. When I've seen Ethan, she makes sure she's nowhere around. Used to have a babysitter there when I arrived, so she didn't have to see or talk to me."

The signal ahead changed to red, and they came to a halt. He sat watching the light, telling himself to leave it there. But he couldn't seem to do it. It was roiling around inside him and he couldn't keep the lid on it. Nor could he help sounding angry when it burst free.

"I've never understood it. How she could stand by me like a rock through all that…crap, but walk away just when things were back to normal?"

"Women," Rafe said, sounding cautious, "have a very different way of looking at some things."

"I've noticed," Blaine answered sourly.

He took a deep breath, calmed himself much as he'd sometimes had to in a combat zone. Played Rafe's words back in his head. Words that sounded as if they were born of firsthand experience.

Then, with a glance at the man in the passenger seat, he asked, "You seem different. Things change for you in that arena?"

"A lot," Rafe said, and there was no mistaking the smile that spread across his face as anything less than happy. He met Blaine's gaze and added, "Long after I thought there was no chance in hell we'd put it back together, we did."

Blaine drew back sharply, wondering if that had been a bit pointed, and aimed at him. He almost missed the change of the traffic light, but was thankful he had to turn his gaze back to the road ahead.

"I'm glad to hear it," he finally said.

It sounded cliché even as he said it, but he meant it. Just because it hadn't and would never happen for him didn't mean he had to begrudge anyone who put their life back together. Especially someone like this guy.

"Never thought it would happen. Never even dared to hope."

Blaine was glad he didn't turn that into advice for him to do the same. But then, Rafe had never struck him as the kind of guy who went around handing out unsolicited advice.

When he made the last turn, onto the street that held the address she'd given him, he slowed to a snail's pace. Not just because it was a small, residential street, but because he felt as if he were approaching the edge of a very steep cliff. When this encounter had been days away he'd been fine. Hours, and he was starting to get edgy. But now, when it was mere minutes, and that in a single digit, it was all welling up inside him—the pain, the longing, the anger.

"It's a mission," Rafe said. "Just like any other. Eyes on the goal."

So now the man was a mind reader? Something he maybe picked up from whatever woman was tough enough to take him on?

"She must be really something," he said.

"That she is," Rafe said softly. Then he gave Blaine a sideways look. "Don't go thinking it's easy, though. She's tough, smart, stubborn and determined."

Blaine had the thought that it would take all of that to deal with this man as he looked back at the road, at the numbers on the houses they passed.

His heart took a leap, then seemed to stop in his chest. The instant he'd spotted the little house on the next corner, he'd known. The sharply angled roof that went up on one side then dramatically dropped off vertically on the other to meet the rest of the building caught his eye, but it was the garden that told him. The glorious garden, with several trees, including a couple he thought looked like orange trees. The lower level was green with splashes of color everywhere, even in November. He recognized her beloved snapdragons, something else shorter but similar in color and profusion, and even a couple of what looked like Christmas things—poinsettias, was it?—only they were pink rather than red.

"That's it," he said, his voice tight. "She always wanted the most garden she could get, but...never had it before, because she never knew when we might get transferred."

She did it, and she did it without me.

He parked at the curb in front of the place, feeling, oddly, that assuming it was okay to park in the driveway would be... presumptive. He got out, walked toward the house and suddenly stopped, unable to take another step. He'd faced active battle zones with less trepidation than he was feeling now.

He felt a nudge on his right leg and glanced down to see Cutter looking steadily up at him. Automatically, he reached down to touch the dark fur on the dog's head with a gentle pat. And felt it again, that flow of comforting warmth. After a moment he straightened up, thinking he might be able to do this now. Rafe had understated his furry partner's capabilities.

"Just how much extra are you paying her a month?" Rafe was looking around, as if inspecting the neighborhood. Then he looked back at Blaine.

He shrugged. "As much as I can. After what she went through getting me back on my feet, I didn't want her to have to deal with being broke."

"Even after she left you."

"She's still the mother of my son." *And the only woman I've ever really loved.* He didn't say the last part, but he had the feeling Rafe, this Rafe, the new Rafe, just might understand.

Chapter Seven

Erin had thought she had braced herself. And maybe she had, but it just wasn't enough. Maybe nothing would have been enough. Maybe there was no way she could prepare for the kind of impact Blaine Everett had always had on her.

The moment she opened the door and saw him, saw those deep blue eyes that used to take her breath away when he smiled at her, it was as if her world, her carefully constructed world, slammed to a halt in an instant.

Now he didn't even have to smile at her—as if he ever would again. All he had to do was exist, and she felt as if she had to concentrate on the simple matter of keeping her heart beating and her breath going.

He'd changed, a little, but he hadn't gotten any less beautiful, to her. It wasn't just his eyes, although they had always been enough to disrupt her pulse. He still topped her own five foot six by five inches, he still had that lean, wiry build that sometimes made people think he might be less strong than he actually was, still had that thick, dark brown hair that now wasn't quite as short as she was used to, and she sillily remembered how he used to say longer hair was a pain under a flight helmet. There was also the faintest touch of silver at the temples, new since she'd last seen him, and she wondered how much of that was from what he'd gone through. Or what she'd put him through.

Sure, because it's all about you.

She abruptly realized he wasn't alone.

Not only was there another man with him, there was a dog.

But the man with him was standing back several feet, as if he wanted to give them privacy to deal with this…awkward moment. And the dog was sitting at the other man's feet, looking at her, but not making a move. Well-trained, she thought, rather inanely. And the man was familiar. She'd seen him before, but—

"This is Rafe Crawford. He's the guy I pulled out on that last mission before the—"

"I remember," she said, before he could mention the crash that had eventually ended everything.

And she did remember, since Blaine had been given a medal for that rescue he'd single-handedly pulled off under fire. And she'd proudly been there when it was presented, having put her shivering, weak-kneed fear behind her. Again. Until the next time. It was lucky she'd only heard about most of his heroics after the fact, because if she'd known while it was happening she probably would have cut and run much sooner.

She also remembered how, when she'd first started dating, her mother had spent a lot of time telling her to never fall for a liar, a cheater, a pushy salesman or a politician. She'd teased back, asking if they weren't all the same thing.

What her mother hadn't told her was to never fall for a hero.

But then, she already had done that, at about age seven, when Blaine Everett had moved in across the street. True, they'd both tried being with other people while in high school, mostly at the prompting of both sets of parents, but later, when they were back together, they'd both admitted they'd known it would never work, because they were meant to be.

But that was before she'd had to face the bitter truth of her own lack of courage. Spoiled, that was what she was. Spoiled and needing a life without risk, without danger, without loss.

And now you may have lost the only thing that's kept you going all this time. Your son.

Blaine's son.

"And you came to the hospital, too, I remember," she said belatedly to the other man. "I'm sorry, come in."

She had been cleaning madly ever since he'd said he was coming. Not that her place was ever dirty or even untidy, but it was all part of proving she was doing fine without him. A lie she almost had herself believing before she'd walked into Ethan's room and found it empty.

She stole a glance at the tall, rangy man who followed Blaine inside. He had that same look she remembered from when he'd visited Blaine in the hospital and then rehab, that look of having seen a lot and too much of it bad. But at the same time there was a glint in those eyes and in his expression that…lightened it somehow. As if he was someone who'd gotten through it all in one piece, despite the injury she knew had been quite severe. Not as bad as Blaine's, and only his leg, but that was just degrees of hell.

Something brushed her knees. She looked down to see the dog who had come in with Rafe. She'd never had a dog as a kid—her mother was a cat person—and later it had never seemed fair when they were transferred so often. This one was interestingly colored, black fur over his head and down to his shoulders, where it transitioned to tan with a tinge of what in a person she'd call auburn. He didn't look like the traditional military dogs she'd seen over the years, but might if he didn't have all that soft, fluffy fur.

As she looked at him, he sat at her feet.

"This is Cutter," Rafe said, his voice oddly quiet, almost gentle. "He belongs to my boss, but he's here to help."

Help? Was he some kind of tracking dog? That was silly, how would that help after all this time? Maybe if they found someplace Ethan had been recently. But there was something in the way the dog looked up at her, those dark eyes fastened on her face. No, there were flecks of color in those eyes, like amber, or gold. Then he leaned into her, looking up almost pleadingly.

"That's his 'please pet me' expression," Rafe said.

That seemed so out of character for…well, both men standing here, she couldn't help but smile. And she reached down to stroke the animal's dark head.

Her hand stopped before she'd finished the first stroke. What on earth? She stared down at the dog as she moved her hand again, then lifted it to start the movement anew.

It was real. She didn't know what it was or what to call it, but she could not deny the strange sense of warmth and peace and calm that practically flowed into her. And several long moments passed before she could pull her hand back. She looked up at Rafe.

"Is he a therapy dog?"

"He's had some training in that, yes," Rafe said. "Among a ton of other things. Including mind reading, emotion reading, bad guy reading…"

"Hope he's good on that last one."

Blaine had spoken for the first time since they'd stepped inside, and Erin's gaze snapped to his face. That face that she had imagined beside her so many times, the face she had ached to wake up to so many times she'd stopped even trying to track how long it had been. That face that had always showed his hunger for her as he made long, sweet love to her.

She'd resigned herself to the apparent fact that he would forever and always haunt her, and she might as well get used to it. And now he was here, looking at her not in the old, loving way but in the cool, calm, collected way she guessed his brothers-in-arms always saw.

"He's also got quite a track record with kids," Rafe said, and she turned back to him, not even trying to deny the relief she felt at looking away from Blaine. "Both finding them and helping them. And we have a lot of people we can call for help, if we need it."

That puzzled her. And while Blaine didn't look the same to her, apparently he could still read her easily, because he said, "He works for a foundation that helps people. It's called Foxworth."

Her eyes widened. "I've read about them." She looked back at Rafe. "They're big. Surely they wouldn't help on something like this."

"Things like this is what they were founded for. Helping people who can't get it elsewhere," he said.

And she suddenly remembered who this man was. The award-winning sniper who had saved countless lives in those wars and battles that haunted her dreams. Blaine had told her about him after the rescue, in that wide-eyed way that she'd loved. Saying "Holy moly" rather than something cruder. The way he always did around Ethan. She remembered teasing him, saying he'd saved just as many lives himself.

"Maybe, but I do it from a safer distance, with a built-in escape module," he'd joked, clearly seriously impressed with the man who was now here with him. The man who apparently had answered his call for help immediately, and had brought reinforcements.

So she had two heroes on her side, temporarily. And apparently a very capable dog with a knack for soothing frazzled nerves, among other things. Although it wasn't really her side they were on, she reminded herself. It was Ethan's. They were here for him, and until he was home safe she didn't matter. Nor did her jumbled feelings. She would just have to set them aside. The focus needed to be, had to be Ethan.

And she would do worse than deal with her ex-husband for the sake of their son.

Chapter Eight

"I have coffee on," Erin said.

As she stood up from where they'd taken seats in the living room to head for the kitchen, she rubbed her hands down her legs in that way she'd always had. Especially if she was nervous. Blaine supposed he should be thinking about why she was nervous, but all he could think about in that moment was those legs, and how it had felt to have them wrapped around him while he buried himself in her.

Not now, idiot.

He took the chance while she was gone to look around. The gardening had extended indoors, he saw, with several potted plants adding a touch of greenery to the room. The couch they were on was comfortable, arranged so it faced what looked like a gas fireplace, and a flat-screen atop a cabinet beside it. The other side of the fireplace was taken up by a floor-to-ceiling, full bookcase. She'd always loved to read, had preferred print, and that clearly hadn't changed.

The color scheme was appropriately beachy, given they were only about five miles as the seagull flies from the Pacific. White, sand, and a light blue seemed to be the theme, both in furniture, pillows, and a framed painting on the wall opposite the fireplace, between two large windows that looked out onto the remarkable garden she'd created.

But what really caught his eye were the three photos on the wall opposite where they were sitting. One was of her parents, who lived in Florida. The next was of her getting what looked like a degree, given she was wearing some kind of school robes like people wore at graduations. But it was the third photo that snagged his full attention. Ethan, at eight years old, wearing the child-sized flight suit Blaine had tracked down when his son had announced he wanted to be a pilot just like his dad.

How had he gone from that little boy in the jumpsuit to... whatever he was now?

Don't be stupid, you know how.

He shook off the unsettled feeling that had taken over his gut. Saw Rafe watching him, but thankfully the man didn't say anything.

"You finally got your garden," he said to Erin when she came back with a tray carrying three mugs and a bowl of sugar and a small jug of cream or milk, he wasn't sure. She took both if she hadn't changed, while he took just a spoon of sugar. Rafe accepted his mug with thanks, and shook his head to the offer of either. She'd always made good coffee, and at his first sip he knew it was still true.

"I did," she said. "It wasn't much when we got here, but now it looks good, I think."

"It's incredible," he said, past the knot in his throat. He'd never been able to give her that.

"Labor-intensive," Rafe commented, but he said it admiringly.

"Yes," she admitted. And then, with a slight shakiness Blaine couldn't miss, she set her mug down. "Maybe I spent too much time on it. Maybe if I'd spent more on Ethan he wouldn't—"

"Stop it," Blaine said. "Don't blame yourself for this."

For the first time she met his gaze head-on. And it didn't matter how long it had been, he still recognized the pain in her blue eyes. "How can I not? I'm the one who—"

She cut herself off and looked sharply away.

The one who what? Blaine wondered. Didn't notice any trouble? Expected too much from the kid? Was too hard on him? He didn't think any of that was true. It just wasn't who Erin was.

But that left only one thing he could think of, one thing that could have made Ethan angry enough to run away.

She'd broken up their family.

But that had been two years ago. Why would Ethan take off now, after all that time? Was it simply that he was older now, going through those early teenage years? Or had something else triggered this?

He stood up abruptly. "Where's his room?"

"The far end of the hall," Erin answered, starting to rise as well.

"No. Stay here." He didn't want her with him when he looked at Ethan's room. He wouldn't be able to focus, and he wanted to look at every inch of it.

"Erin." He heard Rafe's voice, low, gentle, but commanding. Blaine didn't look back but kept going in the direction she'd pointed.

She didn't follow.

ERIN WASN'T SURE why she'd felt compelled to stop herself from following Blaine down the hall. But something in the way the other man had spoken…and then the dog had gotten up and put himself between her and the hallway, not aggressively, not like a dog who wanted something, or a dog who was hungry or wanted out, but one who wanted to tell her she shouldn't take another step.

Politely.

"He needs a minute," Rafe said, nodding in the direction Blaine had gone. "Maybe a few." He hesitated before adding, as if he wasn't sure he should, "This isn't easy for him, either."

At least he'd acknowledged this was uncomfortable for both of them. She sat back down and looked at him again, studied him in a way she hadn't before, because she'd been so distracted by Blaine's presence.

"Blaine said, back then, that you were…a sniper?"

"I was."

"He said you were one of the best ever, short only of the man the trophy you kept winning is named after. Sorry, I can't remember—"

"Hathcock. Carlos Hathcock."

She nodded, recognizing the name now. But she couldn't quite suppress an inward shudder, which she hoped didn't show. She knew they were crucial, that they saved lives, but…

"That makes you nervous?"

"Not nervous. I admire anybody who does such a…rough job. I just can't imagine what it must be like. Killing like that."

He studied her for a long moment, and she wondered if she'd offended him. It would figure, he comes to help a friend, and she screws it up.

Finally he spoke, and if he was angry, it didn't show. "Hathcock probably said it best. He said he never enjoyed killing, but it was his job. And if he didn't do it, they were going to kill a lot of kids dressed up like Marines."

"I…never thought of it quite like that."

"He had a unique viewpoint. And saved a lot of our guys."

"Blaine said you saved another pilot he went through training with. Who was about to get shot down with an RPG."

"I remember," Rafe said after a moment of thinking. "And Blaine told me he came home, got married and has three kids. So far."

She smiled at that. And didn't miss his point, that if not for him that father would be dead and those kids wouldn't exist.

"So," she began again, shifting to what he'd said, that Blaine had told him about the other pilot, "you and Blaine have stayed in touch? I didn't realize."

"Sort of," Rafe answered. "I mean, we touched base now and then. Probably should have done better, given he saved my life, but…reality gets in the way."

"And yet when he does call you, after all that time…"

"I come running." He smiled, a little crookedly. "A little lopsided, but running."

She shook her head. "Men. It's amazing how you can do that, just drop into each other's lives after months, even years, and pick up as if nothing's changed."

He studied her for a moment. Then let out a compressed breath. And when he spoke, she couldn't help thinking there was something deeply personal in what he said. "And I don't get how women have to do constant maintenance. But I guess I'd better learn."

"Someone you need to get to know?" It was a guess, but she would have bet money she was right.

"Someone I've known for a long time, loved for a long time. But…we fell apart years ago. Because of me."

She sensed there was something more. "But?"

He smiled then, widely, warmly, and it changed everything about him. "We've put it back together. Stronger this time." He held her gaze a moment before saying quietly, "It can be done. Even if the breach is…huge."

She knew that was aimed at her. But she shook her head. "Too much damage."

"That's what I thought, too."

She tilted her head as she studied him. She wouldn't have expected this man to be so…open with someone he didn't even know. But maybe this was part of the debt he felt he owed Blaine. She was getting the feeling there wasn't much this man wouldn't do to help.

But he couldn't help with this. She hadn't just broken up their marriage, she'd shattered it.

"I was young," she said, unable to stop it from pouring out. "I'd always loved Blaine, and I had some silly ideas about being married to a pilot. The pride, the…the glamour, I guess. Before I realized what came with it, the constant fear."

"Being a military wife is a job like no other."

She couldn't shake the feeling that this was…unusual for this man. He clearly wasn't saying all this easily. She could almost feel he was having to work at opening up like this, but yet he was doing it.

"It is a job," she agreed. *One I wasn't very good at.*

"Especially when there are children involved."

She sighed. "Yes. And now they both hate me. Blaine and Ethan."

"You're wrong," the man said, a little gruffly. She stared at him. "This isn't my business, but I've been there, so I'm going to say this and then shut up. Blaine feels a lot of things about you, but I guarantee hatred isn't one of them."

She couldn't miss the utter certainty in the man's voice and expression. *I've been there…*

"The one you put it back together with?" she said softly. "She's a lucky woman."

"I'm the lucky one," he said, just as softly, although she guessed his earlier gruff tone was more the norm for him.

Just then Blaine emerged from the hallway. He had something in his hand but she couldn't see what it was.

"What stuff did he take? And what did he put it in?"

She blinked. "What?"

"A pile of schoolbooks was dumped in the closet. Did he have a backpack for those?"

"I…yes. A blue one." She should have mentioned that. At the moment she was just surprised that he'd figured that out.

"What's missing?"

"What?"

His voice took on that tone of extra patience, and she didn't blame him this time. She was so rattled she wasn't thinking straight.

"What things did he take with him?"

"He emptied my wallet of cash. Didn't take credit cards or anything else, though."

"What about clothes, shoes… It might be a clue to where he went."

"Oh." She'd noticed a couple of things that were gone, that she'd mentioned to the police officer who sadly looked as if he took reports like this every day. But she hadn't thought to go through all his clothes. She stood up. "I'll go look."

She started that way, but had to pass Blaine to do it, and stopped when he lifted his hand and showed her what he'd been holding.

"I found this."

She winced when she saw it was the photograph Ethan had always had up on the mirror over his dresser. Or rather, half of that photo. It was from their wedding, and the half left behind was her in that flowing dress she had so loved.

The other half, Blaine, looking sharp, impressive and impossibly handsome in full uniform, was gone. Carefully, almost surgically removed, as if Ethan had wanted every trace of her gone, without doing any damage to his father.

She couldn't blame him, not anymore.

"I'm not surprised. He'd want the half he took with him." Somehow, she managed to keep her tone neutral. Although she wasn't sure if she hadn't, whether it would have come out cold, or just bitter.

"When did it become a half?" Blaine asked, sounding as if it was a strain for him, too, to keep his voice even.

"It must have been when he…decided to leave."

"Where did he keep it?"

"Tucked into the frame of his mirror. With me hidden underneath the frame. So he could see you all the time." Okay, some of the bitter had crept in that time.

"I found this on the floor, under the bed. So he didn't throw it away."

"Or burn it?" she suggested. The bitter was starting to win.

"If he was in a hurry," Rafe said, "and rushing around, it might have ended up there unintentionally, if it wasn't taped or pinned."

"It wasn't," she said. "I wouldn't let—" She broke off suddenly, thinking how bad what she'd been about to say would sound, under the circumstances.

"You wouldn't let him mess up the furniture," Blaine said, his tone so neutral she knew it was intentional just as hers had been.

"It was new," she said, knowing how lame it sounded. How demanding it made her sound. How hard to live with. Was he thinking no wonder Ethan had run away? Was he thinking he was lucky to have escaped?

"We never had new furniture." Now there was something different in his voice, something gentler, almost understanding.

"No," she said. "We never did."

"We didn't need…things."

Heat, and she was sure color, flooded her cheeks. Because he was absolutely right. They hadn't needed things. Because they'd had each other. And that was all she'd ever wanted.

And now that he was here in front of her, alive and healthy, she was afraid she still did.

Chapter Nine

"Let's lay this out," Rafe said. "Erin, you said you talked to him that night, before he disappeared?"

She nodded. "Late, too. I had to go in and tell him to shut down."

"What was he doing?" Blaine asked, knowing they needed every bit of info they could get, even if it didn't seem important now.

Erin grimaced. "Playing one of his games. He wasn't happy when I told him he had to go to bed."

"How unhappy?" Blaine asked.

"Unhappy enough that he refused. I had to threaten to cut off the Wi-Fi." His ex-wife gave him a pained look. "If you mean was he unhappy enough to run away, then probably. I told you, he hates me."

"Erin," Blaine began, but Rafe cut him off. Probably didn't want to hear them fighting, and he couldn't blame the guy.

"What kind of game?"

"Something about kids—well, teenagers—riding dragons and battling...some other creatures. You get to pick a character to be."

"Did he play it on a computer, or a game console?"

"Both, depending on where he was." She grimaced again.

"I have a feeling he was playing it a lot lately, because I got a call from his school that he'd cut a few classes."

"Did he take the computer with him now?" Blaine asked.

"Yes, his laptop is gone. He actually got a part-time job last year to pay for it, because he wanted one capable of running the game. I would only give him enough money for one that would handle his schoolwork, because he already had the console." She sighed audibly. "And I only got him the console because he kept sneaking into my office to use my computer to play whenever I wasn't home. He inadvertently destroyed some important work."

"This game," Rafe said slowly, "is it one he plays with others?"

She nodded. "A lot of them, apparently. I think he spends as much time messaging with them as he does playing."

"Do you know what name he signed in with?"

"I…no. Not his real name, though. I did ask that, and of course he looked at me like I was an idiot."

Blaine watched as Rafe reached for the phone in his jacket pocket, a slightly different sort of model with some extra buttons he'd never seen on a phone before. Erin was looking at him warily.

"I didn't think it was bad, or dangerous," she said, sounding a little anxious. "And at least he was home when he was playing."

"The game may be fine," Rafe said as he tapped the screen. "The other people who play—and message—may not be."

Blaine heard her breath catch. He had to admit he hadn't thought of that, either, but then the world of online video gaming, especially what he thought were called RPGs, role-playing games, were out of his experience. He'd been busy enough fighting the real villains of the world.

"Ty?" Rafe said into the phone. "Yeah. I need some help, and it's right up your alley."

He walked toward the other end of the room, talking rapidly into the odd phone. Which left him and Erin essentially alone together. Something that hadn't happened in two years, since the divorce had been final.

She didn't—or wouldn't—look at him. Or speak. His jaw tightened, but then he consciously released it. He'd given up trying to figure out how she could throw away what they'd had over something that was already over and done. Yeah, he'd been pretty messed up, and it had taken him a year to get fully back on his feet and operational, but he'd done it.

Only because she was there fighting beside you.

He'd never denied that. She'd been there every step of the way, fighting alongside him, and many times fighting for him, against medical people who made assumptions she thought they shouldn't, or a couple of times when, as she'd put it then, the right hand wasn't talking to the left hand and some important wires got crossed.

He wouldn't be here now, pretty much back to his old self except for a few scars and a shoulder that tightened up on him now and then, if not for her. When he thought back to those early days, he wondered if he'd have pulled through at all if not for her. So many times he'd just wanted to quit, to take the easier way out. But how could he give up when she was there, fighting so hard for him, for them?

And then she walked away, after all that, just when things were right again.

"Thank you. For coming."

The quiet words, uttered barely above a whisper, snapped him out of the old, useless, ever-repeating cycle of memories. But the effect lingered, and there was an edge in his voice when he answered her.

"Ethan's my son. Of course I came."

"I was afraid you might not. Because...of me."

He stiffened. "You really think I'd put that above Ethan? That I'd abandon him because—"

He cut himself off. Stopped the words that would have been downright pitiful. *Because you abandoned me? Threw us away?*

He was beyond grateful when Rafe walked back toward him. He was focused on Erin. "How long ago did he last play that game on your computer?"

She looked as relieved as he felt when she shifted her gaze to Rafe. "He got the laptop right before school started, so probably August?" she answered, her answer a question in itself.

"Ty?" he said into the phone. "August." A pause. "All right. You'd better tell her what you need. Give me a second."

Rafe lowered the phone and gave Erin a look Blaine could only describe as intense. "I've got the Foxworth tech expert on the line. I want him to track down the name Ethan used on that game, and who he talked with. There might be a clue there to where he went, or if someone there talked him into it."

Blaine saw Erin go pale as she swayed slightly. "I never thought...could that be..."

He instinctively reached out to steady her. He supposed it was a measure of how distraught she was that she let him grasp her arm without pulling away. But she kept her attention on Rafe.

"You'll have to trust us, Erin," the man said. "I know you don't know me, but you know of Foxworth, and I swear to you we live up to the reputation."

He felt as much as saw her pull herself together. As she

had so many, many times in various hospital rooms and rehab facilities. "What do you need?"

"Access to your computer." He gestured with the phone. "Ty can set up a way he can remotely connect, but you'll need to install a piece of software. He'll walk you through it."

She glanced at Blaine. "Trust him. Trust them," he said.

She took in a breath. "All right," she said, sounding determined. Sounding like the Erin he used to know, the woman who had never let go of his hand on their walk through hell.

The Erin who had loved him.

She took the phone Rafe handed to her and headed with him down the hallway. Blaine followed, because he was curious, wanted to see this office of hers. Ethan had told him she was doing something with designs for advertisers, but that was about all he knew.

When he stepped into what probably would have been a den but had been set up as an office, he stopped dead. Stared at the walls, which contained several framed graphics, some dramatic, some graceful, some clever, but all undeniably effective. The one on the wall above the computer desk really caught his eye, and if he'd been in the market for a dog groomer, it would be enough to have him checking this one out. Which was, after all, the whole point of advertising. Maybe he should point this one out to Rafe, for Cutter.

She was good. Really good.

Erin apparently saw him gaping, because she said, rather sharply, "Is there a problem?"

"No," he answered quickly. "I just never realized... I didn't know you did this. So well."

"Because of course I have no skill or talent for anything." There was no denying the snap in her voice.

"I never said—"

"Later, both of you," Rafe interrupted. He gave them both a pointed look. "Look, I know exactly where you are. But it can't matter now. You can fight it out after Ethan's home safe."

Blaine felt a kick of inward disgust that they'd done it again. Rafe was right, this was not the time. And judging by Erin's suddenly flushed cheeks she felt the same. She sat down at the desk and began to follow the instructions the Foxworth guy on the other end of the phone was giving her.

"When you've talked to him before, has he mentioned this game?" Rafe asked.

"Not by name, so I can't help there," Blaine said. "I know he was playing a lot, but I didn't know if that meant one game or a bunch of them." He let out a compressed breath. "I just knew that was the only thing he sounded enthusiastic about."

He was surprised at how quickly the program was installed, giving the man on the phone access to Erin's computer. She ended the call and pushed back from the desk after barely ten minutes. Then she looked up at them.

"He said to just give him time, and not to do anything on it while he's working on it from… I forgot to ask where."

"St. Louis," Rafe said. "At our headquarters. Well," Rafe added with the slightest of smiles, "what was our headquarters. Our chief financial genius has relocated, and I think the headquarters designation went with her."

Blaine studied him for a moment. "Is she the one?" he asked.

"She is definitely the one."

There was such satisfaction in Rafe's voice that it rattled Blaine. From what he'd told him, they'd been as blown up as he and Erin were, and yet…

The phone Erin had handed back to Rafe rang. He glanced at the screen, then answered. He listened for a moment, smiled and nodded, as if an expectation had been fulfilled.

"Just getting started here, so no need yet," Rafe said to the caller. "I'll let you know. And thanks, my friend."

When he'd ended the call he looked at Blaine. "Teague, the guy from the office I work out of that I mentioned." He shifted his gaze to Erin as he added, "Also a former Marine, so he was offering any help we needed."

Erin gave a tiny, wondering shake of her head, then flicked a glance at Blaine. "Just like that."

Blaine nodded. He would and had done the same. Some people thought that brothers-in-arms stuff was made up, but he knew it was utter truth. And even if he hadn't believed it, he'd have to now.

Because when he'd called for help, one of the most famous Marines in sniper circles had come running.

Chapter Ten

Erin supposed she would never fully understand military men, especially Marines. Maybe she wasn't supposed to.

Maybe she just didn't understand the male of the species, period, and that was why Ethan had run away.

Maybe that was why she'd lost Blaine.

You didn't lose him, you threw him away.

You had to.

The old, pointless argument ran through her head as it had countless times before. It didn't matter now. What mattered was that she had help, tough, competent help, to find Ethan and bring him home.

But even that wouldn't solve the underlying problem. That her son hated her so much he couldn't stand to be under the same roof with her. She suppressed a shudder, or tried to, wondering how she had made such a huge mess of her life. Then she felt a warm, strong arm come around her, holding her, supporting her.

"We'll find him, Erin. We'll find him."

Blaine's quiet, confident words reassured her as nothing else could. Except holding her.

She couldn't help herself, she leaned into him. Savored the heat, the power of him. All the memories boiled up inside her, of how wonderful, how sweet…how utterly hot their time together had been. And for a moment it was like it had once been, this strong, steadfast man always at her side, always there for her. She ached for it to be that way again, them, together, unassailable, indivisible.

When he wasn't off fighting some stupid war somewhere.

And that easily she was back in the muddle again. Telling herself it was her own fault. For never realizing until it was too late that loving a hero required some bravery of her own, which she obviously didn't have. No wonder Ethan hated her. No wonder Blaine hated her.

Blaine feels a lot of things about you, but I guarantee hatred isn't one of them.

She glanced at the tall, rangy man who had come at Blaine's call, bringing some incredible help with him. How did a man like that, whose job in the military had essentially been killing people, end up working with a group that did nothing but help people?

More importantly…was he right? Did Blaine really not hate her? And what if he was right? That didn't mean the rift between them could ever be mended.

And again Rafe Crawford's words ran through her mind.

It can be done. Even if the breach is…huge.

She felt a sudden, fierce longing to see that look he'd worn when he'd said it, that expression of undeniable and complete satisfaction, on Blaine's face again. She tamped it down. She had to. Especially when he was looking at her as if he knew exactly what she was thinking. As if he could still read her so well.

Another memory, odd for the moment, struck her. Of another military wife complaining that her husband not only never listened to her, but would never, ever admit that he was wrong about anything.

Blaine was not like that. He never had been. Sometimes it took some convincing, but if he came to see he'd mistaken something, misinterpreted something, or hadn't had all the relevant details, he had no problem admitting it and changing his mind. In fact, he had shown her how to do it in turn, with grace and lack of ego. Because when he knew he was right, there was no budging him.

He looked at her now and said quietly, "We have a battle to fight."

She let out a long breath, and was about to pull away, to stand up on her own and face what they had to face, when he said softly, "But remember what you were just thinking, too."

Then he let her go and stepped back. And she tried not to feel bereft.

She wasn't sure she'd managed it.

BLAINE WAS BEYOND RESTLESS. He wanted to get moving, but he didn't know where to go. He wanted to go on the hunt, but didn't know where the objective might be hiding. He wanted to do something, anything, but everything felt like just flailing around blindly. And now it was dark out, and he'd be blind in that way, too.

Erin was in the kitchen, where she'd been washing those coffee mugs for nearly an hour. They were likely sterile enough for surgery by now. Rafe, who had been across the living room on the phone again with who knows how many people in that last hour, finally put the thing back in his pocket and walked back over to him.

"Got through to one of Walker's police contacts this time, gave him a heads-up on why we're here. He's going to look into the case and see if there are any developments or leads they haven't had the time or manpower to look into. We compared lists—" he held up the list Erin had made out, of friends and places Ethan might contact or be at, although they were only the ones she knew of "—and he helped us eliminate a couple that they did check out thoroughly."

Erin set down the last mug with an audible thump. She looked at Rafe in surprise. "They actually did something? The officer who took the report wasn't optimistic about that. Said they were too backed up."

Rafe turned to look at her. "They are. But it turns out the juvenile detective for the area is former military. Once he knew Ethan was the son of an active-duty Marine pilot, he was all in." He shifted his gaze to Blaine. "He owes one like I owe you. But I think he would have done it anyway. He'll call if he turns up anything. And expects the same from us, of course."

"He didn't tell you to stay out and let the police handle it like he did me?" Erin sounded a bit offended.

"You're a civilian, of course he told you that," Blaine said, feeling a little sick at the idea of her out there when there were possibly street gangsters involved. Especially here, where the influx was so high, less than a hundred miles from the border. Before Erin could say whatever it was she was about to, Rafe thankfully, tactfully, and probably intentionally cut it off.

"I also talked to the attorney Walker's wife, Amy, works for, Marcus Rockwell," Rafe went on.

"I've heard that name," Erin said.

"He's pretty well known in the area, has handled a few gang-related cases, and gave me a couple of locations to check. He can help with any aftermath issues for Ethan as well."

"You got information from both a detective and an attorney?" Erin asked.

"Foxworth did," Rafe corrected. "The name opens a lot of doors. We work with the police, often. If we get information they can't, we share it. And they know if it turns into something big for them, we don't care about getting credit. But we're not bogged down by their rules, so we have more freedom to do what's necessary to help and protect our client."

Blaine noticed he wasn't at all irritated at having to explain again what he'd already told him. He really was proud of his work. The thought caused a pang in Blaine's gut.

"Client? Is that what I am?" Erin asked.

Rafe studied her for a moment before saying quietly, "I think in this case Ethan is our client."

Blaine could tell by the look on her face that she felt the same way he did at those words.

"You're not going to get in trouble with your boss for using that influence, are you?" Erin asked, and Blaine felt a soft, warm recognition. This was the Erin he knew, always worried about everyone else, sometimes to her own detriment.

Rafe smiled at her. "If we needed him, my boss, his wife, Teague, our other team member Liam, they'd all be on their way down here. Or Quinn would order Walker and his team back here by morning. He was ready to stay and help after he flew me—" he paused and grinned at the dog "—us down here."

She looked a little awed as she stared at him. Blaine knew the feeling. When he'd called Rafe he'd had no idea it would be like calling out an entire squad to back him up.

Then, as if a bell had rung somewhere, she said briskly, "Shall I tell you where I've been, who I've talked to, so you can take that off the list?"

Rafe hesitated, and Blaine guessed he knew why and said it for him. "We're going to talk to them, too. Just in case."

He knew some people who would have no problem lying to a woman might think twice about lying to a guy like Rafe. Or him, especially if he had Cutter with him.

Blaine was afraid she'd take offense, but she didn't. Instead, she simply shocked the heck out of him.

"It's getting late," she said. "And you must be tired, both of you, traveling all this way. I have a guest room, and the couch isn't awful to sleep on."

That startled him. She wanted them to stay? Here, with her? Her ex under the same roof?

The thought of being here with her set off all kinds of danger signals in his head. He opened his mouth to say they had someplace else to stay, but Rafe spoke before he had the chance.

"That will be fine," he said, and Blaine blinked.

"We're staying here?" he asked, warily.

Rafe met his gaze then. Steadily, betraying nothing. "I think it's best somebody stay where Ethan just might return to. It's been long enough now he might need or want something he left here, or he might get over whatever crisis set him off."

Damn. He hadn't thought about that, and he should have. But then, Rafe had said they'd stay at Foxworth. He hadn't mentioned staying here until Erin had. So what had changed?

Maybe it was just meeting Erin. That's all it took for you to want to do anything she asked.

"Fine," he said abruptly. "But I'll take Ethan's room. You take the guest room." He heard Erin's breath catch, and spun around. "You have a problem with me sleeping in my son's room?"

"I...no. No, of course not." Her cheeks were pink again. They always betrayed when she was upset.

Of course, they also betrayed other things. He'd never forget the time he'd discovered that that slight pinkening of her cheeks could mean something else, too. That time in the middle of the grocery store when he'd noticed and asked, wondering what on earth could have embarrassed her in the condiments aisle.

I was thinking about how much I'd like to pour some of that honey on you and lick it off...

He'd about lost it right there. Because unlike him she never, ever said things like that, especially out in public. He'd wanted to press her up against the shelves and kiss her until she moaned like she did in bed. Only the fact that they'd probably break those shelves had stopped him.

But he'd tossed three squeeze bottles of honey into the cart.

And that night she'd followed through in one of the hottest, most mind-blowing nights of his life. Of course the cleanup after had been a chore, but they'd done it together, laughing about how neither of them would ever look at a bottle of honey the same way again.

And they both suspected that was the night Ethan had been conceived. Had even joked when they found out that if it was a girl, they were going to have to name her Honey.

Ironic that that night with the honey had fifteen years later brought them to this.

Chapter Eleven

Erin heard the movement inside Ethan's room and sleepily had the door open before she remembered who was inside. And all sleep vanished, despite the early morning hour.

Blaine straightened up from where he'd been checking the drawers in Ethan's dresser. Normally, she probably would have been irritated by the prying, but if digging through Ethan's stuff would help find him, she was all for it.

But then Blaine spun around and her mind went blank. She'd managed not to stare at his backside—well, for long anyway—in those nicely fitting jeans, but she only realized when he straightened up and turned to face her that he was shirtless. And the view of that broad chest and shoulders, those ribbed abs, set her pulse racing as they always had. And the fact that his jeans were half-unzipped only kicked up the pace.

Her mouth went a little dry as she tried to suck in air, and she spared a brain cell to be thankful she wasn't drooling instead. But then her gaze sharpened, and she focused on the scar on his right side, where a piece of shrapnel had hit him across the ribs. Oddly, it had done the least damage although it had left the biggest scar. There were others, true, some just as jagged, but the scary ones were the tidier ones from all the surgeries to deal with the rest of the injuries he'd suffered, which had been internal. She'd stolen a look at his hospital chart one afternoon, and the list of them had sent her reeling into the small bathroom to throw up before she'd gotten halfway through it.

That he was here, now, as steady and strong as he looked—*and as beautiful*—was nothing short of a miracle to her. The doctors had told them he would be hurting for a long while. They hadn't lied, but the only way she knew that was because she knew him. Someone who didn't would never have noticed the slight tightness of his jaw or the way he bit the inside of his lip when a movement hurt him.

But she had.

He had never complained. "I survived to come home to you and Ethan," he'd told her anytime she brought it up.

She and their son had been the lodestar of his life. The reason he did what he did, to assure them a safe country to live in, and why when badly injured he fought to survive. To come home to them.

And she'd thrown it away.

Of course, that was easy to say now, two and a half years after she'd filed the papers to end it. Now that enough time had passed that she felt an ache inside at the loss of what they'd had. Now that her fears, her horror at what had happened to him had ebbed.

Ebbed enough that you call on him to do it again?

She couldn't deny that there was possible risk here. She was hoping beyond hope that the possibility of a gang-related connection was merely that, a slim possibility. But if it was not…

For the first time she thought she understood the "mission first" mindset of the military. And so she stamped on her instinctive sensual, erotic response to him being half-dressed.

"Come here," he said. And she had to stamp on it again.

"Why?" she asked warily.

For a moment he just stared at her, brow furrowed. Then she saw realization dawn. "Jeez, Erin, do you think I'm going to jump you? Now? Especially here in Ethan's room?"

If I get the front door closed before I jump you it'll be a miracle.

His words from long ago careened into her mind. She didn't know why that was the occasion that kept coming back to her. Maybe because it had been one of the hottest, sexiest nights of her entire life.

"I just need to know what else he took with him," he said when she didn't—couldn't—speak.

"Oh."

She felt ridiculous. Of course he wasn't going to jump her. Why would he? She'd made sure he would never want her that way again.

She tried for the most businesslike tone she could manage. "I haven't pulled out everything, but what I know is missing are two pairs of jeans—the others are in the laundry, I checked—all of his clean underwear, socks, about half of his T-shirts." She hesitated, then went on. "His favorite shirt, the Marine Corps one he's almost outgrown, was in the laundry basket. He pulled it out and took it, too."

She thought she saw that move she'd just been thinking about, that bite of his inner lip. But she went on.

"From the closet, his favorite sneakers are gone, and his lace-up boots, They're bulky and would take up most of the backpack, so I assume he wore them." She took a deep breath and finished it. "And the Marine Corps jacket you sent him is gone."

For a moment those dark blue eyes of his closed. And

he looked as if he'd absorbed a blow he couldn't quite hide. She herself felt as if she'd been kicked in the gut.

"He made it pretty clear which side he's on," she said, remembering the nausea she'd felt when she realized he'd taken with him anything connected to Blaine, and left anything that had to do with her—including excising her from that wedding photo.

Blaine had turned back to the bed he'd slept on last night and grabbed up his shirt, but when she said that he spun back sharply.

"Side? Why did he feel like he had to pick a side?" She felt as if his gaze was some kind of laser she could feel. "We swore that wasn't going to happen, we weren't going to hurt him like that!"

"And I didn't," she said, her own voice a little sharp now. "I have never said anything to him against you. Ever. In fact…in fact…" Her voice wobbled as her throat tightened unbearably. She tried to swallow, but the tightness was too much, she couldn't even do that.

"In fact what?" he demanded.

"I told him to blame me. That I was the one who wanted the split. That I was…" She wiped at eyes that were swimming yet again, furious at herself. "That I was the one who couldn't take it."

"But you did take it!" He didn't quite shout it, but it was close. "You got me through it, you were there fighting for me when I couldn't. And then when the worst was over you were gone."

She couldn't seem to get enough air to speak. He'd never understood. He never would, because he didn't have a cowardly bone in his body. The silence stretched between them, taut as if it were some visible wire about to snap.

There was a cough from behind them. She saw Blaine's

head snap to his right in the instant before she whirled around, just as startled. Rafe stood in the doorway, the dog at his side. The slight waft of cooler air she felt told her they had probably been outside.

And then the dog walked into the room. For a moment the strikingly colored animal just looked from her to Blaine and back again, and she had the oddest feeling they were being assessed. And for a moment all she could do was wonder what would have happened if she'd given in to Ethan's desire for a dog. She remembered the discussion they'd had, about how it wasn't fair when they had to move so often. That had ended as so many had, in anger and yelling. And once they'd settled here, where it might have been possible, he hadn't even asked.

But now she wondered if the presence of a pet might have held him here. Or would he simply have taken the dog with him? Never having had one in her life, she had the feeling she didn't quite understand the bond that developed between dogs and their humans. But looking at this one had her wondering if there was more to it than she'd ever realized.

Rafe's tone was a little too neutral when he said, "If you two can manage not to punch each other out, I'll fix breakfast." He smiled crookedly. "I'm told I make some mean scrambled eggs."

She felt hideously embarrassed that this man who had come only to help had witnessed their little screaming match. And relieved when he left it at that and headed down the hall toward the kitchen. The dog, however, stayed behind. And continued to look at them both in that assessing way.

"Why do I get the feeling you're rendering judgment, dog?" Blaine muttered.

"Maybe because we deserve it," she said. "I'm sorry, Blaine. I keep doing this, when there's no energy to spare for old, tired emotions. We... *I* need to be focused solely on Ethan."

"Agreed." He sounded as brusque as she had. But then, in a softer tone, he added, "But tuck this away to think about later. That maybe telling him he should blame you were instructions he followed, not how he really felt."

He was gone before she could react to that unexpected olive branch.

And for the first time ever, she considered the possibility that if she hadn't been so mired in her own misery, hadn't been neck-deep in blaming herself, Ethan might not have blamed her quite as much. Either way, she had driven him away. And that was something it was going to take a very, very long time to get past. If she ever did.

That it was Blaine who had made her think about this, that he, who had suffered the most in all this, had the grace and kindness to try and ease her burden, made her...she wasn't sure how it made her feel.

Other than that, running away from not him, never him but his life, was probably the stupidest thing she'd ever done.

Chapter Twelve

"Those eggs really were incredible," Blaine said as he and Rafe got ready to head out.

Rafe shrugged, and said only, "Don't ask me to do anything more complicated or you'll regret it." As he spoke he didn't look up from his phone, where apparently he had a checklist set up.

Blaine hesitated a moment, then went on. "I'm sorry you had to hear all that, earlier."

"I've heard worse." Rafe looked up at him then. "I've *said* worse."

Blaine had a hard time picturing this man losing his cool that much. Not after seeing his utter unflappability under fire. But then, he was usually pretty calm himself.

Except with Erin.

"That lady you made it up with?" he guessed.

"Gets to me like no one else can," Rafe admitted.

At the light sound of toenails on the floor Blaine looked around to see Cutter approaching. "That dog…" he began.

Rafe chuckled. "Let me guess. He stared you both down while you were…discussing."

Blaine's head came up sharply. "Yeah. How'd you know?"

"Because that's one of his other skills."

"What, he's a…a peacekeeper?"

"That too, but he reads people, especially people who are—or should be—connected."

"Connected?"

"You know what I mean," Rafe said with a steady look.

He did know, but his gut shied away from that "should be" part. So he tried to focus on the dog, who stood there now, looking up at him with that same, assessing gaze. He had to admit, it was a bit unsettling.

"And," Rafe added, "if he decides you need to be reconnected, you'd best listen to him."

"You make him sound like a matchmaker or something."

"I could tell you tales," Rafe said, shaking his head as if he found it hard to believe his own words. "But personally, I've learned to take his advice. It has always paid off."

"This is a dog we're talking about, right?"

"Or an alien in a dog suit."

Blaine stared at him. "Who are you and what have you done with the Rafe Crawford I used to know?"

Rafe laughed. "Nobody was a harder sell than me. But I'm telling you he knows. About humans who should be together, I mean. He corralled us and guarded the door until we talked it out. And when I tried to run—again—he stopped me. The hard way. Put me on my ass."

He couldn't believe what he was hearing, from the most unfanciful guy he'd ever met, in uniform or out. Blaine shifted his gaze to the dog again. Those dark eyes, seemingly flecked with gold, sort of like that piece of amber he'd given Erin that she'd loved so much she'd had it made into a necklace, just stared at him. As if the admittedly clever animal could see down to his very soul.

And suddenly what Rafe had said didn't sound quite so silly.

Erin came into the room from the kitchen, where she'd been tidying up. "Please," she'd said when Rafe said he was used to cleaning up his own mess, "nobody ever cooks for me. Let me say thank you this way."

"All right," Rafe said with a nod. Then, with a glance at Blaine, he added, "We'll be heading out momentarily."

"I feel like I should go with you."

The worry in her voice tugged at Blaine all over again. But Rafe said calmly, "Somebody needs to be here, both in case the police find something, or Ethan comes back."

Her mouth—that lovely, soft mouth—twisted rather painfully. "I think I gave up on him just coming home."

"He might reach out," Blaine said, a little surprised at his own need to soothe her.

She looked from one to the other before saying suspiciously, "What's the other reason you don't want me to go with you?"

Blaine let out a tired breath. "You've already been to or talked to most of the people we'll be reaching out to."

"So?"

"So maybe they…didn't want to talk to you for some reason."

"Because I'm some hysterical mother?" she asked, her tone kicking up a notch. As it did, Cutter let out a low sound, something between a tiny growl and a whine. Remembering what Rafe had said, he looked down at the dog, who was looking at Erin much as he'd looked at Blaine earlier.

Somehow that made him able to keep his tone even. "I didn't say that. I'm only saying that he—" he jerked a thumb toward Rafe "—is a lot harder to say no to."

She seemed to consider that for a moment. "Especially if they're bad guys," she finally said, her tone bleak.

He wanted to hug her, reassure her, but he didn't trust himself to touch her. Even now the connection between them pulled at him.

Connection.

He looked down at Cutter, who was again looking from him to Erin in that rather unnerving way. He didn't think he'd share what Rafe had told him about the dog's other talents just yet. Maybe ever. Because when this was over and Ethan was back home and safe, he'd be out of her life again.

But maybe not so far away.

It wasn't the first time he'd had the thought. That when he got out this time, it would be for good. And that he would relocate, to somewhere close enough that he could see more of Ethan, become part of his son's life again. He hated only seeing him every few months. He remembered too well the chaos of his own teenage years, and if this was any indication, Ethan's was even more tangled. He needed to be closer. It had been too long. The two and a half years since Erin had left him felt like forever—and yesterday.

You thought it would be easier now, that you'd been apart long enough that she wouldn't get to you anymore. He nearly snorted with audible laughter at his own thought. *How's that going for you?*

He felt a nudge to his leg, and looked down to see Cutter still staring up at him with that unsettling gaze. He leaned down to touch the dog's dark head, and froze. He'd forgotten that crazy effect the animal had. The comfort and easing just stroking his fur gave.

One of his other skills, Rafe had said. Just how many hidden talents did this furry beast have, anyway?

He straightened up, looking at his fingers as if they held the answer to that effect. But he was unable to deny he did feel a little better, a little steadier.

Rafe came over to them. He looked at Erin and asked, "You have something Ethan wore that hasn't been washed yet?"

She blinked. "I...yes, I'm sure there are a few things, in the laundry room."

"Get them," Rafe said, and followed her down the hall, with Cutter glued to his side.

When she handed him a couple of shirts and some underwear, he crouched down in front of Cutter and held them out. "Search," he said, and the dog poked his nose into the wad of clothing. He seemed to sniff deeply, then pulled his head back and looked at Rafe, who stood up again and handed the items back to Erin.

"He'll know?" Erin asked. "Just from that?"

"He'll know his job is to find him." Rafe's mouth quirked. "Now, if I'd said 'target,' that'd be a whole other thing."

Blaine could imagine. *Target* had an entirely different connotation.

"Let's roll," Rafe said and headed for the door, Cutter now at his heels. Blaine looked at Erin, who still didn't look happy about staying back, but she nodded resignedly.

"We'll find him," he vowed. "Sooner or later we'll find him."

"All the sooner you can manage, please," she said, her voice sounding the same as her expression looked.

He nodded, saw Cutter was still in the doorway, looking back at him, and headed that way.

He didn't realize quite how wound up he'd been until they were in the car and pulling out of the driveway. Rafe had told him to drive again, given his familiarity with the area, including a couple of the places on the list.

They were at the stop sign on the corner when he looked

at Rafe and, only half joking, asked, "So did the dog here make you change your mind about where we should stay?"

Rafe actually looked startled. Then a little sheepish as he said, "No. That one's on me. But the reason's still valid."

"Yeah."

They were going to check in at the sheriff's office for the area first, to "stay on their good side," Rafe had said, "And see if they've turned up anything since we called."

He pulled away from the stop, driving slowly in the quiet, residential neighborhood. The neighborhood Erin had chosen probably for that very reason. "You think they really will look deeper?"

"I think the Foxworth name gets a lot of things done."

Blaine thought about that. Wondered what it must feel like to have gone from the behemoth that was the military, ruled so often by people who'd never even been close to a uniform, to working for an organization like this Foxworth of his, where apparently they all had the same aim and goals and bosses who were behind them one hundred percent.

Even as he thought it something buzzed from the small console on the roof of the SUV near the rearview mirror. Rafe reached up and tapped a button.

"Crawford," he said, speaking upward at what was obviously a built-in system.

"Hey, Rafe, Jace." The voice was steady, calm. "Quinn just told us about your case. I'm with Walker in Arizona, but we can be back by this afternoon if you need us."

Blaine glance over in time to see Rafe smile. Obviously this must be one of the local Foxworth people. "We're good for now," he said. "But I'll give you a call if that changes. How goes it there?"

"Still checking out locations. Lot of nice people."

"Our kind, then."

"Yep. Hey, Walker says to stick around until we get back, even if you're done. He'd like to see you."

"You mean he wants to see Cutter." Rafe's tone was so exaggeratedly dry Blaine knew it had to be a joke.

"Well, that too," the man on the other end said, and he was laughing.

"Later," Rafe said, chuckling himself as he ended the call. He looked a little bemused, as if he wasn't quite used to kidding around like that.

They were out of the residential area now, and things were looking more familiar. Some places had different names, housed different businesses, but the buildings were the same as he remembered, and that helped him make the turns necessary.

As he drove, passing those familiar places, he gave a wondering shake of his head. "I actually miss this place."

"You sound surprised."

"I am. I thought it was behind me. Especially after the divorce."

He'd told Rafe once about how he and Erin had started, and he remembered how the idea of childhood sweethearts, the proverbial girl next door "except across the street," had seemed to boggle the guy.

"Hey, it became a cliché for a reason," he'd said.

But that had been back when they were still together, when Rafe had come to see him after his crash.

"Thinking about coming back?" Rafe asked now.

"I have been. Never thought I would, but... I feel like I need to be closer to Ethan. Maybe if I had been, this wouldn't have happened."

"Maybe," Rafe said. Blaine felt that steady gaze on him. "Going to give up flying?"

"I hope not," Blaine said fervently. "It's the only job

I love." He gave Rafe a sideways glance. "Although you sound pretty darned happy with yours."

"I am," he agreed. "So you'd be willing to fly civilians around?"

"Fly with a very low likelihood of getting shot out of the sky? You bet."

"There is that," Rafe said, sounding amused now.

Blaine marveled anew at the change in the man. But he supposed being reunited and rebuilding with the only woman you've ever loved could do that for you.

Too bad he'd never find that out for himself.

Chapter Thirteen

Erin wondered how many miles she'd covered just pacing her own living room. Those people chasing ten thousand steps a day would be proud of her.

She had snapped out of a haze of thought to find herself standing and staring out the back window into the garden she'd worked so hard to create. She had made sure Ethan was a part of that, because she wanted him to be certain they would not be packing up and moving again, as they had so often during the first dozen years of his life. This was home, would stay their home, and she had wanted him to be sure of that. Because it was so important.

You think the place matters? It's not home. It'll never be home. Because Dad's not here.

Ethan's words, screamed at her as he'd thrown down the trowel she'd handed him, rang in her head now like the church bells from the mission she could hear when she happened to be nearby at the right time.

He had never forgiven her. He never would. She knew that now.

She didn't blame him. He'd been there, too, through the worst of it. Through the time when everything had focused on getting Blaine back on his feet and as healthy as possible. He had even helped, willingly, as much as he could as an eleven-year-old could. If Blaine needed something he'd run to get it. If Blaine got down, he'd talk about all the stuff they'd do when he got well.

You gotta get well, Dad. I need you to show me that curve ball thing again.

That curve ball thing. She suppressed a deep, powerful ache. He could have done that. He could have played baseball, maybe even made the big leagues, with that snaky, impossible curve ball of his. She remembered the opposing players muttering that the damn thing changed direction twice just going over the plate. His strikeout record at the local high school still held.

But no, Blaine Everett had some patriotic idea that he wanted—no, *had* to serve his country, and had enlisted instead. She had hated the idea, not because she didn't love her homeland but because she was terrified at the idea of him possibly being hurt.

And you were right to be.

When it had happened, when she'd gotten word that his helicopter had been shot down by some random fanatic on what should have been a routine flight, all the fears she'd tried to keep hidden had burst free. She knew right then this was it. She would get him through this, get him on his feet and functional again, and then she was done. She couldn't deal with the fear anymore, let alone the reality.

She spun on her heel, searching for something, anything to do. Because she knew if she let herself, she would sink into the mire of self-recrimination and regret and be lost for hours. She strode down the hallway, pausing to check the guest bath. The only sign anyone had been there was some remaining droplets on the shower floor.

She steeled herself and opened Ethan's door. The first

thing that hit her was like a slap in the face. The bed was made, perfectly. Ethan never made his bed. It was a major bone of contention between them, him saying he was just going to get back in it again so what was the point, while she tried to explain it was like setting your mind right for the day, to start out organized.

He'd called her a controlling witch, and she was pretty sure that first letter of the noun was different in his head.

But it had started her thinking. Was she? Was that the core of it all, that she wanted to control everything? And that the one thing she could never, ever control was what might happen to Blaine as long as he wore the uniform?

She gave her head a shake and continued down the hall. The guest room looked as if no one had set foot in it, except for the duffel bag on the chest at the foot of the bed, and the water bowl on the floor for the dog, a cleverly crafted collapsible thing that probably fit neatly in a side pocket of the large duffel. The bed here was also made, and perfectly.

Those Marines.

Nothing to do here, she told herself. Except be grateful Rafe Crawford had come with Blaine. Not only because he seemed more than qualified to help find and rescue Ethan from whatever he'd gotten into, but because he was a buffer of sorts. And now that her ex was here, she needed that buffer. Not because she hated him, or wanted to yell at him for never understanding why she couldn't go on, but because...because...

Face it, Erin. He's still the only man on the planet who gets to you. You're as hot for him as you ever were.

She'd known that from the moment she'd opened the door and looked into those deep blue eyes. But she hadn't really admitted it in so many words until now.

She'd kept telling herself she'd built a nice, solid wall

around those old feelings, a wall built of bricks formed during that horrible battle to get him back on his feet. She was nowhere near as brave as the man going through it all firsthand. She'd never denied the problem was her, not him. She didn't care that it was exhausting to her, or sucked up every bit of her energy. It was seeing him so destroyed that destroyed her.

She loved him too much.

She let out a smothered sigh, knowing that to most people that probably made no sense at all. Sometimes it made no sense to her.

She tried to think of something, anything that needed doing that she hadn't already done three times since Blaine had told her he was on his way. She thought of that water bowl, and wondered if the dog needed food, or if that obviously prepared former Marine had brought that along, too. She should have asked, if there was anything he needed that she could pick up at the store.

It struck her then there was something she could do, something she hadn't thought about. Assuming Blaine's choice of foods to have handy hadn't changed, she could go pick up his favorites. But then she'd be facing how much to buy. Enough to last a couple of days? A week? God help her, a month?

A horrendous wave of guilt swamped her. Her beloved—even if he had been so difficult to deal with—son was missing, and her first thought when contemplating a month of continued searching was to wonder how she'd survive that long under the same roof with Blaine without…

Without what? Jumping him? She certainly felt the need, just as she had when she'd first reached the age of understanding what this sensation of need and longing for him was. They'd waited—and only because their parents were friends and they knew they'd somehow get discovered and it would be beyond embarrassing—until their senior year of high school, when the need had become too strong and they'd been away on a senior class trip. It had only gotten better since then, and now, twenty years later, she felt it just as strongly as she had then.

That had been one of the hardest things after her leaving, the gradual realization that she would never feel the same way about any other man. Never ache with want, never breathless until she saw him again, never feel as if your world was completely off-balance without them.

They said you never forget your first, but she hadn't counted on never wanting anyone else.

Chapter Fourteen

The kid looked at the dog, a bit nervously, but answered Blaine's question.

"Nah, like I told his mom and I told the cops, haven't seen Ethan and I don't know where he is."

Blaine studied the kid named Connor intently, gauging, assessing, trying to decide if he was telling the truth. Wondering if being able to deduce that was some skill that could be learned, or if you had to be born with it. But all he could see was wariness, and a touch of antipathy. They'd found him down the street from the middle school where Ethan should be right now. For that matter, where the kid they were talking to should be right now. They'd already had a chat with the principal and a counselor Ethan had dealt with, which hadn't produced much except what they already knew, that Ethan was not happy at home.

The boy was very wary, and Blaine explained again how they didn't care that he was apparently cutting classes by being here at ten in the morning. They just wanted to know if he'd seen or talked to Ethan.

Just when Blaine had the feeling the kid was about to bolt, Cutter moved, taking a step forward. Rafe didn't try to hold him back. He'd explained earlier that at home the dog was used to being off leash most of the time, because of the more rural surroundings and the simple fact that he was perfectly behaved unless told he could cut loose. But he tolerated the leash now because he knew they were working. Blaine had seen similar behavior in the MWDs he'd seen, so he accepted the assessment.

The boy they were talking to, that Erin had said was one of Ethan's close friends, one she had already talked to twice, shot a glance at the man at the other end of that leash as Cutter nudged him with a gentle nose.

"It's okay. He'd like you to pet him."

The kid, a gangly redhead with freckles who looked as if he'd had a growth spurt he hadn't quite learned how to handle yet, reached out and touched the dog's head. Curious, Blaine watched the boy's face. And knew instantly he had felt the same sort of soothing sensation he himself had felt when he'd stroked that dark, soft fur. He started to speak, to question the boy again, but stopped when Rafe put a restraining hand on his arm. He glanced at him, and saw him give a slight shake of his head.

He wasn't about to ignore the advice of this particular brother-in-arms, so he waited. Silently. After a long moment the boy crouched down beside Cutter so his face was at level with those dark, amber-flecked eyes. The dog nudged his cheek with a cold, damp nose, and the boy smiled.

And then he looked up at Blaine. "You're really Ethan's dad?"

"I am."

"He misses you."

Blaine's throat tightened until it was almost hard to breathe. "I miss him, too."

Connor grimaced and looked away. "It's his mom's fault, isn't it."

It wasn't a question, and Blaine was glad of that because he didn't want to get into a "who's to blame" debate, here and now or with Erin herself.

"Right now I don't care whose fault it is," he said. "All I care about is finding Ethan and making sure he's all right."

The boy fastened his gaze on the dog, kept stroking the dark fur, and after a moment said very quietly, "I don't like his new friends."

Blaine went still, knowing this could be important. He flicked a glance at Rafe, who nodded at him to pursue it. But how to do it without making the boy clam up all over again? He wanted to demand details, who these friends were and, more importantly, where they might be. But for some reason the question that came out was both simpler and more complex.

"Why?"

The words came out in a rush, as if once the dam had been breached there was no stopping the flood. "They're mean. They pick on people who haven't done anything to them. And they think they're a big deal, because they've got a bunch of tats and dress like gangsters."

"They ever really hurt anybody?"

The boy lifted a hand to his right eye in a seemingly unconscious movement. "Only if you try and fight back."

"Like you did?" Blaine suggested quietly.

"Yeah," Connor admitted. "I had a black eye forever, felt like."

"Did Ethan ever fight them?" The boy flashed him a suspicious look, as if wondering why he'd asked that particular question. Which Blaine supposed was sort of an answer in itself. "He did, didn't he?"

After a moment Connor nodded. Then, looking down at the toes of his scuffed sneakers, he said embarrassedly, "Only he won."

Blaine couldn't help the jolt of pride that went through him. Before the world had fallen apart on them, back when Ethan had turned ten, Blaine had started to teach him a bit about defending himself. Maybe he'd actually done some good, if Ethan had managed to best one of the wannabe gang members.

He crouched down beside Cutter, pretending he only wanted to pet the dog, too, when in fact he wanted to better see the boy's face. But he did stroke that dark fur, and again that sense of calm washed over him.

"What did winning get him?" he asked quietly.

The boy's mouth twisted. "He got to hang with them." His eyes shot up to Blaine's face then, as he said in a rather defiant tone, "I don't think that's any real prize."

"And I think you're right, Connor," Blaine agreed. The kid didn't quite smile, but he thought he saw something there in those young brown eyes. And the boy was still stroking Cutter, so he risked it. "Where do they usually hang out?"

With a half shrug Connor said, "Coupla places. Near the mission sometimes, 'cuz Isaac, the big guy, likes to flip off people who go there. And there's a store just down from there that'll sneak them beers. I think somebody's brother works there. The rest of the time, they've got some hideout somewhere. I don't know where."

Blaine saw Cutter suddenly change posture, as if going on alert. A moment later he heard Rafe's voice, barely above a whisper, saying "Incoming, from the north."

He glanced that way and saw a group of kids who appeared to be a little older than Connor on the corner, headed their way. Four of them, the biggest one twirling what looked like a short chain in one hand. He saw that Connor suddenly seemed frightened.

"That some of them?" he asked.

"Not the ones Ethan's been around. But they're bad guys." The boy stood up, clearly nervous.

"Will they recognize you? Know you live here?" Rafe asked.

Connor nodded again, fear in his expression and his posture as the other boys got closer. "They go to my school. When they go."

"Okay. We're tourists and you just stopped to look at the dog," Rafe said. "That's all."

"I...okay," he said hastily.

The foursome slowed, looked as if they were contemplating...something. But then Cutter moved, shifting so that he was facing them, not making a sound but clearly focused on them.

They noticed. And picked up speed again.

"Now, which way's the mission?" Blaine asked when they got close enough to hear, as if he really were that tourist instead of someone who'd grown up just down the road.

Connor pointed, and Blaine nodded. "Thanks."

The four passed them hastily then, eyeing Cutter warily as the dog shifted yet again to remain facing them, as if he wanted to be ready to leap at them if necessary. The four wannabes kept going, a little faster now that they'd gotten a good look at Cutter, and probably Rafe, too. That steely gaze of his would scare anybody with sense into behaving. Not that those four came across as boys overly gifted with sense.

"Wow," Connor said. "They almost ran."

"My buddy here has that effect on people with bad intentions," Rafe said.

Connor looked from the intimidating Rafe to Blaine. "Is

that why he was nice to me? Because I didn't mean to do anything bad?"

"Probably," Blaine said. Then, with a smile, he added, "So keep it that way, okay?"

The boy sighed. "I guess I better go back to school, then."

"You going to be in trouble there?" Rafe asked.

Connor nodded. "I…kinda been cutting class lately." He shot a sideways glance at Blaine. "Since Ethan went away. We used to hang out together, and now…"

Cutter headbutted the boy, who again stroked that dark head. Blaine could almost see the tension flowing out of the kid. And then he looked up again.

"You're gonna find him, right?"

"Yes," Blaine said firmly.

"Do it fast. Those guys'll get him in trouble he can't get out of."

Blaine felt a knot in his throat. "That's the plan," he said. And driven by an instinct he didn't quite understand, he went on. "Why don't we walk you back to school? Then we can tell them you were helping us, and maybe you won't be in quite so much trouble yourself."

The boy brightened. "That'd help."

"Then let's go," Blaine said, wishing that helping his son could be this easy.

Chapter Fifteen

Erin finished the last call on her list. Mrs. Larson, Connor's mother, was running out of patience, she could tell. She tried not to be a nuisance, but it wasn't like she could quit looking. She'd even tried texting, knowing a lot of people preferred that method of communication, actually including her, but somehow she needed to hear other human voices.

When she had realized people were getting irritated—something she didn't quite understand, given the circumstances—she'd broken the names down into two lists and rotated them, so she only called each person every other day. But lately her calls had been going straight to voice mail, and a couple of people had even blocked her.

Sometimes, when she was exhausted after a sleepless night of worrying, she wanted to ask them how they'd feel if it was their own child who was missing. But she knew it would come out angrily, probably almost hysterically, so she bit back the words and reeled in her temper. Or tried to. She needed their help, not their antagonism.

When she caught herself pacing the living room floor repeatedly for the third time today, she broke.

She had to *do* something. She couldn't go see the people on her lists and irritate them even further, but she could revisit the places she knew about, that Ethan hung out. Or at least, where he used to hang out, before he got sucked into whatever he was into now. She didn't expect to turn up anything, but at least she'd be doing something. She had to try, or she'd go mad. Besides, the odds of Ethan showing up after all this time seemed beyond slim to her. And she suspected making her stay home was just as much—if not more—that Blaine didn't want her with them.

So she spent a couple of hours going from place to place to place and finding out nothing, before she got to the commercial block that was last on her list of possibilities. She parked in the first spot she found, mentally making a list of all the places she could think of that Ethan might have gone to. The first two, first only because they were the nearest to where she'd parked, turned up nothing. She'd not expected anything, but the next she had higher hopes for.

There was a new cashier at the small game store she knew he used to visit. The girl, who looked about eighteen, shook her head at Ethan's photograph. "Nope, never seen him."

"You're sure?"

The girl, whose name tag read Hannah, nodded. "I've only been here a few days, so there's not a lot to remember yet. But I pay attention." She glanced around, as if to see if anyone was close enough to hear, before adding, "We get some guys coming in here who scare me. As in already looking for another job scare me."

Erin's breath caught before she recovered and asked, "You mean gang types?"

"Yeah. Well, younger, like junior high age, but the same look." She grimaced. "Like those gangsters are something to emulate."

Erin had to calm her breathing, and wished she could

do the same for her pulse rate, which had just kicked up. It was the first connection she'd found, the first location that both Ethan and the gang wannabes had in common. Assuming, of course, this group was the same one he'd gotten tangled up with.

She asked a few more questions, got a couple of descriptions that might be useful, and the interesting news that none of that group had been in for almost a week.

Almost the same amount of time Ethan had been gone.

"Good luck finding that other job, Hannah," Erin said, meaning it as she handed the cashier her business card with her phone number.

"Thanks. I hope you find your son." The young woman smiled. "And I'll call if I see him come in."

She exited the store and headed back to where she had parked, a couple of blocks down. She was both up and down, up that she might have confirmed at least the likelihood of a connection between Ethan and those other boys, and down for the exact same reason.

She'd known early on that that connection was a possibility, but she kept hoping it wasn't true, so she hadn't spent much time considering what might happen if it was.

Something Blaine's intimidating friend had said, about the attorney he'd talked to, came back to her now.

He can help with any aftermath issues for Ethan as well.

Aftermath issues.

It hadn't registered at the time but it did now. He meant legal trouble. He meant if Ethan had been lured into breaking any laws while in the company of those kids she'd hoped against hope he wasn't involved with. She'd been so focused on worrying about his safety, and whether their relationship had been fatally fractured that she hadn't even thought about other kinds of repercussions. For instance, ending up having to visit her son in some juvenile detention facility.

The very thought made her faintly nauseous. Images rose in her mind of prison jumpsuits and a glass wall always between her and Ethan. And that was what she was lost in thought about when she was jolted out of the reverie by a sharp exclamation of her name.

"Erin! What are you doing out here?"

She snapped out of the fog to see Blaine headed for her, now barely six feet away. When he reached her he grabbed her shoulders and pulled her to the narrow grass parkway that ran along the side of the street, out of the pedestrian lane.

"Let go of me," she snapped, not because he'd hurt her or even because he'd made the decision to move for her, but because his touch still had that crazy effect on her and she hated the fact.

"Sorry," he muttered, releasing her instantly with an exaggerated movement of his arms, his hands wide-open now. As if she'd burned him. As perhaps she had.

It was a moment before he asked again, "What are you doing out here?"

"What do you think?" she asked, waving the photo she'd shown to Hannah. "Looking for my son."

She saw a flicker of something in his eyes. Pain? Belatedly she realized it was at her referring to Ethan as her son, not *our son*. But he didn't call her on it. Instead he just said, "We're doing this. Why aren't you at the house?"

"I didn't realize I was under house arrest!"

She hated the way she sounded even as the angry words left her mouth. What was it about him that just broke all her governors?

"You're not," he said, more gently than she deserved. "It's

just someone needs to be there, just in case. And we're the new eyes, with a bit more experience in search and find."

She only noted he didn't use the more traditional phrase search and rescue, and for some reason that really registered. Maybe because it told her he, too, was trying to avoid thinking the worst.

"I'm sorry," she said, meaning it. "Really, Blaine, I am. I was just going crazy sitting at home, waiting, not doing anything about finding him."

Something flickered again in his gaze when she said his name. But it was different this time. As if it had nothing to do with their son and everything to do with them.

Before she could get lost down that rabbit hole, she said quickly, "But don't be mad. Because I found something. Maybe."

"Come on," he said. "Rafe and Cutter are just up here."

He gestured in the same direction she'd been heading, and they started to walk. He said nothing more, and the silence seemed more tense to her than it probably was. She was floundering in her mind, trying to think of something to say when she saw the tall, rangy man and the distinctive dog exiting a shop a few doors down. The pet store, she realized, and for some reason that made her smile just as Cutter apparently spotted them, his head coming up sharply. Rafe seemed to react almost as quickly, and they both headed toward them at a fast walk.

"Erin says she found out something," Blaine said to the man without preamble.

She felt a little uncomfortable at the way that sounded. "It's not much," she said hastily. "But I know Ethan likes that game store back there, and I just talked to the clerk. She's new, and hasn't seen him, but she said that some other kids about the same age have been hanging out there, and they make her nervous because they look like a younger version of some adult gang types she's seen in the news."

"So we have the same sort he's reportedly hanging out with frequenting one of his regular locations," Rafe said.

She nodded, grateful that he hadn't dismissed the tiny tidbit as useless. And that was what made her say, "I know it's not much, but it's something."

Rafe nodded, then said, "I got a little something, too, thanks to Cutter here." At her startled look a slight smile crossed his face. "I thought he was just being a dog when he wanted to go into the pet store. But he insisted, and I've learned not to say no when he gets that way. Anyway, the guy who owns the place was there, and he recognized Ethan from the photo. Said he comes in fairly often."

Blaine let out an audible breath. "So this is definitely an area he frequents."

"I should have thought of checking there," Erin said, upset at herself. "He's always wanted a pet of some kind, but the timing was never right."

"For who?" Blaine asked.

The two words stabbed at her as if they'd been obscenities. Because she knew he was right. She had been the one who hadn't wanted the added responsibility of an animal when she was barely hanging on as it was.

She was grateful when Rafe stepped in before she could think of a thing to say to the question that had seemed an accusation.

"He told me when Ethan first came in a couple of months ago, he was asking about a hamster they have that he seemed to like, asking if they made any noise."

"Noise?" she asked, puzzled.

"Probably wondering if he could keep it hidden," Blaine said. There was no accusation in his tone this time, but she knew that if he'd finished that sentence it would have been with "from you."

She wanted to be angry at him for the sniping, but how could she when he was absolutely right?

"There's more," Rafe said, cutting off her unwelcome thoughts. She obviously didn't know the man well, but something in the way he said it sent her pulse up a notch and made her almost afraid to breathe. "He said that Ethan was in looking at the hamster again, with a couple of other kids he didn't like the look of."

So that proved it. Ethan had definitely hooked up with the last group of kids she'd have ever wanted him involved with. She felt that faint queasiness again, but fought it down.

"Rafe?" Blaine said, looking at the man as if he sensed something else was coming.

Rafe's gaze shifted from her to Blaine, then back as he added quietly, "That was yesterday."

Chapter Sixteen

Blaine couldn't stop himself from closing his eyes and letting out a rather harsh sigh of relief.

Yesterday.

Ethan had been gone a week, but as of just yesterday he was alive and clearly well enough to make this apparently regular stop. Meaning he was also still in the area; he hadn't taken off for some gang-infested big city.

Belatedly he tuned back into what Rafe was saying.

"—owner said he's worried that they were scoping out the place."

"Ethan would never…"

Erin's voice trailed away, making Blaine look at her again. He had no trouble reading her expression, but then he'd always been fairly decent at it. Except when it had counted most, apparently.

He didn't have to ask what had stopped her declaration. She could no longer say with certainty what Ethan would or wouldn't do. He'd be willing to bet that a week ago she would have said he'd never fall in with the kind of trouble-makers these other kids seemed to be.

"That wasn't the point," Rafe said gently. "The point is, he has surveillance cameras."

Blaine's head came up sharply. "He does? Did they get Ethan? Can we see the—"

He stopped when Rafe held up a hand. "I already have. It's a little short on clarity, but he let me send a copy to St. Louis. Ty's working on it now."

Blaine blinked. "He just handed it over?"

Rafe gave him that satisfied smile again. "He never hesitated, once I told him who I work for. He's heard of Foxworth. The branch here helped somebody he knows. Besides—" Rafe leaned down to scratch the dog's ears "—he liked Cutter. We should have a cleaned up copy at the office soon."

Erin had been silent since the mention of the hamster, but now she asked, "Is your office close by?"

"It's just a few blocks from the mission," Blaine said, knowing that to any local that pretty much pinpointed the neighborhood. Belatedly he realized why she'd asked. "Planning on joining us?"

"Planning on keeping me from it?"

There was no denying the snap in her voice, but then, his own had been a little sharp, too. Enough that Cutter let out a low sound, not a growl, but not quite a whine, either. He felt the craziest urge to apologize to the dog for upsetting him.

Erin, on the other hand…

But when she spoke again her tone had shifted completely. "I'm sorry. Again. If I try harder, can we set this aside until Ethan is home safe?"

He wanted to tell her that was up to her, since she was the one doing most of the sniping, but he didn't. All he said was, "Fine. Truce."

Cutter moved again, and he glanced down to see the dog looking from him to Erin and back again almost assessingly.

"You two," Rafe said sounding more amused than anything, "remind me of a couple of other people."

Blaine wondered if he meant himself and the woman he'd been so estranged from. He wasn't sure how that would make him feel, given where they seemed to be today, all healed and moving forward.

He couldn't even imagine that happening with Erin. Not after what she'd done. Not after she'd thrown away nearly thirty years of being together, from childhood right up until the day she'd walked out without an apparent second thought.

Not even if he still wanted her more than he'd ever wanted a woman in his life.

She opted to follow them to the Foxworth headquarters, and although he thought it, he said nothing about her needing to be back at the house in light of the newly declared truce. But he watched her walk toward where her car was parked fifty feet or so down the street. Watched the way she moved, watched that sweet backside and the long-legged stride.

And again that memory of those legs wrapped around him nearly swamped him. Sex with Erin had been like no other, not that he'd sampled much. Only a couple of times before they'd faced the fact that they were meant to be, and only once since she'd walked out on him. And if he was honest, he'd admit that last time had been as much to see if he could still function as anything else. Erin had treated him as if he were made of fragile glass after he'd been hurt, backing away from anything sexual. At least he'd thought it was because of his injuries, then. Now he knew better. She'd even then decided she was going to leave, and only stayed as long as she did because she'd felt she had to.

His gut was starting to churn again, as it had so many

times since he'd arrived here. He felt a nudge at his left knee and looked down to find Cutter staring up at him. Wondering if that soothing knack the dog had would work for this, too, he reached down to stroke the dark head.

It worked.

The calming ripple went through him, and he could feel himself settle. He shot a glance at Rafe, who shrugged.

"We call it the Cutter Effect. I can't explain it, but I've been glad of it many times," the tough veteran said with a crooked smile at both Blaine and Cutter. "But we'd better get going. She can't follow us if we're not moving."

On the short drive she kept a safe distance, but as they turned onto the side street a block away from the main road she was the only other vehicle moving. She slowly pulled into the long driveway after them. Rafe waved her past the gate, then to a spot beside them on the wider part of the drive.

Blaine got out, then turned to look at the older-model sedan as she maneuvered into the spot Rafe had indicated.

"That thing sounds like crap," he muttered.

"I noticed," Rafe said as he got out and opened the back for Cutter to exit. Then he walked toward the other car, motioning to Erin to roll down the window. Blaine couldn't hear what he said over the noise, but when she pulled in beside the Foxworth SUV, she left the car running. Rafe walked around and lifted the hood, and the clatter got louder. Blaine walked over to look himself.

"Fan belt," he said.

Rafe nodded. "Plugs, too. And it sounds like the timing's off." He pulled out from under the hood and looked at Erin, who was looking worried. "How long has it been sounding like this?"

"A couple of weeks, maybe a month."

"Okay. Probably hasn't built up too much carbon yet." He went back under the hood.

Blaine kept looking at Erin. "When did you have it serviced last?"

"I…it's been a while."

It wasn't like Erin to let things pass like that. He studied her for a moment. Then deciding that he couldn't make their relationship, such as it was, much worse, he went ahead. "Why?" When she didn't answer and looked away, he had the answer. "What'd you spend money on instead?"

Her gaze shot back to his face, and this time stayed. Sometimes he almost forgot just how sky blue her eyes were. He could almost see her reading his suspicions. Could she blame him? He already sent her as much as he could, and more often than not did without so she could have more, to see to their son. She shouldn't have—

"The new edition of Ethan's game. They're expensive." Her expression shifted then, to something less worried and more defensive. "Yes, I bought him the game that got him into this trouble. So it's all my fault. Happy now?"

"I'll be happy when he's home safe," he said, a little sharply.

He heard a faint sound and looked down to see Cutter had stepped in between them again. The dog was looking up, from one of them to the other, with those dark, knowing eyes.

"Rafe said he's sort of a peacekeeper, among a ton of other things," he said.

"And it seems we need one," she responded. "Or at least, I do."

Blaine was startled by how sad she sounded. Cutter seemed to hear it, too, because he moved to nudge at her hand with his nose. Automatically she moved her fingers to stroke his dark head, while Blaine watched her face, curious. There was no mistaking the change when it came. Her expression went from tension and sadness to, if not happiness, at least calmness. And then, as he looked, it changed to nothing short of amazement. And she turned her head to meet his gaze.

"Crazy, isn't it?" he asked.

She nodded, and looked back at the dog, shaking her head in wonder. It was a shared moment like those they'd always had before. A moment in the life he wished they could go back to.

Rafe dropped the car's hood, startling him out of the useless reverie. Blaine looked over just as he started toward them.

"I'll deal with the car later. Let's get to that video."

And that quickly Blaine was back in the present, dealing with a potentially disastrous situation that would blow up the present as thoroughly as Erin had blown up their past.

Chapter Seventeen

As offices went, this one was very nice, Erin thought. With its comfortable gathering spot around an adobe fireplace it had a homey, welcoming feel to it, as if all the people who worked here would get along. Like a family. If she'd ever had the chance to work in a place like this, she might never have bailed on the corporate world. She tried not to dwell on the fact that the only reason she'd been able to do that at all, able to pursue the one vocation she truly loved, had been Blaine.

She watched as Rafe went over to the nearest desk, sat and pulled out the computer keyboard that was in a tray beneath the desk surface. She didn't see an actual computer so assumed there was a central unit somewhere that powered all three of the workstations in the main room, and probably another in what looked like a more private office in the far corner, beyond what looked like a small meeting room with a large table and several chairs.

She walked over to watch, taking care to keep space between her and Blaine. The screen in front of the Foxworth man lit up. In the same moment she heard a faint musical chime that, she gathered from the way he reached for the phone in his pocket, signaled a call or a text. He started to put the phone face down on the desk, clearly intending to silence it. He glanced at the screen in the same motion, and suddenly stopped.

Erin watched his expression change, from all business to something different. Not softer, she doubted that word could ever be used about this man, but gentler. Even tender.

"I...have to take this," he said, almost awkwardly, as if he were completely unused to having anything take priority over work.

And she knew who was on the other end of that call. The woman he'd put it back together with. The woman he'd been estranged from for years.

The woman he loved enough to put that look on his rugged face.

When Rafe got up and walked across the room for some privacy, she didn't dare look at Blaine, for fear everything she was thinking and feeling would show in her face. This was hardly the time to ask him if he thought they could ever do the same, put the pieces back together. Besides, why would he ever want to?

For a moment all she could do was stare at the screen showing what was apparently the Foxworth logo, simply the name in a stylized font. She would have given them something different.

"Erin?"

Blaine's voice was quiet, but still made her pulse leap. But then, it always did. She realized she'd been standing there probably looking blank, so she went with the first thing that came to mind.

"I was just thinking I'd design them a different logo. Something with more...feeling. They should have that, if they always jump in to help people like this."

"I think they do," Blaine said. He glanced over at Rafe. "And Rafe's a different guy because of it."

And because the breach between him and the woman he loves is healed.

She didn't say it, but she wanted to. She hated thinking of Blaine with everything in past tense. And hated herself for causing it, even though at the time it was the only path she could see.

Rafe was heading back toward them now, sliding the phone back in his pocket as he came, and a slight smile that warmed even though she barely knew the man. But now that she thought about it, the simple fact that he was here, and had called in his employer to help, told her all she needed to know.

"Your lady?" she asked when he reached them.

The smile widened. "Yes." Then, with a glance at Blaine before meeting her gaze again, he added, "Thankfully."

"I'm happy for you."

"It wasn't easy. But it was worth it."

She wasn't sure if that was aimed at her and Blaine, but it felt like it. He didn't wait for a response, but sat back down at the desk. With a few clicks and keystrokes there was a program open, and a message alert flashing. He gestured to them both to pull up chairs within camera range, then clicked on the alert. A video window opened, showing a young man with a stubbled chin and rather spiky hair almost the same color as her own, and a smear of what looked like tomato sauce at the corner of his mouth.

"Sorry," he said, "pizza. I was in the middle of dinner when your call came in."

"You didn't have to drop *everything*," Rafe drawled.

"Are you kidding? You asking, for personal reasons? Everything gets dropped." The guy grinned then. "Besides, I wouldn't want Charlie mad at me. She's one tough cookie."

Rafe chuckled. "Can't argue with you there."

"I hear she doesn't get mad all that much anymore, though."

It was a moment before Rafe said quietly to the man on the screen, "I hope not."

"Y'know, I kind of miss her. Not her hanging over my shoulder, mind you, but sometimes she made those mind leaps..."

"I'm well aware," Rafe said, smiling now. Then he indicated both her and Blaine with a gesture. "Ty Hewitt, meet Erin and Blaine Everett."

Erin saw the last name, Blaine's name, register with the young man. "Blaine Everett? The pilot who—"

"Pulled me out of hell, yes," Rafe said.

Ty's gaze shifted to Blaine. "Then we owe you great thanks, Mr. Everett. Foxworth wouldn't be what it is without Rafe."

Erin couldn't not notice that both Blaine and Rafe looked uncomfortable with the praise. She knew Blaine was proud of his service, and rightfully so, but after what he'd been through, she wasn't sure all the thanks in the world would be enough. For her, anyway.

"Now," Ty said, "let me send you that video. The file's kind of big, so this'll take a while. It wasn't the greatest quality, kind of pixelated, but I got it smoothed out a bit and I think they're recognizable now."

She saw a circular gauge in the corner of the screen gradually filling as the file downloaded.

"Any questions or anything else I can do, just holler. I'm here," Ty said.

"Finish your pizza," Rafe said.

Ty laughed, and then that window vanished. The gauge continued to slowly fill. Erin felt tension building anew inside her as they waited. She grasped at the first thing she could think of for distraction.

"That photo over there," she said to Rafe, "with the two men shaking hands. Is that… Gavin de Marco?"

"It is," Rafe confirmed the identity of the world-famous lawyer who had dropped out of sight. "He works out of our northwest headquarters."

"With you?" Blaine asked, and by his tone she was guessing he, too, had heard of the man.

Rafe nodded, then gestured toward the photograph on the wall. "The other guy is Marcus Rockwell."

"The attorney your guy's wife works for?" Blaine asked.

"Yes. He wasn't real sure about Amy getting tangled up with us, so Gavin flew down here to reassure him."

Erin blinked. "He came all the way here just for that?"

Rafe leaned back in his chair and gave her a steady look. "Welcome to Foxworth."

"No wonder you sound happier now than you ever did in uniform," Blaine said.

"Let's just say the guidance at the command level of Foxworth sees a lot clearer."

Blaine's mouth quirked in that wry way of his. "Not," he said, "that that would take a lot these days."

"Truer words," Rafe murmured, but he was turning back to the screen now, and she saw the file had finished downloading. He hovered the mouse over the file name, then looked at both of them. "You ready for this? You might not like what you see."

"If it's Ethan and he's alive, I'll deal with the rest."

Blaine's head turned rather sharply, and she could almost feel the look he gave her before he went back to looking at the screen. And belatedly it hit her that if she'd been that certain a couple of years or so ago, this man she'd never stopped loving would still be her husband.

And Ethan would still have a loving, full-time father, and they probably would never have ended up sitting here like this, waiting to see just how much trouble their boy was in.

Chapter Eighteen

It didn't matter that he hadn't seen Ethan in three months, he recognized him instantly. And even if he hadn't, Erin's quick, audible intake of breath would have told him. There was no audio on the recording, but he didn't need that, either. This was his son.

"He's looking a little skinny," he said.

"That's more because he's grown three inches in the last few months. He's only a couple of inches shorter than me, now," Erin said.

He knew she didn't mean it that way but it hit him like a punch to the gut. She shouldn't have had to tell him that, he should have known. He should have been here to watch it happen.

His jaw tightened. He should have pushed harder for a relocation. A desk is a desk is a desk wherever it was, and as long as they would only let him instruct and push paper, what did it matter? True, being where there was an airfield mattered, because at least they let him teach the basics of flight school, and he got to get in the air—although it wasn't at all the same without the pulse-hammering addition of combat—but there were several places that fit the bill on this side of the country.

Hell, he could be stationed at Pendleton, barely ten miles away from this place, or from Erin's house, once you got on the freeway.

He'd asked about it, way back, but they'd said no for whatever reason they had that they didn't care to divulge. And once his initial desperation had faded a little, he'd realized he might be better off a little further away, if only because Erin had made it so coldly clear that casual, unplanned drop-in visits would not be welcomed.

And judging by the tension that crackled every moment he was around her, that hadn't changed.

"Smooth," Rafe muttered, yanking Blaine out of his thoughts.

"What?"

Rafe reached out and backed the video up about thirty seconds. He watched closely this time, and saw that one of the other boys who had come in with Ethan had engaged the man behind the counter in a rather animated conversation. The second one stood looking at a nearby aquarium that apparently housed a reptile of some persuasion, drawing an occasional glance from the owner.

And while that had all been happening, Ethan had walked to the end of the main aisle and grabbed something off the shelf, stuffing it inside his jacket and quickly zipping it closed.

"So the first two were in charge of distraction, and Ethan handled the stealing," Blaine said.

"How can you say it like that, so calmly?" Erin burst out.

"I believe he was admiring the tactics," Rafe said. "As was I."

She looked at both of them, appearing utterly nonplussed. "Tactics," she muttered. "Sometimes I just don't understand you. Either of you. I guess I just don't understand men."

"Back at you," Blaine said, a little sharply.

"A little focus, please?"

Rafe's words snapped their attention back where it belonged. "Sorry," they both said, quietly and simultaneously.

"Having recently been there myself, I can say with certainty, it'll keep," Rafe said dryly.

Blaine speculated for a moment about what all Rafe and his lady—Charlie, Ty had called her—had had to work through. But only for a moment.

"I wonder what he took," he said.

"Wondered that myself," Rafe said, picking up his phone.

Oddly, both he and Erin turned away from the screen at the same moment, as if neither of them wanted to stare at that image a moment longer.

"Let's go sit down, and work out what's next," he suggested.

She didn't speak, but she did start toward the big, curved couch that faced the fireplace, where, he belatedly realized, a gas fire had come on by itself, obviously tied to a thermostat. She sat in the section nearest the fire, as if she were chilled. He took a seat a safe distance away, thinking vaguely that he didn't link California with ever being chilly, even in winter.

"At least it wasn't the poor hamster," Erin said. "Ethan would take care of it, but those other two looked like they'd just torture it or stomp it and toss it in the trash."

Blaine stopped himself from asking why, if she was so sure he'd take care of it, she'd never let him get a pet once they were settled, without a re-stationing in the future. It would do no good to open that subject again. And he wondered if he'd ever really understood her at all, this woman he loved.

Or maybe the woman he'd loved had never really existed

at all. Maybe he'd made some assumptions, just because of their long history together. Maybe he'd never seen the real her.

But the woman he was seeing now was the same woman who'd been an absolute rock through the worst time of his life.

That wife of yours is something else, Captain Everett. If everybody had someone like her in their corner, we'd clear out this place a lot faster.

The words of the rehab therapist who'd finally signed him off as ready to go echoed in his head. He knew it was true, once he'd felt recovered enough to take in the way she handled things.

He remembered the time they'd tried to wheel him out of his room for some kind of medical test, and he'd watched in more than a little awe as his five-foot-six wife stood down a six-foot-two orderly until he called in the doctor who'd ordered the test. Then she chewed out the doctor, regardless of his rank, with that phrase that had almost become her trademark, that the right hand needed to talk to the left hand around here because he'd just had that test yesterday, ordered by a different doctor.

For the first time it struck him that perhaps that had been her battle. He'd heard guys talking about great heroes who had fought one big, crucial, turning-point battle and then retired from the field forever. They'd only had that one battle in them, but it had been a battle that had to be won and they'd won it.

Maybe he'd simply drained all the fight out of her.

Not the temper, though. She'd still take your head off if you tick her off enough.

"Are you going to say it, or just sit there staring at me like you've never seen me before?"

He blinked. She was glaring at him. "Say what?" he asked cautiously.

"Whatever you're thinking."

"I was just...remembering."

"Remembering what?"

"That day you faced down Captain Francis. He ran the whole place, but you were so fierce you scared the guy."

Her expression changed, the glare vanishing, replaced by a soft, warm look. "You were already going through so much, making you have the same test twice when there was no reason, it wasn't to monitor anything for changes, was just...stupid."

"I'll never forget when you told him no matter who got their wires crossed the buck stopped with him."

She grimaced. "You mean when he laughed at me?"

She'd thought that? "He wasn't laughing at you. That was approval, not judgment."

She was staring at him now, shock clear in her face. "How could you know that?"

"Because he told me. Told me how lucky I was to have a wife who had no fear of staring down the officer in charge if it would help me."

Her eyes widened. "But I was afraid."

"And you did it anyway," he said softly. "Honey, what do you think bravery is?"

She stared at him wide-eyed for a moment before she said, "Bravery is what you did, all the pain you went through and never giving up."

"I never gave up because I couldn't, not when you were still there, fighting for me every step of the way. Literally and figuratively."

"Funny thing about bravery," came Rafe's voice from

behind them. "It comes in all kinds of forms, and they feed off each other."

He was a little embarrassed that the rugged sniper had clearly overheard at least part of the personal discussion, but after a moment, remembering what the man had been through, putting his own personal life back together, he decided maybe he could learn something from that. He'd have to have a talk with the man. After this was over and Ethan was home safe.

As Rafe joined them in the sitting area, Blaine refused to consider any other possible outcome for this. Ethan would come home, and he would be safe and unhurt when he did.

The rest was merely cleanup.

Chapter Nineteen

Honey. He'd called her honey.

The word opened up a flood of memories, all tangled up with that word. For a moment she could barely breathe.

"—whole bag of it."

She was startled back into the present. "Mouse and rat food?" Erin asked. "That's what he took?"

Rafe nodded.

"Maybe he got that pet he always wanted," Blaine muttered.

She winced inwardly, although he didn't seem to be aiming that at her. That didn't stop her from feeling guilty. She'd worked so hard, tried so hard, to provide a stable home life for Ethan, one where he didn't have to pack up and move all the time. But what he'd really wanted was…a pet? A creature to be responsible for, that he'd have to feed and take care of and who might not like the constant moving any more than she did? An animal who would always need attention, care and feeding—

She felt a nudge, realized Rafe's dog had moved, and was now right next to her. He'd done it so quietly she hadn't even realized it. The moment their eyes made contact the dark head came to rest on her knee. The animal kept looking up at her with those gold-flecked eyes. Because it seemed like the thing to do, she reached out to touch the dark fur. And there it was again, that soothing warmth, as if somehow the dog had the knack of infusing calm, comfort.

A thought struck her suddenly and she went very still.

"What?" Blaine asked, observant as always.

"I just…had a thought."

"About what?"

"That…maybe I was looking at the whole pet thing all wrong. I was looking at it as another responsibility, another weight to carry."

"Like an adult, not a kid." Blaine's voice was quiet, almost understanding.

She stared down at her fingers, still stroking that soft, black fur. It was as if the dog had brought the idea with him, and had somehow given it to her. That was silly, but she couldn't deny the notion made sense.

"I never really thought about it from Ethan's point of view. That maybe…maybe he just wanted a companion he wouldn't lose every time we had to move."

"Like he lost whatever friends he made on base or at school?"

She nodded, and finally met his gaze. "God, I feel so awful. Why didn't I realize—"

"Because it was as hard on you as it was on him," Blaine said. "Don't think I don't know that."

For a moment she just stared at him, looking into those deep blue eyes, so much darker than her own. A silly memory struck her, of the day they'd joked that Ethan's medium blue was what happened when you mixed their two colors together.

She nearly jumped when Rafe stood up suddenly. He held out a hand toward her. "Give me your car keys," he said.

For a moment she just stared at him, wondering how one man could look so intimidating and yet be as kind as he'd been to her. Somehow she trusted him, and pulled the keys out of her pocket and held them out to him.

"Here's the deal," he said briskly as he took the keys, with a slight snap in his voice now. "We've done all we can until I get some answers on those last calls I made."

"I should go home, then," she said. "Be there just in case, like you said."

"Yes. But not this instant. I'm going to do a little work on your car, and the tools are here."

Erin blinked. "What?" She hadn't realized he'd meant he would personally deal with her overdue vehicle service.

"I'll see what we've got in the garage here, but I'll probably have to pick up some parts. While I do that, you two are going to sit here, on neutral ground, and talk."

She stared at the man, because there was no doubt that that had been an order. "I don't think—"

"This isn't the time to overthink it." Rafe shifted his gaze to Blaine. "Either of you. Just talk it out until you can work together. For Ethan's sake."

He turned as if to go. As if assuming they would of course follow orders. She wondered if anyone had ever dared not to, when given by this man. And she was suddenly very curious about the woman who had the backbone to stand up to him.

But then he turned back slightly. "Cutter?" The dog's head came up. "Peacekeeper," he said, in that same tone, that of command.

The dog let out a little yip of acknowledgement.

And then Rafe was gone, and she and Blaine just sat staring at each other.

"He can really order him to…do that," she said.

Blaine nodded. "Rafe told me he—" he reached out to scratch behind the dog's ear "—has done this job before."

"I'm sorry he has to do it for us." She looked down into the gold-flecked dark eyes, remembered the feeling of soothing warmth that seemed to emanate from the animal whenever she touched him.

Silence spun out between them for a long moment. Then Blaine grimaced and stood up. "It just feels wrong."

"Sitting here doing nothing while Ethan's out here, somewhere?"

He turned to look at her. "Yes."

"Yes, it does," she agreed. "That's why I had to leave, even if it was just to walk around. But I did do a little research, when I was going crazy just sitting at home. Foxworth is quite an operation."

"Seems like it."

"They don't promote themselves much, but if you check out the places online where they're mentioned, when you read the statements and comments and posts from people they've helped, they're so heartfelt and the people are so grateful for whatever they did. I saw it over and over and over. It's staggering. They all said that if you're in the right and can't get help anywhere else, they'll help. And that no case is too small, if Foxworth believes in it."

"Rafe told me one of Quinn's—Quinn Foxworth, who started the foundation with his sister—first cases was finding and returning a stolen locket. It was a little girl's only memento of her dead mother."

Erin stared at him, amazed at what he'd said. "That's… wow."

"Better yet, the guy who stole it got his head straight and now works for Foxworth, helping other ex-cons who want to go straight."

"Wow," she said again, and now she could feel her eyes stinging, and a tightness in her chest. "It's…wonderful to know that there are still people out there who care that much."

"Yeah." Blaine flicked a glance toward the outside. Her car had fired up again, making what sounded like even more noise than before, but it shut down after a moment and he went on. "And now they're on our side, Erin. The people who have done that small thing to taking down a sitting governor are on our side."

"Thanks to you," she said softly.

He half shrugged. "Thanks to me being in the right place at the right time and having a bird to fly."

She studied him for a moment. "You never were comfortable with the hero hat, even when you'd earned it."

The look he gave her then was so startled it startled her. What, did he think she'd forgotten what he'd done, how he'd served, the lives he'd protected and saved? She sighed.

"Just because I'm not hero material doesn't mean I don't recognize it when I see it," she said. "Like in you two," she added with a nod toward the door, which had opened again, just enough for Rafe to lean in.

"I'm going to pick up some parts. If Ty pops up again—" he gestured at the computer screen where they'd watched the video "—go ahead and answer him. I should be back in fifteen or less."

Before she could even ask about how much this was going to cost, the man was gone.

"I can't afford a big repair bill," she said, hating how anxious she sounded.

"We'll work it out," Blaine said.

So, what, he was going to pay for this, too? He already gave so much that she wondered what he lived on himself.

She couldn't even look at him, her emotions were so tangled up. She buried her face in her hands.

She didn't know how much time had passed before she heard Blaine say, very quietly, "You were wrong, you know."

She nearly laughed out loud. She'd been wrong about so much. "You're going to have to narrow that down a bit."

"You were as much a hero as I ever was."

She jerked her head up sharply. "What?"

"Don't belittle what you went through. I don't, because I know that if you hadn't been there, fighting for me, I would probably have given up."

"I doubt that," she said, but she couldn't deny the words pleased her. She'd wanted to be there for him, the way he'd always been for her, and Ethan.

It was the nights between the long days of pushing and trying that nearly did her in. Because every night she dreamed of them getting past this, of him getting back on his feet, and then…it happened again. And again. Endlessly, in her nightmares, he would heal, then get broken. Heal, get broken. Every night.

He hesitated, then added, "I know what you told everyone. That nobody was supposed to tell me how bad it was, just how many bones I'd broken, or that my left arm might never work right again. Dr. Hadley told me, right before he released me from rehab."

"I just didn't want you to think any damage or limitation was permanent, before you had to."

"And because of that, because of the way you never let me hear what the staff, what the medics were saying, never let anyone tell me, I had no idea that I couldn't be doing what I was doing."

"I didn't want to hear it, either," she said honestly.

He smiled. "Because you did that, because I never knew how bad the prognostications were, I never lost hope. I just thought it was taking so long and hurting so much because I'd been so busted up, not because I was never going to get on my feet again."

"And so you did," she said softly.

If she was proud of anything she'd done in that long, hard battle they'd fought it was that. She believed in the power of the mind to convince the body to heal itself, and it had worked.

Too bad she hadn't been able to power her mind into preparing to go through it all again someday.

Chapter Twenty

"How can you be so calm?" Erin knew how the words sounded, so she quickly added, "I don't mean that as a jab, I just want to know how you do it. Because I'm a wreck, knowing there's nothing we can do but wait."

Which they had been doing, for a couple of hours now. Restlessly, on her part. Blaine was still where he'd been on the couch, so outwardly calm it had made her ask.

"Years of practice. Waiting for a mission. Waiting for a team to return. Waiting to hear if an operation was successful."

She stopped her pacing to look at him. "I…never thought about it like that. I always worried about the time you were active, under fire. Not the downtime in between."

"The worst was waiting to find out if your buddy or co-pilot had been found dead. Or injured. Then it became waiting to see if he was going to live."

She shook her head slowly. She'd never been able to wrap her mind around that part of what he did, and so tended to shy away from just the idea. But now she asked, "How do you deal with that?"

"You find a distraction. For me it was reading. For some guys it was drinking. For some it was working out, or run-

ning a ten-mile circuit around the base. Others found something else to work on."

She turned to look out the window where another man
with that kind of experience had his head under the hood
of her car.

"Which is why I have a trophy-winning sniper working
on my car?"

"Exactly."

She walked back over to the couch and sat. She felt a
sense of awkwardness she'd never felt around Blaine before. She'd been angry with him, worried about him, and
above all she'd loved him with her whole being, but she'd
never felt awkward. She never had to, because he always
seemed to understand when something was gnawing at her.
And usually, after some effort, had her laughing about it
eventually. She missed that. More than she ever could have
guessed she would.

She wondered if he ever missed that, too. Missed them.
She wasn't sure she wanted to hear the answer to that, so instead went with something she already knew the answer to.

"Do you really miss flying?"

He studied her for a moment, in that way she'd just been
thinking about. Then with a half shrug, he said, "Flying
itself, no. Because I still do it."

A chill rocketed through her. She stared at him, feeling
a rush of that old, horrible sensation. She'd thought it was
over, that time of worrying about him. It was a moment
before she could even speak.

"You're still flying?"

"I just don't get shot at anymore." At her no doubt
stunned expression he added, "I'm teaching now. The new
kids, coming up."

She swallowed, almost engulfed by a flood of relief that

at least he wasn't in combat any longer. She grabbed for the first thing she could find words for. "You say that like you don't like it."

Another shrug. "I kind of miss the high, the adrenaline rush when you're under fire. It's different, when you're not in a combat situation."

"Thank God," she murmured under her breath. "How could you possibly want to go back to…that? Being shot at, people trying to kill you?"

For a long moment he just looked at her, with that thoughtful Blaine look she knew so well. When he finally spoke, what he asked seemed a total non sequitur to her.

"You want to go back to the accounting firm?"

She blinked. "What?"

"You know, go back to the steady, known paycheck, the income that doesn't rely on your talent, your artistic eye, and whether you can convince a customer you're the best one for the job."

"No, of course not, but what does that—"

She cut herself off as she realized the analogy he was making.

"You want to do the work your heart's in," he said quietly. "And it took a lot of nerve to make the break to do it."

She couldn't deny that, although she was a little surprised he realized it. Which she shouldn't have been. Apparently she had forgotten just how on the nose he could be when he put his mind to it.

"It's not that much different," he said.

"Except for the getting shot at part," she couldn't help pointing out.

"Point ceded," he agreed. "But I always was more of an adrenaline junkie than you."

"I got that the time you jumped off the garage roof onto that trampoline," she said dryly.

"Hey, I was seven," he said, suddenly grinning. It nearly took her breath away. As did the fact that they were actually managing to talk without sniping at each other.

But she couldn't deny he'd made her think. Hard. She'd never put what he did in that context before. And if she set aside the risking your life part—which was a darned big ask—she could see the similarities. She could have stayed with that accounting firm, endlessly, and it would have been steady work that she didn't hate.

But she didn't love it. Not the way she loved what she did now, not the way she loved letting her imagination—the same imagination that manufactured horrible ideas of what could happen to him—flow and come up with the perfect images for her clients, from logos to ad campaigns. Not the way she loved looking at what she'd built, from a small thing she did in her spare time to full time work she could live on, albeit it required some penny-pinching.

And more help from Blaine than he was legally required to give. Because he loved Ethan, just as much as she did.

She should have made it easier for him to see more of their son. Or at least not have made it more difficult by insisting on not being there. She should have done a lot of things differently.

And then there was the big one she maybe shouldn't have done at all.

"I've been the worst sort of ex, haven't I?" she said quietly, hating that two letter descriptor of what she was now.

"No. I've seen worse. One of the guys in my unit doesn't even know where his daughter is. Her mother vanished with her, cut him off completely."

That made her stomach churn, but she was still amazed that he was giving her any credit at all.

She heard a car start up outside. She turned her head to look, expecting to see the Foxworth vehicle pulling out. "Do you suppose he has to go get even more parts? I can't do that, Blaine, I can't—"

She stopped when he laughed. Her head snapped back around. "That's your car, not his. I'd say he got the job done."

Erin looked out the window again, staring now. She hadn't heard her car sound like that in…she didn't know how long. Smooth. Powerful. No clanks, no pops, no misses.

She watched as Rafe closed the hood, then stood as if listening just as she was. Then he nodded in obvious—and well-earned—satisfaction.

"Do you know what happened? With him and his girl-friend?"

"All I know is he blamed himself for something bad happening, overseas. While he was deployed. Something that wasn't really his fault, but he didn't—maybe couldn't—see it that way."

"Something to do with her?"

"No. Something that made him feel he didn't deserve her."

She let out a weary sigh. "Sometimes nobody's harder on us than ourselves."

"I don't know," Blaine said, his tone a little too casual as he stood up. "Sometimes the ones we love can sure as hell do a number on us."

He was out the front door and headed toward Rafe before she could react to the bull's-eye he'd just struck.

She guessed the truce was over.

She felt her eyes begin to sting. Remembered all the tears she'd shed, from the time she'd gotten word that Blaine had been hurt, throughout his long, hard recovery, until the day she'd made that fateful decision. The decision that had ended her life as she'd known it, and tossed her into the chaos of single parenthood. And the furious, understandable emotions of her son.

That had stopped the tears, for a while. She hadn't had the time or the energy.

But nothing had ever stopped the pain. That she'd been the one to walk away didn't make it any easier to bear. In many ways, it made it harder. Especially in one of those shouting matches with Ethan. She knew how selfish she seemed, given it was Blaine who had gone through the agony, Blaine who had fought so hard to get back on his feet, Blaine who had never given up, and never would.

And in that moment she understood exactly how Rafe Crawford must have felt. Because she didn't deserve Blaine.

And he deserved better than her.

Chapter Twenty-One

"Just listening," Rafe said as Blaine came up beside him. "Making sure I didn't miss anything."

"I doubt you did," Blaine said. "That thing sounded like a berserk sledgehammer before."

"A quick test drive and she'll be mobile again." Rafe glanced toward the house. "You two okay?"

"We had a fairly civil conversation, if that's what you mean."

"Good start." He walked over to the driver's door. "Thought I'd go throw some gas into it. It's pretty low."

"She's worried about paying for all this," Blaine said frankly, "so let me give you—"

Rafe cut him off with a shake of his head. "You're Foxworth clients now."

"But that can't include vehicle maintenance. Not to mention the price of gas here."

The former sniper smiled. "It can if the Foxworth agent in charge says so. And right now that's me."

Blaine studied him for a long, silent moment before saying, "Man, no wonder you like this job."

"I do," Rafe agreed. "It's the best thing—"

He stopped as the door opened behind them. Erin stepped

outside. Blaine braced himself. He didn't really regret that parting shot, since it was pure truth, but he didn't expect to walk away unscathed. Although as he watched her come toward them, she did not look like someone looking for payback. In fact, she looked like someone barely hanging on. And that got his gut churning.

Just as she reached them Rafe's phone rang. He looked at it, and answered so quickly Blaine figured it had to be his lady or his boss. Boss, he decided, when Rafe explained to the caller about what the pet store video had shown them, that as of yesterday Ethan was still okay and still local.

If it had been the brave lady he would have walked away to give the guy some privacy. *Or to avoid hearing him talking to the woman he loved, and who still loved him despite whatever it was that had pulled them apart?*

Rafe was listening now. Then he said, sounding a little surprised, "He doesn't have to—" He stopped, and for a moment closed his eyes. Then, quietly, in a tone of utter respect Blaine doubted he gave many, he said, "Yes, sir… thank you."

The call ended and Rafe looked at them. "Let's go inside. We have a couple of things to talk about."

He leaned in and shut off the car, then handed Erin back her keys. "It sounds…new," she said.

"Should run better. I wasted some gas doing it, so we'll top it off later," Rafe said as he headed for the office door. The guy had learned some tact along the way, and he wondered if the lady had managed that.

Maybe she could teach me.

He smothered a sigh as he followed Erin back inside. Rafe walked over to the workstation they'd been using, hit a few keys, but then came back and indicated they should go back to the couch, specifically together, in front of the flat-screen on the wall.

Erin gave him a sideways look, but sat. And feeling he had no other choice, he sat down beside her. Only when he looked up did Blaine realize the flat-screen on the wall had come to life.

"Call coming in in a few," Rafe explained.

Then he sat down to one side and looked at them both. In the manner of someone giving a briefing, he said, "Quinn's going to fly Walker back to help. He's been here long enough now that he's got some more local contacts. Plus he's got some special experience that might help."

"Special experience at…?" Erin asked.

Rafe shifted his gaze to her. "Do you remember that big terrorist sleeper cell the Feds took down a while back? The ones behind those bombings at local arenas in Chicago and Philadelphia?"

"Yes." Blaine saw she looked horrified, no doubt wondering what that had to do with Ethan. As he was.

Rafe continued. "Remember the civilian they credited with getting all the intel necessary, and saving thousands of lives? The one who just happened onto them, but risked his life and practically lived undercover with them for five years to help take them down?"

"Yes," she said. "I do. I remember thinking how incredibly brave he was."

"That guy," Rafe said with more than a touch of wonder himself, "was Walker Cole. My boss's brother-in-law, his wife Hayley's brother."

Blaine stared at him. "The Walker you said runs this office?"

Rafe nodded. "And apparently he's adapted that undercover experience to where he's got some connections with the local gangs that have been occasionally...helpful."

Blaine let out a low whistle. This had to be what Rafe had been so...awed by, when he'd been on the phone with his boss. He himself was a bit awed, that his boss would have somebody drop everything to come back and help a guy he'd never even met. "And he's coming back here?"

Rafe nodded again. "Should be here by late this evening. Jace—" He stopped and explained to Erin that this was one of the local Foxworth guys, then went on. "Jace is going to stay there to finish the location search, and Quinn has to head back home, but he'll drop Walker off on his way, and I'll go pick him up. That way I can read him in on the way back."

"This Walker...he's really coming back here to help look for Ethan?" Erin sounded a little stunned.

Rafe looked at her again. "You're a Foxworth client now. You've got the full power of the Foxworth Foundation behind you."

A sound came from the workstation where the video call from St. Louis had come in.

"Speaking of power," Rafe said, his mouth quirking slightly. He leaned forward and pulled open a drawer beneath the coffee table in front of them. He grabbed a remote control from inside and aimed it at the flat-screen. It came alive, an image immediately appearing on the screen.

Blaine wasn't one who followed such things as famous lawyers, and the man on the screen didn't look quite like he had in the days when the media had so adored him for his gorgeous looks, dramatic presence and his brilliance in the courtroom. But Blaine still immediately recognized the world-famous Gavin de Marco, if only because he'd recently seen that photograph on the wall here.

The man was less…polished now, his hair a bit longer, a little stubble on his jaw. And there was no sign of the custom-tailored suits that had made him look as expensive as he no doubt was. Instead he had on what looked like a long-sleeved Henley-style shirt, as dark as his eyes appeared on the screen.

He also looked a lot less wound up than he had, back in the days not so very long ago. Just as Rafe did. And Blaine couldn't help wondering if going to work for the Foxworth Foundation had the same effect on everyone. If it did, he envied them all.

Rafe performed quick introductions. Blaine felt a little edgy when the legendary attorney fastened his gaze on him. "I understand we have you to thank for Rafe's life."

Feeling a bit awkward as he always did, but even more so now that he had called in that debt, Blaine said simply, as he usually did, "Right place, right time."

"And the right man," de Marco said. Then he shifted his gaze to Erin. "You've got the best on your side now. They'll find your boy. I'm just here to talk to you about what happens then. What might arise if there are any legal ramifications."

"You mean if he's broken any laws?" Erin asked. "He's already—"

She stopped abruptly as Blaine tensed. Should they not tell the man that they already knew he'd stolen at least one thing?

"Anything you tell me," de Marco said, clearly not having missed a thing, "is subject to attorney-client privilege."

"I don't care if he's in legal trouble, as long as he's home safe," Erin said flatly.

Blaine nodded in agreement. Inwardly, he was recovering from the little shock that had gone through him when

Erin had instantly sensed his concern and stopped midsentence. It had been like the old days, when they'd been so in tune people joked that they could read each other's minds.

So they told the man everything they could think of, and answered all the questions he asked. Blaine figured the guy was probably pretty adept at hearing what they didn't say as well. You didn't reach the heights Gavin de Marco had without being able to read people.

The man on the screen nodded. "All right. I've already spoken to Marcus Rockwell, and he's agreed to help. He served in the Navy himself, and does a lot of work with active and former service members, so he gets it. And if it comes to proceedings, I'll be there."

"That oughta do it," Rafe said, giving the man on the screen a rather crooked smile.

"Might as well use all that fame for something good," de Marco said.

"As you often have," Rafe agreed.

"Thanks to Foxworth." There was such satisfaction in his voice Blaine felt that tug of envy again. "Keep in touch. Oh, and Rafe?" de Marco said with a grin, "Charlie wants to know if you'd mind a red house."

Blaine saw Rafe pull back slightly, and saw a look that was probably as close to fear as the man ever got. After a moment he grimaced and said, "I'm guessing 'I don't care' isn't the right answer here."

"Good call," de Marco said. "I'd say 'Depends on the inside,' would be better."

"Thanks," Rafe muttered. De Marco was laughing as the image on the screen clicked off. Rafe glanced over at them. "Time was he could have charged a grand for that one sentence of advice."

"Given the two options, I'd say it would be worth it," Erin

said, and Blaine was glad to see she was smiling. "That is, assuming Charlie is your lady."

"Yeah," he said, and that half smile was back. Then, with a clearly self-directed eye roll he added, "The financial brains behind the whole foundation. Charlaine Foxworth."

They both drew back in unison. Blaine figured he was gaping, because the last name hadn't come up before.

"Foxworth?" Erin asked.

"The boss's sister."

"Well, that must keep things interesting," Blaine said, smothering a laugh.

"You don't know the half of it," Rafe replied, but he said it with the look of a man totally in love. A look Blaine had once worn.

A look he wished he could have back.

Chapter Twenty-Two

"You went from second looey to captain faster than anybody I know."

Erin heard Rafe's voice from the living room. They'd come back to the house and—after she'd finished marveling at the difference in her car—she'd hastened to check for any messages. There had been a few, but none with news, only friends checking on her, or asking for news.

Then she heard Blaine's reply to Rafe's comment. "Eyes on the prize."

She suppressed a little shudder. How could flying into a combat zone, getting shot at, be the prize?

I don't understand. How can being sent into some big battle, where you could get killed, be rewarding?

It's the walking away afterward. Especially if you won.

That long-ago exchange with Blaine, one of the ones that had convinced her she would never understand that part, ran through her mind for the first time in a long time. But on the heels of that had come his whispered follow-up.

I do it so you, and others like you, don't have to. So you can live a good life, in peace.

That was when she'd realized that this was just who he was, that he'd always risk himself for those he loved, and that in his mind that was what serving in the Marines was.

That night had ended up with them in bed, and her riding him fiercely, showing him in every hot, physical way she could what those words had meant to her.

That had been the night she had at last comprehended she had married a hero. She just hadn't understood yet how high the price for that was.

Now she realized she'd tuned into her thoughts instead of the present—something that happened far too often, something she feared may have been part of the reason Ethan had run—because Blaine was standing now, Cutter at his feet, and staring at the well-used tennis ball in his hand.

"C'mon, dawg," he drawled, "let's go wear you out a little."

"Thanks," Rafe said. "He's a little restless today."

"I know the feeling," she muttered as Blaine and the dog stepped out into the backyard. She was glad she'd kept a long open space between her flower beds, so the dog at least had room to run.

"I know it probably feels like we're not doing much," Rafe said as he took a seat on one of the barstools pulled up to the kitchen counter.

She turned to look at the man who was only here because Blaine had asked for his help. But she couldn't deny what he'd said was true.

"It's just…"

"I get it. So much of what we do in cases like this these days is internet-related. But I understand the feeling that it doesn't count if you're not out there physically looking."

"Only because my son is out there somewhere, getting involved in who knows what, already stealing, and… I'm sorry, I'm just getting more frantic the more time passes."

"Of course you are. But this way we can search so much more area so much faster. Which Ty is doing as we speak. He developed our own recognition software, and that goes beyond facial to body type and way of moving, too. He's looking for any other matches in videos we can access—which is more than you might think. The Foxworth name opens a lot of doors."

She found herself relaxing a little. "You've already found out more than I did, or the sheriff. Are all of you this good at this?"

The still rather intimidating man laughed. "If there's a low man on the tech tier at Foxworth Northwest, it's me. I've gotten better, because I've had to, but believe me, my first instinct is the same as yours, to get out there and physically look."

She smiled, rather wanly she was afraid. "You'd think I'd be okay with it, given almost all my work is done on a computer."

"This is different. This is your son, not a customer or some tech problem."

"And having Blaine here—" She cut herself off before she could say something truly stupid. Then, with a long sigh, she said, "He's done nothing but try to take care of Ethan, over and above what the court declared as mandatory support. He sends us so much sometimes I wonder what he's living on."

"It's cheaper to live on base, in many places."

"So he does. And if we need something, he does what he can to see that we get it." She gestured around the room. "The only reason I was able to afford this place at first was because he pays for almost everything else."

"He's a good man," Rafe said, his tone a little too carefully neutral.

"I know," she said, her throat tightening and making it hard to get the words out. "He's done nothing but try to see to Ethan, and to me. Which is why I hate, truly hate the way I get mad at him. He doesn't deserve that."

A long and—for her at least—painful silence spun out. When she finally looked at the man across the kitchen counter from her, she saw him swallow as if his own throat was tight. Then, very quietly, he said, "Maybe…maybe you're not mad at him, or not solely. Maybe you're mad at yourself."

She blinked, drew back. "What?"

He grimaced. "Voice of experience here. Charlie and I butted heads constantly for years. We…hated each other. Were constantly mad at each other. Or so we thought."

"But?"

"She was only…reacting to me being always angry when she was around. And it wasn't her I was mad at."

She remembered what Blaine had told her. "You were mad at yourself?"

"Yes."

He looked as if it pained him to even remember, so she didn't pry. He didn't seem like the kind of guy who would easily share deeply personal things with essentially a stranger, and she understood. She didn't explain to even her closest friends that the reason she and Blaine had split had been her own cowardice and she was—

She was mad at herself for it.

She stared at the man with those eyes that looked as if he had seen far too much, and too much of it awful. Was that how he had read her so accurately? Because he recognized what he'd felt in her?

His phone chimed an alert.

"And that," he said flatly as he reached for it, "is the end of my poking my nose into what isn't my business."

"I think they call that 'mission accomplished,'" she said quietly, feeling she needed to acknowledge what had obviously not been easy for him—and what had struck such a chord in her.

His gaze shot back to her face as if she'd startled him. But when he went back to tap the phone screen, he was smiling.

A while later Blaine came back in with Cutter.

"Man, my arm is tired, but he's still ready to blast off."

Rafe chuckled. "I think I'm the only one to ever wear him out. And it wasn't from chasing a ball."

He had a look on his face that told Erin there was a lot more depth to that statement than appeared on the surface.

The dog came over to her and nudged her hand. She stroked his dark head, savoring the soft fur, again felt that sense of calm and comfort, and wondered why on earth she'd been so adamant about not letting Ethan have a dog. Of course, this one was obviously special, from what Rafe had told them. But she had the feeling every dog was special in its own way, and maybe, just maybe, she'd deprived both of them of something good by clinging to her old reasons for not adding a pet to their little family.

She was aware of Blaine coming to sit down beside her—close, but not too close—but she wasn't prepared for what he said, because she'd almost forgotten how good he was at reading her.

"Second thoughts about the 'no pets because we're always moving' rule?"

Her gaze shot to his face, and she looked into those blue eyes that she so loved. Still. And driven by that admission she gave him an answer she'd never given anyone.

"It wasn't just that. It was…it felt like it would be trying to replace you in our lives. And nothing could ever do that."

His eyes widened, and he looked actually shocked. At the words, or at the fact that she'd said it, she didn't know. "Then why—"

He cut off the question she didn't want to answer when Rafe got up and walked over to them. "Walker's inbound, due to land in about fifteen, so I'm going to head up to get him. We may need to make a stop or two—he wants to make some calls, plus he'll want to see Amy. By then it'll be late, so I'll crash at Foxworth. We'll be here bright and early for a planning session." He looked at Cutter. "Dog?"

The dog looked up at Rafe, then he turned to face him and sat down practically on Erin's feet. He just looked at the man who was his surrogate owner at the moment.

"Really?" Rafe asked, one brow lifting. Then he looked at her and Blaine, and she saw that look of understanding again. "Ah," he said. "Okay, your call, dog."

He shifted his focus to her and Blaine, and she wondered what those long-distance gray eyes had seen. "He self-regulates on food, so just leave some of that kibble in the bowl."

"You're leaving him here?" Blaine asked, sounding as surprised as she felt.

"Problem?"

"No," Blaine said quickly. "He's great, I just figured he'd want to stick with you."

Rafe nodded toward where the dog was sitting. "That's his 'staying here' position."

Erin blinked. "He decides that?"

"He does." One corner of Rafe's mouth quirked upward. "He knows where he needs to be. And who needs him," he added as he dug his keys out of his pocket.

She didn't know what to think of that. Or to think of a dog who had seemingly convinced his humans that where he went and what he did was up to him. Or a dog apparently smart enough to see that it all worked out.

All of which kept her from thinking about the one thing that was hammering at her brain demanding to be let in.

She was going to be spending tonight alone with Blaine.

Chapter Twenty-Three

It had happened so fast the ramifications were only hitting him now. And suddenly Blaine was very glad Rafe had left Cutter behind, because he was a buffer of sorts, something to focus on beside the fact that he was here alone with the only woman who had ever been able to tie him into knots.

Erin was up on her feet, pacing, as if with Rafe gone she couldn't bear to sit anywhere close to him. He watched her for a minute or two, but realized as he focused on the way she moved and how good she looked in those snug jeans and that silky top that flowed over her, that he'd better find something else to look at.

"I can't stand this!" she suddenly exclaimed.

And there it was. The reminder he needed. With a long sigh he stood up. "I'll get out of your way. Unless you want me to leave altogether."

She stopped midstride and turn to look at him, a strangely puzzled expression on her face. "What?"

"Is it okay if I just go back to his room, or do you want me to get out from under your roof?"

Understanding dawned on her face. She let out an annoyed-sounding breath. "I didn't mean you. I meant what we talked about before, just hanging around here again, and not doing anything to find Ethan."

Well, that was what he got for assuming she was thinking about him. He should have known better.

"We'll find him, Erin."

"But what if they quit just shoplifting and start robbing stores? He could be hurt, or in worse trouble, and what if… What if he's starting to use drugs or something, and—"

"Hold on," he said, and despite his better judgment he walked over to her and grabbed her shoulders. She was shaking. He could feel the small tremors going through her, and his gut knotted. He remembered the days when he would have done anything to keep her from ever feeling like this.

He wasn't sure he wouldn't do the same now.

"Don't make it worse than it already is," he said.

"How can you be so—" She cut herself off. "Never mind. I know how you can. You fly into combat zones, so a missing kid is nothing."

Nothing. She thought Ethan being missing was nothing to him.

Anger flared, triggering already stressed nerves. He tightened his grip on her shoulders. He wanted to—

A short, sharp bark cut off the thought. He looked down to see Cutter had edged his way between them and was looking from one to the other as if to say, "Knock it off, you two."

Peacekeeper.

"Thanks, dog," he muttered. He let go of her shoulders. Then he sucked in a deep breath. And managed to take his voice down a notch or two from the yell he'd been about to let out. "This is *my* son we're talking about. There is nothing bigger or more important to me than that."

She looked up at him then. He saw moisture pooling in

her eyes as she took her own deep breath and said, "I'm sorry. I know that. I'm just so scared."

"I know."

"And you've fought in wars. You've been shot at. You nearly died. You're too brave to be scared."

"At the risk of dragging out something I've told you before, brave doesn't mean you're not scared. It means you saddle up and head out anyway."

A tear was tracing its way down her right cheek now. "And you always have. It's me who ran, who was gutless, who ruined...everything."

He might be a little slow on the uptake, but he realized she was no longer talking just about Ethan. Something sparked deep inside him, something he didn't even dare name as hope.

He shoved aside the thought and tried to focus. His mind was churning, turning over possibilities. Only then did he become aware Cutter had moved, and at a slight metallic sound he turned in time to see the dog had reached up and grabbed the leash Rafe had left on the table near the front door.

He turned back to Erin. "Do you agree that at this point the odds of him just...showing up here at home are slim?"

"Yes," she said, and he wondered what had made the faintest of smiles flicker across her face at the word *slim*.

"And if he did, he has a key, right?" he asked.

She nodded.

He reached down and took the leash Cutter was holding delicately. "Let's take Cutter here for a walk." He hesitated, but decided he had to say it. "What about that file cabinet in your office? Can you lock it?"

"Yes, why?"

"Grab anything crucial or valuable and stuff it in there, then lock it."

Her brow furrowed. "Why would—" She stopped suddenly and he knew it had hit her, that if Ethan did happen to show up here, he likely wouldn't be alone. And if they were right about who he'd been hanging out with, they would have no qualms about ripping off anything of value.

"Yes," he said, telling her she was right. "So do that, grab your phone, a jacket, and a few of those flyers you did, and let's go. We'll cover every street in the neighborhood, and I want to have a look at that park down the way, just in case."

She stared at him for a long, silent moment. "You're just doing this to keep me busy."

"Maybe," he admitted. "But me, too. I need something for my brain to fix on before I go stark, raving mad myself."

Something flashed in her eyes. It had been a long time since he'd seen it, but he recognized the look she'd always given him when he'd hit on the right answer.

They'd been walking in silence in the chilly evening air when Erin, who had been watching Cutter with obvious interest, said, "He walks nicely. Doesn't pull like a lot of dogs do."

"Only if you need to go where he's pulling you." She gave him a sideways look and he shrugged. "Just quoting Rafe. Who said it took him a long time to learn just how smart this critter is."

They'd reached the end of the block when she asked, "Do you think he could really scent Ethan, if he was close by?"

"Rafe said he's done it multiple times before. Once he's fixed on a scent he's got it. He said they even tested him, on picking out only objects handled by a certain person out of a big pile, and he never missed."

"So a good nose and smart," she said.

"Apparently." He gave her a sideways look. "He realized we needed to do something before we went nuts. So he went and got his leash."

She let out a faint laugh, but given how close to the edge she'd been a short while ago, he'd take it gladly.

"Now, that's smart," she admitted.

He hesitated, but then decided to go for it. "Rafe also said if it wasn't for Cutter, he and his lady Charlie would have never made up. That he tried to walk away, like he always did, and Cutter wouldn't let him."

She was staring at the dog now, and he wondered if it was because of interest in the animal, or disinterest—maybe even repulsion—at what he'd said. Before he could dig the hole any deeper, Erin was hailed by a neighbor, who asked how she was doing and if there was any word on Ethan.

The woman looked at him, and he was about to speak when Erin finally said, a little tightly, "This is Blaine. Ethan's father."

"Oh!" She sounded surprised. She flicked a glance at Cutter, then back to Blaine. "I thought perhaps you were someone using the dog to track Ethan."

"It is something the dog can do," Blaine said. "And if there's a sign he's been in the area, I'm told he'll find it."

"Good idea. And good luck, Erin. I know we're all watching out for your boy." She looked at Blaine again. "Nice to meet you finally, Mr. Everett."

He winced inwardly, although judging from the woman's seemingly genuine smile he didn't think the "finally" had been meant to be a jab. He was just a little touchy, that's all.

"She seems nice," he said neutrally as they walked on.

"She's one of the nicer neighbors. I did some work for her husband's company after we moved here, so we got to know each other a little."

He seized on the more impersonal topic. "What did you do for them?"

She shrugged. "Redesigned their logo, brochure info and packaging. Worked with their website designer to blend it all together. They were happy with it, and their business picked up shortly thereafter, so I count it a success."

"How about your business?"

She smiled at that. "It picked up, too. I even had to hire a bookkeeper because I couldn't keep up with it all."

She took in an audible breath as they stopped at the next corner. Blaine looked across at the spacious park he'd noticed before, thinking it had several places a kid could hide out, if he wanted to. Places he wanted to check for any sign, even if he couldn't know if it was Ethan or not.

But Cutter would.

He wasn't sure why he was so certain of that, other than he knew just how much it would take for Rafe Crawford to trust as much as he clearly trusted this dog.

"I'm glad you brought that up," Erin said, yanking him back to the moment. "I wanted to tell you…you don't have to keep sending so much extra money. We're okay."

His head snapped around and he stared at her.

"We needed it, at first, and that we have our house is because of you. But I'm doing well enough now that I can manage. You don't have to…be so generous."

"I never *had* to be in the first place."

She winced, but he couldn't help his sharp tone. "I know. But you were. You have been. And I thank you for it, a thousand times. But you don't have to do without for our sake anymore."

He had, in fact, done without a few things, but it had been worth it to him. Sure, sometimes his base housing was cramped; in fact he'd had one where he thought his college dorm room had been bigger. But he hadn't really cared, because he knew that whatever extra he sent went to Ethan's care. Not every divorced dad could say that, and he knew a few of them. Too many had exes that blew even child support on themselves, instead of spending it on the child.

But not Erin. She would do without just about anything if it meant Ethan had what he needed. Blaine knew if he sent her money for new clothes or shoes because Ethan was growing so fast, he knew that was what it would go for. Never would Erin be decked out in the latest, trendy attire if Ethan was wearing things that were worn out or too small.

Oddly, he was proud of her, for making a go of what had been the one thing that had always appealed to her.

"I'm glad you made your dream happen," he said as they started across the street, figuring that was safe enough. When she glanced at him he added hastily, "And I don't mean because you don't need as much money now."

"I never thought you did," she said, her voice very quiet. "You always encouraged me before...before everything."

"Before it all fell apart, you mean?" he asked, and he couldn't help his sour tone or the way his mouth twisted.

She stopped on the opposite corner and looked up at him. He would have sworn he could see her steeling herself before she said, "It—we—didn't fall apart. I blew us up."

"Erin—"

He stopped when she shook her head. "I did it, Blaine. And not a day since has gone by that I didn't hate myself for it. Because I threw away what our son needed most, because I didn't have the guts to live with a hero."

Chapter Twenty-Four

There. She'd said it.

It had been eating away at her for two and a half years, since the day she'd filed the divorce papers. And every day since she'd lived with the vivid, searing image of Blaine's look of utter and total shock when she'd told him what was in the envelope she'd given him.

You can't mean this. I thought... I love you. I thought you loved me.

I do. Too much. Don't you see, that's why I can't stay?

But I'm fine now. The worst is over.

Over until the next time. I'm sorry you married a coward, Blaine. You, of all people.

She had expected to be relieved. She should have been relieved. But the peace she'd expected had never arrived. Instead there was just that gaping hole in her life, which hurt almost as much as seeing him so damaged had.

And, of course, the fact that her son hated her now.

Hated her enough that he couldn't stand to be under the same roof with her. That even hanging out who knows where with kids headed for big trouble—if they weren't already there—was better than having to be around her.

And the worst part was she understood. Because there were days on end when she felt the same way. When she wished she could…not be who she was. She wondered if she had any courage at all of her own, or if she'd borrowed it all from Blaine. If his courage fighting for his life had some-how seeped into her, giving her enough—just enough—to get through.

And left her, when it was over, drained, empty and feel-ing utterly hollow inside.

Blaine was staring at her. She was grateful there was no one else out and about, at least not close enough to hear as they stood on the corner. And still glad she'd chosen here to do this, so she wouldn't have the echoes of this pain-ful admission inside her home. Not that she hadn't admit-ted that she didn't have the guts to live with a hero there. Sometimes out loud.

Blaine finally spoke. "After what you went through when I was injured, how can you say you don't have guts?"

"I couldn't walk out on you when you were so hurt."

His eyes widened. "Erin, what on earth do you think courage is?"

"I know what it's not, and that's leaving because I couldn't take it if it happened again."

She expected him to go back to what he'd often said be-fore, that that was a big if, but instead he just looked at her for a long, silent moment. Then, quietly, he said, "But you had the guts to call me now, even though you hate me for what I put you through."

She sucked in an audible breath, shocked at the inter-pretation he'd put on her lack of contact. "I don't hate you. I could never hate you."

His mouth twisted with obvious disbelief. "So, that's not the reason you can't even tolerate speaking to me un-less it's an emergency? Why you never call, or talk to me when I call Ethan?"

"No, I—"

"Or maybe you're just so done with me it's not worth your time?"

She gave a slow shake of her head as her mouth tightened and she swallowed hard, painfully. She looked around, almost desperate for something else to focus on, but found nothing.

Because nothing was enough to distract her from this.

"No, Blaine," she whispered. "That I don't talk to you isn't because I'm done with you." It took every bit of nerve she had to look up at him again. "It's because I'm not."

He was still staring at her, looking utterly shocked, when Cutter gave a soft bark that sounded almost apologetic. They both looked at the visiting dog, and as if he'd been waiting to be sure he had their attention, he started walking into the park. By necessity—and for Erin with relief, they followed.

At first she assumed the dog had some business to take care of, and tried to remember where the park's cleanup supplies were. But it shortly became obvious the dog had a destination in mind. He stopped at the base of the ladder that led up to the small, cabin-like structure that was the top of the various play equipment structures. A slide went down the other side, and the set of swings out from a third side, and the big sand pile on the fourth.

Blaine nodded at the dog. "That's what I wondered, boy."

She didn't realize until he started up the ladder what Blaine had meant, that this was the place in the park he'd wanted to check out. But Cutter had led them here, and smart as he seemed, he couldn't have understood that. But could he have scented something? She'd seen some videos of search and rescue dogs doing some incredible things sometimes days after an incident.

Blaine disappeared into the structure, and she heard him moving around. A couple of minutes later, he reappeared in the doorway. She nearly gasped when he dropped straight down to the ground, skipping the ladder. And all she could think of was how hard he had worked to get his left leg functional again.

But he obviously thought nothing of it. Or what he'd found up there outranked it. Which he proved with his next words.

"Somebody's been there, probably for a couple of nights at least."

Her breath caught. Could Ethan have really been so close? All the time she'd spent walking the neighborhood, could he have been there, watching her? She'd walked around the park, but never really looked near the playground area, since Ethan was a teenager now and looked on such things with disdain. But she'd never thought of the little structure as a possible place to hide.

Because you didn't want to admit your son wanted to hide from you.

She saw then that Blaine was holding something, what looked like a crumpled paper bag from a local takeout. He held it out to Cutter, who nosed it and let out a low whuff as he reached up to paw at it. Her mind was racing, wishing she knew more about dogs, especially very well trained ones like this.

She wanted to believe this meant Ethan, that he was picking up the scent Rafe had made certain he knew. And surely if it had just been the scent of whatever food had been in the bag, the dog would have tried to take it, to see if there was more food, or maybe lick that grease that had stained the bottom?

But Cutter did none of that, only pawed at it and looked

up at Blaine. And once more let out that whuff, as if to be sure he'd gotten the message. And Blaine, being Blaine, understood.

"I got it, boy. It's his. Thanks."

"How can you be sure? It must smell like food to him."

"If Cutter says Ethan's scent is on this, it is. Rafe said trust him. And I trust Rafe."

Once he would have said that to you. Until you proved to him you didn't deserve his trust.

He stroked the dog's head, and then dug into the bag. When he pulled out the narrow white strip of paper, her pulse gave a sudden kick. A receipt. Which would be dated.

"Saturday," he said.

She smothered a gasp. That had been the day she had broken and called Blaine. That day, Ethan had still been that close? If she'd been more thorough, if she'd thought about this little place as a shelter, if she'd—

"Stop." Blaine's voice was sharp. "Quit blaming yourself."

"But it's my fault—"

He reached out and grabbed her hand. A jolt went through her at the contact. "Erin, think. Does it really matter a damn right now whose fault it is? What matters is finding Ethan. Nothing else. There'll be time enough when he's home safe to blame yourself from here to Alaska if you want to. But now, you need to—"

"Get over myself," she finished for him.

He grimaced. "I wasn't going to say quite that."

"I know. You're too kind to. Which is why I said it for you. Because you're right."

She dug down deep, tried to remember how she'd gotten through those awful days four years ago—when she'd gone from sitting at his bedside waiting for those infernal machines to send out that hideous sound that meant his battered body had surrendered, to watching him win every challenge of his recovery, then fight his way through rehab and therapy until now, when you'd never guess what he'd been through, if you didn't know. He looked...normal. Strong. Moving as if nothing had ever happened. That pilot's gaze as sharp as ever.

That gaze that rarely missed anything. Except it had missed how little sand there was in her, how little courage.

But she knew she'd been right about that: she could never go through that again. But surely she could use what it had taught her about perseverance and never giving up? What Blaine had taught her, just by watching him never give up? For the sake of their son, she could—she would—find whatever was left of that strength and pour it into finding him.

They walked for another two hours, Cutter finding nothing more of interest other than another dog out for a walk with his kid. The passerby was about a quarter the size of Cutter, but with about the same amount of fur. They talked to the girl who was holding the leash for a few minutes, and found out that yeah, she'd seen some older kid hanging out near the slide house last week, but hadn't seen him lately.

Erin quickly pulled out her phone and showed her the picture of Ethan she'd been using.

"Yeah, that looks like him. If his hair was longer."

"He was overdue for a haircut," she said.

Blaine's jaw tensed for a moment, and she wondered if it was because he missed out on all the ordinary, mundane aspects of parenthood, like haircuts and nagging about homework.

"I gotta go," the girl said. "I'm late and Mom will be worried."

"I know the feeling," Erin said, stifling the jab of pain as she said it. "So hurry home."

She watched the girl and the ball of fluff hurry on, until they turned up the sidewalk leading to the house on the corner opposite the one they'd stopped on before.

"So she lives in a good spot to see the place," Blaine said quietly, as if he was thinking out loud.

"Yes." Something belatedly struck her. "And if it truly was Ethan, then...he didn't go to those kids, the wannabe gangsters, right away."

The slightest of smiles curved Blaine's mouth, then vanished. A brief flash of hope. She'd been afraid to even name the emotion.

"No, he didn't," Blaine said softly. "So it wasn't his first thought. He didn't leave to join them. He joined them after he'd left. And maybe didn't know what else to do."

She wasn't sure how this tiny bit of information they couldn't even be sure was true comforted her, but it did. But then, Blaine had always had the knack. She stared up at him. He stared back, his eyes moving as if he were searching her face for...something. After a long, silent moment, he leaned down. And kissed her.

It was the lightest, briefest of touches, almost casual, but it took her breath away nevertheless. Because Blaine Everett had always been able to sear through all her defenses.

Standing still had made the chilly air more evident. And after the flash of heat he'd just sent through her it felt even colder. Blaine stepped back, as if he were having second thoughts about that brief but all too sweet kiss. She shivered slightly, from the cold or his absence she didn't know. She pulled her lightweight jacket a little closer around her.

"I think that's about enough for tonight," Blaine said, his voice showing nothing of the turmoil she was feeling.

"Hopefully the Foxworth guy in charge down here has some connections that will help, when he gets here."

"They seem like…really good people."

He nodded as they started to walk back toward her house. "Rafe did some pretty incredibly heroic stuff when he was in the Marines. But he says he's prouder of what Foxworth does than anything else."

"Sounds like a good place to be."

Blaine nodded again. "He's really happy. And he deserves it."

So do you, Blaine Everett. So do you.

With a smothered sigh, she followed as the Foxworth dog led them back home.

And tried not to replay that kiss in her mind on an endless loop.

Chapter Twenty-Five

Well, that had been one of the longest nights of his life.

That had been the stupidest move he'd ever made, kissing her like that, now, when he was only here because she was desperate. And that kiss had brought on memories of hotter, even sweeter kisses. Which in turn had brought on dreams of what that kiss would once have led to, unreeling in his mind like some adults-only movie.

He was grateful to see the faint lightening outside, telling him they were at least in astronomical twilight, probably close to nautical twilight. He told himself not to even guess at how much sleep he'd gotten, because it didn't matter. The mission was on, and he would roll out.

At least in the hospital he'd been drugged up enough that he hadn't really been aware of exactly how much time passed. Crazy how this seemed almost as painful as those seemingly endless days full of pain and fear. Fear that this was never going to end…and fear that it would, abruptly, when his heart finally gave out or his brain decided he'd had enough and shut down.

But somehow, every time he had gotten close, close to giving up, to surrendering, he'd felt slender, warm fingers wrap around his hand, felt a soft, tender kiss on his cheek, and even when he wasn't entirely clear on why, he knew he had to keep fighting.

"She takes copious notes," one of the ICU nurses had told him. "And never misses a thing. We're all on our toes when she's around." The man had said it with an appreciative smile. "She's one gutsy lady. In that part of life, you're a lucky guy, Captain."

He had the sudden thought that he'd never told Erin what the nurse had said. Maybe it would mean something to her, coming from a stranger—although he'd felt like a friend by the time they finally said goodbye to him—but one who had observed her firsthand.

He sat up on the edge of his son's bed. He'd started out the night as he had both nights he'd been here, sitting on the front porch, in the dark, watching for any activity, not so much hoping Ethan might come home, but that he might try to sneak back to get something. What he'd taken might have been enough to get through a few days, but then he was going to be out of money. Which would mean starving, or stealing. Since he'd already started the latter, it wasn't that big a jump from rodent food to people food. Or worse, expensive items that could be converted to eating money. Or worst, drugs.

With a smothered sigh he got to his feet. He walked over to the small desk under the bedroom window. He flipped on the desk lamp, and sat in what he guessed was a gaming chair, like he'd seen some of the guys using in the rec hall. He wondered how hard it had been for Ethan to leave that pretty fancy-looking game rig behind.

Methodically, he started going through the drawers. He'd done the dresser that first night, looking for anything his son might have hidden, a clue to where he might have gone, but had found nothing unusual. He'd looked at the desk, but had only done a cursory search. He'd remedy that now.

The only thing that had grabbed him was when Erin had appeared in the doorway and said quietly, "I did a more thorough check. He took your shirt with him."

He remembered giving her a puzzled look. "What shirt?"

"He has one of your T-shirts from flight school."

Realization dawned. "The one with the Huey on it? I wondered what happened to that."

"He wears it on his birthday." She had taken a deep breath before adding, "And on yours."

It had been like an RPG straight to the gut. He'd bent over to put his hands on the dresser, afraid his knees were going to give out. He remembered wanting to go out and ask Rafe if they could go back to plan A and crash at the Foxworth headquarters.

He shoved aside the image in his head and went back to searching the desk. Erin said she had gone through everything, but there was always the chance she'd missed something, or that there was something that was meaningless to her but not to him. Or Ethan.

In the center drawer he found a few school papers, with big red A's marked at the top. One math, one science, it looked like something about weather. A manual for his gaming system, still sealed in plastic. Obviously he hadn't needed it to get up and running. In the top, side drawer he'd found some other boxes and paper instructional inserts for various cables and smaller tech items, all tossed in loosely. There appeared to be more of the same in the bottom drawer, except...

He pulled out the brochure from the very bottom of the drawer.

The USMC recruiting brochure. And inside that one he found the flyer on becoming a Marine Corps pilot.

He didn't know what to think. Was Ethan just curious, because of him? Or was he thinking about...joining?

Maybe he had been. And maybe he'd gotten over it, and that was why the stuff was buried at the bottom of this bottom drawer.

Or maybe he'd been hiding it from his mother.

The thought of how Erin might have reacted if she'd found this made that a more distinct possibility.

He put the things back in the drawer and shoved it closed. No real clues there, except a peek into who his son was. A kid capable of excellent grades, a gamer, and one who, thankfully, hadn't forgotten his father.

He stood up again, yawned widely and stretched. Then he walked to the foot of the bed, grabbed up the clothes he'd set out for today, and headed for the bathroom down the hall for a shower.

He managed not to look toward her bedroom door at the far end this time, unlike the first two nights he'd spent here. It did not, he found, help much. His imagination was still quite capable of filling in the blanks. Remembering how she used to like to sleep, that some part of her had to be touching him, even if it was only a toe to his calf. How when she woke she would turn to snuggle up to him, often whispering her recommendation for an effective wake-up call into his ear. He used to tease her by saying he needed a fuller description to decide. And she gave him one, although they usually only got halfway through before he was so hot for her he had to start on her suggested path.

Hell, he was getting hot now, just remembering.

He had his hand on the doorknob when the slight sound from his right made him snap his head to that side.

She was there, standing in her doorway, staring at him. Her hair was tousled, and she was wearing a pair of clingy shorts—damn, her legs really were that long—and a T-shirt cropped enough that it showed her trim abdomen.

And you're standing here practically buck-ass naked, already hard from just thinking about her.

Yet he couldn't seem to move. He told himself he was imagining the desire he thought he saw in her gaze, but those words she'd said kept coming back to him.

That I don't talk to you isn't because I'm done with you. It's because I'm not.

He knew what he wanted to do. He wanted to run down that hall to her, sweep her up in his arms like he used to do, and carry her to bed. And when she suddenly looked away and darted back into her bedroom, he wanted to call out to her, stop her, somehow put them back the way they'd been, together, whole, and meant for each other.

He remembered the urge that had driven him to kiss her, and how futile it had been to fight it. How he'd had to count on them being out in public to rein himself in, since he was apparently incapable of doing it himself. And the feel of her mouth beneath his, even that slight, short brush of lips, had nearly done him in out there on the street.

The sight of her now, disheveled from sleep—or had her night been as restless as his own?—had been like that punch to the gut all over again. And he faced the truth he'd managed to mask for a long time now, that wherever he went, whoever he met, nobody affected him like Erin did.

When he hit the shower he never even touched the hot water faucet. And thought that even in November California wouldn't produce water cold enough to cool him down.

Chapter Twenty-Six

Erin closed the bedroom door behind her and sagged against it, trying to slow her heart, her breathing.

She knew if she'd been closer she'd have seen the various scars, one of the things that had enabled her to leave. Not because they repelled her but because they reminded her of how easily she could have been looking at them as they prepped him for a coffin.

But she hadn't been closer. And that was a good thing, because she'd seen enough even from twenty feet away to kick up her pulse and make her suddenly feel as if it were midsummer and she was baking in the sun. Her heart was still pumping madly, and closing her eyes to block out what she'd seen did no good. The image of that fit, taut, gorgeous body she'd made love to so many times seemed etched into her eyelids.

She wanted nothing more than to race down there and join him in the shower. She even knew he'd likely be interested, judging by his semi-aroused state, as she'd seen too well through those clingy, knit boxers, while she stood there gaping at the beautiful sight of him. And he had kissed her, after all. True, it had been barely a kiss, the lightest of touches, but all things considered she could hardly expect more.

You're my center, Erin. Without you I'd be spinning around out of control, crazy, damaged...

He'd said that long before he'd been hurt. And she'd treasured it, tucked it away in that special corner of her heart dedicated to only him.

And when he had been hurt, it had become her mantra, what told her she had to stay until the damage was repaired. Judging by the look of him, all of him, it definitely was. He was as beautiful as ever.

I think you'll regret it, Erin. I understand, I truly do, but I think you'll one day regret it. A lot.

Her mother's words, spoken the day she'd told her parents what she'd done, that she'd filed for divorce, echoed in her head now.

I already regret it, Mom. But I'll regret it even more if I stay and next time he dies. I don't want him to be the center of my entire life when that happens.

She was just pulling on her shoes when she heard the knock at the front door. She got to the living room just as Blaine was opening it. Cutter trotted in, followed by Rafe, who turned back to look at the man behind him.

Erin went still. This was the man who'd been recalled to help? The man who ran this branch of the famous Foxworth Foundation? His dark hair was a bit unruly, and his eyes were a striking combination of gold and green. All in all, he was quite a good-looking guy. But in her current mode, she mostly noticed he looked more like some kind of street thug, with his neck chains and tattoos.

The moment she thought it she realized it was likely intentional.

Rafe had clearly seen her reaction, because he looked back at the other man and said, "I see you've still got it."

The other man laughed, and then Rafe introduced him

as Walker Cole. She smiled—how could she not when she knew he'd come back just to help?—and shook his hand.

"The tats are temporary," he said as he saw her looking at the one that crept up the side of his neck. "But it helps to blend in. My wife didn't care for that one either, until I showed her how if you looked at it right, it's her name."

Erin's smile then was genuine. "Lucky lady."

Walker shook his head. "I'm the lucky one."

Then he turned to Blaine, who also shook his hand but was looking at him differently. Not just with welcome and thanks, but respect. And just that look brought back the history of this man, in the moment before Blaine spoke it.

"That was a hell of a thing you did, Mr. Cole. I doubt I'd have had the nerve to stick it out as long as you did. But you saved a lot of lives, and put away some atrocious people."

"Just Walker, please. And they had to be stopped," the man said simply.

Suddenly Erin was struck with the simple fact that she was standing with three heroes. Men who, as Blaine had told her, had done what they did so others didn't have to.

Walker smiled then, briefly, and for that moment he was a different person, a good-looking guy who no doubt had women looking twice just walking down the street.

"Let's get to it," Rafe suggested.

"Right," Blaine said briskly, and proceeded to tell them what they'd discovered last night, that for a while at least, Ethan had been close by in the park.

Walker nodded. "All right. Good to know he didn't start out intending to connect with those guys in the video, or plan it ahead of time."

Erin was glad he'd reached that conclusion, just as she had. That was the reason finding out he'd been here in the park for at least a couple of days had so relieved her.

Walker went on. "I talked to a friend of mine at the local sheriff's office." He glanced at Rafe. "A guy Brett Dunbar put me in touch with when I first got here."

Rafe smiled, then looked at Blaine and Erin and said, "Detective we often work with up north, but he used to work down in this area."

"And has a rep the size of Alaska," Walker said with a brief grin. "Anyway, the guy here looked at the video Ty found, from the pet store. And he thinks he recognizes one of the kids, although it's fuzzy enough he can't be sure. But he told me a couple of places they frequent. So I'm going to go hang out a bit, see if I can find out anything. And he's going to try and rattle Missing Persons a bit, make sure they're working it." He grimaced. "They're understaffed these days, but what department isn't? Anyway, he'll try."

Erin felt a little overwhelmed. She'd felt so alone in the first days after Ethan had vanished. She'd spent that time worrying, but also assuming he'd come home on his own, or the local law enforcement would find him. When neither happened, she'd broken and called Blaine.

And now she felt like she had a veritable army at her back. Or better yet, the Marine Corps.

"Thank you," she said. Or tried to, it came out as barely a whisper.

Cutter stepped over to her and nudged her hand. She almost automatically stroked his head. And felt it again, that odd sense of...not peace, but calm. As if he were telling her it was safe to believe it would all come out right.

She stared down at the dog, but it was herself she was bemused at. Had she been passing up this kind of comfort all her life simply because she'd never had a dog and didn't know? Was this what Ethan had wanted, and she had denied him? If so, she was the fool, because this was...amazing.

"Amazing, isn't it?" Blaine's voice was quiet as Rafe took Walker down to Ethan's room, to get a feel for him. "Just petting him calms you down."

That he would use the exact word she'd thought didn't surprise her. Blaine had always been on her wavelength. She'd never realized how truly precious that was until he was no longer in her life.

You had what many people search their entire lives for, and you threw it away.

Belatedly—very, very belatedly—a thought struck her. He hadn't given any indication, but suddenly she had to know. "Is there…did you leave someone to come here?"

His brow furrowed. "I got leave to come, from my commanding officer," he said. "We're between flight classes at the moment, so they won't miss me."

"I meant…personally."

He drew back slightly as understanding dawned on his face. "No, Erin. There's no one. There hasn't really been since you left."

In two years—because being Blaine she knew he wouldn't even think about it until the divorce was final—he hadn't found someone to replace her? Someone with the courage to live with his life and the potential for disaster?

"How about you?" he asked, his expression unreadable now. "Should I expect some guy to show up this weekend and ask what I'm doing here?"

"No!" It came out much more sharply than she'd intended. She took a breath to steady herself. "I haven't had time."

It was true. She'd been so wrapped up in getting her business up and running she hadn't even thought much about it. Except when she went to bed at night, missing him. Aching for him.

And now he was here.

She looked up and held his gaze. "And I haven't wanted to," she said.

She waited, every muscle tense as she wondered what he would say, but Rafe and Walker came back out before he could speak. Rafe headed outside, saying he had something he needed to give them. But Walker came over to Blaine, looking at him rather curiously.

"Rafe tells me you're the pilot who pulled him out of that battle zone when he was wounded."

"I…yeah."

"He said you went in alone, without your copilot because it was an emergency and you were the closest. That he would likely have been dead if you hadn't."

Blaine smiled rather crookedly and gave one of those annoying half shrugs, usually seen when he'd done something wonderful but didn't seem to want credit for it.

"It worked out," was all he said.

"Yeah, especially for Foxworth. And Foxworth will make this work out for you."

Rafe was back, with what looked like a couple of rather odd-looking cell phones, with the extra buttons like his had, in his hand. He handed one to each of them.

"These are especially designed for Foxworth. That first button will connect you to us, live, wherever we are. The texting app there—" he pointed to an icon that looked, logically, like a fox "—will go to everyone who's live on the circuit. And that red button there is for emergencies. Either you're in trouble and need immediate help, or you've got something that needs top-priority attention."

"Wow," Blaine said, looking down at the device. "Slick."

"Brainchild of Ty and Liam Burnett, another of our guys from up north. Keep them with you, and don't hesitate to use them. Here, listen," he said, and triggered the unique-sounding notification tone.

"And I'll use it to let you know if, when, and where I find out anything," Walker said. "Plus," he added, "I'm going to borrow our furry compatriot there, since he's the one with the nose and will know if Ethan's been somewhere, even if it's being denied."

"Be sure to tell him to put on his tough guy demeanor," Rafe said dryly.

Walker only grinned. "I have a feeling he'll know when to do that, scarily brilliant critter that he is." He glanced at her and Blaine. "I'll have to tell you about my first run-ins with this guy sometime. But now, let's get your boy home safe."

As they began to lay out a plan, it took Erin a moment to realize that she was feeling...different. Better. Blaine slipped an arm around her. He was rock-steady, as usual.

And in that moment she realized the difference was hope.

Chapter Twenty-Seven

Blaine looked down at the screen on the Foxworth phone, now showing a map of the entire south county, with three areas highlighted.

"We're going to need Cutter to go through them all," Walker said. "But I'll hit this one first—" he pointed to the one farthest inland "—because I know some folks there. Or at least, this guy does," he added, flicking the thick gold chain he wore. He pointed at the second area. "Rafe, this one is for you. Not quite as touchy about strangers there. Blaine, this is where you first hit something, right?" Walker asked, pointing to the third area, which included the shopping area with the pet store. Blaine nodded, and Walker went on. "Okay, if you can take that, we've got the most likely areas covered."

"If you think I'm just going to sit here at home on the very slim chance he comes back," Erin began.

Blaine held up a hand. "Nobody said that."

"Funny, I didn't hear my name mentioned."

He saw Rafe and Walker exchange glances. "I'll get those set up," Rafe said, and quickly turned and headed outside.

Walker coughed lightly, then said, "I brought some concealable security cameras from Foxworth. Rafe's going to set them up outside, and one in Ethan's room, just in case that happens. They're programmed to notify anybody with one of those phones if they're activated. If they are, then whoever's closest heads back here. Fast."

"Sorry," Erin said. "I'm a bit on edge."

"Understandable," Walker said.

"And me being here doesn't help," Blaine said, and he couldn't quite keep the sour undertone out of his voice. "We seem to be…at odds a lot."

To his surprise, Walker laughed. "Hey, I saw Rafe and Charlie back when they were going at each other's throats all the time. You guys are downright tame."

As he watched Walker and Cutter leave a short while later, Blaine thought of what Rafe had told him, about how he and his Charlie had worked it all out and rebuilt something even better. He glanced at Erin, wondering. Pointlessly, no doubt. No matter how she'd looked at him this morning, and no matter how his heart and body had responded.

She looked down at the map again, and he guessed she was figuring out where she would go to search. He didn't like the idea of her out there alone, if only because she'd be looking for gang types, and they weren't the sort to welcome scrutiny. Even from a beautiful woman. And being that beautiful, plus being alone, poking around, could put a nasty target on her. But he knew if he suggested she might not be safe, she'd blow up at him, because right now all she cared about was Ethan.

He quashed the single, tiny bit of pleasure there was for him in all this, that Ethan loved him enough to act out like this. That he missed him that much. But there was no room for that, not now, not when his boy was out there, quite possibly headed for much bigger trouble, if not already there.

Today was the tenth day since Ethan had taken off, and in his mind that was a fairly grim marker.

"Come with me," he said abruptly.

She looked up at him. "We can cover more ground if I don't."

He knew better than to say what he was guessing was true, which was that if Ethan did see her, he would dodge out of sight. She was the focus of his anger right now, deserved or not.

"True," he said neutrally. "But if we go jointly, and happen to get lucky enough to hit the right place, the shock of seeing us together might freak him out enough to let himself be seen."

He watched as she considered that. Finally she nodded. And so they both headed out to the district near the pet store where they'd gotten their first lead. She parked her car in a public lot near the closest intersection, but didn't get out immediately. After a long moment of watching her stare out the windshield as if she wasn't seeing anything in front of them, he finally spoke.

"I was thinking we'd stop in at the pet store. In case he came back."

She visibly snapped back to the present. "Okay. Yes."

"I'll pay the guy for what he took, too. Might make things easier when we get him back home."

She gave him a long, steady look. "You're…used to this," she said quietly.

He blinked. "What?"

"Situations like this, I mean. Nail-biting ones. Searches with crucially important goals. Life-or-death missions…"

Her voice trailed away as she said that last part. "Erin," he began, but stopped when she shook her head.

"You're used to this, so you're good at it. I just seem to…fall apart."

A sudden memory struck him, of a day long ago, when ten-year-old him had determined he was going to climb that ancient tree that spilled over into the backyard at his childhood home. He'd told her to stand guard and let him know if Mr. Edgar came out. The old guy was pretty cranky, and he didn't want him coming over to yell at him, or worse, his parents.

"Then why are you doing it?" she'd asked, sounding exasperated.

"Because it's there and needs to be climbed," he said, as if it were self-evident.

"What if you fall and get hurt?"

He had scoffed. "Won't happen."

"Well I'm not helping you do something that could end up with you in the hospital."

He didn't know how his expression had changed, but when he snapped out of it she was watching him.

"Where did you just go?" she asked.

He shrugged, letting out a rather embarrassed chuckle. "Long ago but not so far away."

She drew back slightly. "What?"

"Mr. Edgar's tree."

He could tell by her reaction that she'd gotten there immediately. Her eyes widened slightly, and then took on that look again, that of staring into the distance but not seeing what was in front of them right now.

"Even then," she finally whispered.

His brow furrowed. "Even then?"

She focused on him. "That day…it was a preview, wasn't it? Of what our life together would be. You taking off on some dangerous task, and me…staying back and being afraid for you."

"Funny," he said. "What I remember is you quite logically trying to talk me out of it. For my own sake. To protect me." He managed a sad smile. "As you've always done."

"You needed someone to cheer you on, not someone too afraid to even face what you were doing."

He couldn't stop himself, he reached out then and cupped her cheek. "You smiled and waved me off, even when I could see you were scared. You think acting happy that I was going would have been better?"

"More supportive, maybe."

"No, Erin. Supportive is letting me go even when you hated the idea, because you know it was what I had to do. What I needed to do, deep down."

"But—"

"Supportive," he said, gently cutting her off, "is fighting for me when I couldn't fight for myself, when I was barely aware of what was happening, and knew only that you were there so it would be okay. Supportive is standing up to medical folks who couldn't seem to grasp the concept of mutual communication."

She was staring at him now, and he thought he might never get a better chance to tell her. To tell her what he hadn't in all the chaos, in all the agony, both physical and mental. Especially in the pain of her finally declaring it was over, she couldn't take it again.

"If it hadn't been for you I would have given up, Erin. I would have taken the easy way out. I thought about it, a lot, on those days when every breath, even the slightest movement hurt like such hell. I even figured out a couple of ways to do it, to end it all. But I couldn't give up, not when you were there, fighting as hard as I was."

He saw the moisture pooling in her eyes. "But you were the one hurting so much."

"And you weren't? It was just different battles, Erin. Different kinds of pain, but no less."

A tear overflowed and streaked down her cheek. "After all the years together, since we were kids, I should have known."

All those years, and he thought he'd known her pretty well. But apparently not as well as he thought, because he couldn't read her now, just as he'd never been able to understand how she could have just walked away.

"Should have known...what?" he finally asked.

"I should have known what I was getting. That you'd never change. That you'd always be what you were—a hero, a fighter for what you believed in."

"Erin—"

"I should have let you go long ago, so you could find someone who was tough enough."

He reached out and tilted her head back with a gentle finger under her delicate chin.

"Only one problem with that. I never wanted anyone else."

Chapter Twenty-Eight

He'd stunned her into silence. Only the fact that finding Ethan outweighed everything right now enabled her to get moving, and she seized on that. Which, she thought tiredly, was typical.

It had always been Blaine who'd confronted…everything. Including how they felt about each other when they'd been old enough to understand where it would lead. He'd always said it was destined, because they'd been born on the same day, and ended up living across the street from each other. And she'd always believed it, because no one else had ever held an attraction for her.

Especially the kind she felt for Blaine. And, as he'd just said, the kind he felt for her.

Did he…still? Was it even possible, after what she'd done, that he could still feel that powerful pull, that feeling that this connection was not just inevitable but unbreakable?

But you broke it.

The words she'd said to herself so many times rang in her head yet again, but for a different reason now. Because now she knew it wasn't completely true. She may have broken them, but she hadn't broken that spell, that connection, at least on her end. Because it was pulling at her as strongly now as it ever had. Just looking into those eyes of his, and remembering how it once had been, was enough to swamp her.

As they got into her car she didn't say much because her brain was spinning, analyzing that momentous decision she'd made as she hadn't done in a very long time.

She knew she wasn't incapable, or helpless. She'd accomplished a lot. She'd built a business, bought a home, and even with Blaine's extra financial help it hadn't been easy. And now she'd gotten to the point where she didn't need that extra cushion anymore, and she was proud of that.

There was only one area of her life where she had truly failed, and that was the day she'd run. She'd considered it a seriously-thought-out decision then; in fact she'd believed it not just the smartest choice but her only choice. And she'd done her best to build a sane, steady life for herself and for Ethan.

And how'd that work out?

She winced inwardly. But she had to face it. How sane and steady could any life be when it was built on the rubble of what had once been a firm foundation? Obviously not steady enough, because here they were, out here searching for her not-so-little-anymore boy, who had found the life she'd built—she'd thought for both of them—so intolerable he'd run away.

"Maybe," Blaine said as she drove toward their area on the map, "once Ethan's home and safe and all that's worked out, we could…talk."

She shot him a sideways glance. He'd ever been the doer, not the talker. For him to actually suggest it, especially with the import that pause gave it, warned her he was quite serious.

He probably still didn't understand why she'd done it. She wasn't sure she herself completely understood anymore. But it was easy to think that now, when he was here beside her, strong, well and looking as damned sexy as ever. When he'd been bloodied, broken and hooked up to machines, not so much.

"Maybe," she said neutrally, not looking at him, pretending to be searching for a parking place when she'd already spotted one up ahead. Thankfully, he let it drop.

It felt strange, walking elbow to elbow with him down the street. Time was they would have done it holding hands, or with his arm over her shoulder and hers around his waist. Unlike some, he'd had no qualms about such public displays; he was hers and she was his, he used to say, and he didn't care who knew it. Her oldest friends had told her how lucky she was, and she'd agreed.

She had never told them about the awful, long nights spent alone when he was deployed. That was something only to be shared with fellow military spouses who would understand what it was like to have the worst possibilities hovering over their heads at all times.

She'd just been one of the unlucky ones who'd had it come true.

As always, she silently chastised herself, because what she'd gone through had been nothing compared to what Blaine had gone through. And yet here he was, strolling along as if it had never happened, as if he were back in that time before, as if—

No, he wasn't. Because he'd never been this tense before. She'd heard the phrase "high alert" many times, but never had it been more personified than in the man beside her right now. His head was rarely still, and his eyes never were. He was constantly scanning, looking, searching.

They were headed back the way they'd come, although on the opposite side of the street, still with no sign of anyone familiar, either personally or from that video. It appeared this had been a useless effort.

She wondered what Ethan would do, if he saw them. She knew Blaine had been right—he'd be stunned to see them together. He'd likely want to avoid her, but surely the temptation of his father would overcome that? Surely—

She cut off her own thoughts with a heavy sigh. "You're right."

"It happens," he said evenly.

"In trying to save Ethan from horrendous pain, I've just driven him away."

She felt his gaze on her, could see him thinking, as if he were considering whether to say something or not.

"Please, say it," she said. "If we can't be honest now, then when?"

He grimaced slightly. "It's just something I've wondered now and then. Since you left, I mean."

"Go ahead. I can't feel much worse than I do already."

"I don't mean to make it worse—"

He broke off as that distinctive sound Rafe had played for them sounded from two different locations, his jacket pocket and the small purse she had slung over her shoulder.

He got to his first and answered. "We're both here, go ahead."

He held it out so she could also hear, although she had to lean in to do it. She got it, this might be something they didn't want the world to hear on speaker, but being essentially head-to-head with him set her pulse jumping again.

But what Rafe said kicked it into overdrive.

"Head for Foxworth headquarters," he ordered. "We just got something from Walker's contact at the local sheriff's office we need you to look at."

There was enough of an edge in his voice, and he ended the call so abruptly she looked at Blaine for explanation. But he was already moving, clearly reacting to that tone of command in the former sniper's voice.

And the next thing she knew they were running.

Chapter Twenty-Nine

If nothing else, the way Erin was driving—fast, chance-taking, and on the edge of reckless—would have told him how wound up she was. Usually she was smooth, careful and polite. He used to joke about how she'd spoiled him, that passengering with anyone else made him carsick. With her he could read a book if he wanted to.

Says the man who can autorotate without getting airsick.

Her usual rejoinder to that joke rang in his head now. That she had that ammo was his own fault, since he'd made the mistake of letting her see a video of what could have been an ugly crash when his engine began to misfire at about a mile up and he'd had to make the dive.

He'd explained as she'd watched, how when the aircraft stopped powering the rotor's spin, you had to use the airflow itself, from a steep dive, to keep it turning and maintain some kind of control.

"Then at the last minute you flare up, to get the skids under you again, and you're down."

He remembered glancing at her expression then and trying to lighten it by joking about the heavy jolt. It didn't work. She'd just gone from staring at the screen to staring at him.

"It's just something you learn," he'd said. "Like knowing that if you're driving on ice and you start to skid, you turn in the direction of the skid."

"I have a better idea. When it's icy, stay off the road."

"And it's a good idea," he'd agreed. "It's just that the world doesn't always cooperate."

He was yanked back to the present when she cut someone off and earned an angry sounding of the horn and an obscene gesture. He wasn't sure if the jolt he felt was that or the last part of that memory that had been going through his mind. The ever-vivid image of her holding his gaze and saying softly, "Then it's a good thing there are men like you to make up for that."

She'd meant it then, he knew she had. Her voice had rung with the sincerity of it. Up until that day when the crash had come. No autorotation that day, because there'd been no rotor left to spin. They'd gone down like the nearly ten tons of bricks they essentially were without that big blade.

His life had nearly ended that day.

Life as he'd known it ended because of that day.

He hated this, the almost constant revisitation of a past he'd tried so hard to put behind him. He'd known when he'd gotten on that plane to come here that he was opening the door to a lot of things he wasn't going to like, but it wasn't like he had any choice. Not when Ethan was at stake.

He hadn't realized he was clenching his jaw so tightly until a bump in the road made him tighten it even more. But he remembered the bump, at the end of the street that was their destination.

The gate was open when they reached the Foxworth building, and Rafe's vehicle was already there. Erin started to pull in behind it, but changed without protest when Blaine suggested she pull over beside it, so they could either or both exit in a hurry if they had to.

"The kind of thing I never think of," she muttered as she turned off the engine.

"The kind of thing civilians shouldn't have to," he said as they got out and headed, nearly at a run again, to the office door.

Rafe was standing with the remote in his hand when they stepped inside. He turned to look at them, and Blaine once more had that feeling that he would never, ever want to be in this man's sights.

He didn't waste any time with niceties. "Walker's still working his area, but says no sign yet, and Cutter hasn't signaled anything. But this just came in from the sheriff's detective he contacted." At Erin's curious look, he took a moment to explain. "Foxworth helped him find his kidnapped daughter when all else had failed. So he knows a bit about what you're going through."

"That's why he's helping?"

Rafe nodded. "That's all Foxworth ever asks in payment, the willingness to help someone else down the line."

He turned then to the flat-screen and hit a button on the remote. The screen flared to life, showing a slightly grainy black-and-white image.

"This place is right at the east edge of the area Walker's working now," Rafe said.

It looked to Blaine like a convenience store of some kind, apparently at a gas station, since he could see the pumps through the glass front of the structure. For a moment nothing was happening. There were no cars parked, or even at the pumps. The front counter was deserted, too. He assumed whoever was running the place at the moment was out of range of the camera.

Then the door opened and a tall, gangly figure came in. A moment later—thirty-two seconds, according to the timer in the lower right corner—the door opened again and two more people, shorter, younger, came in.

Blaine heard Erin gasp in the same instant his gut clenched. Because the second kid who came in was Ethan. There was no mistaking it—the image was much clearer than the one from the pet store.

And then he was swearing under his breath as it became clear what was happening. It began when Ethan and the other kid started a scuffle at the back of the store, near one of the refrigerated cases, at the very edge of the camera's range. The clerk, a middle-aged man with a bit of heft to him, stepped into the frame, clearly headed to break up the scrap. In the center of the image, the bigger, older kid snuck around the counter and began to work at the cash register.

Ineffectively, as it turned out. He couldn't get the cash drawer to open.

"Amateur hour," Blaine muttered, wondering how much cash would actually be in there anyway, given the propensity for electronic payments these days.

"I'd say they planned everything but that little detail," Rafe agreed, freezing the image just as the older kid slammed a fist on the register in frustration.

"You're saying this was planned out?" Erin asked.

Blaine looked at her. "Obvious, isn't it?" He gestured toward the corner where the clerk had pried Ethan and the other boy apart. "They were the distraction. I'd guess he—" he shifted to the kid behind the counter "—figured all he had to do was push a button and it would fall into his hands."

"But…why? There can't be much money there," she said, echoing his earlier thought.

Blaine exchanged a glance with Rafe. "Initiation?"

"A little light for that. A line on the résumé, maybe."

Erin's gaze was shifting from him to Rafe and back. "You mean they did this to…try and get into that gang Walker was talking about?"

"To get noticed by them, maybe," Rafe said. "They likely wouldn't take kindly to some kids horning in on what they see as their territory."

Rafe's phone chimed a notification. He grabbed it, put it to his ear and said only, "Go." Then, a moment later he said, "Hang on. We're all here, just watched the video, so let me put you on speaker."

Walker's voice came through clearly. "I just talked to the clerk at the store. He's also a co-owner, by the way. Couple of things. First, they got sort of lucky, because the leader couldn't get the register open, so they spooked and just ran, didn't even grab any stuff on their way out. So that'll keep the legal situation banked a little."

"And second?" Erin asked, tensely.

He seemed to hesitate, then said, "The guy said when he went back to break up the fight, the older, bigger kid just cussed a blue streak."

"But Ethan?" she prodded.

Blaine thought he heard the other man take a breath. "The clerk said he looked scared. Said it looked like more than just getting caught, that the way he kept looking toward the front of the store, where the leader was, it seemed like that's who he was afraid of."

Erin winced visibly, and lowered her head. But when Walker started to say something more and then stopped himself, it came up again.

"Say it." Her voice held as much command as Rafe's had earlier.

"This is nothing but the guy's feeling, okay? But he does have three kids of his own, so he's not coming completely out of nowhere. He said he had the feeling that if he could have, if they'd been alone, Ethan would have asked for help."

Blaine saw the shudder go through her. He moved automatically, instinctively. He put his arms around her and held her, because this was Erin and this was what he did when she was upset. And no amount of time or distance could kill that instinct, apparently.

At the same time he was fighting the urge to go charging into that space Walker said was theirs, guns blazing. He was not in a war now, at least not the kind he'd been trained to fight. No, this was a much deeper, more personal war. A battle for his son. And, he thought, almost overwhelmed by the feel of Erin in his arms again, possibly for even more.

And he would do whatever it took to win that battle.

Chapter Thirty

She was exhausted.

Erin could no longer deny it. She was so tired she should be asleep on her feet, and yet she knew if she went to bed she would lie awake half the night as she had the entire ten days Ethan had been gone.

Actually, it would probably be worse tonight. Because all she could think about was what Walker had told them the clerk had said.

...he looked scared.

Her little boy—she caught herself, he wasn't so little anymore—was out there somewhere, caught up in something he hadn't intended, or at the least had changed his mind about. Oddly, that gave her hope, but that hope was swamped by the rest of the situation.

...if he could have... Ethan would have asked for help.

She tried to focus on the progress they'd made, more since Blaine and his friends had begun to help out than she'd made the entire time since Ethan had taken off. They were getting closer, and thanks to Foxworth, they knew so much more. But that only made her feel again as if she ought to be out there, pushing harder, searching. They had the cameras here now, she could do it. It would be better than this. But then almost anything would.

She rolled over and sat up on the edge of her bed. She rubbed at her burning eyes, wondering if she had any moisturizing drops left. She got up to go into the bathroom to see, but stopped short of the doorway when she heard something from the front of the house.

Something that had sounded a lot like the front door opening and closing.

Ethan?

Her heart leaped with hope. Had that robbery been the last straw, had he broken free and come home?

She pulled open the bedroom door and started quickly down the hall. But the moment she saw the figure in the darkened living room she knew it wasn't Ethan. No, this was a man, tall, broad-shouldered, strong. A man who moved in a way she knew all too well.

Blaine.

But he had clearly just come in—using the spare key she had given him, because it was the only practical thing to do—from outside, because he was pulling off his heavy canvas jacket. But what had he been doing? Rafe and Cutter were back at the Foxworth headquarters, she suspected intentionally leaving them alone together. She wasn't sure why she thought that, except that Rafe had said, when he'd told her he would be staying there, "He's a good man, Erin. Even if you don't love him anymore, let him be a bigger part of your son's life."

He was wrong about one thing, but she wasn't ready to admit that yet. And on him being a larger part of Ethan's life, well, she'd already decided that. Maybe if she'd done that earlier on, Ethan might not have taken off at all. She grimaced, tired of feeling this way, of self-critiquing her every thought and action. But it was hard not to, when this had been the result.

She flipped on the living room light. Blaine spun around, startled.

"Sorry. I tried to be quiet and not wake you."

She shook her head. "I wasn't asleep." She let out a sour laugh. "Not sure when I did sleep last, truly."

He just looked at her then, wearing that worried expression she had once known meant he cared, so much. Now she wasn't sure what it meant.

"Where were you?" she asked.

"Out walking around. Just in case."

Just as she had lain there wanting to do, only he'd already done it. How very like him. Even if it seemed futile, Blaine just never quit if it was something that had to be done. She could only remember once he'd lost his temper with her, after she told him that she was leaving because she could not ever go through anything like this again.

A sudden image flashed through her mind, of the moment when her words "I'm leaving," had hung in the air between them. He had stared at her as if she'd spoken them in ancient Latin, as if he had no idea what she could possibly mean. But when he'd finally understood, what she'd said and that she meant it, he'd had a few choice words to say.

And every one of them had been true.

"I kept thinking," he said now, "about what Walker said about that clerk's impression, that Ethan was scared and wanted help."

She quashed the painful memories of the destruction of a beautiful life. "So did I. It's why I couldn't sleep."

He crossed the room to her, put his hands—those strong, powerful hands that could make such delicate adjustments while flying that his bosses called him one of the best they'd ever seen—on her shoulders. She looked up at him, at a loss for words. Maybe because it used to be when he touched her, words were the last thing she wanted, except to maybe say "Hurry up."

"He's going to be all right, Erin. We're getting closer, we'll find him and get him free of whatever he's gotten himself into."

She drew in a deep breath to steady herself. Rafe's suggestion once more went through her mind. And then, still looking at him, she nodded.

"And when we do find him, when he's safe again, things have to change. You have to be in his life more, Blaine. I'm sorry I've made it more difficult than it should be. But I was…afraid."

He drew back slightly, but didn't let go. "Afraid? Of me?" He looked beyond upset, almost horrified.

"Not you. Never you. I was afraid of…me."

"You?" he said, brow furrowed.

She took another deep breath. And said what had to be said. What he deserved to know.

"I know I'm the one who left, the one who destroyed us. The one who thought Ethan and I would be better off if we weren't always worried about it happening again. Weren't always worrying that the next time, you might not survive." She let out a harsh, short laugh. "Ethan's answer to that explanation was that I might be a coward, but he wasn't. That he wanted to live with you, wherever that was, and no matter how often he had to pack up and move. He obviously inherited your courage."

He gave her a look then that she couldn't quite interpret. Not happy, not now under these circumstances, but… pleased?

"Erin, I understand how bad it was, what you went through."

And there he was, that kind, understanding Blaine, the

gentle part that lived behind the tough, self-confident warrior. The Blaine who had ever been able to put her back together when she fell apart. Except for the time when she made sure she was too far away for him to even start.

She shivered slightly and lowered her gaze. "But there was one huge flaw in my grand plan."

His hands slid down her arms and he clasped her hands. "What?" he asked.

She stared down at those strong hands wrapped around hers, those tough, protective hands. She drew strength from them, from his touch, as she always had. And it was that strength that helped her look up once more, and lock onto those beautiful blue eyes.

"The huge flaw was… I couldn't… I never stopped loving you."

"Erin," he said, and it was a low, harsh, almost broken whisper.

And then he was kissing her, not the light, tender kiss of before but deep, fierce and absolutely luscious. She leaned into him, helpless to do anything else. This man, and only this man, had ever stirred her like this. The feel of him, the heat of him, the taste of him, fired nerve endings that had been dormant for so long she'd almost forgotten they existed.

It was like rereading a well-loved book that she hadn't looked at in years. All the things she'd adored were there, but it had been so long it all felt new.

But when, half-dressed and just outside her bedroom door, he stopped and threaded his fingers through her hair to tilt her head back to look at him, and asked in that deliciously rough tone she knew so well but had tried fruitlessly to forget, if she was sure, she knew this was still Blaine.

Her Blaine, and if she said no he would stop. Because that was who he was.

"I'm sure I don't want to go another minute without you."

"But how are you going to feel…after?"

"I'll deal with that then. But I swear, I won't take it out on you."

The only time she felt any hesitation was when, after freeing her of the last of her clothes and putting her gently on the bed, he shed the rest of his and she saw the scars. Not because they repelled her, but because they reminded her. Not just of the horror of what had happened, but of how pitifully incapable she'd been of handling it.

Look at them as proof he's a survivor.

The words of one of the Navy doctors who had noticed her state of mind came back to her now. She'd shoved them aside then, but now…

The moment he was on the bed beside her, hot, powerful and fully aroused, she forgot everything about those horrible days, and knew only how much she had missed this, the perfection of them together. From their first time she'd been stunned, but Blaine hadn't. He'd merely smiled and said he'd always known it would be perfect.

And it was perfect now as the door on that knowledge she'd kept locked away burst open, and everything she'd learned about his body, about what he liked, and where he liked to be touched, stroked, licked and kissed, came flooding out. At the same time he made it clear he hadn't forgotten a thing about her, either, and it was a reunion she'd never expected to have.

And more explosively spectacular than she could have hoped.

The moment he started to slide into her, she arched involuntarily, wanting that feeling of utter completion she knew would happen when he was inside her. And it did, and the groan of pleasure he let out when he was fully there told her it hadn't changed for him, either.

She shuddered at the sensation and whispered, "Only you. Only you do this to me."

"Because—" he began to move, to stroke "—we were—" he drove hard and deep "—made for each other."

She could not deny it, didn't even try.

And when she felt her body hit the peak, tightening around him until he let out her name on a gasp, she remembered how she'd always thought in this moment she understood him, because this was as close as she could get to flying.

Chapter Thirty-One

The signal from the Foxworth phone interrupted the sweetest dream Blaine had had in two years. Then he opened his eyes and realized it hadn't been a dream. The faint, early morning light proved it. He was in Erin's bed, she was snuggled up behind him, her arm draped over his ribs, and he was instantly hot enough to ignore the electronic sound and roll over and start anew that glorious joining he'd thought was gone forever.

Ethan.

He jolted upright, scrambling for the jeans he'd shed in such a hurry last night, digging into the pocket for the Foxworth device. Erin was awake now, so he put it on speaker so they could both hear.

"We've got something. Two somethings, in fact." Rafe's voice was sharp, as if he were on alert. "I'm on my way to you, ETA fifteen. Then we rendezvous with Walker and Cutter. Be ready."

"Copy," Blaine said, almost reflexively.

The phone went silent. He looked at Erin, who was staring at him. "Well, that was…abrupt," she said.

"This is something," he said, his own voice tense. He rolled out of bed, his dreamed scenario of a joint shower and a revisiting of the joyous union that had clearly never faltered despite it all shoved back for now.

In fact, he was relieved—in fact downright grateful—that there was no time for discussion, no time to obsess about what had happened last night. No time for her to say she regretted it now, the morning after.

And she thinks she's a coward?

He, of course, knew better. Erin was many, many things but a coward she was not. A coward wouldn't have stuck it out when he'd been in such bad shape. Which was why he'd never understood why she'd left, after the fact, after fighting through the worst.

He'd almost forgotten how efficient she could be, under pressure. But she showed it now, when she beat him getting washed up and dressed, and had coffee ready to boot. Just as Rafe pulled into her driveway they exchanged a look, one he guessed they both knew said this was temporary, this time of setting themselves aside for the sake of their son.

"You know the park off the Ortega Highway just east of the freeway?" were Rafe's first words. When Blaine nodded, Rafe gestured at the driver's seat and walked around to the other side. Erin didn't protest, but Rafe spoke as if she had. "Dark tinted windows in the back," he explained. "I'll update you on the way."

Blaine pulled out of the driveway, wondering how Erin must feel knowing that she was possibly a hindrance to their search that needed to be hidden, because they had to assume Ethan was still angry at her.

But she didn't react, other than to quietly take a back seat. When he glanced at her before he turned back to face front after clearing the driveway, he saw her slender jaw was set, and knew that she'd do whatever it took to get Ethan back home safely.

"Walker picked up something late last night, cruising his target area. He thinks it's solid, so we're going to meet up with him at that park. But in the meantime Ty came up with something. From the message boards in one of Ethan's games, that Ty also happens to play."

"I thought those were private," Erin said.

Rafe's mouth quirked. "Frankly, I don't think anything online is safely private when Ty goes after it. But he found a couple of exchanges, with different people but locals to here. All about a place they called Caspers."

Blaine shot a look at Erin. She knew the place as well as he did. As kids they'd spent a lot of time in the big, regional park, hiking, and more than once camping out, to pretend they were on a vacation far from home.

"You know it," Rafe said.

"Yes," Blaine confirmed. "We've…spent some time there."

"Big, from what I could find," Rafe said.

"Eight thousand acres big," Erin confirmed.

"Lots of places to hide?"

"Lots," Blaine said, his mouth twisting sourly.

"But it's November, so the trees will be mostly bare. They won't provide as much cover as the rest of the year," Erin pointed out.

Rafe nodded, looking thoughtful, as if an idea had come to him, but he didn't say anything.

A few minutes later Blaine pulled the car into the small parking area at one end of the park. He hadn't been to the long, narrow greenbelt-style community park just off the Ortega Highway in a long time, but he remembered how to get there. It was, he noted, on the inland side of the freeway from the convenience store in the robbery video. He appreciated the choice of a residential neighborhood, blocks away from the main drag, making it a bit less likely they'd be noticed.

The Foxworth phone signaled again. It was a different sound than the ring of a call, but memories of last night still flooded his brain, and he almost wished this hadn't come up, so he could have made love to her yet again. They had, after all, two years to make up for. But it was not the time, and this was the Foxworth phone and so could not be ignored.

Blaine pushed the flood of memories from last night out of his mind—and again resisted looking back at Erin in the back seat—when he saw the vehicle Walker had been driving, a slightly older version of the Foxworth one they were in, parked near the farthest boundary of the greenbelt. He realized the phone notification must have been a signal.

"Up close?" he asked Rafe.

The man nodded. "It'll be quick. Don't even get out."

Walker had Cutter out on the grass on a leash, and Blaine heard the dog let out a low bark of greeting as they pulled up. Rafe rolled down his window as the second Foxworth man walked over to the passenger side door. And again he didn't waste time on niceties.

"You should have an envelope somewhere in the glove box."

Blaine blinked, puzzled, but only looked at Rafe, who already had the compartment open and was digging through the contents. He pulled out a small manila envelope, showed it to Walker, who nodded. Rafe pulled out the contents, which looked like the registration papers for the vehicle and put them back in the compartment.

"Okay, we're negotiating here. When I say so, hand me the envelope, and I'll give you the trained guard dog I just sold you."

"You think they're watching?" Rafe asked.

"Can't be positive they're not. They put up with me because I don't pull anything on their turf, but they don't take that for granted, either."

"So," Blaine said, "we're what, buying drugs?"

Walker's mouth quirked. "Nah, that would tick them off. That's their main business. They put up with me because I don't mess with their trade, so we're warily in balance. And now I'm just selling a guard dog," he said, nodding at Cutter.

Blaine shook his head slowly, wondering how the guy did it. And Erin asked from the back seat, "What about when you're not doing this kind of…undercover thing? Don't they think that's suspicious?"

Walker gave her a crooked smile. "You'd be amazed the difference a haircut, shave and losing the tats makes." He looked back at Rafe. "Anyway, wanted to meet up because I'm going to have to do that cleanup tomorrow. Amy's boss has a client who needs some help. But I think this might do it."

Rafe nodded. "Go ahead."

"I was talking with one of the big guy's lieutenants around two a.m. I got the same mention from two other lower-down guys. About some kids, some wannabes that the boss is starting to take notice of. They all confirmed he was thinking about it because having juveniles to pull stuff off is handy, because they do less time if they get caught."

Blaine grimaced.

"Charming. Not," Erin said, sounding as sour as he felt.

"Yeah. But the important thing is, they all referred to them the same way. Called them the Caspers kids."

Blaine went still. He sensed Erin's sudden tension from behind him. But before either of them could speak Rafe did.

"Because?" Blaine could hear the alertness in the man's voice, and knew he was just making sure the conclusion they'd already leaped to was right.

"Because they're supposedly hanging out in Caspers Park. About another six miles up the road from here. It's a big park and wildlife preserve—"

"I know," Rafe said quickly, and explained what Ty had also discovered.

"Leave it to Ty," Walker said with a grin. "Anyway, apparently one of them—I'd guess the big guy from the robbery vid, who looks about sixteen or seventeen—has a car."

"Makes sense," Rafe said. "Somebody with a driver's license ID would make things easier."

Walker nodded and went on. "Putting some pieces from different sources together, I think it's an old, beat-up, maroon sedan with some bumper sticker on it, but that was about all I could get. But it was worth a check with the park personnel, and one of them thought it sounded familiar, and that it might be connected to some kids they had to kick out of one of the regular campgrounds because you're only allowed two weeks out of a month."

Blaine smiled at the guy who had disrupted everything to come back and help. "I feel like there really should be some money in that envelope we hand you."

"Nah, Foxworth pays fine. And brought me back to Amy, thanks to this guy—" he bent to stroke Cutter's dark head "—so I'm good."

Blaine noticed Rafe was smiling. And Walker Cole looked like a happy man. He suddenly remembered what Rafe had said about the dog being, among his many other skills, a matchmaker.

"I haven't been there in a while," Blaine said, "but if I remember right, there are a lot of places you could hike into that the rangers wouldn't know you were there. Problem would be the car, and the lack of paved roads."

"And the park staff monitors those pretty well," Walker said. "But there are places you could get to, if you weren't too worried about what shape your car would end up in. Problem is, it's a huge area to search."

"Got an idea about that," Rafe said as he handed over the empty envelope with the same care as if it had held a big payout.

Walker took it the same way, but all he said, with a nod toward the dog, was, "Amy's gonna want to see this guy before you leave."

"And she will," Rafe promised as he reached out and hit the control that opened up the back of the SUV. Walker took the dog around, and he jumped willingly into the vehicle.

"Good working with you again, buddy," Walker said as he gave the dog a final pat. Then he looked at Rafe through the interior of the car. "You, too," he added with a grin. "Give me two or three days for this new case, and I should be able to get back with you, if you need it. But knowing you, I'd say you'll have it safely wound up by then."

Blaine watched the man walk back to his car and drive off, as if what he'd done for them was just to be expected.

He silently hoped Walker was right about this coming to an end that fast.

And safely.

Chapter Thirty-Two

Erin knew something was up the moment Rafe asked Blaine, "Feeling a bit grounded lately?"

"Yeah, a bit," Blaine answered, looking at the other man curiously while he tapped edgily at the steering wheel. "Why?"

"Thinking a flyover might be a good start."

Erin watched Blaine go very still, but could also feel the sudden alertness in him. "You have access?"

Rafe nodded. "We can have. We have somebody here with a small fleet, who owes us a favor. If you think you can manage without all the armor and weaponry."

Blaine's half grin and nod were confident. "Yeah, I'll manage. I've done it before."

And it hit her what Rafe was talking about. An aerial search. A flyover. As in Blaine doing the flying.

The search part made perfect sense. The Blaine flying part had her once more weighing the risk against the hoped-for result. If they could find where Ethan was hiding, wouldn't that be worth…everything?

I just don't get shot at anymore.

She remembered his words, when he'd told her he was still flying, but teaching now. That made it different.

Ethan made this different.

"—too bad Walker had to start that other case, but Foxworth committed to it, so it's done. We'll need Cutter on the ground, but you need an observer."

"Without all that armor and weaponry, I can fly and observe both," Blaine said.

"Hello?" she said, not bothering to mask the tinge of sarcasm in her voice. Both men looked back at her. She pointed at her face with two fingers. "Eyes? Twenty-twenty vision?"

Blaine stared at her. "But… I thought you hated flying."

She couldn't blame him for that, so reined in the temper that had flared at being left out of this too often. Ethan was her son, and she would do a lot worse than climb into a helicopter to look for him.

"I hated *you* flying," she corrected. "Because I always worried. But this is way beyond worried already, so can we get moving?"

"Yes, ma'am," Rafe said, sounding as if he'd just been given marching orders. And that made her smile, inwardly at least.

That didn't mean she wasn't nervous about it. Because she was. And she was going to have a twenty-minute ride to the airport to stew about it. But then Cutter stuck his head over the back seat to nudge at her. Again, as if he'd sensed her tension. She didn't hesitate this time to stroke his head, and felt anew that soothing calm.

Blaine started the engine and headed back to the road, while Rafe began making arrangements on the phone. She could only hear his side of the conversation, but she couldn't help but notice that once the name Foxworth was mentioned, the pace picked up immediately, and faster than she could have ever guessed, arrangements were made.

When Rafe put down the phone, all he said was, "It'll be

ready and waiting when we get there. They offered a co-pilot, but it'd be a couple of hours and I didn't think you'd want to wait."

"No," Blaine said firmly, "no more waiting."

"All right," Rafe said. "You'll need to be in touch with air traffic, although my guy with the bird says it's not heavy in the area. As long as our fellow Marines just five miles away don't lose track of the base boundaries."

"If they do, I'll deal," Blaine said.

Rafe shifted his gaze to her. "I'll be back in the area by the time you get airborne. Any possibility you spot, I'll head Cutter that way, and he'll let us know quickly if Ethan's there, or ever been there."

She no longer doubted the clever dog would perform exactly as described. And whoever those kids were, they were no match for one of the best snipers in military history. Or one of the best pilots.

The private helicopter, a sleek, blue-and-white number she thought she might have seen now and then flying along the coastline, was already out on the tarmac and waiting for them. Blaine and Rafe were talking about the make and model, something about an Airbus, but she didn't pay much attention except to notice how big it was.

"Seats up to seven plus the pilot," said the man in a polo shirt bearing a logo that was the same helicopter they were standing next to, with the name Southwest Air Tours beneath it. Rafe had told them this was Matt Russell, the man who'd started this business two decades ago with one much smaller craft and grown it to a fleet of eight and a reputation for safety and efficiency that was unmatched in the area.

"I'm liking the enclosed tail rotor," Blaine said. "They're a lot quieter."

"Fifty percent," said the man proudly. Then he considered Blaine. "Mr. Crawford here tells me you're a great pilot."

"I won't hurt her," Blaine promised, patting the side of the craft as if it were alive.

"Wouldn't matter if you did, if it'll help Foxworth," he said. "I owe them…everything."

"How is your daughter?" Rafe asked.

"She's doing great. She'll graduate this year, and she wants to go to work for you guys."

Rafe's mouth quirked. "Might just happen."

The man got into the helicopter with Blaine and started pointing out various controls. After the crash refresher and Blaine pronouncing himself ready, the man gave Rafe a rather fierce handshake, then walked back toward the office and hangar. Erin asked, "What happened to his daughter?"

"She was kidnapped," Rafe said. "Along with three other girls, by a sex-trafficking ring. Foxworth got a lead and had an in, and ended up bringing her—and the others—home safely."

Erin just stared at him for a moment. Then, softly, she said "No wonder he just handed a gazillion-dollar helicopter over to you."

Rafe just smiled, and the quiet satisfaction in it made her remember what Blaine had said about him being happier with what he did now than anything else.

"Go," he said simply. "Let's find your son."

She clambered into the helicopter. Rafe retreated to the Foxworth vehicle, where Cutter was watching with apparent interest. She took her seat beside Blaine, noticing that the craft was built for visibility. Big windows at the sides, and with the front glass sweeping down to below floor level on each side of the trim control panel, giving a full view downward. That was going to be her job, to utilize every bit of that visibility.

She felt a new vigor pulsing through her. In fact, she felt more energized than she had in days, because this felt… real. So much more than blindly driving around looking with no clue to actually follow.

And it felt good. Doing something felt so much better than just…waiting. She needed to think about that a little. And the fact that after last night she just couldn't imagine going back to life without Blaine.

But now they had to find their boy, so all she gave him was a quick nod. He didn't smile, just nodded back as he said, "Here."

He was holding out a pair of heavy-looking headphones. She took them, listened carefully as he pointed out the controls, then put them on. It was a bit awkward, since she wanted to keep one ear clear for the Foxworth phone, but she managed to finally achieve a balance of sorts.

She watched as he readied the aircraft. He was talking to someone she couldn't hear, and guessed it was the control tower at the small but busy airport. She watched his hands, the hands that had driven her mad last night, on the controls she remembered him explaining to her. More than once, since she couldn't quite believe it involved not just both hands but both feet as well. The throttle she got—it was like the ones on motorcycles. But that the same stick was also the pitch control —the collective?—threw her. And the main control, the cyclic, boggled her even more. Throw in the antitorque pedals, and she was thinking flying an airplane had to be easier.

A plane wants to fly, it's designed that way. A helicopter wants to tear itself apart.

It had been a ten-year-old Ethan who'd told her that, with

such a tone of glee she'd wondered for a moment about his sanity.

But Dad's so good it wouldn't dare.

He'd added that with a blissful pride that had made her grab the boy and hug him, never mind his protests. Their lives had been good then. But just over a year later...

She shook off the painful jab. *Focus. You have to focus like you never have.*

You can't rebuild until you have all the pieces.

Chapter Thirty-Three

It felt good to be at the controls again, even if it was a very different kind of aircraft. One designed not to kill or blow things up, but to carry people having a good time, to beautiful places. Or in this case, to help in a desperate rescue. Which spoke to Blaine on a deep level, making him wonder if he should have focused on medevac work more all this time.

The takeoff went smoothly, and he had to admit he liked how much quieter the closed-in cabin of the craft was, compared to the often open-sided military choppers. And that enclosed rotor made a difference, too. He got them out of the airport traffic pattern as quickly as possible and moved inland, to be able to fly faster than they could near the more popular coastal area. It was only a few minutes before he had it pretty much down, the way the helicopter responded and how he needed to adjust his instinctive moves for the lighter—and unarmed—craft.

Mr. Russell had kindly uploaded a fairly detailed aerial map of the park, making it easier for them to determine where the boundaries and roads were.

"Coulda been worse," Blaine muttered.

"What?" came Erin's voice in his ear, almost startling him, he'd been so focused on being in the air again.

"Just thinking at least we've got something the size of a car to look for. Could have been a motorcycle or bicycle."

"He wants a motorcycle."

He gave her a brief glance before going back to scanning, aware from the radio traffic he'd heard that there was a local agency police helicopter aloft to the north. "He does? How'd you feel about that?" he asked, although he guessed he already knew the answer.

"I told him no way."

"How'd that go over?"

He thought he heard her sigh, although it was hard to tell. "Like anything I tell him since…"

She didn't finish the sentence. She didn't have to. He knew she meant since they'd split. He smothered a sigh of his own. He'd reach out to touch her, reassure her that they'd work it out somehow, but there was that pesky detail of needing hands and feet on the controls. He smothered the urge and kept flying.

He had the feel of the Airbus now, and pushed the speed up to as fast as he thought safe. Maybe a bit beyond. But as was long ingrained habit, he never lost track of where they were, and never stopped scanning the ground.

Just in case.

"We're not there yet," Erin's voice came in his ear. "What are you looking for?"

"Likely spots, if we have to set down in a hurry." He'd said it almost absently, but when she stiffened he glanced at her. "It's second nature, like watching the fuel gauge and the compass. Like you check for cross traffic at an intersection in a car. That's all."

"Oh."

When they neared the park area he slowed. He'd already planned out a search grid for the park, but before they started he flew along the few paved areas, road and parking, and the main campground areas to check for any sign of the maroon sedan. Nothing.

He was about to begin the grid search they'd worked out when he saw a rhythmic flash of light from just ahead and to their right side, along the northern boundary of the park.

"There's Rafe," he said.

"That flash...it was a signal?"

He nodded.

"Let me guess," she said, her tone a little dry, "that's another thing you two didn't have to discuss because it's just habit?"

He glanced at her to see if she was upset for some reason. But she was almost smiling, so he just said, "Once a Marine..."

The Foxworth phone signaled. Erin lifted it to her head. He pulled the right side of the headset off his ear so he could hear. When she saw that, she turned on the speaker.

"You could have used this and foregone the semaphore," she said, and he could imagine Rafe's grin.

"Saves time," Rafe said, sounding unoffended. Then, briskly, "Air's clear at the moment."

"And no sign of the car in any of the campground areas, or parking areas," Blaine said.

"There are a few off-road tracks on this side they might know about. Or have caused," Rafe said. "It would definitely put them off the beaten track. I'll check those with Cutter while you do the area scan. Let me know when you're changing sectors and we'll shift position."

"Copy. Starting section one now."

They'd divided the map of the park into sections of about

a hundred acres. They were able to eliminate the more frequently used areas that held visitors even now in the off-season, which narrowed it a bit. But eight thousand acres was a lot of ground to cover, and it was going to be a long day. And would likely require a return to the airfield for refueling before they were done, if they had to cover the whole thing.

They'd decided to start on the outer edges, the less visited areas, on the assumption the kids would think it a better place to hide. Then they'd work their way toward the middle. Those areas, with campgrounds and hiking trails and overlooks, would take longer, but they would get it done.

Erin was as intent on the task as he'd expected she'd be. More than once she went for the high-power binoculars Mr. Russell had loaned them. They were truly needed because of the promise they'd had to make that they would stay as high as possible, to avoid spooking all the wildlife that called this place home. He knew only the Foxworth name had gotten them permission to make this search at all, and he was once more in awe of this place Rafe had landed.

But every time Erin raised them, she eventually lowered the binoculars with a shake of her head. He flew on, fiercely intent, as if he were hunting armed insurgents who would slaughter his fellow troops on the ground. Because to him it had become even more important. This was Ethan they were searching for, that precious boy who meant more than any other human being to him—except for the woman beside him, who was searching just as intently.

Memories of last night started to intrude, but he knew better than to let them in. Because if he started thinking about how spectacular it had been, how incredible, how it had surpassed even the vivid images that so often blew up his dreams, he'd lose focus, and he couldn't risk that. He hadn't been at all surprised, it had always been that way between them, but he'd had to admit time—or his efforts at avoidance—had dulled the vibrancy of the memories a bit. But after last night, everything was as vivid and powerful as ever.

Maybe you didn't ever get over a woman who'd been at your side since childhood.

He slammed the door shut on those thoughts with the ease of long practice and the fierceness of a hard-won determination.

Although he had to admit he'd had worse observers aboard than Erin. She was both intent and intense, and had no qualms about telling him to circle back for a better look at something. At least he didn't have to worry about enemy forces trying to blow him out of the sky. Although dodging that red-tail hawk a moment ago had been a bit jolting. But he didn't want to hit it—he liked the birds who seemed to love flying as much as he did.

He couldn't help smiling at the memory that surfaced then.

"What?" Erin asked.

He was a little surprised she'd noticed, as intently as she was focused on surveying the ground beneath them.

"Just remembering my dad joking that if he believed in reincarnation, he figured I'd come back as one of those red tails."

"Hmm," she said, as if seriously considering the idea. "I would have thought a bald eagle would be more appropriate."

He gave her a startled glance for the instant he could spare. She seemed to sense it, and glanced back. And the cabin of the helicopter seemed suddenly full of an electricity he was surprised didn't short out all the instruments.

He almost said something, but the Foxworth phone signaled again.

"Cutter hit on something," Rafe said. "Just south of your location. Near some off-road tire tracks. Faint, so not recent, but something."

"Copy."

He'd made the adjustment to the search area before he finished speaking the word. Erin had the binoculars up to her eyes again just as fast. It was nearly a minute, which seemed like a week to him, before she spoke.

"There's Cutter."

He shifted, while she scanned the area. He changed their angle as much as he could, putting some strain on the engines to keep them aloft, so she could use more window to see. He spotted the dog, who was forging ahead like some unstoppable force, his nose working hard. Rafe was a few feet behind, and without looking away from the intent Cutter, he waved at them to indicate he was aware.

Blaine began to make rhythmic sweeps, covering a swath on either side of the search path Cutter had made so clear.

They'd been at it a few minutes when Erin asked, "Can you drop down, just a little?"

He did so, and at the same time resumed the visual scan he'd begun the moment Rafe had spoken, always looking for someplace to set down if need be.

"There!" Erin yelped. "I swear, I saw a glimpse of something maroon or purple! Next to that tree that's still got some leaves on it, down and to the left."

He dropped down even more, until the rotors set the branches of everything he could see swirling.

"It's the car!"

"A car," he cautioned, and sent them upward again.

"What are you—"

"Tell Rafe," he said, not caring that he'd cut her off at this point. "I'm going to set down over there near that tree you pointed out."

She grabbed the phone and spoke into it as he negotiated the slightly cramped clearing. He could only hope the Foxworth good name would cover him landing on county property—or maybe it was state out here?—without getting permission first.

Because he wasn't about to stop now.

Chapter Thirty-Four

He touched the bird down so lightly Erin wasn't even sure they had landed until he ripped off the headphones and reached for the door handle. She echoed his action, on instinct alone hanging on to the binoculars. By the time her feet hit the dirt beneath the helicopter's skids, Blaine was already running toward the car parked almost hidden under what she could now see was a live oak. There was no sign of any other people close by, kids or adults.

She bent a little as she followed, not even sure if she needed to dodge the rotor but remembering one of Blaine's earliest lessons. She tried to visualize the map, estimate how far they were from the park entrance and the more frequented areas. She thought a long way—enough to make it a good place to hide—but the rolling hills made it hard to judge.

She got to the parked car just as Blaine, who had been walking around the area next to the half-hidden vehicle, crouched down beside what looked like a roughly made firepit. She glanced at the car, saw there was a bumper sticker on the left rear. Something about coexisting, ironically. But it made it even more likely that the scratched and dinged vehicle was the one they'd been looking for. A quick glance showed her there was nothing immediately visible inside, at least in the way of clothes or backpacks—Ethan's backpack in particular.

She turned just as Blaine straightened up. He was brushing ash off his fingers. As if he'd actually stuck his hand into the pit. As it struck her why he'd probably done it, he spoke, proving her right.

"Slightly warm, way down. I'd say a fire going last night, burned out this morning."

"But where did he—they—" she needed to remember her boy wasn't likely alone "—go, and leave the car?"

"Don't know." He turned and walked over to the car. Tried the doors, which were apparently locked. Stood there, considering.

"Thinking about breaking a window?"

He shot her a sideways look. "Definitely under consideration. I want a look at the glove box and the trunk."

Her brow furrowed. "But you do think this is the car, don't you?"

"Yes. But there's some sign there might have been a tent pitched over there," he said, nodding toward the other side of the firepit. "And I want to know if they took it with them."

Understanding hit her. "Because if they didn't, they'll be back here sooner. Not camping out somewhere else tonight."

"Yes. And if they didn't, that might indicate they plan to vacate this spot soon, otherwise why bother to take it down." His mouth twisted slightly. "Not like they could have expected an aerial search with Ms. Eagle Eye on watch. That was a good spot."

She couldn't begin to describe how that made her feel. She'd felt up until now that she'd been useless, practically in the way. "Thanks," she said, meaning it rather fiercely.

This was the Blaine she'd known and loved since she was seven years old.

Turning her head so he wouldn't see the moisture pooling in her eyes, she murmured, "Where would they have gone? Hiking? If this car is their only transportation…"

"No idea. But," Blaine added as he turned to look at something she hadn't even heard, "I'll bet he can tell us."

She spun around just in time to see Cutter, unleashed, break through some underbrush, heading toward them. Close behind him was Rafe, unexpectedly geared up with a backpack and…

A rifle.

Rafe the sniper.

Her heart slammed in her chest. She glanced at Blaine, but he didn't seem to have reacted to the presence of the weapon. Of course, he was a lot more used to such things, saw them every day.

She did not.

Rafe came to a halt beside them, and Blaine quickly gave him a summary of what they'd found since they'd spotted the car, which Blaine admitted wasn't much.

"A lot more than we had," Rafe said. And then, clearly having noticed her glance at the weapon strapped to that backpack, he met her gaze. "A precaution, Erin. For Ethan's sake. We don't know for sure somebody isn't armed."

"Oh."

Since there had been no weapon used at the convenience store, she'd assumed, sillily perhaps, that they didn't have one. But that didn't mean they didn't have one now. Or more. That older kid, the one who had gotten so angry when he couldn't get the register to open…

She noticed Rafe was doing something at the car door, and when it swung open a moment later she realized he was somehow opening it. She saw him slide a small case of something back into a side pocket on the pack, and guessed they should be grateful the old car had the kind of locks you could pick.

Blaine was already inside, reaching over to the glove box. He pulled out some paperwork, glanced at it, started to reach in further, then stopped.

"I see some weed, and a little baggie of pills. Figure I'd better not touch it."

"Good call," Rafe agreed, while Erin tried to process the presence of drugs without freaking out.

Blaine found the right latch and popped it, then got out. Rafe was already at the back of the car, lifting the trunk lid. A sudden horrible image hit her, born of dozens of movies and television shows, of people unsuspectingly opening the trunk of a car to find a body. She slapped it down, hard.

No wonder Blaine doesn't want you involved. You aren't equipped for this, mentally or physically.

But she had found the car. She'd done that much at least.

...Ms. Eagle Eye on watch. That was a good spot.

His words played back in her head, and did more to calm her than any self-recrimination could.

"No tent," Rafe said, straightening up. "But a tarp that looks like it might be a rain cover for one. And a couple of spikes." He looked as if he were about to say more, but stopped. Erin wondered if she'd imagined the slight ramping up of tension.

"So they took it with them," Blaine said.

"Maybe they wanted a camp spot farther in, away from where cars could reach." *Or helicopters.* She glanced at Blaine. "Good thing we came in on a tourist-looking thing, in case they saw us."

He nodded. "Good cover." He shifted his gaze to Rafe.

"Which I'll thank you again for later. After," he added, rather tightly, "you tell me what you found in there that ratcheted up your alert level."

So she hadn't imagined it.

Rafe remained silent, but he held something out to Blaine. It looked like a small, flattened cardboard box. Blaine took it, looked. His gaze immediately shot back to Rafe.

"Crap," he said.

"Indeed," the other man agreed.

She held out a hand, and without comment—or, thankfully, hesitation—Blaine handed the thing to her. And she read, with dismay, that she was holding what had once held fifty rounds of 9mm ammunition.

They all turned to look when a short, sharp bark, came from the trees toward the front end of the car. Cutter stood there, looking back at him with obvious impatience.

"He's got the scent," Rafe said. "We'd better move."

And now, Erin thought grimly, they weren't just looking for some kids hiding out on some crazy adventure. They were looking for some kids with lousy judgment and misguided ideas, who apparently had a gun.

But they were closer to Ethan than they'd been in more than ten days, and she'd risk a lot more than confronting those kids to save her son.

Chapter Thirty-Five

"You're sure it's Ethan he's scenting?"

Blaine saw Rafe look back at Erin. "I can only say that in the more than three years I've worked with him, he's never been wrong." He paused, and with a crooked smile that reminded Blaine of how much the man had changed, he added, "About anything."

"Or anyone?" Erin said softly.

"That, too," Rafe agreed.

Blaine looked at Erin. Had she gotten the point? The point that even couples who thought they had nothing left but debris could rebuild and be stronger even than before? Sharing all that seemed a bit touchy-feely for the rugged former Marine, but Rafe himself admitted he wasn't who he used to be.

And neither are you.

They followed the dog. Cutter was clearly both intent and intense. Even a rustle of some creature in the bushes off to one side, and a raucous call from a raptor above didn't sway him. He moved like someone who knew what his job was and wasn't about to let anything distract him from it. Blaine had the feeling only a direct order from Rafe would even slow him down.

And they were moving fast now, fast enough that Blaine said to Rafe, very quietly, "We're making some noise."

Rafe nodded, but also spoke quietly. "He knows when to shut it down. Knows we less skilled humans need time to assess before we barrel ahead into whatever it is."

Blaine smiled in spite of the situation. "You said he just appeared out of nowhere on your boss's wife's doorstep one day."

Rafe nodded again. "After her mother died. As Hayley says, when she needed him most."

"Sounds like he was a gift, then." Erin said it just as quietly as they'd been speaking.

"He is," Rafe said. "To all of us."

Well, that proved more than anything yet just how much Rafe had changed since he'd last seen him. The tough guy had never, ever been given to such whimsy; in fact had had a darker, grimmer view of life and the world than most.

"I'd like to meet your Charlie someday," he said.

Rafe gave him a quick glance. "She'd like to meet you, too." His mouth quirked. "She might even like to thank you."

They trekked, Cutter never wavering, forging on. And when he looked ahead of the dog, Blaine could see traces of passage, a footprint here, a broken branch there, all looking fairly fresh. He wondered if the failed robbery attempt had convinced them to lie low for a while.

He also wondered what they were eating. Wondered if there was some grocery store in town questioning where half their supply of that darned sugary cereal Ethan loved had gone.

You don't even know if he still eats the stuff.

He smothered a sigh. Sometimes that was what he hated most, that he didn't know his own son's tastes and habits anymore. He'd thought he would always know all of those things, as he had known them up until the day Erin had walked out on him. Yes, he'd been gone, on deployment for months at a time, but he'd been luckier than some and never completely out of touch for more than a day or two. And when he was home he focused completely on his family.

He had, perhaps foolishly, assumed that the mathematical fact that he spent more cumulative hours with them than most nine-to-five guys would make up for the times when he was gone altogether.

They kept going, as he wondered just how far back in these kids had gone. He tried to picture Ethan, overlaying the latest photo Erin had, which was newer than his own, trekking out here through the brush and occasional oak tree. The Ethan he remembered would have been excited to see the wildlife, like that deer that had scooted away from its tasty meal of leaves when they got too close, the skunk that had thankfully waddled away, or that coyote that had trailed them for a while, until apparently deciding they weren't worth his time and Cutter was no kin. He saw tracks of others, including some he was fairly sure were from one of the cougars that lived here, and hoped they hadn't become so accustomed to humans they wouldn't stay clear.

He was startled out of his thoughts when Erin, who was a couple of steps ahead of him, suddenly grabbed his arm and pulled him to one side. He gave her a startled look.

"Rattlesnake," she whispered. "One of the red ones, with the black-and-white tail above the rattle."

He couldn't, never had been able to stop the shiver that went through him. He'd been bitten by a snake as a toddler, and it had left him with an instinctive fear so deeply ingrained he'd given up trying to fight it.

He'd gotten better about the nonvenomous ones over the years, with Erin's help. She was just normally wary, and actually interested in the beasts that weren't poisonous. She even liked a few of them. But one sound of that rattle and his nerves were buzzing crazily.

"It was headed away," she assured him, "but I didn't want you to freak if you saw it."

He grimaced. "And I would have. Never have beaten that one."

She just slid her arm around his waist and gave him a hug. God, he'd missed this. The quiet understanding, the knowing each other so well, the sweetly teasing way she'd always said, "Even you have to be afraid of *something*."

His mind wanted to rocket into the future, into pictures of them putting it back together, as Rafe and his Charlie had. But he reined it in, knowing nothing, not even that, could take precedence over what they had to do now.

And if he failed in this task, nothing else ever would.

Even as he made that mental vow to concentrate on nothing but Ethan, Cutter let out a short, low sound, not a bark or a growl, but something that sounded oddly like a gruff whistle. The dog had slowed as well, and Blaine saw he was no longer searching the ground for the scent he'd been following, but had stretched his head out, holding it up slightly.

Then Cutter stopped dead, his head went up further, and Blaine saw that incredibly sensitive canine nose twitching. And suddenly it hit him, what had happened. The Foxworth dog was no longer following a trail on the ground. He was picking up the scent in the air. Which meant…the quarry had to be close.

Ethan had to be close.

And then that crazily brilliant dog sat. He stared up at Rafe, who clearly understood. "Got it," he whispered to the animal.

Blaine scanned the area, looking for some higher ground.

At this time of year the foliage wasn't as thick as it could be, and he wanted to use that.

"What now?" Erin asked, her whisper even quieter now, telling him she too had understood what Cutter's actions meant.

He'd found his spot, a small rise just to the west. "I want to get up there, where I can see better."

"I was thinking there," she said, pointing toward a rather similar place in the opposite direction.

"Good idea, cover both," Rafe said just as quietly. "Cutter and I will hold watch here. Just stay silent. If you spot something, double-click on walkie-talkie button on the phone, don't speak. Whoever didn't signal, head back here."

They both nodded. "Glad I brought these," Erin murmured, reaching for the binoculars.

"Me, too," Blaine whispered back and, unable to stop himself, leaned over and kissed her. A light, quick brush of his lips, but at the way she blushed he wasn't sorry. And spared a split second for the time when they could lay this all out and see what they had. See if they could rebuild.

When he got to the top of the rise he was both glad and disappointed. He could see, as he'd hoped, down into the small gorge that headed south, but it was empty. At least of humans, and there was no sign any human life had ever intruded. He thought he saw a coyote moving through the brush on the other side, and wondered if that meant there were no humans around. Then again, coyotes these days adapted so well to the human invaders it probably welcomed them and all the goodies they lugged around when in places like this.

He moved slightly, but the underbrush was too thick to penetrate without making noise. The dense stand of prickly pear cactus was a factor, too. He could work his way around—

Two short, sharp spits of static from the phone in his shirt pocket froze him in place.

Rafe had seen something or… Erin had.

When he got close to the rally point they'd left, he found Rafe watching for him. The moment he spotted him the sniper swept his arm in the direction Erin had gone, and started that way. Blaine moved as fast as he could without risking too much noise, and followed.

He spotted Cutter first, and the always alert dog looked as if he were vibrating, he was so intent. When he neared the top of the rise Erin had chosen, Rafe already had the binoculars to his eyes. He wasn't scanning, but was holding them fixed on one spot. Blaine looked in that direction, toward a small cluster of live oaks…with a tent pitched beneath them.

Erin was at his side in the moment Rafe lowered the binoculars, and she threw her arms around him. "He's there," she whispered excitedly. "I saw him, Blaine, he's there and he's okay."

He hugged her back, but his gaze was fixed on Rafe, who had finally lowered the binoculars. He just looked over at him and nodded to confirm Erin's words. Then he gestured them back down the way they had come. Blaine guessed to keep the slight hill between them and the makeshift campsite. Once they were below the crest he stopped.

"The one with the blue baseball cap on backward. He's armed," Rafe whispered. "Semiauto pistol. Chrome. No holster, just stuffed in his belt."

Blaine's jaw tightened, but he only nodded. Then Rafe handed him the field glasses and told him to sneak back and watch for a minute, to assess Ethan's state of mind as best he could. Erin started to speak, but stopped when Rafe held up a hand.

"We need another assessment from someone who knows him," Rafe whispered, and she went silent again and nodded.

Blaine wasn't sure he qualified anymore, but he went. Slowly, carefully, a difficult task given his every instinct was screaming at him to charge this place, grab Ethan and get him out of there. When he was in the same spot Rafe had been, he lifted the binoculars.

Every muscle he had tightened the moment he spotted the boy sitting on a rock just outside the tent. His head was in his hands and all Blaine could really see was that his hair was the right color, the same sandy blond as his mother's. He wore a stained hoodie sweatshirt, and jeans that had a hole in one knee and were a bit ragged around the bottom edges. He felt a ripple of an emotion he couldn't name when he saw the boots the boy had on.

The lace-up, military-style boots he'd bought the boy for his fourteenth birthday just a few months ago. They were the only thing he wanted, Ethan had told him. Boots like his.

He tried to swallow past the sudden, constricting tightness of his throat. It really was Ethan. It had to be. And then the boy looked up, to his left, and Blaine saw his face, which confirmed it.

But seeing his son's face confirmed something else. And this was what Rafe had wanted, he knew. There was no mistaking the slumped posture, the hunched shoulders. But even if he hadn't been certain, the way the boy took a sudden swipe at his eyes told him what he'd sensed in his gut was true.

Ethan was miserable.

Another person, a bigger kid Blaine immediately recognized as the boy with the temper from the robbery video, came around the back of the tent, followed by the other, younger boy who had helped stage the distracting fight. Ethan watched both of them warily, and the bigger kid said something to him that made him lower his gaze, to his knees apparently, judging by the way he started picking at the hole in his jeans.

And Blaine did not like the way the apparent leader was looking at his son. He wondered if the guy was perceptive enough to have noticed Ethan's unhappiness, his restlessness. If maybe he guessed the boy wanted to bail.

There were a couple of other kids back farther under the trees, apparently collecting firewood, who looked about Ethan's age or even younger. And they were close enough to mess things up unless they played this right.

Ethan said something, and the leader cuffed him on the side of the head. Every muscle in Blaine's body tensed, and it was all he could do not to go racing down the slope and put the guy on his ass. But he could see the butt of the handgun the older boy had stuck into his belt, and stopped himself.

The bigger guy—funny how he didn't seem much like a kid now, after that—shoved Ethan into the tent and said something to him. Through the binoculars Blaine could almost read his lips, and thought he'd said "—and stay there!"

He'd seen enough. He made his way silently down the rise to where Erin, Rafe and the amazing Cutter were waiting. Rafe lifted a brow at him silently.

Keeping his voice as low as he could he said, "Five of them, total. The older one with the gun, two more about Ethan's age, and one younger." He looked at Erin. "He's scared, just like the clerk said. And he's miserable."

"Yes," Erin said instantly, confirming she, who would know better than he, had seen the same thing.

Rafe nodded. "Then he won't fight you. That's what we needed to know."

"And," Blaine added by way of warning, "I don't like the way the leader's treating him."

"He's watching him really carefully," Erin agreed.

"Like he doesn't trust him?" Rafe asked.

Blaine nodded. "And he just slapped him, and ordered him into the tent."

Erin tensed even more, but didn't speak.

"Time to move, then." Rafe began to slide off his backpack.

They had discussed on the way here what would happen at this point, and while Erin hadn't been happy, she'd understood. Both of them, he knew, would risk anything to get their boy out of this. It had been a tough call, but she had agreed she was out of it, because while she would appear less threatening to the kid with the handgun, even she admitted—painfully—that if Ethan saw her he was likely to be uncooperative. And Rafe was many things, but easy to overlook or take casually wasn't one of them.

So for now, they would stay back, out of sight. Rafe would stay with her, but ready to make whatever move was necessary, while they hoped that the surprise of seeing his father would put Ethan off-balance enough that, if nothing else, Blaine could grab him and run.

"Here," Rafe said, digging into a side pocket of the pack and then holding out what looked like an earbud. "Keep this in so I can relay any larger view changes, and can hear how it's going on your end. It's on VOX, so just talk."

"Vox?" asked Erin.

"Voice-activated," Blaine answered as he seated the tiny device in his right ear. Rafe did a test count that came through clearly, and he nodded. Then he quietly called Cutter back to them. The dog obeyed, although he immediately turned back to face that scent as Rafe handed Blaine the leash he'd had stuffed in a pocket. Blaine clipped it onto the dog's collar, amazed at how the animal looked at him as if in acknowledgement of who was now in control.

"He's downright scary," Blaine muttered.

"Yep," Rafe agreed cheerfully. "But he knows what the leash means and he'll look to you for orders. And," he added, "he knows what it means if you let him off it."

"That he's in charge?" Erin asked. "You trust him that much?"

"Everyone at Foxworth has trusted this guy with their life, at one time or another. So have our clients. So far he's batting a thousand."

"Good enough for me," Blaine said, reaching down to stroke the dog's head. When he saw Erin watching, as if she completely understood the comfort just touching the dog gave, he asked her quietly, "A pat for luck?"

"Yes," she said, reaching down to stroke the exact same spot Blaine had. Cutter gave them one of those steady, intense looks he was so good at. And Blaine had the strangest feeling it was something along the lines of "We'll work on you when this is done."

Lord, he was losing his mind, putting such thoughts into the mind—although an admittedly very clever mind—of a dog.

"Ready?" Rafe asked. He nodded, straightened and took the leash into his left hand. "You sure about no weapon?"

Blaine nodded. He could shoot, had been trained, but this was different. Nothing was clear-cut here, and his son was involved.

"One-on-one isn't really my ballpark. I don't want anything they could grab while I'm focused on Ethan." His mouth quirked upward. "I'm counting on one of the best Marine snipers in history to handle that, if necessary. And to keep Erin safe."

"We'll get it done," Rafe promised.

And that they would, Blaine vowed. One way or another. Ethan was coming home.

Chapter Thirty-Six

If you'd asked him two weeks ago if a dog could be taught to understand the concept of undercover, Blaine would have laughed. But when Rafe bent down and whispered something that sounded like "casual" to the dog, and the hyperalert stance vanished and he seemed to shift into an ordinary creature that could be any family pet, he wasn't laughing.

"He'll be the biggest doofus around if necessary. But he'll never lose focus. He knows Ethan's the goal."

To keep any attention away from the rise where Rafe would be waiting, he headed back down and to the faint trail where they'd been before. And then he put on the most casual, out-for-a-day's-hike-with-the-dog demeanor he could manage, although he doubted it was nearly as good as the dog's.

It took several minutes to work their way down to the cluster of oak trees. Ethan was still inside the tent—he knew Rafe would have updated him if not—while the other two were fussing with something near the tent flap, the older kid with the gun yelling something at the youngest one, "stupid" being the only word Blaine could make out.

He worked his way through the brush to where, when he emerged, he would be as close as possible to the tent, and also for the startle factor. Cutter, as usual, seemed to understand and pretty much ignored the branches that caught at his fur and neatly dodged another small group of prickly pears.

He let Cutter lead, keeping his gaze fastened on the leader, who was standing in front of the tent almost protectively now. All while trying to present as just a guy out walking his dog.

"Hey," he called out with all the fake friendliness he could muster. "Nice day."

The leader spun around, clearly jolted.

Hurt my boy and you'll feel a real jolt.

Then the guy's gaze fastened on Cutter, and Blaine could see the wariness come into his eyes. Cutter hid the more aggressive looks of his kin beneath a fluffier coat, but the intensity was still there to those who looked.

And maybe those who knew they should be looking.

"What are you doing here?" the leader asked, in a tough-guy tone Blaine thought—and hoped he was right—was a little put on. As if he were speaking as the guy he wanted to be, but wasn't necessarily there yet.

Blaine gave him a rather wide-eyed look. "Walking my dog in a public park," he said, trying his best to sound puzzled by the question.

"This is pretty far out."

"Off the beaten path, yes," he answered, still doing his best to sound like an innocent bystander. At the same time he was watching as one of the younger kids opened the tent flap behind the leader. "But that's what the dog likes."

The guy asked, both looking and sounding suspicious, "How'd you get here?"

"Flew, actually. Maybe you heard us, a few minutes ago? Or maybe you didn't, that helicopter's pretty quiet."

Rafe's voice snapped in his ear. "Ethan heard you. He's headed out."

Even as Rafe finished the warning, Ethan appeared in the tent's opening. Blaine had, when he'd been the most down about it all, wondered if his own son would even recognize him when he saw him. Three months—three and a half now—wasn't long in his life, but it was a lot longer in a fourteen-year-old's.

That doubt was vanquished the instant their gazes locked. Ethan's eyes widened.

Three things happened simultaneously. Cutter yipped. Ethan yelped, "Dad!"

And the leader pulled that pistol from his belt.

"Dad? This guy's your father?" he snapped.

He aimed the pistol at Blaine. Cutter let out a low sound, not quite a growl but menacing nonetheless. The leader shifted the weapon to the dog, but he was still looking at Blaine. He obviously didn't know where to focus, so Blaine decided to further distract him. Anything to keep that weapon pointed anywhere but at Ethan. Even if it was at him. He could see now it was a 9mm, matching the ammo box they'd found. So unless the kid hit him smack in the head or heart, he could take one and keep moving. Long enough for Rafe to take his shot, anyway.

"Now that you know who I am," he said, "who are you?"

"None of your business." He turned the weapon on Ethan, who looked terrified now. And that look steeled Blaine in a way nothing, not even combat, ever had.

"What should I call you, then? Boss, maybe?"

He didn't think he was wrong about the slight shift in the kid's expression. He'd liked that.

"Yeah," the leader drawled, "you can call me that."

"Okay, Boss. Enjoy the title while you have it."

The rather shaggy brows lowered. "What's that supposed to mean?"

"They won't let you in, you know," he said, his tone conversational now. "Not after you couldn't even get that cash register open."

Shock flashed across the guy's face, wiping out any trace of satisfaction. "How the hell do you know—" He cut himself off and shifted the weapon to Ethan again. "You've been talking to him?"

Whoa. He hadn't expected that mind leap.

"Careful, he's panicking," Rafe's voice said in his ear.

Just as the assessment came Blaine saw, as if he'd read it in the kid's face, that he was indeed panicking. And he was going to bolt. In the same moment, the kid in the baseball cap grabbed Ethan's arm and ran, half dragging him along with him farther into the brush beyond the tent.

Cutter let out a snarl and a sharp bark. Blaine moved after them instantly, although the brush slowed him down because of the simple difference in his size and the kids'.

"I'll be right behind you, with him in the scope," Rafe assured him in his ear.

"Good," Blaine muttered, the first thing he'd said directly to the man backing him up.

"Say 'follow' and cut him loose." Blaine knew Rafe meant Cutter. But he hesitated. The dog had never met Ethan, could he really—

As if he'd read his doubts Rafe said, "He'll know. Trust him." Blaine bent down and unclipped the leash. Cutter darted ahead. "He won't attack unless you say so."

I'll try not to get him shot.

Blaine smothered the qualms as he'd so often had to before lifting off on a mission. He forged forward in the dog's wake, although making a lot more noise because he didn't care anymore—stealth had left the equation. Still Cutter got ahead of him, and he had to hustle to keep the dog in sight. He heard Rafe some distance behind him but closer than he'd expected. He'd obviously come over the rise and down, with the reason for concealment blown now. He just had to hope Erin was safely out of range.

When Blaine reached the edge of the thicket of tall brush and was able to see out to a bare spot, it was like a scenario from a film. Cutter had them cornered. Ethan was huddled on his knees, staring at the dog. The armed target—he had no problem thinking of the guy that way, even if he was a teenager, not since he'd turned that weapon on Ethan—was jammed up against a V-shaped tumble of large rocks, boulders that were taller than he was. It looked like the result of a long-ago landslide.

The wannabe boss's gaze was fastened on Cutter, who looked beyond threatening as he snarled at him. The kid was trying to get a bead on the dog with the pistol, but apparently Cutter was smart enough—or wolf enough—to keep moving side to side, so the kid couldn't really do it. He obviously was a few steps below amateur with the weapon. Which of course made him even more dangerous.

Blaine stepped quickly out of the underbrush.

"I wouldn't try that, if I were you. He'd take offense at you shooting at him, and that is not a dog you want coming at you."

"Go to hell," the kid spat out uselessly.

"Don't think so," he said. "Here are your options, Isaac." He saw the boy react in shock to the name, but kept going. "You take the dog down, I take you down. You take me down, the dog takes you down. Either way, you lose."

The wannabe gangster's lip curled. Blaine hoped it was just false bravado. He gestured at Ethan with the pistol. The winter sun glinted off the chrome. "And what if I just shoot him?"

"Then I kill you where you stand."

Blaine's tone was deadly serious and icy cold. And it registered with the kid, who tried to back up a step but came up against the towering boulder.

"And," he added in the same implacable voice, "way out here it would take a long time before anybody found your body."

"That's big talk for a guy who's not even armed," the kid blustered, shifting his focus—and the gun—away from Ethan.

In that instant Blaine lifted his right hand and snapped his index finger forward. A crack rang out from the trees in the same instant the kid's backwards baseball cap flew off his head.

Isaac shrieked. He fell back against the boulder. Blaine dived forward, grabbing Ethan. Using the same momentum he kicked out with his right leg, striking the kid's gun hand hard. The weapon went flying, landing near the baseball cap that now lay a few feet away, a bullet hole obvious in the brim. Isaac stared in shock at them both.

"Fair warning, he didn't miss your head because he couldn't hit it," Blaine said, his own voice almost shaky from the wave of relief at having Ethan in his arms, alive and safe.

The former boss sagged against the boulder at his back, and slid down to the ground.

"Cutter, guard!"

The call came from behind him as Rafe cleared the brush, the rifle he'd fired that exquisitely aimed shot from now slung over his shoulder. The dog leaped over to within a foot of the leader who was now just a terrified kid, gave a warning growl for good measure, and stood over him as if he were just hoping he'd try something so he could rip his throat out.

"I'd be scared of him," Blaine said to Rafe when he reached them.

The sniper grinned. "Smart man."

Blaine felt Ethan move, looked down to see him shifting his gaze from his broken captor to Cutter, to Rafe. And then, finally, he looked up at him.

"You came for me," his son whispered.

"Of course I did." He saw the moisture pooling in the boy's eyes, and added with a smile, "And I brought the cavalry."

Ethan threw his arms around Blaine's waist. Blaine heard a sound, realized the boy was crying. He hugged him back, fiercely, breathing easily for the first time since he'd gotten that phone call.

His son was safe.

"Was that really you flying that helicopter?" The question was a bit muffled, since apparently Ethan didn't want to let go. Which was fine with Blaine, because he didn't, either.

"Yeah," he answered. "And now I have to take it back. Want to go for a ride?"

Ethan tilted his head back then, the fear fading, and excitement growing. "Seriously?"

"Seriously," Blaine said, looking down at the head that now nearly came up to his chin. How had he grown so much so fast? How much else, what other kinds of growth, had he missed out on?

That had to stop. And it would. Somehow.

Even if last night hadn't meant what he hoped it had.

Chapter Thirty-Seven

"Dad, that was so slick, the way you just kicked that gun right out of his hand!"

"Thanks," Blaine said, "but that's not what you should be thinking about right now."

Erin had come out of the bathroom at the separate living quarters at the Foxworth building just in time to hear that exchange. Her pulse was still elevated. The fear had abated the moment she realized her son was safely in his father's arms, but the adrenaline from the whole operation was taking a while to ebb. That was one reason they'd come back here instead of to the house. Neutral ground, Rafe had called it.

And she understood what Ethan had meant. That moment when Blaine had grabbed Ethan and in the same smooth, powerful movement punted that gun right out of the older kid's hand had been...beautiful. Almost dance-like in grace, and martial arts in power.

She hesitated there in the doorway for a moment. Back out there, as she'd taken to calling it, her son had been so shaken he'd let her fuss over him, as if he felt like a child again instead of the angry, rebellious youth who had vanished. But she had known even then it wouldn't last, that once he got over the fear, the reason he'd run would still be there. And the excitement of the ride back in the helicopter seemed to have done that.

She felt a nudge at her leg, and looked down at Cutter. She'd been surprised when the dog had refused to leave with Rafe when he'd gone back over to the Foxworth office across the courtyard to do the "drudge work" as he'd called it, which she assumed meant paperwork. She was more than amazed when Rafe told them he'd handle the details, the kid with the gun and the others. He'd run interference, and what he couldn't handle the Foxworth name would. There would be fallout, but they'd help with that, too.

And when his—well, Foxworth's—dog had sat at Ethan's feet and refused to move, Rafe had simply looked at them and said, "Peacekeeper. Work it out," and gone on his way.

Ethan himself had seemed a bit boggled at the change in demeanor of the animal, from fierce, well-trained attacker to what seemed to be a soft, fluffy house pet who wanted his ears scratched. And she had a feeling the dog's presence, as he leaned into the boy while he sat in one of the armchairs, had a lot to do with her son's calm as she came back into the living room.

This was a nice place, she thought. Maybe built as a guesthouse at the same time the main building had been constructed. It had the same look and feel. There were two bedrooms with a connected bathroom between, and a small but fully equipped kitchen in the front corner.

Blaine was in that kitchen, readying the meal they'd picked up on the way here from a local Mexican restaurant Rafe said Walker had recommended. Rafe had taken his with him, saying this was going to take a while. She could only imagine, what with Ethan stealing things from stores, an underage teenager with a handgun, and who knew what the details were on those younger kids whom Rafe had, after a phone call with Walker, safely turned over to the local CPS.

But Ethan was safe now, and whatever fallout there was, they would deal with it. Somehow.

Blaine called them to the table and set down what was an indeed luscious-smelling spread of burritos, tacos, rice and beans, all of which Ethan loved. And Blaine had remembered.

Ethan waited standing until she had taken a seat at the rectangular table near the windows out to the courtyard. She'd like to think it was gentlemanly conduct, but she knew it was much more likely he just wanted to be sure he was as far away from her as possible. That he'd let her fuss over him when he'd been shaken and scared didn't mean he'd forgotten or forgiven.

Ethan didn't sit until Blaine had, and as she'd expected he sat as far from her as he could get and still be next to his dad.

She ate a couple of bites of the admittedly delicious meal before saying to Blaine, "We owe Rafe so much."

Before Blaine could respond Ethan said, in the belligerent tone she'd gotten used to hearing from him, "Dad's the one who did it. He flew there, confronted the guy, faced him down without even a gun, just Cutter here."

The dog had been plopped on the floor just watching, but at Ethan's words—or perhaps the sound and tone of his voice—his head came up. She saw his ears twitch at the mention of his name.

Blaine set down the tortilla-wrapped yumminess he'd been about to take a bite of. "We only found you at all because of help from Rafe's colleague here at this office, which he arranged. I flew out there in a helicopter Rafe got for us. Tracked you only with Cutter's help, which he also provided. And that shot that distracted your badly chosen friend was taken by one of the best and most well-known snipers in Marine Corps history."

Ethan was staring at him, cheeks flushed slightly. And Erin was remembering how Blaine's innate sense of fairness and never stealing credit he hadn't earned—now even with his own son—had been one of the reasons she loved him so much. And that was why she didn't mention that Rafe wouldn't even be around to help if it hadn't been for Blaine.

"Wow," Ethan finally muttered. "I...didn't know."

"You assumed some things?"

"I guess so."

"Eat," Blaine instructed. "And then we're going to have a...briefing. About making assumptions and other things."

Ethan blinked. Leave it to Blaine, she thought, to come up with a word other than talk or discussion, a word that wouldn't send Ethan running for cover to avoid it.

But when the time came and they were all gathered in the living room around the gas fire Blaine was turning on against the chill of November even here, she realized she was the one who wanted to head for cover. Ethan had taken that armchair again, and she wondered if it was because he wanted to be alone there, or just didn't want to sit on the same couch she was on.

She smothered a sigh. *For once, it really is all about you.*

And then Blaine startled her by coming over and sitting, not just on the couch with her, but so close they were touching. A united front. And it hit her with a blast warmer than the flames now burning on the hearth, just how much she'd missed this. The simple act of just being together. On the same side.

But were they?

She sucked in a deep breath and looked, not at the boy who had been the burning focus of her life the last ten days, but at the man who had held that spot for thirty years, since she was seven years old.

"I'd like to tell you something."

Blaine shifted his gaze to her. "What we're here for."

"I just wanted to say that… I finally understand. I always knew you were a protector, but I didn't get it, not all of it. Now I do. Not just the…adrenaline rush of doing something that has to be done, but the willingness to do it." He held her gaze, and she saw a glow that wasn't just the reflection of the fire in his eyes. She finished it. "Whatever's necessary."

Ethan snorted, loudly. They both turned to look at him. "Like you ever would," he said, his disgust clearly aimed at her. "You coddle everyone, want everyone completely safe all the time. What kind of life is that, never taking any chances, ever? She never even stands up for herself—"

"Do you know why I'm still alive, Ethan?"

Blaine's seeming non sequitur stopped the boy's outburst dead.

"What?"

"You were only nine when I went down. Did you even understand completely what death meant, then? That it was forever, and everything, all the memories, all the things, would be forever tainted by that?"

She was staring at him then. He'd never talked about it like this, even to her.

"I know now," was all Ethan said.

"So do you know why you didn't have to learn back then? Why you didn't have to go to my funeral and come home with the flag that was over the box they buried me in?"

She felt an echo of the old fear from that time. Ethan was simply staring at his father, brows lowered in that way she knew meant he was trying to figure something out.

"You got better," Ethan said, sounding confused.

"Yes. I did. And there's only one reason I did. Because someone else was fighting the battle I couldn't. Someone else was confronting the doctors with every question I couldn't ask, who fought them when necessary, stood up to them, made them do what was best, and not do a couple of things that would have done more harm just because their egos got in the way."

"Fought doctors?" Ethan sounded quite puzzled.

"Specialists, mostly, who kept doing things that clashed with what other specialists were doing," Blaine explained. "Only one person stood up to them. And that same person was the one who pushed, prodded, and had my back through month after month of rehab. The one who made me fight on even when all I wanted to do was give up. The one who would not let me quit. The one person who is the real reason I'm still alive and functional today. The one person who is why I was able to do what I did today. And she's sitting right here, just taking those dirty looks and angry words you're throwing at her."

Ethan was staring at her now. She didn't speak, couldn't think of a single coherent thing to say. It wouldn't have gotten past the tightness of her throat anyway.

"It seems," Blaine went on, "that one of those assumptions you've made is that your mother knows nothing about fighting, about rebellion. That she knows nothing about reality and how it can bite. That seems to have become a habit with you."

"How would you know?" Ethan snapped back defensively.

Blaine leaned back then. "And that one's true, and my fault. I could have forced things, could have come more often—"

"You would have, if she hadn't made it so hard."

"I—"

He stopped when Erin put a hand on his arm. "No, he's right about that. I was trying to make it easier on me, but that doesn't change that it made it harder for you."

Ethan stared at her, as if she'd shocked him. How? By just saying he was right? Had she truly been that rough on him? She took a deep breath and held his gaze.

"If I've been hard on you, Ethan, overprotective, it's because I knew death was forever, and we'd come so close with your father. I knew, and I was afraid to face it again. I wasn't brave enough to face it again. Especially with my son, the boy I love more than life itself."

The boy's shocked expression changed, slowly, into something more thoughtful.

"Your mother's been to hell and back once already, with me," Blaine said. "Don't blame her if she doesn't want to make the trip again with you. She loves you more than anyone in the world."

"She doesn't," Ethan muttered.

"What?" Erin exclaimed, more shocked than he'd looked.

He met her gaze then, and it was the most tangled look of defiance and hurt that she'd ever seen. "You stopped loving Dad, and now you don't love me, either."

Erin was moving before she even thought. She pushed off the couch and ended up on her knees in front of her son. Appropriate, perhaps. And the words tumbled out just as fast.

"I never stopped loving your father. And I will never stop loving you."

She heard a sharp intake of breath from behind her. And Ethan wasn't looking at her. He was looking at his father.

The man she'd just admitted out loud to them all she still loved. And Blaine had to know better than anyone that if she'd said it aloud to Ethan, she meant it.

Chapter Thirty-Eight

Blaine told himself she'd just been trying to get through to Ethan. But he knew that wasn't true. No matter where else she might have gone wrong, she would never lie to Ethan to his face. Telling him that in the heat of the moment was one thing, but saying it out loud to their son...

Memories of last night rose up to swamp him. He knew Erin, knew she never would have done what she'd done, never would have made love to him as much as he made love to her, if she hadn't...if she didn't...mean it.

At the time, he'd been grateful they hadn't had time to discuss it. Thankful there had been no time for her to admit she regretted what they'd done. Although how anyone could regret the kind of impossibly hot, all-consuming sex they'd had—the kind they had always had—was a bit beyond him. That was why he'd made sure before, because he knew he wasn't going to be able to think after.

...how are you going to feel...after?

I'll deal with that then. But I swear, I won't take it out on you.

And she wouldn't, he knew that. No, Erin would just walk away. Saying only she couldn't do this again. Just as she had before.

I never stopped loving your father.

The words rang in his ears. Had they been just to calm Ethan, or…had she truly meant them?

He gave a shake of his head. She'd meant them. Erin wouldn't say something like that unless she meant it. But there were different kinds of love. Maybe she'd just meant she loved him as Ethan's father, not the mate she'd had for decades. Maybe it had been too long, maybe they'd burnt it out, maybe, in her heart, there was nothing left but ashes.

If there was, he had to know. But this was not the kind of discussion to have in front of the boy they'd just pulled out of potential disaster. At the same time, he didn't feel like letting his son out of his sight just now, either, because of what they'd just gone through—

Cutter moved. The agile dog jumped to his feet, trotted over to the door of the guesthouse, nosed around in a basket Blaine hadn't even noticed before, and came back with a bright lime green tennis ball in his mouth. He trotted back and dropped the ball over the arm of the chair into Ethan's lap. The boy looked startled. Cutter nudged the ball, then Ethan's hand, and let out a tiny whine, sounding for all the world like any dog who wanted to play.

Ethan picked up the ball. And Blaine realized this was his chance. "Go ahead. We'll…finish this later. There's room in the courtyard. He's earned some playtime, don't you think?"

"Yeah," Ethan said, his expression brightening.

The dog would also keep Ethan safe. And here. Blaine knew that deep in his gut now, and apparently so did Erin, because she made no complaint as the two headed for the door.

"And hey," Blaine called out. "Think about calling your buddy Connor. He's been worried about you."

Ethan looked embarrassed, but nodded, and then followed Cutter out the door.

Erin got up from her kneeling position, but instead of coming back to him she turned and sat in the chair Ethan had been in. And he didn't know how to interpret that. And was too fearful of saying the wrong thing to speak at all.

"Aren't you going to ask?" she said.

"Ask...what?"

"If I meant it."

"No, I'm not going to ask."

Her head tilted slightly. "Why?"

"Because I'm afraid of the answer."

To his shock, she laughed. "You? Afraid? The man who's faced combat, the man who flies a machine that wants to tear itself apart, the man who faced down death and won?"

He had the feeling this was important. Very important. So he held her gaze when he said, slowly, "Do you really think I wasn't afraid? Erin, I was always afraid. All those times, I was afraid."

"But you did what had to be done anyway. And that is the difference between you and me, Blaine. You always will, and I...can't."

"But you did. When it mattered most, you did what has to be done. You fought those doctors when I couldn't, you left when you had to for your own sanity, and you set aside your feelings and called me when you had to for Ethan. That's not cowardice, Erin. You keep saying it, but you're not a coward. I meant what I said—bravery isn't not being afraid. It's saddling up and heading out anyway, because it has to be done."

He heard her let out a long breath, and she seemed to slump a little. And he had the thought that if they were going to have this all out anyway, and it seemed they were, maybe this was the time. He'd have to work up to it, but... now or never.

"I want to ask something...about what I've never understood."

She looked up then. "Go ahead." She gave him the faintest of wry smiles. "As long as we're digging down to the bone."

"I would have gotten it if you'd left when I was such a wreck, but... I never understood why you left when you did. After the hard part was over."

"I couldn't have left when you were so hurt!" It broke from her in a burst, as if she were pointing out the obvious.

And there it was. The perfect opening for the question he'd lugged around for two years now. Yet still he hesitated.

He made himself say it.

"Then tell me. What would you have done if...if I hadn't been able to get back on my feet? If I'd continued as broken as I was in the beginning. If I'd given up the fight and just decided to live that way?"

He saw her eyes move, away from him, but then she was meeting his gaze again. Another deep breath, and she said. "I would have stayed."

His own breath jammed up in his chest, tightening it almost beyond bearing. This was why it had been so hard to ask. "So my getting better destroyed us? You wanted me...helpless?"

He shot to his feet. As he would not be able to do if it had happened that way.

"Blaine, no!"

"Sounds pretty clear. My getting better ended our marriage."

He turned on his heel as sharply as if he'd been given an about-face order. And walked out, ignoring her calling his name.

He was a couple of steps into the courtyard, not really sure where he was going or what he was going to do, when he heard his son.

"Dad, watch!" Ethan yelled. "He's amazing!"

He turned to look at boy and dog. Ethan threw the tennis ball high into the air. Cutter watched the arching sphere, dancing sideways as it started its downward trajectory, until he was in the perfect spot. When the ball reached about Blaine's height, the dog jumped high into the air and snatched it in a perfectly judged and timed leap.

"That he is," Blaine said, grinning at his son, letting the relief soothe and calm him again. "You keep at it. I'm going to go talk to Rafe for a minute."

He hadn't really planned that when he'd left the guest-house; he'd just had to get away. Had to think, and he couldn't do that in the same room with Erin. But now that he'd said it, it seemed like the thing to do. The guy was sane, and he'd been there. Here.

Damn, I can't even think straight.

Rafe was typing at the keyboard of that same workstation, using Blaine's own "two-fingered and the occasional thumb" method. Erin could put them both in the dust, as fast as she typed. He yanked his thoughts away.

Rafe looked up as he came in. "That was fast," he said, then paused before adding, "That is, assuming you got things straightened out."

Blaine grimaced. "Not exactly."

He hadn't planned this, either, but before he could stop he was explaining what had just happened.

"So if you'd been disabled for life she would have stayed, but because you weren't, she left?" Rafe said.

"Yeah." He shook his head slowly. "How the hell do I deal with that?"

Rafe looked thoughtful, and it was a moment before he said, "But you've said she's the one who got you to that point."

"Yes."

"So she fought for you."

Blaine nodded again. "Hard."

Rafe leaned back in his chair, looking up at Blaine. "Sounds like she already did her part. Do you want to do the same?"

"What?"

"Fight for her. Do you want to put it back together?"

Blaine had never really put it into concrete words like that. And once Rafe had, there was only one possible answer. "I love her. I have since I was seven years old."

"Then take it from two guys who nearly blew it," came another voice from behind him. He spun around to see Walker Cole coming out of the office in the far corner of the building. His hair was neatly combed today, and the tats were gone. "I knew my Amy almost as long, since she's my sister's best friend. When we first reconnected, she hated my guts. And now, I'm drunk with happy to be with her."

Blaine looked back at Rafe, who just sat there with a blissful, crooked grin on his face, an expression he never could have imagined the tough, gruff sniper ever wearing.

He gave them both a sour grimace, but one that his heart wasn't in. "You two are a walking advertisement for mushy endings, y'know?"

"Yeah," they both said simultaneously.

"Or for guys who got their heads on straight," Walker said.

Rafe reached out and picked something up off the printer

and handed it to him. "Something that might help a bit," was all he said. "Read it before you take that next step."

"And say yes," Walker put in, nodding toward the printed page.

He glanced at it. His eyes widened, and he looked back at Rafe. "You're serious? Your boss is serious?"

"Which one?" Rafe asked blandly. "I have two now."

"Me, too," Walker agreed. "And I've never been happier."

"So," Rafe added, wearing that grin again, "go make us a trio."

Chapter Thirty-Nine

She shouldn't feel so bad. Shouldn't feel as if the entire earth had crumbled beneath her feet. Because she was back where she started, Ethan back but Blaine still gone.

Maybe she shouldn't have been honest with him. Maybe she should have told him she would have left anyway, eventually. But she knew she wouldn't have, and they'd always been honest, even when it sometimes hurt.

She heard Ethan calling out to Cutter outside, and silently thanked the brilliant dog for once again seeming to sense what was needed and handling it.

Ethan.

Just because he was back and safe didn't mean things were fixed between them.

You coddle everyone, want everyone completely safe all the time. What kind of life is that, never taking any chances, ever?

For the first time she faced a truth she'd denied for a long time. That she had been not just protective but overprotective of Ethan, probably because she hadn't been able to protect Blaine.

You wanted me helpless?

Another aspect hit her, hard. Had she? Had she felt she

could handle it if he didn't get any better, because at least then he wouldn't be out flying into danger anymore?

She felt a wave of nausea sweep her, strong enough that she dashed for the bathroom. All the lovely dinner came right back up and out. When she could move again she flushed away the evidence, rinsed her mouth, and when that wasn't enough dug into the medicine cabinet and found some toothpaste and a small stack of packaged toothbrushes. When she was done she sank back down onto the floor because she wasn't feeling like this was over. She'd never felt this kind of…self-loathing before. She'd always thought she'd simply done what was best for her and Ethan.

And now all she could think was that there was nothing, not even perpetual safety, that was worth losing Blaine.

Especially when it had nearly cost her their son, too.

"Erin?"

Blaine. He'd come back. She'd half expected him to take off. Maybe even take Ethan with him. And she wouldn't have blamed him.

In the rush she hadn't shut the bathroom door, and he quickly found her. And almost as quickly he was down on the floor beside her.

"Are you all right?"

She tried to smile but was pretty sure it came out more like a wince. "Dinner came back for a visit."

"Didn't agree with you?"

"Figuratively and I think literally. Because right now I don't agree with me, either."

"Agree with what?"

"Something just hit me. Hard. About why I've been… the way I've been with Ethan."

He seemed to hesitate, then said, "Cautious?"

"You can say it. Overprotective. Or as Ethan put it, coddling." She let out a disgusted breath. "And there's another phrase for it that seems appropriate. Helicopter mom."

That one got a slight twitch of a grin out of him. And that enabled her to go on.

"I've been overprotective of Ethan because I couldn't protect you."

Again he hesitated, but then he said softly, "I thought I was the protector."

"You are, in all the ways that matter. I was just...trying to control what I could, because I was terrified of what I couldn't."

He slipped an arm around her. And because it was what she'd always done with him, she leaned against him, resting her head gratefully on his strong shoulder.

"I have to let Ethan be himself. I know that now." She sighed. "It's going to take him a while to get past this, but he won't at all unless I give him room."

"Within reason," Blaine said. "There have to be limits. He is only fourteen."

"I think he'll only accept those limits from you. For now, at least."

He was quiet for so long she had to wonder what he was thinking. Then, at last, he said, "Then I guess I'd better stick around."

She straightened abruptly, turning to stare at him, fixing on those eyes she'd once teasingly called "clear flying blue."

"Just how," she said carefully, "do you mean that?"

He shifted on the floor then, turning to face her. She had a brief flash of memory, from the time when that simple movement, when getting down here with her would have been impossible. She'd always looked at that time as him doing all the fighting, she was just the support staff. But now, thanks to his insistence, she was thinking maybe she had fought, maybe as hard as he said.

"You said you never stopped loving me," he said bluntly.

"And I meant it."

"So do I."

Her breath caught. "Are you saying…you want to try again?"

"I'm saying I'm tired of not having the woman I love in my life."

Her heart leaped, but this was too important to go on impulse. She thought about what she'd admitted, that if his injuries had been permanent, she would have stayed.

"But…how could you want me back, after what I told you?"

He reached out and cupped her face. "I still don't like the idea that you would have stayed. But…something Rafe said made me think. All that fighting you did for me, when I couldn't? And all the grit and determination you've shown these last couple of weeks? That was you paying in advance for a second chance. For us."

And then he was kissing her, and she wondered not for the first time how this man, and this man only, could make her feel safe, cherished and more than a little wild, all at the same time.

Wild enough to have crazy sex with him on a bathroom floor with their son playing right outside. But after thinking about that for a moment, she decided there couldn't be a better time.

And afterward, when they finished tugging clothes back on, he gave her a cautious look.

"I'm not changing my mind, if that's what that look is for," she assured him.

"You might still, after I tell you something. Well, a couple of things, actually."

She went still, but her determination held. "Nope. Not a chance. What?"

"Well… I'm transferring to Pendleton. You'll have to put up with me under the same roof. In your house."

"*Our* house!" She threw her arms around him in delight. "Why on earth would you think that would upset me?"

"Not done yet. The second thing is kind of two connected things. No, make that three."

She was laughing now. "Can we get back to where you don't walk on eggshells anymore? Just out with it."

"You really want it all at once?"

"Fire when ready," she said, and to her inner glee, she meant it. If it meant having Blaine back, she could—and would—take anything.

"I'm leaving the Corps after this re-up. Foxworth has offered me a job here at this office, but I'll still be flying now and then."

She stared at him. "You're leaving the Marines?"

He nodded. "I decided that before you even called about Ethan."

"Why didn't you tell me?"

"Because it wasn't important while Ethan was missing, and now… I didn't want that to be the reason you said yes."

For a long moment she kept looking at him, processing what he'd said. Finally she nodded. "Okay. I get that."

He looked startled. "And you got that I'll still be flying?"

"Yes. I've been okay with that since you mentioned you weren't getting shot at anymore." She kissed him, long and hard and deep. And then she pulled back and met his gaze again. "I meant what I said, Blaine. Nothing matters more than you and Ethan, and I've realized I can't hang on to either of you with a choke hold. That's done, over. I love you."

"Say that last bit again?"

"I love you, I love you, I love you."

He looked oddly thoughtful. "Okay, about twenty-seven hundred more times and you'll have made up for three times a day for the last two and half years."

Erin burst out laughing. "Oh," she said when she could, "I'm going to beat that by a long shot."

"Promise?"

"I do," she said, purposely choosing the vow they'd made all those years ago. He kissed her this time, full of promises old and new.

Then they went outside to collect their son.

Epilogue

Cutter warned Rafe long before he himself heard the car coming down the quiet street. He glanced at his watch. They were a few minutes early, but that didn't surprise him. And Rafe didn't mind, because they were heading home as soon as this was wound up. Heading home, Cutter to his beloved Hayley and him to his beloved Charlie.

He didn't get all choked up even thinking those last words anymore, but he didn't think he'd ever get past the throat-tightening stage. What had seemed impossible had happened. And not just for him, but for Blaine, too. And having some small part in that made him understand why everyone—including himself now—took such glee at Cutter's matchmaking skills.

Walker came out of his office with the tall, straight-backed man with a touch of gray in his dark hair at the temples who had arrived about twenty minutes ago.

"I'll leave you to it, Mr. Rockwell."

The older man smiled. "Someday I'll get you to call me Marcus."

Walker grinned back. "You're my wife's boss. It'll be tough." He looked at Rafe. "You're heading out when you're done here today?"

Rafe nodded. Walker came over and shook his hand. "It's been great working with you."

"Ditto. You're doing great work here, Walker. You've built a good thing in the last eighteen months." He paused to give his fellow operative a crooked smile. "And I don't mean just Foxworth."

Walker grinned back at him, a far cry from the worn, wary man who had knocked on his sister's door after years away, only to get decked by the brother-in-law he'd never even met.

"Don't be a stranger," Walker said. "And keep working on that word."

Rafe rolled his eyes before saying, "Tell Amy that Hayley expects you for a visit soon."

"I will," Walker said as he waved and left the office, Cutter dashing over to sneak out with him. Rafe saw him pause to talk to the Everetts as they were getting out of Erin's car, while Cutter greeted Ethan with a furiously wagging tail.

"What word is it you're supposed to be working on?" Rockwell asked.

Rafe smiled crookedly. "He thinks there should be an official word for the connection between us."

"Connection?"

"He's married to his sister's best friend, so he thinks that ought to have a word. But he thinks we should have a word, too, since he's also married to my future wife's brother's wife's best friend."

Rockwell stared at him for a moment, then burst out laughing. "English is an amazing language, but I don't think that one's going to get much use if you do come up with it."

Rafe guessed that the fact the attorney was laughing made the Everetts relax a little when they came in.

It had been several days since he'd last seen them. He

hadn't been in the least surprised when Blaine told him they were going to try again, and if he judged by the look on all three faces—and the ring with the stone that looked like amber on Erin's left ring finger—it was going well. The change was obvious, and as a man who had recently rebuilt his own life from what he'd thought was unsalvageable rubble, he recognized it immediately.

Yes, he really was starting to like this matchmaking stuff Cutter always seemed to pull off. Especially with people like Blaine and Erin, who were almost as messed up as he and Charlie had been.

When they were all seated near the fire, Rafe formally introduced the man who joined them.

"Marcus has been dealing with the legal aspects of your case," he said.

Ethan looked suddenly glum. "How much is that gonna cost? Lawyers cost a lot, right?"

"Usually," Rockwell agreed, unruffled. "But working with and for Foxworth is a privilege I don't charge for."

Rafe noticed Blaine relax a little, and guessed he'd been wondering about that himself.

"How's it going?" Rafe asked, although from the way Blaine and Erin were holding hands he figured he already know.

"Good," Blaine confirmed.

"Ethan?" Rafe asked.

The boy looked up from petting Cutter. "Great. All I ever wanted was my family back."

"You got that," Blaine said, but there was a not stern, but firm note in his voice. "But don't go thinking you won something by putting us through this hell. You got what you wanted, but like we talked about, it comes with rules."

"I know," Ethan said, sounding chastened. "I'm still… learning."

"If I can, you can," Erin said quietly. And when the boy looked at her and nodded, totally without the antipathy Rafe had seen before, he knew they were going to be all right. In fact, he'd known it when he'd seen Ethan taping the photo he'd cut in half back together again.

"Good. Then I'll turn this over to Marcus," Rafe said, and leaned back to let the attorney take over.

"I'm going to lay this out, then you tell me if you agree with what we've arranged. Ethan, in the video from the convenience store you're simply in a fight with another boy, correct?"

"Yeah," Ethan said, but with a glance at his father he sat up straight and said, "but it was a distraction so Isaac could rip them off."

"I appreciate the honesty. But no proof of you being involved in the actual attempted theft is in the video, thankfully, so the owners have agreed to press charges only against Isaac. But you are on video stealing from the pet store near the mission. And you were the only one committing a crime in that instance."

Ethan lowered his gaze and said, "I know. Stupid."

"Rafe and I, and Cutter," Marcus added with a nod at the dog now parked at Ethan's side again, "had a talk with the owner of that pet store. And he has agreed he will not press charges if, and only if, you come and work for him every weekend for the next ten weeks."

Ethan's head shot up. "Work? In the pet store?"

"Is that a problem?" the attorney asked.

"No!" The boy actually looked excited at the idea.

"So you'll do it," Blaine said, "even knowing you'll still have to get your schoolwork done and any chores at home?"

He glanced at both his parents. "I'll even walk if I have to. It's not that far."

"And you're looking at summer school next session, too, to make up the time you lost," Erin said.

Ethan grimaced, but it was a normal kid look, not angry, not hostile or hateful. "I know. I'll do it. All of it."

Once it was all worked out and agreed to, Ethan went outside with Cutter for a last round of tennis ball catch. Marcus gave them his card, but said this should do it and he'd let them know if there was any problem. Rafe walked him to the door, thanked him, then turned back to look at the two who were once more a couple. If he had to guess, he'd say unbreakable this time.

They walked to the door themselves, and watched Ethan and Cutter playing. When the boy saw them he came over, Cutter at his heels.

"Mom says once Dad's all settled in and everything, we can get a dog," he told Rafe.

Cutter barked, happily, as if in agreement with the idea.

"Yeah, I know, mutt," Rafe said. "Everybody's happier with a dog."

"And Dad says when he's out of the Marines he's going to work here."

"That he is," Rafe agreed.

"I'd say that big debt you thought you owed Blaine is more than paid up now," Erin said to him with a wide smile.

"Nope," Rafe said. "It's just changed. Now it goes both ways."

Blaine smiled. "You got it, bro."

Cutter's bark this time sounded exactly like the sharp rap of a gavel, and Rafe grinned. "That's his 'case closed' bark."

Erin grinned back. "We'll never find a dog that smart, but that may be for the best."

"For sure," Blaine agreed. "Keeping up with this one must be a full-time job in itself."

"That it is," Rafe said as Cutter came to stand by his side and look at the others. He reached down to stroke that dark head. "But it's worth it."

And later, at the private side of the airport awaiting Wilbur's touchdown with Quinn at the controls, Rafe sat on the small couch with Cutter beside him, the dog's head resting on the injured leg that likely would have ended up a death warrant if not for Blaine Everett.

"Thanks, buddy," he whispered to the dog.

Cutter lifted his head and swiped his tongue over Rafe's cheek.

And if anyone had pointed out that his eyes got a little wet, Rafe would have denied it.

Maybe.

* * * * *

COMING SOON!

We really hope you enjoyed reading this book.
If you're looking for more romance
be sure to head to the shops when
new books are available on

Thursday 18th December

MILLS & BOON

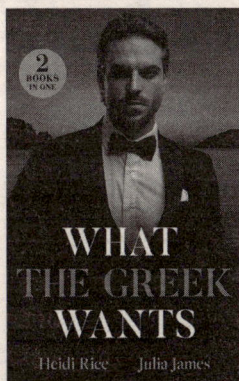

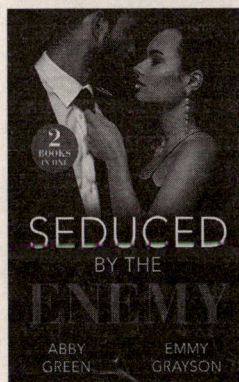

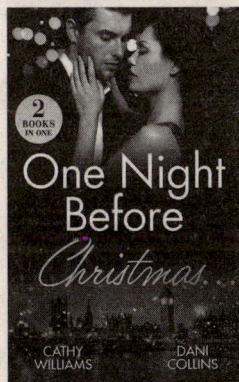

LET'S TALK
Romance

For exclusive extracts, competitions and special offers, find us online:

- MillsandBoon
- @MillsandBoon
- @MillsandBoonUK
- @MillsandBoonUK

Get in touch on 01413 063 232